PRAISE FOR *The Last True Vampire*

"Full of sexy vampires, strong women, and excitement."
                                        —*Fresh Fiction*

"The chemistry is electric . . . Kate Baxter has done her job, and masterfully."   —*San Francisco Book Reviews*

"A jackpot read for vampire lovers who like sizzle . . . brimming with heat!"   —*Romance Junkies*

"Mikhail and Claire's love story ha[s] that combination of romance, steam, and suspense."
                                        —*Book-a-holics Anonymous*

"If you like the Black Dagger Brotherhood . . . pick up *The Last True Vampire*, you won't be disappointed."
                                        —*Parajunkee Reviews*

"Kate Baxter has done a remarkable job of building this paranormal world."   —*Scandalous Book Reviews*

ALSO BY KATE BAXTER

THE LOST VAMPIRE

KATE BAXTER

St. Martin's Paperbacks

THE LOST VAMPIRE

Copyright © 2017 by Kate Baxter.
Excerpt from *Wicked Vampire* Copyright © 2017 Kate Baxter.

For information address St. Martin's Press, 175 Fifth Avenue, New York, NY 10010.

ISBN: 978-1-250-12541-5

Our books may be purchased in bulk for promotional, educational, or business use. Please contact your local bookseller or the Macmillan Corporate and Premium Sales Department at 1-800-221-7945, ext. 5442, or by e-mail at MacmillanSpecialMarkets@macmillan.com.

Printed in the United States of America

St. Martin's Paperbacks edition /August 2017

St. Martin's Paperbacks are published by St. Martin's Press, 175 Fifth Avenue, New York, NY 10010.

10 9 8 7 6 5 4 3 2 1

CHAPTER
1

The bright lights of the Seattle cityscape appeared like stars in a vast universe as the 747 made its descent. The Space Needle jutted into the skyline like a sentinel, alien in its shape and form in comparison to the structures surrounding it. As alien as Saeed Almasi felt now, surrounded by humans who might have looked like him but, in truth, couldn't be more different.

A woman watched him from across the aisle. The scent of her anxiety and fear reached his nostrils. The color of his skin, his features that so clearly identified him as someone from the Middle East, put her on edge. He didn't have to hear her thoughts to know what worried her. Saeed turned toward her with a tight-lipped smile. The urge to grin and flash the dual points of his fangs overwhelmed him. She feared the color of his skin, his dark eyes and hair, and the possibility of his intentions. What Saeed wanted to tell her was that there were far more dangerous things in this world than a man from another country or a man who spoke another language. She sat across from a vampire, not a terrorist. And had his thirst been overwhelming, the scent of her blood would have awakened the predator in him.

Luckily for the woman who continued to watch him, and every other person on the flight, he'd fed before take-off, glutting himself on Sasha's blood in an effort to keep his thirst at bay. Closed up in a metal tube with little ventilation, he might as well have been trapped within the confines of an all-you-can-eat buffet with strict orders not to eat.

Saeed turned his attention from the woman and her judgment and focused his gaze on the city beyond his window. The two and a half hour flight hadn't been long, but to Saeed, centuries had passed. He'd taken enough of Sasha's blood to manage his thirst, but it seemed that lately no amount of blood could keep him from the memories that plagued him. For months, Saeed had given himself over to the Collective, the memories of every vampire that had ever existed, transferred through blood at the moment of a vampire's turning. With practice, and regular feeding, the memories became nothing more than white noise in the back of a vampire's mind. No more distracting than music in an elevator or the chatter of small talk in a crowded restaurant. To Saeed, the Collective had become a lifeline that connected him to the only thing on earth that could save him.

Through the memories of vampires long since dead, the Collective had shown him the female that would tether his soul.

The members of his coven thought him mad. Sasha and Diego, his most trusted advisors and friends, considered him lost. He'd made them vampires, just as he'd promised Mikhail he would, and when he'd been assured of their stability, he turned the leadership of his coven over to them. It was a decision Mikhail still wasn't happy about. The vampire king wasn't burdened with the matter of Saeed's soul, however. Mikhail Aristov's singular concern was that of replenishing the vampire race. As far as Saeed was concerned, Mikhail could turn every dhampir in Los Angeles. He certainly didn't need Saeed's help for that.

The plane touched down and Saeed said a silent prayer of thanks. He could remember a time when the only modes of transportation were horses, camels, or boats. The modern world moved much too quickly. Jets, sports cars, bullet trains all designed to get you from point A to point B in the shortest amount of time. He supposed humans had no choice but to move quickly. After all, their lives were so short. They had so little time on this earth, it seemed foolish to waste even a single second.

Saeed's life had spanned millennia. Before his turning, he'd been one of the oldest dhampirs in existence. Now, he was nothing more than a fledgling vampire. As new in this world as a child. Perhaps it was his soulless state that kept him from feeling even an ounce of wonder over any of it. He was empty. Hollow. As void and black as the night that stretched out before him. It seemed odd he'd be concerned at all for the return of his soul in his seemingly apathetic state. But Saeed wasn't simply concerned, he was obsessed. So obsessed, he'd relinquished control of his coven and flown to Seattle to reclaim what had been taken from him. He wasn't even sure if he'd find what he was looking for in the Emerald City. But he had to start somewhere, even if he was following the inarticulate ramblings of a child Oracle.

The plane taxied slowly down the runway and came to a stop at its gate. Impatient to get on with their very short lives, the people around him hustled to retrieve their carry-on bags from the overhead compartments, only to waste more of those precious minutes standing in a line. Saeed sat, hands folded neatly in his lap, gaze cast straight ahead.

He'd waited this long to begin his search, what was ten more minutes when compared to the eternal soul?

"Excuse me? Would you mind if I stepped past you?"

Saeed looked up to find a woman no more than twenty-four or twenty-five years of age staring down at him. Young. Pretty. Her expression pleasant. Her dark auburn hair was piled in a haphazard mass on top of her head, and the thin white cords of her earbuds dangled from either side of her head.

"Of course." Saeed held out his hand in invitation and scooted his legs to the left. She gave him a sweet smile, her dark brown eyes sparking with interest as she looked him over one last time before sidling past.

Humans were such easy prey. Drawn to predators like Saeed. It really was a shame their blood didn't offer more sustenance. In reality, vampires needed dhampirs to survive and vice versa. Like the delicate threads of a spider web, their existences were intertwined. Dhampirs couldn't thrive without drawing from a vampire's life essence and likewise, vampires often fed from dhampirs to keep their organs and bodily functions from going dormant. The stronger the creature, the more powerful their blood. Because Saeed had fed from Sasha—a vampire—before leaving, it would be at least a couple of weeks before he would need to feed again. With any luck, he'd find his mate before then.

The fae with hair like fire.

Saeed had seen her in the Collective so many times her features were ingrained in his memory. Throughout time and history, from memory to memory, he'd tracked her. Italy, Spain, England, and Mongolia. Australia, China, Russia, and Africa. There wasn't a corner of the earth she hadn't occupied, nor a space of time when she hadn't been present. Sasha doubted her existence and thought her dead but Saeed knew better. The fae would tether Saeed's soul. He needed only to find her to prove it.

As the last human shuffled down the narrow aisle to exit the plane, Saeed rose from his seat and retrieved his bag. A thrill raced through him. He was a predator after all, and this was the ultimate hunt. Seattle was a vast city, nearly as large as L.A. But the supernatural community was much smaller, narrowing the scope of Saeed's hunting grounds. He would find her. Because he had to. His soul, his very sanity, depended on it.

A shiver of anticipation raced down Cerys Bain's spine as she crossed East Denny and headed north on 10th Avenue East. She gave a quick look over her shoulder. Nothing. Electricity charged the air and caused the fine hairs along her forearms to stand on end. Fatigue tugged at her eyelids and weighed down her limbs. Gods, she could sleep for a year if only Rin would give her the opportunity to rest. A soft snort escaped her lips. There was no rest for the wicked, and Rinieri de Rege was as wicked as they came. Cerys supposed that as his property, and under his command, that made her wicked by default. She'd certainly carried out enough wicked deeds for him over the millennia to warrant the opinion. Too bad she didn't have a soul to gauge the severity of her offenses one way or the other.

At least tonight's errand wouldn't take too much out of her. True, Rin wanted retribution from the shifter that had cheated him, but the mage must have been feeling magnanimous tonight. When she found the shifter, he'd walk away with a few scratches, maybe a broken bone or two, which was much better than the alternative. Cerys would say he could thank her later, but in truth, it would be Rin who would receive the shifter's gratitude.

Cerys guessed she could say she hated her job, but that would require her to get the benefit of an actual paycheck from the wily mage in order to make the complaint in the first place. Slavery had its benefits she supposed. Sure, she didn't have cash in her pocket, but she didn't have to worry about things like covering her rent, paying her bills, grocery shopping, car insurance . . . Rin took care of everything. She was his collared pet, his property, the tool that carried out his will. She was certain her position seemed a hell of a lot more prestigious than it actually was.

It wasn't like he kept her in a kennel or chained her up in a basement when she wasn't being put to good use. On the contrary, Cerys lived a fairly lavish lifestyle. Rin provided for her. Fed her, put a roof over her head, made sure she had clothes to wear and outfitted her with the finest weapons. But even a prized poodle ate filet mignon every now and then. Cerys knew her place, knew what was expected of her, and Rin had made certain a long time ago that she would never bite the hand that fed her.

Another tingle of anticipation danced over her skin. She was much too seasoned for nerves. Too hardened for anxiety of any kind. Something was coming. And Cerys had a feeling that whatever it was would stir up all kinds of trouble.

She stopped on the sidewalk and looked up at the sign that read The Caged Canary. She snorted. The name was sort of fitting considering her situation. The club was primarily a supernatural hangout, which meant Cerys wouldn't have to operate with too much discretion. Fine by her. Duplicity had never been her thing. She threw her shoulders back as she walked through the entrance. The bouncer, a rough-looking werewolf she'd seen around, gave her a once over and took a cautious step back. Most every supernatural creature in Seattle knew she worked for

Rin, but that's not why they tended to give her a wide berth. No, it was because Cerys was an *enaid dwyn,* a stealer of souls, and that's why she was regarded with a certain level of fear. The notoriety should've been a nice boost to her ego. Instead, it only made Cerys long for autonomy.

From across the bar she spotted the shifter hanging out at the pool tables near the back of the building. As if he sensed her eyes on him he looked up and met her gaze. He stood up straight and dropped the pool cue to his side. His eyes darted from one end of the club to the next as though looking for a route of escape.

Sorry buddy, there's only one way out and that's through me.

Cerys made a beeline for the pool tables. She was tired and not a little hangry. She just wanted to get this business over with, scarf down a burger, and go to bed.

"Cerys, what's up? I was just getting ready to go see Rin."

She rolled her eyes. *Sure.* That's what they all said when they were caught. "I don't have the patience to deal with your bullshit tonight, Derek. You know what Rin wants."

Derek shifted his weight from one leg to the other. He was getting ready to bolt. It wouldn't do him any good. There wasn't anywhere in the city he could go that Cerys wouldn't find him. "I need a few more days. I can pay him interest."

"No interest. No leeway. You owe Rin thirty large, due immediately. You have it or not?"

Derek's fear thickened the air. It settled on the back of Cerys's tongue, thick and cloying like honey. She knew what he thought. What he assumed she was here to take. Cerys didn't have friends, hell, she didn't even have acquaintances. No one could stomach her company for more than a few minutes because they were too busy being afraid of what she had the potential to do. That, coupled with the notable absence of remorse, made what she was about to do to Derek that much easier.

So fast the movement was a blur, she grabbed Derek by the wrist and pinned his hand to the pool table. She might have been nothing more than a diminutive fae, but Cerys's strength surpassed even the most stalwart of males. Derek cried out, the sound high pitched and frantic.

"Don't do it!" he screamed. "I'll pay Rin tomorrow! Every damn cent! Don't take my fucking soul!"

Cerys reached for the dagger sheathed at her hip. In one fluid motion, she pulled the blade free from the scabbard and stabbed down, severing Derek's pinky finger at the second knuckle. She released her hold on his wrist and he fell backward to the floor. He cradled his injured hand, his frantic, sobbing breaths reaching her ears over the din of the dated nineties music. A smirk curved her lips as she scooped up the severed digit and tucked it into her pocket. He was damn lucky to be walking away tonight having only lost a finger.

"Tomorrow." Cerys pointed the dagger at Derek to drive her point home before cleaning the blood off on her pants and sliding it back into the sheath. "Thirty-thousand, delivered to Rin, in person. If you don't show up by midnight you'll be seeing me again and it definitely won't be a pleasant experience."

She took Derek's incoherent blubbering as a positive affirmation. She gave him one last appraising look before turning on a heel and leaving.

Cerys paused at the door. She waited for a string of profanity, angry shouts, the threats that should've inevitably followed her out the door. The only sounds to fill her ears were that of the retro dance tracks pulsing around her and the murmur of voices as she walked past. She pulled open the door with a derisive snort and stepped out into the cool spring air. The scent of rain filled her nostrils as she took a deep breath and held it in her lungs before letting it all out in a rush.

Just once she'd like to see someone treat her with open hostility and disdain rather than cower in fear. Or perhaps have someone look upon her fondly, offer up a genuine smile, or treat her as a friend for no reason other than they enjoyed her company. Over the course of her existence, Cerys had learned there was nothing more hurtful than being feared. But as long as she remained Rin's property, she would never be regarded as anything other than a creature straight out of a nightmare.

Soul stealer.

Reaper.

And thanks to Rin, she deserved every bit of it.

CHAPTER
2

"Vampire!"

"What is he doing here?"

"They are expanding their territory."

"Mikhail Aristov is power-hungry. He won't stop until he controls the entire West Coast."

"He looks dangerous. His eyes are wild. Steer clear of him, or he'll tear your throat out."

Saeed tucked away his amusement as he sauntered down Summit Avenue and negotiated the crowded sidewalks of Capitol Hill. This particular district of Seattle was heavily populated with supernatural creatures, though none of them like Saeed. In his world, he wasn't gawked at for the color of his skin, his features, or nationality. In the supernatural world, Saeed was a topic of conversation because of his dual fangs. His thirst for blood. The fact that he was only one of a handful of vampires to walk the earth. Perhaps prejudice was inescapable for him no matter who he kept company with.

For decades, the entire dhampir population—including Mikhail Aristov, the last vampire—had been confined to

Los Angeles. But Mikhail's ascension to power and his ability to turn dhampirs into vampires afforded their species the opportunity to wander farther from the epicenter of their population. Something they'd been unable to do for over two centuries. Their newfound freedom was bound to cause a stir.

It had been over a week since Saeed arrived in the city. He'd managed to rent a condo close to Capitol Hill, and every night was spent in search of the fire-haired fae. Dry heat scratched at the back of his throat. It wouldn't be long, five days at the most, before his heart quit beating, lungs quit breathing, and his thirst became unbearable. Saeed refused to take any vein but his mate's. No other's blood would sate him.

If he didn't find her soon, he might lose his mind completely.

The Collective pushed at Saeed's consciousness. Voices called to him, distant memories entreating, seducing, begging him to join their company. Gods he was tempted. So far, he'd been unable to find the fae in the city, but he'd become astute at tracking her throughout the Collective. He could stay there forever, watch her, covet her. But never touch. Never taste. It would be the type of torture impossible to survive.

The tingle of magic drew Saeed's attention as he walked past the open door of a dive bar. Goosebumps rose on his arms, and he brushed the sensation away as he stepped through the door and into the stuffy, crowded space. The air was hot. It weighed him down and seemed to coat his lungs. A fine sheen of sweat slicked his skin as he maneuvered his way past the crowds of humans and supernaturals alike and made his way to the bar.

For the benefit of the humans here, he could pass as mundane in this place. Whether or not he could pass as sane was yet to be seen.

Saeed bellied up to the bar. He asked the bartender for a glass of water and offered up a five dollar bill to temper the human's disdain. Saeed rarely drank alcohol aside from the occasional glass of wine. It annoyed him that bars had become the central gathering places for those out at night. So pedestrian. So unimaginative. But if Saeed had any hope of finding the fae, he had no choice but to suck it up and linger in these carbon copy, crowded, stuffy hotspots.

"Not often you run into a vampire in the city. In fact, can't say I've ever seen one in the flesh."

Saeed sipped from the lip of his glass as he cast a side-long glance toward the source of the gruff voice that spoke beside him. "You must not be very old then," he remarked. "Because the world used to be peopled with vampires."

"Europe maybe," the male went on as though Saeed hadn't spoken. He took a slow breath and determined the male was some sort of shifter. Maybe a werewolf. His scent was canine in nature. "Not in the states though."

Obviously the male knew little of vampire history. Or anything for that matter. "And yet, here I am." The myriad voices of the Collective whispered in Saeed's ears. He muttered a curse under his breath. Commanded them to leave him be.

The shifter's eyes widened a fraction of an inch as he studied Saeed closely. "Well, you're the only one I've ever seen. Lots of talk about you around the city."

"Really." Saeed knew his presence in Seattle wouldn't go unnoticed but that had been his hope. If he couldn't find the fae, perhaps word of his presence would reach her and she would come to him.

"Yeah." At least Saeed could count on the shifter to be easy to bait. "Somebody like you could make a killing here."

Saeed turned to fully face the shifter. One brow arched curiously as he asked, "How so?"

The shifter's Adam's apple bobbed as he swallowed nervously. He brought his hand up to his throat and massaged the flesh there as though to guard it. A corner of Saeed's mouth hitched in a half smile as the bitter tang of the shifter's unease reached his nostrils. It was better the male feared Saeed. It would prompt him to be forthcoming with information without Saeed having to pry it from him later.

"I heard the rumors." The shifter's use of language was enough to make Saeed want to bite him and drink him dry. Good gods. "You're out hunting every night. Killed a warlock last night after the bastard jumped you. Magic wielders, man." He shook his head. "Don't get me wrong," the male added quickly. "Dude probably had it coming. My buddy Randy said the warlock wanted your blood for some dark shit. Ain't no one gonna put up with that. But you're getting a reputation. If you're looking for work, might as well start at the top."

Among those old enough to remember, Saeed already had quite the reputation. But to the ignorant pup standing before him, Saeed was considered formidable because he'd purportedly killed a warlock who'd attempted to attack him. This male had no idea who Saeed was or what he was capable of. If he did, he wouldn't be so foolish as to stand here and run off at the mouth.

"And where is the top?" Saeed took another slow sip of ice water that did nothing to quench the burn in his throat. He'd be surprised if the shifter did little more than point him in the direction of a low-level crime ring. His chest tightened with impending disappointment. Tonight was likely to be a continued waste of his time.

The shifter leaned in close. The scent of his fear intensified and Saeed felt a small amount of respect for him that he'd get so close to Saeed's fangs in order to share the secret. "Rinieri de Rege, man. You think warlocks are trouble? They got nothing on mages."

The breath stalled in Saeed's lungs. He'd never been afforded the opportunity to hear the mage's name. What the Collective had offered him was frustratingly generic. A tease. Breadcrumbs in a dense forest he'd been forced to follow. And though the name had sent a shiver of anticipation down Saeed's spine, it didn't mean this Rinieri was the one he was looking for. Still, it was the most credible lead he'd gotten in a week. He let out a soft snort of amusement that the information would come from a brainless shifter.

"And where can I find this mage?" Saeed asked.

The shifter gave a nervous look around. "He owns a place over on Broadway East called Crimson. He's there every night, the bastard thinks he's pretty fucking special."

Saeed pinned him with a calculating stare. If the male meant to intentionally mislead him or draw him into a trap, Saeed would hunt the son of a bitch down and end him. "Why share this information with me?" he asked. "I've done nothing to warrant the favor."

The shifter shrugged. "Hey, I do you favor, maybe you do me a favor someday. Never a bad thing to have powerful friends. I'm Wes, by the way."

He suspected the shifter wanted more than just a favor in return, though. More likely, he saw an opportunity to move himself up the food chain. Saeed would let him assume whatever the hell he wanted to as long as it got Saeed what he wanted. Nothing mattered more to him than the fae and he would do anything to find her.

Saeed reached into his pocket. He pulled out a money clip and took a hundred dollar bill from the fold and slid it across the bar to Wes. A satisfied smile curved the shifter's lips as he palmed the bill and tucked it away. Saeed smiled wide in turn, making sure to showcase the wicked points of his dual fangs. He drew on his power, held the shifter's gaze. "Tell me, Wes, are you being truthful with me?"

Wes's eyes glazed over as Saeed compelled him. He gave a slow nod of his head. "I wouldn't bullshit you," he replied. "I don't have a death wish."

Saeed released his hold on the shifter's mind. Wes let out a gust of breath and gave a violent shake of his head, giving Saeed a glimpse of his animal nature. He took a cautious step back as though putting a couple of extra feet between them would protect him from Saeed's ability to compel him.

"Thank you for the information, Wes." Saeed was anxious to get out of here and investigate this promising new lead. "If your information proves fruitful, I will indeed owe you a favor." He turned and left without another word. Seattle was vast, but the supernatural community was relatively small. He had no doubt Wes would find him again and expect payment for services rendered. Whatever he asked would be well worth it if Saeed found his mate.

Every freaking night.

Cerys held in a frustrated sigh. Rin was a total attention whore, and he insisted on going out every night to soak up the fear-fueled accolades of those stupid enough to hang around. They sat in the VIP section at Crimson, as usual, with Rin front and center and Cerys hanging out in the back corner trying to be as inconspicuous as possible. She wasn't interested in attention, didn't want anyone's simpering compliments. Honestly, she just wanted to go home and go to bed.

No such luck, Rin was on a roll tonight.

"Cerys! Come here."

She rolled her eyes. When Rin had first enslaved her, she'd treated him with open hostility and welcomed his punishments. As the decades turned to centuries and centuries to millennia, they'd settled into a reluctant camaraderie. It did no good to fight him. Cerys's only option had been to learn to tolerate him. Which, on nights like this, was hard enough.

The crowd of would-be worshipers parted as Cerys made her way to him. She wasn't merely feared, she was reviled. Others were loath to touch her, worried the simplest contact would leave them bereft of their souls. If only it were that easy.

Rin clucked his tongue at Cerys's grim expression. "Gods, have a drink, would you? You look like you're at a damned funeral."

Cerys pursed her lips. She was in a sour mood and no amount of alcohol was going to change that. "Haven't you had your fill of adulation for one night?"

Rin's robust laughter rang in her ears. Obviously he hadn't. And as his bodyguard, she was required to stay by his side until he was ready to tap out for the night. He reached for the bottle of Tito's and pulled it from the bucket of ice. He poured a shot and slid the glass across the table toward Cerys. His dark gaze leveled on her and his lips thinned. "Drink."

A knot formed in the pit of Cerys's stomach. His serious expression told her he wasn't about to suffer her snarky attitude tonight. Her jaw clenched so hard her teeth ground. She snatched the glass from the tabletop and threw back her head as she downed the shot in a single swallow. "Happy?" she asked without an ounce of humor before slamming the glass back onto the tabletop.

Rin's expression softened and he gave her a wan smile. "Sit with me," he said. "I hate it when you skulk in the corner."

Rin had made her an assassin. Skulking sort of came with the territory. She took a seat beside him and propped her legs up on the opposite chair before folding her arms across her chest. She'd sit with him, but she'd be damned if she looked like she enjoyed his company.

"You still look pissy."

Cerys shrugged, unconcerned. "I'm hungry. And that makes me cranky."

Rin snorted. "You're always hungry."

Cerys gave him a pointed look. "And whose fault is that?"

Rin looked away as though bored with the conversation. The absence of her soul left Cerys feeling perpetually empty. Hungry. If not for her supernatural metabolism she'd weigh five-hundred pounds by now. Food did little to fill the void. She'd tried alcohol centuries ago but all it managed to accomplish was to make her feel even emptier. So yeah, food was her vice. She stuffed her face, filled her stomach, and for a while it made her feel as though she were more than just an empty shell. *Gods*. She was a total shit show.

Rin brought his hand up into the air and snapped his fingers. A server rushed over from across the building and bent over Rin's left shoulder. "Cerys is hungry," he replied. "Have the kitchen whip her up something."

The server, a sylph with long, wild blond hair turned her attention to Cerys. "Sure," she said. "What do you feel like tonight?"

"A burger and fries will work." What she really wanted was a hot fudge sundae but that wasn't exactly bar food. "Can you bring me some mozzarella sticks too?"

"Can do," the sylph said with a bright smile. "I'll bring it out to you in a few."

"There. I've fed you." Rin seemed pretty damned pleased with his magnanimous gesture. "Now cheer the fuck up."

Magnanimous, but never kind. Indulgent, but never selfless. He wasn't suggesting that Cerys adjust her attitude.
It was a command. One she'd best obey, or be prepared to
face the consequences if she chose to blow him off. She
sat up straight in her seat and unfolded her arms. Rin retrieved her discarded shot glass and poured another jigger
of vodka before sliding it back to her once again. Cerys
forced a pleasant smile to her face as she picked up the
glass and brought it up in a silent toast before tipping it
back and letting the liquor burn a path down her throat into
her stomach. She knew what was expected of her. Knew
how to play the game. And she knew all too well what
would happen to her if she misbehaved.

While Cerys waited for her food, she made exhausting
small talk with the members of Rin's fan club that littered
the private lounge. Out of respect for Rin, they were all
friendly with her but beneath that façade Cerys tasted their
fear and it nearly stole her appetite.

"Vampire!"

Cerys's head whipped around toward the witch who'd
issued the surprised word from behind her. She followed
the female's line of sight across the bar toward the
entrance. Vampire? In Seattle? It had been centuries since
Cerys had laid eyes on a vampire. For some unexplained
reason, Rin had always kept the company of vampires. But
after the race's near annihilation, he'd found new acquaintances to entertain him. Cerys had found herself fascinated by vampires as well. She wondered if their thirst for
blood rivaled the hunger she felt on a daily basis. She'd
always sensed a kindred connection to vampires even
though they couldn't have been more different.

Cerys scanned the crowded bar for a glimpse of the
creature that had caused such a stir. The curious murmurs
reached Rin's ears and he sat up a little straighter in his
seat, his expression serious. "Where?"

Yes, where? Cerys forced herself to remain nonchalant when what she really wanted to do was launch herself from her chair and comb the bar herself. She'd heard the rumors. That the vampire king had come out of hiding and resurrected his race, but she'd paid the gossip little attention. It had little to do with her world as it was. But now that a vampire had come to their very door, Cerys couldn't help but be intrigued.

Rin leaned back in his chair, angling his head toward the witch. "What have you heard?"

Her eyes went wide and an excited smile grew on her slender face. She was pleased as punch to have Rin's full attention and eager to keep it. "The rumors have been circulating for days," she said. "Of course I didn't believe it at first, but now . . ."

Rin urged her on with a flourish of his hand. "Go on."

She leaned in conspiratorially. "He's mad." A wild glint lit her eyes with the words. "And quite violent from what I've heard. He wanders the streets night after night muttering to himself and lashes out at anyone who dares to cross his path."

"His name?" Rin ventured.

The witch worried her bottom lip between her teeth. "That I don't know." She leaned back in inch or two as though concerned she would stir Rin's ire. "Others speculate that he's old. Perhaps older even than Mikhail Aristov. A Saracen and quite a frightening specimen."

Cerys's heart raced in her chest. She glanced over at Rin, knowing the witch's words would only serve to pique his interest more. *A Saracen.* The antiquated, and not altogether favorable term gave her pause. Supernaturals had a tendency to live in their pasts and that included their vocabularies. It indicated his heritage but hardly reflected the gods he'd worshipped. The witch wouldn't have referred to him as such, however, if he hadn't been incredibly old. Almost as old as Rin. And likely, just as threatening.

She scanned the crowd once again and near the entrance she spotted him. The familiar anticipation she'd felt earlier in the week danced over her skin and Cerys shivered. He was a male unlike any other. *Magnificent.* Flawless dark skin, dark flowing hair, eyes like midnight. He stood head and shoulders above most of the patrons there and every inch of him was defined with lean muscle. An aura of wildness surrounded him and his gaze remained unfocused as though his mind were a million miles away from this moment. If it were possible, the vast chasm in Cerys's chest opened even wider, threatening to suck her very existence into oblivion.

He was soulless. As an *enaid dwyn*, she could see souls, and where his should have been there was a colorless void. Something tugged at her chest and she reached up to rub the sensation away. Already the two of them had something in common . . .

She'd been right that something was coming, and the vampire definitely looked like trouble.

CHAPTER
3

Saeed swayed on his feet. Memories latched onto him, wound themselves around his limbs, through his body and mind, like tendrils of seaweed grabbing hold to pull him beneath the ocean's surface. The room swam in and out of focus, blurring between memory and reality. He needed to feed. He needed clarity. But until he found her, until she tethered his soul, he was condemned to madness. Saeed cradled his forehead in his palm as he drew a cleansing breath. It had been a long night and an even longer week, and his continued search for his mate was beginning to take its toll.

He just had to keep it together until sunrise. After that he could collapse into blissful oblivion. He would persevere. The Collective would *not* get the better of him.

Saeed shook himself free of the hold of memories and walked further into the club. In most cases, the blaring dance music would've annoyed him, but instead Saeed welcomed the pounding bass into his ears and let the lilting, electronic tones distract his mind. He focused on the sound of the high trills and deep basses, the steady rhythm

that thrummed like a heartbeat, and the tempo that built
to a crescendo before calming once again.

An enticing scent hit Saeed's nostrils and cleared his
mind in an instant. The fog of the Collective evaporated,
leaving in its place a laser sharp focus he hadn't felt in
months. His thirst ignited, burning through him like a fire
through dry kindling. The scent of blood called to him and
he let his senses lead him as he ventured deeper into the
building.

All thoughts of the Collective vanished as Saeed tracked
the scent of blood. His predatory instincts took over, his
singular thought that of pursuit. Near the back of the club
in the VIP section, he spotted a male holding court. Magic
sparked the air and Saeed's gaze narrowed. The mage.
The male was everything Saeed had seen of him in the
Collective: proud, powerful, menacing. And at the mage's
side, Saeed caught a glimpse of fire-red hair. He'd found
her. The one thing he'd coveted for months.

Without a thought to his own safety or actions, Saeed
advanced. His singular focus was the female who stood not
thirty yards away and her inviting scent that beckoned him
closer. He barreled into the VIP lounge, pushed his way
past the mage's supernatural entourage, toward the object
of his obsession. Any creature that dared to try and stop
him would meet a swift and violent end.

His actions were immediately interpreted as an act of
aggression. The very female he sought to possess kicked
out her chair as she stood. Light glinted off metal in a flash
of motion as she drew a dagger from a sheath at her side.
Her arm whipped around in a backhanded motion as she
spun the dagger in her grip. She lunged toward Saeed and
he came to a stop, the razor sharp edge of the blade pressed
tightly against his throat.

Do it.

Even in his madness the thought made little sense. He

wanted her to cut him. Wanted her to draw his blood. He raised his chin, inviting the slice of her blade, and her brow furrowed as she studied him.

"If you have a care for your life, vampire, you won't move another inch."

Gods, the sound of her voice. It resonated through the hollow cavern of Saeed's soulless chest creating a deep, throbbing ache that nearly brought him to his knees. His eyes drifted shut as he waited for the moment of their tethering. Anticipation skittered through him and yet, he remained bereft of his soul.

Nothing.

If it were possible, Saeed felt even emptier. The tether should have been immediate. He'd witnessed it enough times in the Collective to know. Fear and despair choked the air from his lungs. The blood ran cold in his veins and icy fingers of dread speared Saeed's heart. She was his mate. It was the only truth he'd known throughout these months of madness. Something was wrong. Saeed refused to believe otherwise.

"I meant no offense." Saeed's eyes came slowly open with his words. Maintaining composure seemed near to impossible while his world crumbled around him, but at the moment, it was his only choice. "I simply wanted to introduce myself to your master."

A deep groove cut into the flawless skin above the bridge of her nose. Certainly she wondered how he would know such a thing, and it pained Saeed to have caused her any hurt or distress by pointing out she was nothing more than property.

"You'll have to forgive Cerys," the mage said with a smirk. "She takes her job pretty damned seriously."

Her job. As though she had any choice in the matter. Saeed's fangs throbbed in his gums as he was possessed of the urge to sink them deep into the mage's throat and tear out the vein there. Giving in to that violent urge would only lead to ruin however, and so Saeed was forced to maintain his composure.

"Indeed." Saeed pushed the word from between his teeth. "And who could blame her when she serves someone as powerful as yourself."

The mage graced Saeed with an indulgent smile. He flung a casual arm over the back of his chair and regarded Saeed with a narrowed gaze. "What could a newly turned vampire possibly know about me to make that sort of assumption?"

Saeed knew how to play the game. How to play to the mage's ego, lull him into a false sense of security. Had the fae tethered him as Saeed had expected, the arrogant male would be dead by now and Saeed would be escaping the city with his prize. Saeed was adaptive, however, and had learned long ago that things rarely went according to plan. He returned the mage's smile and adopted a relaxed posture despite the fact his mate still held her dagger to his throat.

Tether or not, she was his mate. Saeed refused to believe otherwise.

"I know that Seattle's supernaturals bow to Rinieri de Rege and wait to do his bidding."

The mage broke out into raucous laughter that grated on Saeed's ears. "I'd hardly say they wait to do my bidding. And please, call me Rin."

The invitation for casual familiarity was a good sign. Saeed had expected open hostility and that Rin had so easily let down his guard was one less obstacle for him to surmount. He gave a slight nod of his head which was still hampered by the blade pressed to his throat as he offered up his own introduction. "Saeed Almasi." His eyes slid to the alluring fae, and Saeed tried not to stare. She was the most beautiful creature he'd ever beheld and her mere presence shook him to his foundation.

"Cerys Bain, meet Saeed Almasi."

Cerys. Finally knowing her name after so many months was a gift Saeed cherished. He couldn't wait to say it aloud, feel the roll of it off his tongue, hear the sweet sound of it in his ears. His eyes met hers, and Saeed was once again struck by the notion that the ghostly images of her ingrained in his mind hadn't done her justice.

"Cerys," Rin said with a flippant flourish of his hand. "Sit down and give our guest the opportunity to relax."

Gods, but she was beautiful. No one could ever mistake her for anything other than a preternatural creature. Her hair truly was like fire; wild tangles of curls, multifaceted in their many shades of red and gold, framed her delicate face and made her body appear even more delicate and lithe. Her eyes were like starlight, unlike any color he'd ever seen. Indescribable. Like all of the fae, she was tall and thin—delicate—but he knew she possessed a ferocity and strength that fascinated him. She was beyond description, and worthy only of his awe and admiration.

"Cerys!" Rin snapped. "I said sit down."

A violent urge spiked inside of Saeed and his hands balled into fists at his side. Anyone who spoke to her with such blatant disrespect should've been punished for the offense. Instead, Cerys shot a murderous glare Rin's way before lowering the dagger to her side and dropping back down into her chair.

"She gets cranky when she's hungry," Rin offered the explanation with an air of boredom. "And she's always hungry."

The snickering that came from Rin's entourage told Saeed the issue of Cerys's mood and hunger must have been a running joke. One she obviously didn't appreciate, and neither did he. His own thirst burned in his throat. It was a need Saeed knew all too well and it certainly wasn't a laughing matter.

"Then I suggest you feed her." He kept his tone light despite the indignant rage that continued to burn through him. "It seems prudent to keep a creature as deadly as her as happy as possible."

Rin laughed. He held out a hand toward the empty chair beside him in invitation. Saeed lowered himself into the chair and forced himself to relax though he felt anything but calm. After so many long months, he'd finally found his mate. And she had failed to tether his soul.

Cerys watched the vampire from beneath lowered lashes, careful not to give him her undivided attention. If she showed any interest in him at all, Rin would find a way to exploit it. The last thing she wanted to give him was more ammunition to use against her.

"It seems unfair you know so much about me while I know nothing about you," Rin remarked.

The bastard wouldn't waste any time in learning as much about the vampire as possible. Cerys had been with Rin long enough to know the games he played and why he played them. Saeed seemed unconcerned with Rin's curiosity. A lazy, indulgent smile spread across his full lips, revealing the wicked points of his dual fangs. Cerys's stomach did a backflip before slowly settling back down into place. The reaction was unexpected, but not at all unpleasant.

Interesting.

"Like I said, I am Saeed Almasi," the vampire replied. "Newly turned by Mikhail Aristov, and a former master of one of the thirteen covens."

Dear gods, his voice. Smooth and indulgent like a molten chocolate cake. Cerys would've never imagined that a sound could be delicious but Saeed's voice had managed to make her even hungrier than she already was. He kept his attention focused on Rin with only an occasional glance her way. But when they managed to make eye contact a thrill chased through her that took Cerys's breath away.

"Former master?" Rin ventured. Saeed had managed to pique his curiosity. If only the vampire realized what a horrible mistake that was. "And why is that?"

Saeed gave a shrug that was meant to be casual. Cerys wondered if he'd realized how miserably he'd failed. There was nothing casual about the dark, deadly vampire. His wild gaze, lean, yet heavily muscled form, and the menacing air that surrounded him betrayed his attempt to appear unassuming. The male was deadly. Obviously a killer. Only a fool would let their guard down around him. She could only hope the vampire would realize early on that Rin was no fool.

"The vampire race is reborn," Saeed said. "There is no reason for any of us who've been turned to remain in L.A."

A corner of Rin's mouth hitched in a half smile. He studied Saeed for a quiet moment and Cerys could practically hear the gears grinding away in his calculating mind. "I have to admit I'm pleasantly surprised to learn the rumors I've heard are true. The world has gone too long without the presence of vampires. But why abandon your coven? You could've brought them with you."

Someone as power-hungry as Rin could never fathom why anyone would relinquish power. It would only make Saeed more appealing to him. Saeed's dark gaze slid to the side once again and held Cerys immobile. Rin wasn't the only one fascinated by this stranger. Her own curiosity was a very dangerous thing that could land her in a boatload of trouble.

"I have minded my flock for centuries," Saeed said. "Protected them from the threat of slayers until such a time as Mikhail would rise from his ashes. I have done my due diligence, and my reward is my freedom."

Eloquent. And old. Whoever Saeed was, he'd walked the earth for quite some time, confirming at least part of the rumors they'd heard upon his appearance. His words resonated with Cerys. His need for freedom echoed her own longing and it only served to further hollow out her chest. If only she could sever her own ties so easily.

"Besides," Saeed added. "Mikhail Aristov holds the only true power in L.A. The entirety of the race bows to him."

Uh-oh. Cerys sensed a move would be in their future. The combination of vampires and power would be too much for Rin to resist. He'd be drawn to the vampire king like a moth to a flame. No doubt it would bring them nothing but trouble.

Rin smiled. The son of a bitch was happy as a clam to have this new and very welcome distraction. It hearkened to the good old days—or the *not* so good old days—when they'd spent night after night making their way from one coven to the next. Rin had been even more ruthless back then than he was now. Cerys could only hope the vampire wouldn't reawaken that ruthless bloodlust time had managed to temper, albeit little.

"Do you not wish to bow?"

Saeed let out a chuff of laughter. "On the contrary. I don't mind swearing my allegiance, I'm simply eager to spread my wings. I won't be the only one to leave Los Angeles," he said. "The thirteen covens containing every dhampir alive have been forced to live within miles of the last vampire for centuries. Now that he is no longer alone in his existence, our shackles have been broken."

Rin listened, rapt. "Is it true that Mikhail's mate is extraordinary?"

Saeed's jaw squared, a motion so quick and subtle that

Cerys wondered if Rin had noticed at all. "She is," Saeed conceded. "But to what extent I know not. Mikhail keeps her well protected and covets her secrets."

Strike two. The vampire was either incredibly stupid or working an angle. That information was like catnip to Rin. Vague as it might've been, it was enough to entice him. If Saeed didn't shut his trap, they'd be on the next redeye to Los Angeles. Cerys wasn't interested in relocating, and she certainly wasn't interested in seeing Rin revert to his old ways.

"How many of you are there now?"

Wow. He wasn't beating around the bush. Saeed seemed unconcerned with Rin's straightforward line of questioning and hiked his shoulder once again as he feigned disinterest.

"A handful or so." His noncommittal answer earned him a couple of points. Maybe he wasn't as stupid as Cerys had given him credit for. "It's none of my concern anymore."

"I see."

Rin would play this close to the hip. No way would he show his hand so soon. As intrigued as Cerys was by Saeed, she said a silent prayer he'd come to his senses and leave Seattle as soon as possible. But why did the prospect of him leaving make her feel even more empty than she'd ever felt before?

"Then tell me, what brings you to Seattle?" Rin leaned forward in his chair and fixed Saeed with a serious stare. His lips curled upward with a hint of a smile. "Besides your desire for freedom."

"You do," Saeed said without an ounce of humor.

Strike three. Ugh. The hard-core ego stroking Rin was currently getting would no doubt make him even more insufferable. "Me?" Rin never could pull off humility convincingly. "I'm nothing more than a mage among many.

Surely not as noteworthy as one of a handful of rare vampires."

Saeed grinned, once again showcasing the wicked points of his fangs. "It all depends on your perspective. In Seattle, you are a legend."

Cerys's eyes rolled so hard she worried she might lose them in the back of her head. *Give me a break.* Rin was a lot of things, but legendary sure as shit wasn't one of them.

"I'm humbled by the compliment." No he wasn't. "What can I possibly offer you, Saeed that you don't already have?"

Now they were getting down to business. Saeed turned and looked at Cerys fully. The hunger in his midnight eyes froze her in place. The color gave way to a flash of bright silver and she shivered. The moment lasted far too long and her heart beat a wild rhythm against her rib cage. The intensity of his attention unnerved her and at the same time, she craved it.

"Employment for starters." When Saeed finally tore his gaze away from Cerys to look at Rin once again, she let out a slow and shaky breath. "I might no longer be under Mikhail Aristov's thumb, but that doesn't mean I'm not interested in making a name for myself on my own."

Rin chuckled. "Believe me, you're very existence gives you notoriety."

Saeed inclined his head ever so slightly as though to acknowledge the compliment. "Then allow me to put that notoriety to work for you."

Rin settled back into his chair. He regarded Saeed for less than a second before he said, "How can I possibly refuse?"

Cerys's gut bottomed out. A sense of dread welled up within her to the point that she found it hard to swallow. Nothing but ruin would come to the vampire by associating with Rin. He destroyed everything he touched, her included.

The loud bass of the imposing club music drowned out her thoughts as their server stepped up to their table, a large round tray resting on her right palm. Cerys's stomach growled as she let the food adopt her undivided attention. Some people ate their feelings. Cerys ate her *lack* of feelings.

"Thank the gods." Rin's dramatic tone made her want to sock him in the face. "Maybe now that you've got some food your mood will improve. You'll see," he said as an aside to Saeed. "Cerys is always hungry; she'd eat all day long if I let her."

If she could feel embarrassed, Cerys was certain her cheeks would be flame red by now. But she couldn't muster up the energy or the emotions to care one way or another what the vampire thought of her. His hungry gaze slid to her once again and Cerys suppressed the urge to let out a slow sigh. If it didn't matter what the vampire thought of her, why did he evoke such a visceral reaction? And why did she sense his coming here had awakened something in her she thought long since dead? The vampire's presence was like the promise of . . . *something*. And Cerys knew the only way she'd find out what that promise was, was to keep the vampire as close to her as possible.

CHAPTER
4

Saeed came awake with the setting sun. Dry heat scorched his throat and panic choked the air from his lungs as the unfamiliar surroundings of his Seattle penthouse came into focus. He clawed at his chest as a deep, hollow ache opened up inside of him. An ache that should've been banished the moment he laid eyes on his mate.

Gods, why had he not been tethered?

It was impossible. Inconceivable. And he had no explanation for it. By all rights, Cerys's inability to tether him should've been a clear indicator that her soul had failed to anchor his. Saeed refused to believe that truth, however. He refused to believe anyone other than the beautiful fae would tether him.

The myriad voices of the Collective pushed at Saeed's consciousness. He pressed the heels of his palms to his temples and clenched his jaw. His fangs pricked his bottom lip and his tongue flicked out to swipe the blood away. Cerys's blood had called to him. Her scent had beckoned him like no other's. Only his mate could have accomplished such a feat. There had to be an explanation as to why his soul hadn't been tethered, and Saeed planned to get to the bottom of it.

The low, pleasant tone of his doorbell went off, and Saeed let out a groan as he pushed himself up from the bed. He pulled on a pair of loose workout pants and padded through the bedroom to the front door. The doorbell rang again, this time more insistent. He'd show whoever was on the other side how he felt about being rushed.

He pulled open the door with a jerk, lip pulled back in an angry snarl. The growl that rose in his chest died in an instant as he came face-to-face with Cerys.

A smirk tugged at her full lips as she placed a hand on her cocked hip. Her light eyes raked him from his toes to his head before she fixed a disinterested expression on her lovely face. "Rin wants to see you."

Right down to business. Saeed expected nothing less. He propped one arm high above his head on the door jam and leaned on it as he adopted an equally disinterested posture. He could play her game, and play it better. "So he sent you here promptly at sundown to fetch me?"

"Rin doesn't like to be kept waiting," she replied without inflection.

"I don't doubt it. But that doesn't mean I'm going to jump every time he snaps his fingers."

She cocked a brow. "You should've thought of that before you asked him for a job."

She'd grown colder over the years. Saeed might not have known her, but he'd learned much about her through the Collective. There was a hardness to her that hadn't been there before and disappointment welled within him that he hadn't been able to experience that softer, more vulnerable side of her.

It had been a week since Saeed had struck his bargain with Rin in the dark back corner of the club. A week of longing. A week of unfulfilled want. A week of questions he couldn't answer. A week of gnawing thirst. His heart barely beat, his lungs barely moved with breath. He hadn't eaten in two days and could no longer stomach even water. The only thing that would sate him now was blood. Her blood. And her sweet, inviting scent and proximity to him made her a temptation almost too great to resist.

Cerys's brow furrowed. The hand that rested on her hip twitched and she gripped herself harder as though resisting the urge to reach out. "Hey." The slightest concern flavored her tone, momentarily banishing the hardness that made her seem so cold and unfeeling. "Are you okay? You're not gonna pass out on me are you?"

Saeed swayed on his feet. There was no point in lying to her. "I haven't fed in two weeks." The admission was harder than he'd thought it would be to make.

She fixed him with an appraising stare. "Are you really as crazy as everyone says you are?"

Saeed let out a rueful bark of laughter. *Crazy.* How banal. Had she called him mad there would have at least been an elegant ring to it. The way she made it sound, he might as well be wearing a straitjacket.

"I wouldn't know," Saeed replied without humor. "I rarely concern myself with what others say about me."

Cerys cocked her head to one side as she studied him. Saeed watched her, taken aback by the emptiness of her expression. As though she wanted to conjure some form of emotion, anything, but came up empty. "Well, I never pass up an opportunity for a meal, or a snack, so you must be crazy."

Saeed's fangs throbbed in his gums. "I'm afraid my tastes are a little more discerning than yours."

A slow smile spread across her lips. He liked that she was good-natured enough not to take offense. "Oh yeah?" she asked. "What's your poison then? Dhampirs? I know you rarely feed from anyone other than your own kind. Bet you're rethinking that whole leaving your coven behind thing, huh?"

"Fae," Saeed said. Not exactly the truth, but not a lie either.

Cerys's jaw hung slack. She recovered quickly and hid her astonishment once again behind a mask of passivity. She let out a soft snort. "Good one."

Saeed allowed his smile to grow, showcasing the points of his dual fangs. His gaze didn't waver as his eyes met hers and held them. "Do I look like I'm kidding?"

Cerys's heart fluttered, sending the blood in a rush through her veins. The sound was as sweet as gentle music to Saeed's ears. His eyes drifted shut for the barest moment and it took an actual effort to open them again.

Her gaze narrowed and her jaw took on a determined set. She stepped past Saeed, into the penthouse and he closed the door behind her. He inhaled through his nose, anticipating the scent of her fear. The air around her didn't sour, but instead sweetened with her passage as though the prospect of having him feed from her excited her. Brave. Fierce. Daring.

Mine. Saeed didn't need a tether to tell him that.

She tugged at the snap that secured a wide leather cuff bracelet around her wrist. It came loose and she pulled it free before thrusting her arm out at him. "Go ahead," she dared him. "Two weeks is a long damned time to go without a meal."

She thought to bait him. To antagonize him. To watch with smug satisfaction as he backed down. Instead, Saeed's hand shot out in a blur of motion as he seized her by the wrist and hauled her against his body. Her quiet gasp of surprise only goaded him and he bit down on her tender flesh without preamble. The skin gave way beneath the

pressure of his razor-sharp fangs and an indulgent moan
worked its way up Saeed's throat as the first taste of her
blood washed over his tongue.

Just as he suspected, the taste of her had no equal. With
each strong pull of his mouth, a rush of power flooded him.
It wouldn't have been possible from anyone other than his
mate, solidifying Saeed's faith that Cerys had been meant
for him.

"Stop."

Her breathy plea nearly fell on deaf ears. Saeed was so
caught up in the moment, lost to the frenzy of feeding, her
scent, her taste, that the thought of disengaging his fangs
from her tender flesh seemed nearly impossible.

"Stop."

She issued the command with more force. Her scent did
sour this time, the barest hint of fear beneath her floral perfume. Saeed disengaged his fangs and swiped his tongue
over the punctures to close them before releasing his hold
on her wrist. Cerys pulled away as though burned. She
cradled her left wrist in her right hand and gently smoothed
her thumb over the spot where Saeed's mouth had just
been. A dark scowl passed over her features as she took a
cautious step back. She might've been upset with him for
taking the liberty, but she needed to learn sooner rather
than later that Saeed never backed down from a challenge.

Saeed's tongue flicked out at his bottom lip as he swiped
away the last remaining drops of Cerys's blood. He smiled.
His mind hadn't been so clear in months. "You offered,"
he said without apology.

She had the audacity to look shocked. "I didn't think
you'd actually take me up on it."

Lie. She had to know he could smell it. "You absolutely
did," he countered. "You simply hadn't counted on enjoying it."

Her jaw hung slack. Saeed enjoyed curtailing her stoicism and anger that seemed to boil just under the surface of her composure. Her chin bucked. If it was possible, she was even more beautiful in her indignation.

"Rin expects you in thirty minutes." She fixed him with a hard stare. "I advise punctuality."

Without another word, Cerys turned. She yanked open the door and strode out into the hallway. Saeed took a moment to admire the curve of her hips and the sway of her shapely ass before the door closed behind her and shut her from his view.

It had been centuries since Saeed had been presented with such a challenge. And he welcomed it with open arms.

Arrogant vampire!

Cerys's jaw clenched as she strode angrily through the foyer and stepped into the elevator. She snapped the leather cuff back into place, hoping it would banish the sensation that lingered on her skin. She could practically feel the heat of Saeed's mouth on her, the sting of his fangs as they broke the skin. A pleasant shiver raced down her spine and she forced the sensation away.

You simply hadn't counted on enjoying it.

A frustrated growl worked its way up Cerys's throat. Of course it had felt good! A vampire bite wasn't exactly painful. On the contrary, it flooded the receiver with warmth and gave them a nice little buzz. It wasn't as though Cerys had never experienced it before. Rin had, after all, kept the company of vampires for centuries before their near extinction. Saeed's bite had been especially pleasurable but it could have been that she'd simply forgotten what it felt like.

Yeah, sure. You practically swooned.

She let out another groan. It had been stupid to bait Saeed. She'd known he wouldn't back down from the challenge, and part of her hadn't wanted him to. Something about the vampire intrigued her and made her feel reckless. Or perhaps the monotony of soullessness had finally gotten to her. The gods knew she was looking for any escape she could find.

She reached out to push the button for the ground floor. The elevator doors slid silently shut and the car lurched as it began its descent. Cerys's heart still beat a little too quickly and her breath came in gentle pants. Rin would shit a brick if he found out what happened here tonight and she could only hope Saeed would keep his mouth shut. He'd learn soon enough why no one fucked with Rin.

The vampire had made his bed. Cerys still couldn't understand why anyone would enter willingly into a relationship of any kind with Rin. The male was as selfish and ruthless as they came. He'd exploit his own grandmother for a buck. Cerys snorted. Hell, he probably had. Then again, it was more likely someone like Rin had sprouted from the depths of hell rather than someone's loins. Did it really matter? Rin had Cerys under his thumb and no amount of speculation in regards to his origin or nature was going to change that.

Cerys stepped out of the elevator into the lobby to find Saeed seated on a couch waiting for her. He'd obviously dressed and flown down the stairs with his vampiric speed. *Show off.* She strode past him without so much as a glance. He stood and sauntered after her as though they had all the time in the world.

"You handle all of Rin's business, then?"

A finger of heat stroked up Cerys's spine. She threw her shoulders back and kept her posture straight as she stepped out of the building and into the crisp spring air. The timbre of his voice was an almost tangible thing that affected her much more than it should. "I handle whatever he wants me to," she replied.

Saeed stopped dead in his tracks. Cerys turned to face

him, brow arched curiously. The vampire's expression grew dark. Dangerous. His lip curled back in a sneer to reveal the razor sharp points of his fangs, and Cerys shivered at the memory of what it felt like to have them pierce her skin.

"Is that so?"

His grim tone set off alarm bells. There was a possessive edge to his words that made Cerys's stomach curl into a tight knot. She looked away, unable to meet his dark gaze for another second. "I'm his property," she said, low. "I do what I'm told."

She turned and continued down the sidewalk to where their driver waited with the car. After a moment, the sound of Saeed's footsteps echoed behind her. She had no idea what had set the vampire off, but whatever it was he'd better get the hell over it before they got back to Rin. They reached the car, a sleek Lexus GX. Cerys opened the door and waited for Saeed to get in before climbing into the back seat beside him.

The driver pulled out into traffic and a few moments of companionable silence passed. Cerys expected it to be more awkward, especially considering she couldn't quit thinking about his mouth on her. Saeed seemed to be less affected. He sat beside her, calm, his gaze cast straight ahead.

"Why did you really come to Rin?" It had been something that plagued her over the past week since she'd first laid eyes on the vampire. No one willingly entered into an agreement of any kind with mages as powerful—or as vindictive—as Rin. Saeed had to know he was in way over his head.

"I told you." He didn't turn to look at her. Barely acknowledged her. "The vampires' numbers are growing, and I wanted out from beneath Mikhail Aristov's thumb."

Cerys let out a chuff of laughter. "You do realize you've

jumped out of the frying pan and into the fire, right?" She
didn't know Aristov, had heard very little about the reclusive vampire king, but there was no way he was worse
than Rin.

"That depends on your perspective," Saeed replied. He
turned to look through the window at the traffic passing
by. "Mikhail had nothing more to offer me."

Cerys found herself wanting him to turn toward her so
she could once again look into the depths of his fathom-
less eyes. "And Rin does?" she ventured.

Saeed turned toward her. Her breath caught as he bestowed his full attention on her. "He does," Saeed assured
her. "And I'm not leaving the city until I get what I want."

"Oh yeah?" Cerys asked. That his time in Seattle might
be short-lived caused a ghost of emotion to tug at Cerys's
chest. "What is it that you want?"

Bright silver flashed in Saeed's eyes. "You."

Um . . . what? Cerys stared at him, stunned. She had to
have heard him wrong. "I'm sorry?"

"You heard me." His voice bore not an ounce of humor.
"I came here for you."

The car pulled up to the curb in front of Crimson.
Cerys opened her mouth to demand Saeed explain himself,
but before she could get the words out of her mouth, he
climbed out of the car and headed into the club. She
watched him walk away, his rolling, predatory gait hyp-
notizing in its graceful fluidity. He'd come here for her.

Why?

Their driver got out and rounded the car to open
Cerys's door for her. Her actions were mechanical as she
climbed out of the Lexus. Some small shred of common
sense invaded her brain as her preservation instinct kicked
in. She drew her dagger from the sheath at her hip and
tucked it beneath the driver's chin. "Not a word," she
warned.

She wouldn't put it past the male, a rogue werewolf who'd sought out Rin's protection, to divulge the details of her conversation with Saeed in order to get a leg up in Rin's organization. She'd cut his throat herself before she let that happen.

The male gave a nervous nod. "I didn't hear anything," he said. "I was listening to the radio, didn't even realize you two were talking."

"Good." She tucked her dagger back into the sheath. "Be sure it stays that way."

Rin was dangerous, but mostly because he had Cerys at his side. There wasn't a supernatural creature in the city that didn't respect her personal bubble of space whenever she walked toward them. She'd gotten used to it over the centuries: the fear, the suspicion, the outright hostility. Maybe this was the perfect place for her, doing Rin's dirty work while he reaped the fruits of her labor.

Cerys was fairly confident she'd have nothing to worry about from the werewolf. The only thing scarier than Rin was the prospect of losing his soul to her. She left him beside the car and ventured into the club, her nerves raw and on edge. Her stomach growled, and she placed her palm on the flat plane of her abs. She hadn't eaten for a few hours and she was gods-damned ravenous. She bet Saeed wouldn't want her anymore after he got a glimpse at her monthly food bill.

As she ventured deeper into the club, Cerys tried to push his words to the back of her mind. Rin sat in the VIP section at his usual table, a throng of admirers surrounding him. Didn't he ever get sick of it? His need for attention and admiration rivaled her need for food. She spotted Saeed beside Rin and though his posture remained relaxed, his expression was wary. His eyes found hers and he continued to watch her as she negotiated the crowds on her way to the VIP section.

Cerys snagged a server before she sat down. "Can I get a cheeseburger and fries, and an order of onion rings? Oh," she added. "And a shot of Cazadores Extra Añejo." The top shelf tequila wasn't going to do much good, but she could pretend.

Rin cut her a look as she sat down. "Fries and onion rings?"

She refused to let him goad her. Rin loved to push buttons. "If you served anything other than fast food here I'd order something else," she replied.

"Not high-class enough for you?" Rin laughed.

Cerys's lips pursed. "If I was human, I'd be on my way to open heart surgery from eating your greasy burgers and fries over the years."

He smirked. "Lucky for you you're not human."

Her brow arched as she stared him down. "Lucky for us both, donchya think?"

She'd said she wasn't going to play his game, but here she was, volleying quips. Tension thickened the air and for a second Cerys worried Rin might punish her. It had been a long damned time since she'd done anything to piss him off and it might not be such a good idea to revert back to bad habits.

"Indeed it is," Rin said after a quiet moment. Cerys let out a slow breath and he added, "But I have to say you got the shittier end of the deal."

The barb bit into her heart with razor-sharp teeth. He knew how to cut her without a blade, and she almost wished he would've cut her. At least a physical wound would heal. She didn't think she'd ever recover from the emotional damage Rin had inflicted upon her.

CHAPTER
5

The hurt in Cerys's expression was enough to bring Saeed to his knees. Rage gathered like storm clouds, constricting his chest and causing his muscles to grow taut. The urge to tear the mage's throat out made his hands twitch. He splayed his fingers out on the tabletop and willed them not to move. It was too soon to act and there were far too many unanswered questions.

Cerys belonged to Rin. Saeed had seen it throughout millennia with the aid of the Collective. How had he come to own her, though? A female as strong-willed as Cerys would have never bowed so easily. She was anything but subservient. Which meant the mage held some leverage over her.

What?

Saeed wouldn't rest until he uncovered that secret. She could never truly be his until she was free. Without the tether, however, there was no guarantee she could be his, free or not. The mystery of it all infuriated him. He'd had a taste of her blood—sweeter than any ambrosia—

and Saeed could safely say his interest in her had grown far beyond obsession.

"Like Mikhail Aristov," Rin began, "my territory is expanding."

Saeed's eyes slid to the left and Cerys visibly relaxed with Rin's attention finally away from her. If he could give her some small measure of comfort by occupying the mage he'd do it. Anything to earn her trust. He was going to need it if he ever expected her to believe that she was his mate.

"The West Coast is vast," Saeed said. "And rapidly growing. There are many cities for you to conquer. I certainly don't see any reason for you to limit yourself to Seattle."

Rin chuckled. "Exactly. But I'm not interested in conquering anything. I only want a piece of the action."

Saeed leaned forward in his chair. "I admire your ambition. You are a male after my own heart."

Rin regarded Saeed. He seemed relatively unimpressed with the compliment. "I doubt that," he said dryly. "But if you truly are interested in separating yourself from Aristov, I can use you."

"What do you have in mind?" A male as ruthless as Rin would no doubt have zero qualms about using Saeed to his full potential. He doubted he'd be driving the mage from one night club to the next or shaking down lower-level criminals for money. He already had a formidable right hand in Cerys, which begged the question: what could Saeed possibly offer him?

Their server returned with Cerys's food. She grabbed a napkin and tucked in with gusto, all but forgetting the others at the table as she sated her hunger. A twinge of guilt tugged at Saeed. He'd taken her blood. It had no doubt weakened her. She seemed as ravenous as she had the night of their first meeting. Did she rarely have an opportunity to eat?

"Cerys has been at my side for millennia," Rin said. "A more powerful and intimidating creature you'll never meet." He glanced Cerys's way with something so akin to affection that it caused a hot wave of jealousy to rise in Saeed's throat. "But as formidable as she might be, even Cerys has her limits. I need someone who can pick up the slack. Someone dangerous and just as intimidating to keep an eye on her when she needs backup and make sure my property remains in pristine condition. What could possibly be more unnerving than one of the only few vampires on the planet?"

Saeed's concern for Cerys threatened to drown out everything around him, including Rin's words. His control slipped by a few degrees and with it the voices of the Collective made an unwelcome appearance in his mind. Saeed gave a violent shake of his head, drawing the attention of not only Rin and Cerys, but others nearby. He decided to capitalize on his own weakness. "I am dangerous," Saeed agreed. "And also quite mad."

Rin's expression grew serious and a moment of silence stretched between them before he broke out into obnoxious laughter. "Oh, you're fucking mad all right," he agreed. "But it only makes me like you more."

Of course it did. The city was already abuzz with talk of the crazy vampire who'd abandoned his coven in Los Angeles. He was an outcast. A dangerous variable that no one wanted around. And Rin was an opportunist who wouldn't waste a second to exploit Saeed and the fear he generated.

"As long as we're on the same page." Saeed could conduct business in a civilized manner, and he was sure Rin would appreciate that. "I don't like surprises, and I'm sure you don't either."

"Oh I love surprises," Rin said with a smile. "When they're someone else's."

Of that, Saeed had no doubt. Rin had incredible self-control, and he was well practiced at showing only the parts of his personality he wanted others to see. Right now, he was wooing Saeed. Charming him. Inviting both his trust and camaraderie. Respect would come later, as would fear. Saeed had known many males like Rin, and they were all the same.

"I can help pick up the slack. Whatever you need."

Rin's smile grew and his expression became greedy. No doubt he saw a cash cow in Saeed. "I was hoping you'd say that."

For the most part, Cerys kept her attention on her food. She showed no outward interest in Saeed's conversation with Rin, but he knew she was listening. She ate with gusto, making short work of her French fries before she tackled the burger and onion rings. A few moments later, their server returned and set a shot of tequila and a wedge of lime in front of Cerys. Without preamble, she downed the shot before sucking on the wedge of lime. Something had her agitated. It vibrated from her in palpable waves that pricked at Saeed's skin. He wished he knew what was wrong so he could eliminate the source of her distress.

Saeed needed to be careful. Already he showed too much interest Cerys. He wasn't eager to encourage Rin's suspicion. He needed his guard down so Saeed could slide in and claim the prize for himself.

"I'm curious," Saeed said. "Why you'd need me at all. Why you'd need her at all." He glanced Cerys's way for a brief moment. "You're obviously not without power of your own."

Rin's dark gaze narrowed. A spark of magic singed the air with the tang of sulfur and caused the fine hairs on Saeed's forearms to stand on end. "Careful Saeed," he warned. "No one likes a brownnoser." Beside him, Cerys let out a soft snort of amusement. Rin turned his attention to her and his scowl darkened. "You have something to add?"

She looked up from her food at Rin, her own expression devoid of humor. "Nope," she replied. "I think Saeed is doing a good enough job fucking things up on his own."

She thought he couldn't handle Rin. Saeed planned to prove her wrong. "On the contrary," Saeed said. "I hardly think pointing out the obvious is a gratuitous compliment. Neither do I think it's complimentary to ask why I should do something for you that you could clearly do yourself."

The mage's eyes narrowed. "Let's get something straight right now. The extent of my power and how I choose to use it is none of your business."

Rin's response didn't surprise Saeed in the slightest. There was no doubt he was powerful, but that he didn't flaunt that power piqued Saeed's curiosity. The mage had ego to spare, which made Saeed think he might have some fatal flaw. Something Saeed could exploit to *his* advantage.

"Understood." Saeed had pushed and Rin pushed back. Now it was time to back off a little. "I've served someone else's interests many times over the course of my existence. I'm not opposed to doing it once again, but only because it furthers my own agenda. I'm content to ask no questions but one: what will my compensation be?"

Rin placed his elbows on the chair's armrests and steepled his fingers in front of him. "Sliding scale," he said, right to the point. "Depending on what you do and how well you do it."

Saeed swallowed his annoyance that Rin chose to continue to be vague. The bastard couldn't help but beat around the bush, and Saeed wished he'd hurry up and get to the damn point. "Fair enough. When do I start?"

"Tomorrow night," Rin replied. "You'll be working with Cerys." He leaned toward Saeed and pinned him with a deadly stare. "That female"—he jerked his chin in her direction—"is my most prized possession. Any harm comes to her, and you'll suffer for decades before I finally allow you to die."

Rin's protectiveness of Cerys made the hackles rise on Saeed's neck. He'd die before he let any harm come to her but Rin didn't need to know that. Saeed would protect her from anyone and anything, including the mage. Including *himself* if need be. "I'm fairly certain she can take care of herself," Saeed said. "But believe me when I tell you she has nothing to fear from me. And as long as I'm in your employ"—*Hell, as long as he walked this earth*—"I'll do whatever is in my power to protect her."

"That's good to know," Rin said. "Loyalty is hard to come by. It'll be a while before I believe I've earned yours, but until then, I'm willing to give you a chance."

Of course he was. Because males like Rin wanted only one thing. Power. And they didn't care what they had to do or who they had to use to get it.

Cerys hated to be talked about as though she weren't even there. And it happened more times than she'd like to admit. Rin saw her as a *thing*. A tool to be used at his disposal. A mindless pet. Something he was required to feed and provide a roof for. Offer her a pat on the head every once in a while and in exchange, he expected her total obedience. Something he never would've gotten from her had she not been his hostage.

She took another monster bite of her cheeseburger while she pretended to keep her attention focused on her dinner. She dunked an onion ring in the little dish of ranch dressing and tore off a bite of that as well. For some damned reason she was hungrier than usual. Probably a result of blood loss.

Damn vampire. She sure as hell hoped he didn't think she was an all-you-can-eat buffet. He'd caught her off guard when he'd accepted her challenge and drank from her. It wasn't going to happen again, though. No matter how good it might've felt.

"And as long as I'm in your employ I'll do whatever is in my power to protect her."

Cerys looked up at Saeed's words. The somber tone of his voice seemed to be for her ears alone, as though to let her know he spoke the vow directly to her and the words themselves were simply an assurance for Rin's benefit. Gods, he unnerved her. His presence in the city wigged her the fuck out. She wanted him gone, and yet some hidden part of her knew that if he were to leave, she would mourn his loss. Why? Who in the hell was he? There was more to Saeed than met the eye, and Cerys was determined to find out exactly what that was.

Saeed wanted her to believe he'd come to Seattle for her. And though Cerys doubted the truth of it, she'd sensed no deception in his words. She'd walked this earth for thousands of years but she hadn't lived in a long damned time. Saeed made her feel as though she could reclaim everything she'd lost. And that blossoming seed of hope his mere presence had managed to plant endangered Cerys's very existence.

She needed to get Saeed out of the city before she became as crazy as he was rumored to be.

"You'll start tomorrow night."

Cerys's gaze slid to Rin and her lip pulled back in a sneer. He wasn't wasting any time in putting her back to work it seemed, and now she was getting a sidekick. "I work alone." All eyes at the table turned to her. "And I don't need protection."

Rin's answering laughter only served to further annoy her. "I don't recall giving you an option," he replied. "Or did you conveniently forget who makes the rules here?" As if he'd *ever* let her forget. "Why use me at all then?

Why not let the vampire do your dirty work and you can put me on a shelf for a while."

Rin clucked his tongue at her. "If I didn't know any better, I'd think you were jealous of Saeed."

Cerys let out a derisive snort. "Good thing for you, you do know better."

Rin's eyes narrowed at the insinuation. From the corner of her eye, Cerys caught Saeed watching their exchange with interest. His brows drew down sharply over his dark eyes and a groove cut into the skin above the bridge of his nose. She didn't know what he thought about her open hostility toward Rin and frankly, she didn't care. She'd learned to accept her lot in life. Had gotten used to living in an empty, emotionless state without her soul. Saeed's appearance in the city had only managed to stir up a desperate longing she'd taken centuries to squash. She had as much use for him as she did Rin at this point. She just wanted to be left alone to wallow in self-pity.

"Rin!" A voice shouted from beyond the partition that closed off the VIP lounge from the rest of the club. "Rin! Come on, man. I just need a minute!"

Gods. Cerys rolled her eyes. Instances like these were becoming more and more frequent. Especially with the way Rin had been sending her out to make collections lately. As a race, the fae didn't believe in the devil, but if there was one, his name was Rinieri de Rege.

Rin held up a hand to the security guard at the VIP entrance and crooked his first two fingers to allow his petitioner entrance. He could pretend all day he was humble and nothing more than a business savvy male making the most with what he had. But Cerys knew better. Rin thought himself a king, and he loved to lord his power over others.

Cerys recognized the male who rushed toward their table in an instant. Guilt welled hot and thick in her throat, and she took a sip from the glass of water beside her in an effort to wash it down. She put her head down, focused her gaze on the half eaten burger and onion rings still on her plate. If Rin had an ounce of compassion, he'd order her to leave. But she knew that would never happen. He didn't have to live with the consequences of her actions. He didn't give a shit what anyone thought or felt about her.

"Rin." The desperation in the male's voice stabbed through Cerys's chest. She racked her brain for the male's name . . . Ulrich, she thought. An unfortunate fae who'd fallen victim to Rin's tricks and had been forced to pay the ultimate price. "You have to know I would never intentionally fuck you over. Shit went south, I'll admit that. But give me the opportunity to make it up to you. Tell your *enaid dwyn* to give me my soul back. Please. I'll do anything."

Saeed sat up straighter in his chair. His gaze went to Cerys, and no matter how hard she tried not to meet his eyes, she was powerless not to. She brought her head up to the side, careful not to draw Rin's attention as she looked at Saeed. He studied her with an intensity that stole her breath and caused a lump to form in her throat. The vampire might've been crazy, but he wasn't stupid. It wouldn't take him long to figure out what she was and what she'd done.

"Yes, you will do anything." Rin's tone remained cool and calm. "Anything I ask, anything I want, *anytime* I want. From now until I have no further use for you."

For all his apathy, Cerys wasn't entirely certain Rin had ever had a soul. It was good and intact though, its inky black aura surrounded him, and it did him little good. He was as cold and heartless a creature as she'd ever encountered, and she hated him with every fiber of her being.

"I'm losing my mind." Ulrich raked his fingers through the length of his silver white hair.

Some fae were far too beautiful, far too otherworldly to pass as human, and they wore a glamour to protect the truth of their identities. Ulrich was one of those creatures. Tall, lithe, eternally youthful, and flawless. His hair shone like silver strands and the tips of his ears formed tiny points. This was a private club however, and a glamour wasn't necessary. As shaken up as he was, Cerys wondered if Ulrich would even have the presence of mind to glamour his otherworldly form if he'd needed to.

"It's like I'm me, but not me." His voice cracked with the words. "I'm a fucking shell." He went to his knees at Rin's side and was still a good foot taller. It soured Cerys's stomach to see what had once been such a proud, refined male reduced to a blubbering beggar. "I'm not going to be any use to you like this. I can barely function."

Rin picked up the glass in front of him and swirled the last little bit of bourbon that remained in the bottom. He brought the edge of the glass to his lips and took a long, over-exaggerated sip before leveling his gaze on the fae. "You knew what you're getting yourself into," he replied. "It's not my fault if you can't handle the consequences of your actions."

Leave it to Rin to place the blame on his victim. What an asshole. Cerys couldn't bring herself to look at Ulrich, and so she continued to give Saeed her undivided attention as she wondered what he might possibly be thinking about her right now. No doubt he assumed she was just as sadistic as her master.

"You bitch!" Ulrich stood in a flash of motion and grabbed Cerys by the arm. He jerked her from her chair with so much force it made her teeth rattle. He spun and slammed her against the partition, bracing his large hands on her shoulders. "Give it back!" He lowered his face so close to hers that their noses touched. "Do you fucking hear me? Give it back to me or I'll kill you!"

Gods, she wished he would. If anything to give her respite from her own tortured existence. Before she could respond, Saeed intervened. He grabbed Ulrich and threw him down onto the tabletop. Rin didn't even flinch. He simply sat there with a self-satisfied smile on his smug face, watching as it all went down. Saeed bared his fangs and let out a low hiss that coaxed chills to the surface of Cerys's skin.

"If you threaten her again," he seethed, "you won't have to worry about your soul, because I'll kill you. Understand?"

Ulrich didn't speak, he simply nodded his head. Cerys was sure the male was as shocked as everyone else in the city to see an honest-to-gods vampire. Saeed released his hold and Ulrich rolled off of the table onto the floor. He scrambled to his feet and shot one last accusing glare over his shoulder at Cerys as he rushed out of the VIP lounge and through the club.

That one look summed up everything she felt about herself. The world truly would be a better place if she was no longer in it.

"Excellent," Rin said to Saeed. "I see a very fruitful future with you, Saeed."

Damn it. That's exactly what Cerys was afraid of.

CHAPTER
6

Ian Gregor scowled as he looked out over the cloudy Seattle cityscape. He hated the fucking rain, it reminded him of home. Soggy, wet, dreary. Hopeless. It did nothing but send his already foul mood into a tailspin. If shit didn't start going his way soon, he'd cut a swath of death and destruction that would make the black plague look mild in comparison.

"Did you find the mage?"

He kept his gaze cast straight ahead and out the window. Nothing less than good news was going to placate him now. And the gods have mercy on whoever dared to tell him anything other than what he wanted to hear.

"Oh yeah," his cousin Gavin replied. "He's not exactly hiding. In fact, he seems to like attention."

At least something was going according to plan. He'd waited too long to have his revenge to let something as trivial as a fucking magic wielder get in his way. He never did anything without a backup plan and the mage's slave was his.

"Well?" He did nothing to mask his agitated impatience. "Where the fuck is he?"

"The son of a bitch practically owns the city," Gavin replied. "And he hasn't made many friends. Everyone either hates or fears him."

If not for the fact that Ian wanted the fae, he might've been able to form an advantageous alliance with the mage. Ian himself was either hated or feared and it did wonders in curtailing prospective attacks. At any rate, magic users made him twitchy as fuck. Ian relied on tangible strength, brute force, and a calculating mind. Magic couldn't be seen, it couldn't be measured, and it sure as hell couldn't be trusted. That didn't mean he wouldn't try to use it to his advantage given the opportunity.

"You still haven't told me where to find him." This time Ian swiveled his chair around to look at his cousin. "I'm not interested in wasting any time." He wanted out of this dreary gray city as soon as gods-damned possible.

"He's got his hand in business ventures all over the city. No one knows where he lives, but he owns a club in Capitol Hill called Crimson. Seems to be where he spends most of his time."

Ian would've much rather ambushed the mage in a private place. Males like him surrounded themselves with plenty of protection. Bodies to take bullets when the need arose. Ian didn't want to start a war. At least, not another one. He'd wanted this to be a stealth mission. In and out, take the fae and use her to get what he really wanted. The one thing in this world that would take down that bastard Trenton McAlister and the Sortiari once and for all.

"And the fae?" Ian asked. "What about her?"

"She's always at his side," Gavin answered. "The rumor is she's rarely out of his sight and he keeps her well protected."

Ian didn't expect anything less. If he possessed a creature as reportedly powerful as the fae, he'd keep her under lock and key as well. "It's a complication," he said. "But nothing we can't manage."

"There's something else."

Ian didn't like the nervous quaver in Gavin's voice. "What?" His own tone did nothing to mask his current sour mood.

"There's a vampire in the city," Gavin replied. "A male. It's all anyone is talking about."

Ian sat up a little straighter in his chair. If it was true, the bastards were getting bolder, venturing out of L.A. Like a pestilence, their numbers would continue to grow and they'd infect every corner of the world. Not if he had anything to do about it.

"We don't have time to hunt," Ian said. "But keep your ear to the ground. See if you can find out what he's doing here. In the meantime, we'll do a little reconnaissance, scope out this club and get a bead on the mage."

"And after that?" Gavin asked.

Ian smiled. "Once we discover his weakness, we'll steal his prize."

"Works for me."

And then, maybe, Ian might finally see his plans come to fruition.

"Good." The rain picked up again in earnest, battering the windowpanes. Ian's lip curled and he swiveled back around in his chair to look out the window. "Now get the fuck out and leave me alone."

The sound of the hotel room door opening and closing behind Gavin faded off in the silence. The wind picked up and pushed the droplets of rain harder against the window like tiny missiles searching for a weak point to get inside. Thunder rolled, resounding in Ian's chest with a deep rumble. The storm that raged outside encapsulated every dark emotion Ian felt. There was no room for anything else. His heart had turned to stone centuries ago.

Ian Gregor was everything the world thought of him and more. Ruthless. Heartless. Vengeful. Violent. And those who'd wronged him should be prepared to suffer.

Perhaps the mage's pet would thank him for taking her. After all, Ian knew all too well how tight the bonds of slavery could become, especially over the course of centuries. The Sortiari had shackled him, treated him no better than an animal, and in return had expected not only his gratitude but his obedience. Ian had sold them all into slavery. It was his greatest regret. And he had a dhampir child to thank for it.

For creatures so long-lived, the supernatural community often conveniently forgot their own mistakes and shame. And because of that, history was destined to repeat itself.

Ian could still hear their screams. It was a torture he would forever endure day after day, night after night until the end of time. For all of his strength, for all of his ruthlessness, for all of his prowess in battle and his calculating mind, Ian had been unable to save them. Every last female, gone. Any hope of continuing their race, decimated. Their numbers had been small enough that all it had taken was a sadistic vampire lord and his foolish child to ruin them. The pain of it was as fresh today as it had been over six hundred years ago.

The Sortiari had given Ian and his brethren not only the means, but permission to seek and satisfy their revenge. They would be lauded as tragic heroes, the right hand of Fate, respected and revered. As their leader, Ian had spoken for every berserker when he'd agreed to the Sortiari's terms. A millennium of servitude seemed a small thing in comparison to the eternity of mourning they'd be forced to endure. Gods, how wrong he'd been.

They'd done the Sortiari's bidding and in the course of annihilating the vampire race, they'd become monsters. More violent, more heartless, more ruthless than they'd ever been. Without their mates, their daughters to temper their battle rage, they'd become the stuff of nightmare. Under the disguise of a holy cloister, they'd murdered. Not heroes. Fate hadn't given a shit about them or their plight. And neither had the Sortiari. They were tools. Guard dogs. Mindless killers.

Ian had had enough. If the supernatural world viewed them as monsters he'd show them just how truly terrifying they could be. He'd bring the Sortiari to the ground. Raze their organization. He'd kill the vampires starting with their mates one by one. And after that, the dhampirs. He wouldn't stop until he found the female he was looking for. The one who'd, on a childish whim, given the command to murder every last berserker female. When he found her, she would suffer as no creature ever had. And when she finally begged him for the release of death, he would make her suffer even more.

Ian Gregor was a berserker warlord. And the supernatural world was about to feel the full force of his fury.

"You haven't heard from Saeed at all?"

Sasha Ivanov kept her posture straight, her arms folded in her lap. Mikhail was an intimidating vampire, no doubt about it. But she was the mistress of the coven now—well, more to the point, a co-ruler—and it would not behoove her to be demure.

"Not a word," she replied. It had been almost a month since Saeed had abandoned his coven and left to search for his mate. He'd fulfilled his promise to Mikhail by turning Sasha and Diego, another member of their coven, before relinquishing leadership to them and disappearing. Mikhail wasn't any happier about the turn of events than Sasha was. It was what it was, and no amount of displeasure was going to change that fact.

"Do you have any idea where he's gone?"

Again, Sasha met Mikhail's intense blue eyes. The vampire king was well practiced at maintaining a passive expression. He gave nothing away. "Seattle, I think," she said. "At least, that's where he intended to begin his search." What Sasha failed to tell Mikhail was that the king's own ward, a human girl named Vanessa, had set Saeed upon his fool's errand. The child was an oracle and had apparently predicted Saeed would go off in search of his mate. Hell, she'd pointed him in the right direction and practically pushed him out the door.

Mikhail opened his mouth to speak, and Sasha cut him off. "I respect your position not only as king, but as the father of the race." It would do her no good to ruffle Mikhail's feathers. She wanted them to work together, not against each other. "But Saeed made his wishes clear when he turned Diego and then me. If you try to insert one of your inner circle into our coven, it will only make matters worse."

Mikhail's brow furrowed. "I see your point, but both Ronan and Jenner have had time to adjust to the transition. It could take some of the pressure off of you both if—"

"No." Each individual coven was its own unique ecosystem within the race. Inserting one of Mikhail's own into a leadership role would disrupt the balance. "Diego is unusually self-possessed," she said. "He has the control of a much older vampire."

Mikhail cocked a curious brow. "And you?"

Sasha swallowed against the dry heat that burned in her throat. Her thirst still raged and she'd yet to reconcile with the absence of her soul. But those were both minor annoyances when compared to the well-being of their coven. She'd made a promise to Saeed that she would rule alongside Diego and nothing, not even her own king, would deter her.

"I'm fine," she replied.

"Only fine?"

Sasha met his gaze head on. She didn't look away, didn't falter. "I am just as fit as anyone to rule."

A quiet moment passed. Mikhail studied her as though he could see right through her to inspect each individual cell that constructed her and assess whether or not she was as capable as she claimed.

"You are the king, but this is *my* coven. Let me rule it as I see fit, and I will honor Saeed's pledge of loyalty to you."

A slow smile spread across Mikhail's handsome face. "Mistress of a coven for less than a month and already you're throwing your weight around."

Damn right she was. "Would you expect anything less?"

"No," Mikhail laughed. "I think your coven is in good hands."

The rest of their meeting continued with slightly less formality. Once assured the coven's loyalty would remain intact, his main concern was for Saeed's safety. A sentiment Sasha shared in. She agreed to allow Jenner's mate, Bria, to act as a liaison between Mikhail and their coven. She didn't know much about the female other than she was smart and trustworthy. She served no interest save the well-being of the race. Besides, Sasha could use a listening ear if anything, to help her get a grip on the empty loneliness of her soulless state.

By the time she returned home, the sun was about to rise. The weariness of daytime sleep settled over her, weighing down her limbs and tugging at her eyelids. It'd been a long night and all she wanted to do was collapse into bed and find the peace of oblivion. She didn't get much farther than the foyer before a warm, deep voice called out to her.

"It's not good to go to bed on an empty stomach."

A smile curved her lips as she turned to face Diego. The transition hadn't turned him into a broody, angsty creature that would give any teenager a run for their money. He'd kept his sense of humor and his snarky wit, and for that Sasha was thankful. He had become the sun in her endless dark nights, and she appreciated him far more than he knew.

"I'm not," she replied. "I had a grilled cheese earlier."

He pursed his lips in a chiding expression. "You know what I mean. It's been days. You need to feed."

Had it been days? She'd sort of lost count. There was always so much to do, so many things that required her attention, that her own well-being had taken a backseat. "I'm fine." That seemed to be her mantra of late. As long as she kept saying it, it would be true. "And it hasn't been as long as you say it has."

"I like how you think you can put one over on me," Diego joked. "Like I'm not an observant motherfucker that knows everything that goes on under this roof."

It was true, Diego didn't miss a beat. He knew more than she did about the day-to-day goings-on, which was probably why Saeed had insisted they rule the coven together. "Really, I'm fine."

"No," he said as a matter of fact. "You're not."

Maybe she wasn't as convincing as she'd thought. Her shoulders slumped as she walked back toward the foyer to Diego's side. "Okay, so maybe I'm a little less than fine."

"Oh, I know you are," Diego assured her. "Which is why you're going to let me feed you before you go and shut yourself up in your room for the rest of the day."

"Not here." She didn't want to stand in the foyer like a

kid who couldn't wait to get into her Happy Meal as she glutted herself on Diego's blood.

He gave her a soft, albeit knowing smile. "Not here," he agreed. "Let's go to the study."

Sasha gave a nod of her head and fell into step behind him as they made their way down the hallway to the study that had once been Saeed's office. She supposed now it was their office, though she rarely used the space. It felt wrong somehow, as though by usurping that room she had accepted that Saeed was never coming home.

She refused to believe that. Saeed would come home. He had to.

Once inside the study, Sasha collapsed on a nearby couch. She was exhausted both mentally and physically and the thirst that burned in her throat was downright distracting. Diego was right. She needed to feed.

He sat down beside her. She took in the refined features of his face. His dark skin, deep brown eyes, sharp cheekbones, the straight line of his nose. Her gaze traced the square, strong line of his jaw and downward to the column of his throat and the vein that pulsed there. Diego was strong. Handsome. Intelligent. Caring with a wonderful sense of humor. He was all of the things that made an ideal partner, and yet Sasha felt nothing for him. He wasn't meant to tether her. It was no surprise, really. Her heart had always belonged to Saeed.

Diego offered her his wrist. She reached out and gently guided his arm back to his side. With her other hand she cradled the back of his neck and turned his head to expose the vein in his throat to her. Since her transformation, she'd felt so empty. So lost. The absence of her soul weighed on her, and at the same time she found it difficult to muster the energy to care. She craved some small measure of intimacy. A connection to another creature, no matter how fleeting. Her fangs throbbed in her gums as she lowered her mouth to Diego's throat. She nuzzled the cool, smooth flesh and he stiffened beside her.

Perhaps she was too close for comfort. He didn't stop her however, didn't say a single word. Her fangs broke the flesh and he relaxed, melting against her. She reached up and gripped his shoulder with her free hand as she took deep pulls with her mouth. His blood, warm and sweet, flowed over her tongue and she let out an indulgent moan. Diego would replenish her strength, but he wasn't meant for her. Sasha wondered as she fed, would she ever find the one who would make her heart whole? Or was she destined to feel empty and alone for the remainder of her existence?

CHAPTER
7

After a week of successfully carrying out Rin's wishes, Saeed finally felt as though he was beginning to earn the mage's trust. In fact, it couldn't have turned out better had he planned it. Rin had entrusted the care and protection of his most prized possession in Saeed's hands, which just happened to be the very thing he coveted.

Since that night in his penthouse when he'd taken her vein, Cerys had become increasingly distant. Infuriating, not to mention frustrating, but Saeed had never been one to back down from a challenge. She wasn't afraid of him. On the contrary, her scent became even more fragrant and heady every time she arrived at his door to pick him up for the night. She remained stoic though, never mentioning their previous conversations regarding his admission that he'd come to Seattle specifically for her, or that he'd had her blood.

Like clockwork, she arrived at his door every night at ten o'clock, and tonight was no different. Saeed opened the front door before she even had a chance to ring the bell.

She tried to appear annoyed but amusement sparkled in her unusually light eyes.

"Maybe it's not such a good thing to be a creature of habit."

Saeed's lips quirked in a smile. Her scent invaded his nostrils and ignited his thirst. He'd had her blood a mere week ago, and could presumably go a couple more weeks or longer before he needed it again. Still, he craved her taste. Longed to sink his fangs into her tender flesh. He might've been holding it together physically, but his clarity of mind was another matter altogether. Saeed still couldn't understand why Cerys had failed to tether him. He'd counted on the return of his soul to banish the madness that had plagued him these many months. Instead, he was emptier than he'd ever been, more lost, and even more obsessed.

The Collective refused to release its hold on him. The backdrop of his penthouse blurred out of focus and was replaced with an image of Cerys bathed in early morning sunlight. She stood on the balcony that overlooked the sea while Rin spoke in hushed tones with a vampire seated beside him. Through the dead vampire's memories, Saeed sensed Rin's interest in Cerys. Jealousy burned in Saeed's chest and he rubbed at his sternum as though to banish the sensation.

"I told you, she's not for sale."

The vampire laughed. "Nonsense. Everything *has a price."*

"Not her," Rin replied. *"She is priceless."*

Saeed let out a violent growl. His secondary fangs pushed down through his gums, and he was possessed of an urge to bite and tear flesh. For centuries, she had been treated as a commodity. A resource of great value. Had he known about her sooner, he would have done everything in his power to free her from this life of servitude.

"Saeed?"

He pressed the heels of his palms against his eyes in an effort to banish the torturous visions that refused to release their hold.

"Saeed?"

Cerys's voice came to him as though reaching out through time and space. He held onto the sound, let it become his entire world, as he fought his way through the tangled web of memories and back to reality.

"Hey!" Her earlier concern transformed as she issued the command. "Snap out of it."

Gods, if only it were that easy. The Collective called to him and he wanted nothing more than to lose himself in the churning sea of memories. *No.* He didn't. He couldn't. That time had passed. He needed to stay in the now. She was here with him in the present, and the past no longer mattered. "Leave me be," he murmured to the memories that called to him. "I no longer need your guidance."

He no longer needed the Collective, but apparently it still needed him. Saeed cradled his head in his hands and gnashed his teeth. His knees buckled and crashed to the floor a second later. He kept his eyes squeezed shut, unwilling to witness his reality once again fall out from beneath him. A hand wrapped around his collar and Saeed was hauled to his feet. His back met the wall with a violent shove that rattled his teeth.

"We don't have time for this." Desperation leaked into Cerys's voice. "You need to get your shit together. *Now.*"

Against his better judgment, he allowed his eyes to slowly come open. The details of his penthouse apartment came into focus in the periphery of his vision, and directly in front of him, Cerys pinned him against the wall. Her brows cut angry slashes above her bright eyes and her lip pulled back in a sneer. The tang of her agitation caused him to blow out a quick breath through his nose to clear it of the offensive scent. Get his shit together? Not a chance. At least, not until his soul was returned.

"Saeed." Her voice no longer bore any trace of concern. "Did you hear me? Pull it together!"

Gods, how weak he must've appeared to her. Her blood had fortified him, given him strength, but without the tether to bind them, he would remain lost. The deep cavern where his soul should have been seemed to open even wider. An endless black hole that devoured anything that came near it.

"I'm all right." He gave one more shake of his head to clear the fog from his mind. The voices of the Collective faded until they were nothing more than static sound. His thirst raged with dry heat and his fangs throbbed painfully in his gums. He drew in a deep breath but all it managed to do was tease him with Cerys's tantalizing scent. "You need to back away from me." His voice rasped in his throat. "Now."

The anger melted from her expression, replaced by gentle curiosity. "Why?"

"Because if you don't," he said, "nothing will stop me from burying my fangs deep in your throat."

Her scent changed yet again, blooming with desire. Saeed swallowed down a tortured groan as his head dropped between his shoulders. How could she not know the effect she had on him? Especially after the confession he'd made to her. "Back away, Cerys," he warned once again. "Now."

She released her hold on his shoulders in an instant and took several wary steps back. She was smart enough to be cautious and he appreciated that. Saeed braced his palms on his thighs and leaned over, drawing in deep breaths through his mouth so as not to tempt himself once again with the sweet scent of Cerys's blood. He'd assured her he was fine but that couldn't be farther from the truth. He hung on to his control by the barest of threads. At any second, it could snap and he didn't know if it would be his restraint or his mind that went first.

"I appreciate that you're having some sort of a meltdown," Cerys said from across the room. "But we're on a schedule. You might not know Rin well, but I do, and the last thing he'll tolerate is me showing up late."

Her words helped to calm him. He wondered what sort of punishment she'd have to endure if she angered Rin. Myriad possibilities cropped up in Saeed's mind, and he did his best to curb his thoughts lest he be tempted to go straight to Rin and rip out the bastard's throat. Cerys continued to study him, wary. Her anxiety thickened the air, lent a sharp tang to it. He would protect her with his dying breath and she didn't even understand why. Was there anything in this world more frustrating? To know in his heart of hearts she was his, when she didn't have a single clue.

"I wouldn't dream of keeping Rin waiting." Saeed straightened and dusted his hands down the front of his jeans. He stretched his neck from side to side in an effort to release some of the tension that gathered between his shoulder blades. Cerys shifted her weight, placed her right palm on the pommel of the dagger sheathed at her hip. She watched him with an intensity that tied his gut into knots. How could she not feel this connection when it was the most real thing Saeed had ever felt?

Why in the gods' names had she not tethered him?

"You good?" Cerys asked as she looked him up and down.

Saeed blew out a forceful breath. "I am. What's on the agenda for tonight?"

Holy shit balls, the vampire was seriously a few crackers short of a stack. Cerys wanted to be annoyed. She wanted to be angry. All she could muster was a deep concern that constricted her chest and left her limbs weak and shaky. She'd heard the rumors that Saeed had lost his marbles. Hell, he'd admitted it himself. But up until now she'd yet to witness it with her own eyes.

He'd completely checked out. His eyes glazed over, unfocused. His expression grew wild. He muttered under his breath, words she couldn't comprehend as it seemed he attempted to work through some unfathomable problem that had no solution. She had no idea what to say, how to help him. Likewise, she was incapable of offering comfort, and he'd find no solidarity with her. Cerys had lost her capacity for compassion the day she'd lost her soul. And yet, whenever Saeed was near, she felt a ghost of emotion as though he alone could evoke those things in her that Rin had stolen.

When he was near, she felt something akin to hope. And that was a very dangerous thing for her to feel when she knew she had none.

Cerys headed for the door, more than ready to put this fucked up night behind her. She didn't need to look back to know Saeed followed her. His gaze touched every inch of her like the caresses of thousands of fingers. She'd come to a decision tonight, Saeed had to go. Problem was, Rin was already pretty damned infatuated. He'd gone on and on about how refreshing it was to have the company of a vampire once again. Cerys had almost suggested that Rin make Saeed his slave instead but bit back the words before they could escape her lips. She wasn't looking for trouble. She'd gone decades without managing to piss Rin off. She wasn't about to ruin her track record now.

Cerys could get through tonight. And then she'd do her best to convince Rin to cut the vampire loose and send him on his way.

"I want to explain."

Cerys's step faltered. Saeed's voice reached out from

behind her and the distress in his tone nearly stole her breath. "I don't need an explanation." Cerys kept walking, her gaze straight ahead.

"Whether you need it or don't," Saeed replied. "I want to give it."

If he was looking for compassion, she had none to give. "Don't worry about it." She wasn't interested in explanations, sob stories, or anything else. Everyone had problems. And whereas she wasn't interested in hearing his, that didn't mean she was about to judge. Her own existence was anything but ideal. "Let's focus instead on what needs to be done so we can put Rin's business to bed and call it a night."

"And what business is that, exactly?"

Saeed looked up the street and down, Cerys assumed in search of the black Lexus. Tonight's task required a little more stealth and a lot less flash 'n' flare. The only transportation they'd have tonight was their own two feet.

"Rin did a favor for someone a few months ago," Cerys began. "And this particular individual didn't return the gesture when Rin asked. We're delivering a reminder that when Rin asks you to do something, you do it."

Saeed turned his head to look at her but Cerys kept her gaze straight ahead. "This is what you do for him?" The words ended on a growl. "Exact punishment on those who have wronged him."

"More or less." Cerys was careful not to give anything away in her own tone.

Saeed didn't seem content with a simple explanation. "What is it that you do that makes you so valuable to him?"

Anxiety fueled adrenaline leaked into her bloodstream. If Saeed knew the truth about her, about what she could do, would he be afraid of her too? Would he shy from her as everyone else already did?

"Nothing in particular," she replied.

Cerys didn't bother waiting for the traffic light to change. She darted across Summit, avoiding the oncoming traffic with preternatural speed. Saeed followed close behind, his own speed and agility impressive. She'd forgotten how fast a vampire could move. She hit the sidewalk and kept walking, all but ignoring Saeed. He fell into step beside her, didn't even miss a beat.

"You insult my intelligence if you think I'd actually buy that response."

Cerys cringed. Whether he'd lost his marbles or not, she knew Saeed was no fool. That didn't mean she hadn't hoped he'd accept her response and leave it at that. Something about Saeed made her want to tell him everything. If she'd still possessed her soul, she would have gladly bared it to him. Cerys had never been very trusting. By their very nature, the fae were a suspicious lot. From the moment she laid eyes on Saeed, she'd wanted to trust him. Had inexplicably felt safe when he was near. The words sat at the edge of her tongue, and she wanted so much to tell him the truth. What did it matter? Everyone in the city knew what she was. He might as well hear it from her rather than someone else.

"I'm an *enaid dwyn*." Admitting what she was hurt much more than she thought it would. "Do you know what that is?"

Saeed reached out and seized her by the wrist. He stopped dead in his tracks and spun her around to face him. A deep groove cut through his forehead and his dark irises were rimmed with silver, making his skin seem so much darker. Saeed embodied that dark intensity, and a pleasant shiver rippled over her skin. White hot need flared in her stomach and Cerys swallowed against the lump in her throat.

"*Enaid dwyn* are creatures of myth," Saeed said.

Cerys cocked a dubious brow. "Says the *vampire*."

He continued to study her as if he could see right inside of her. Her stomach curled in on itself, twisting and turning until it formed an unyielding knot. She waited for the look of shock to cross his features, and then the judgment, and finally fear. She'd grown used to it over the centuries but somehow it would be worse coming from him.

"Soul thief." The words left Saeed's mouth in the barest of whispers as he released his hold on her wrist.

Cerys looked away. She clutched her stomach as though to banish the empty, gnawing hunger that never left her. Saeed continued to stare and she wrapped her arms around her middle. Gods, she wished she'd never opened her damned mouth. She should've told him to mind his own fucking business and stay out of hers.

"With power like yours," Saeed said, "you could master anyone. Anything." Cerys looked up at his wondrous tone. His expression softened and he regarded her with a newfound respect and admiration that left her breathless, shaking, and not a little scared. That admiration quickly transformed to concern. "What leverage does Rin have over you that would cause you to bow to him?"

No one had ever asked her that before. Over the thousands of years she'd been Rinieri de Rege's slave, not one single individual had ever wondered how the mage had managed to master her. Everyone simply assumed she was as cold and heartless as he was. The words left Cerys's lips before she could stop herself, "He has my soul."

CHAPTER
8

Saeed's breath stalled in his chest. So many nights of confusion, of worry, of second-guessing his own mind and beliefs. In a single sentence Cerys had made everything so clear. He wanted to laugh at the irony of it all. Beyond that, it once again coaxed thoughts of violence against Rin to the surface of Saeed's mind. Of course she hadn't tethered him.

She had no soul with which to bind his.

How had the bastard managed it? Not even a mage could steal a soul, which meant he had to have found another *enaid dwyn* to do it for him. One of Cerys's own had betrayed her and the injustice of it all made him want to find the fae responsible and dole out a swift and violent punishment.

He reached up and took her chin between his thumb and forefinger, tilting her head to force her to look at him. "Tell me everything."

Cerys's eyes shone like starlight. For a moment, Saeed lost himself in the crystal-like depths. Her flame-red hair framed her delicate face in a wild tangle, and he wanted nothing more than to put his mouth to hers.

"We have somewhere to be." Her jaw once again took on that stubborn set that let Saeed know any attempt to make her talk would fail. "You're not beholden to Rin, but I am. When he gives me a task, he expects it to be carried out in a timely manner. If we're late, or miss our opportunity, it's not you that will pay the price for it."

She'd been Rin's property for thousands of years. Not even Saeed could fathom what that must've been like. He could be patient. He could help her complete whatever this task was that Rin had set out for her. Whatever Saeed could do to give her peace, to make her existence just a little easier, he'd gladly do. Anything for her.

"Let's go then," Saeed said. "But Cerys, don't think I'll let this matter simply go. We have much to discuss."

Her brow furrowed. She didn't agree to revisit the conversation, but neither did she deny him. It was a good sign. He brushed his fingertips along her jawline as he released his hold on her chin. Her gaze went liquid, her full lips parted as a quick breath slipped from between them. An electric sizzle arced in the space that separated them. Saeed's fangs tingled in his gums, his gut curled into a tight ball, and his muscles tensed. No other female had ever had this sort of power over him, intense and absolute. Again, he reminded himself that he didn't need the tether to prove Cerys was meant for him. He could only hope that in time she would come to realize what he already knew. In the meantime, he'd do his damnedest to convince her.

"Rin wants you to learn the ropes." Cerys walked just a beat ahead of him, her shoulders thrown back, spine straight. "And with Rin, the learning curve doesn't exist. We've been at it for a week. He's going to expect you to know what's what by now. If you can't hack it . . ."

"He'll cut me loose?" Saeed ventured.

Cerys turned her head to look at him. Her bright gaze carried with it the chill of winter. "Cut you loose? He'll more likely cut out your heart."

She wanted to scare him, but Saeed wasn't afraid. "I'm not concerned. I can do what he needs me to do."

"You say that so easily." Sadness lent an edge to Cerys's usually smooth voice.

"I might be newly turned," Saeed replied. "But I'm far from young."

Their surroundings transformed from retail to residential apartment buildings as they headed farther south. They cut through a back alley and hit Belmont Avenue, moving away from the more affluent parts of Capitol Hill toward downtown. Streetlights cast eerie shadows on the sidewalk and the other pedestrians avoided them. Saeed was certain the pair of them painted quite a menacing picture. At least he could be assured no one would bother Cerys.

Her voice broke through the silence once again. "How old are you?"

Saeed welcomed her curiosity. He wanted her to know everything about him, and likewise he was greedy to learn everything he could about her. "I was born in the year 1075."

He let her chew on that tidbit of information. He wouldn't offer up anything unless she asked for it first. He wanted her to engage with him, not simply listen to him talk. A wry smile curved her lips as she gave him a sidelong glance.

"I'm older than you," she said with a grin.

He knew that. He'd seen glimpses of her life through the Collective that spanned thousands of years. He returned her smile. "How much older?"

She allowed a small laugh. "A lot older."

"Are you suggesting then, that I give you the respect due my elders?"

Her eyes went wide with her feigned outrage. She reached out and gave him a playful shove. "I might be your *elder*, but you are definitely old enough to know you should never give any female shit about her age."

He liked her this way. Her guard down, mind open. He enjoyed her easy expressions, the blinding brightness of her smile, and the soft lilt of her voice. Through the memories of other vampires, he'd seen her dressed in so many different garbs. Flowing togas, corseted gowns, soft satin . . . The modern attire she wore now seemed more fitting to her personality. The tight skinny jeans hugged every lush curve, over her thighs, her shapely calves, disappearing at her delicate ankles into short brown leather biker boots. A leather jacket of the same shade skimmed her narrow waist and covered the flowing white top that hung past the jacket and swayed with every step she took. A long necklace hung between her breasts, nearly reaching her stomach. And at her wrist she wore the same leather cuff she'd removed the day she offered her vein to him. He'd never once seen her with her hair pulled back. Throughout the years in every vision the Collective offered him, she wore it loose and wild around her shoulders. She might've hardened throughout the decades. The way she dressed might've changed. But her beautiful flame red hair remained the same. Saeed longed to touch it. To let his fingers fall through the silky strands. His hand twitched at his side and balled into a tight fist. He had to bide his time. Patience was his only option.

Unfortunately, he couldn't shake the feeling he was somehow racing against the clock.

"You don't look a day over twenty." Saeed's lips twitched as he fought a smile.

Cerys laughed. Gods, how he loved the sound of it. Like warm rain on a summer day. "You're damn right I don't."

Something else had weighed on Saeed ever since his second conversation with Rin: the mage's indication that Cerys was far more delicate than anyone thought. As though she were an expendable resource he worried might soon run out. Fingers of fear reached into Saeed's chest to squeeze his heart. Was that why he couldn't shake the feeling that time wasn't on his side?

"Rin seems to think you need protection." He made sure to keep his tone conversational.

Cerys snorted. "I don't know if you noticed Saeed, but most of the supernatural community avoid me like the plague. No one wants to come within a foot of an *enaid dwyn*. They all worry that if I so much as touch them, they'll lose their souls. The last thing I need is protection."

"It can't be that simple, can it?"

Cerys cocked a brow. "I've touched you." A corner of her full lips hitched. "Did you lose your soul?"

"Ah, but you see, I have no soul to offer you. Therefore, I'm immune to your charms."

Cerys looked at him as though she already knew he didn't have his soul, though she didn't confirm it. Whether or not she already realized it didn't matter, though. Everything he told her, every bit of information provided, was a tiny building block toward gaining her understanding and trust. He wanted to ease her into the notion that she was his mate and give her what she needed to come to the conclusion he'd reached months ago.

"It's been so long since we've kept the company of vampires." The words came so quietly Saeed strained to hear them.

Saeed sensed her words weren't meant for him. Cerys's

use of the word *we*, as though she and Rin were somehow a set, caused his chest to burn.

"How many vampires are there?" Cerys hooked a left on Olive Way and Saeed followed. "Everyone speculates, but rumors are never accurate."

And for that, Mikhail could be grateful. The vampire king had no desire to let their numbers be known. He'd rather the supernatural community continued to speculate. Saeed wouldn't lie to Cerys. She was his mate and he knew he could trust her.

"Five, including Mikhail, in his coven. Three, including myself, in what was my coven. I believe there are two more but I know very little of them. Who knows how many more there are now. Mikhail moves slowly, though. He is a male who respects order."

"Ten vampires from one in a little over a year." Cerys paused outside of a rundown building. She looked up to the second story window and Saeed sensed they'd reached their destination. "Doesn't seem very slow to me."

She had a point. Time moved at a different pace for supernatural creatures. A year passed in the blink of an eye. It was a wonder the supernatural community as a whole wasn't more wary of Mikhail and suspicious of what his plans were.

Cerys turned to face him. "All right Saeed, time to bare your fangs. You ready?"

He flashed a wide smile. "I'm *always* ready."

Saeed painted quite the intimidating picture. His seductive smile showcased the dual points of his fangs and Cerys shivered at the memory of them breaking the skin at her wrist. If it were possible, his raw sensuality made him appear even more dangerous. More powerful. She doubted he'd complete tonight's task with nothing more than his sex appeal as a weapon, however. Of course, had it been her that Rin needed to keep in line, it sure as hell would've gotten the job done.

"I don't suppose you're going to tell me what's expected of me once we get inside?"

The deep rumble of his voice made it damn near impossible to concentrate. She wondered if he did it on purpose. Used that dark charm to throw her off kilter. Somehow, she doubted Saeed would be quite so sadistic. That was more Rin's speed.

"Several months ago, Rin did a favor for a rogue werewolf who'd deserted his pack to avoid their justice. Don't ask me what he did," she said before Saeed could ask. "Because I have no idea. All I know is Rin gave him a charm that would make him impossible to track. In return, the werewolf owed Rin a favor. When Rin tried to collect, the werewolf refused. We're here to remind him of the importance of keeping a vow."

"Why remind him at all?" Saeed asked. "If he reneged on the deal, why doesn't Rin simply reverse the charm? Or turn him over to his pack?"

Cerys shook her head. If only it were that easy. "That's not how Rin operates. There's no reneging. When you enter into an agreement with Rin, you see it through to the end. Period. If you refuse, he gives a gentle reminder as to why it's important to hold up your end of the bargain. If you refuse again . . ." Cerys's voice trailed off. She didn't want to finish the sentence. Didn't want say out loud exactly why she was so valuable to Rin.

Saeed finished the sentence for her. "He sends his soul thief to exact a steeper payment."

She should have known he'd force her past her comfort zone to address what she didn't want to talk about. Somehow, Saeed seemed to know her better than she knew herself. As though they'd been acquainted for much longer than a couple of weeks. She didn't like it. Didn't like to think she could be bared in that way—left so vulnerable—to anyone. It was bad enough that Rin had power over her. She didn't want Saeed to hold any sway over her as well.

"He does." Cerys looked away. "And once Rin has your soul, you're his slave until such a time as he sees fit to cut you loose."

Storm clouds gathered in Saeed's dark gaze and silver flashed in his irises like lightning. His lip pulled back into a snarl and a low growl gathered in his chest. "And how many of these slaves has Rin released from his service?"

Their eyes met and Saeed held her gaze. "None," she answered on a breath.

Silver completely swallowed the brown of Saeed's eyes. His anger caused Cerys's stomach to rocket up into her throat and she did her best to swallow it down and put her own encroaching fear on the backburner. Strange, the absence of her soul had allowed her some measure of apathy over the many centuries she'd been without it. But the more time she spent with Saeed, the more she realized he evoked something in her so akin to an emotional response that it left her shaken. It shouldn't be possible, and yet he'd managed it with ease.

"Then I think we should do our best to convince the werewolf that it's in his best interest to repay Rin as soon as possible."

"That's what you're here for," Cerys agreed.

"Why is that exactly?" She'd hoped he wouldn't pry too deep, but Cerys should have known a male like Saeed would never blindly do what he was told without asking a few questions. "It seems to me that Rin would prefer to collect as many slaves as possible."

"If he could manage it, he would," Cerys said darkly. Rin's hunger for power was insatiable. If he could, he'd own the entire world.

"Why can't he?" Saeed's voice thickened with suspicion. "He has *you*."

Nope. It was impossible to pull anything over on the vampire. He didn't miss a beat. "Because even I have my limits," Cerys said. "The more I take, the more of myself I sacrifice. Rin is very selective of whose souls I take for this very reason. It's not like there are many *enaid dwyn* in the world."

"It hurts you?" Saeed's voice broke on the words as if it caused him pain.

"It's killing me," Cerys said with a rueful laugh. "But what does it matter? I've been dead for a long time."

Tired of the conversation, of her own damned tragic life, of trying to keep it together while Saeed's gaze devoured her, Cerys took off toward the building's stoop.

"Cerys!"

She started at the command in Saeed's tone. She turned abruptly to face him and was taken aback by the sheer rage and determination that shone in every detail of his handsome face. "I'm going to free you of this prison." The words were spoken with the sanctity of a vow. "I promise."

Her heart pounded with so much force that it sent the sound of her rushing blood to her ears. Cerys turned and headed up the stairs, too afraid to acknowledge Saeed's words. She couldn't allow herself even the slightest glimmer of hope. It was too dangerous, the possibility of disappointment too great. Most of all, though, she couldn't allow herself to feel anything for Saeed. Whether he liked him or not, if Rin found out, he'd kill Saeed. And he'd make Cerys watch as he ran a stake through his heart. Detachment was her only option. That or death. And it would only take a few more souls to get the job done.

"What's the werewolf's name?" Saeed asked from behind her.

"Nick," Cerys replied. "Why?" It's not like Saeed

needed it. This wasn't a pleasant social visit. Rin had sent them to lean on the werewolf, plain and simple.

"What time does Rin expect you back?"

What was up with the weird questions? It was moments like this that reminded Cerys that Saeed's mind wasn't exactly on solid footing. She pulled a lock pick from her pocket and jimmied open the door to Nick's building. She paused inside the open doorway. "Tonight? Last call." She hated that Rin deemed it necessary to give her a curfew. If she wasn't back to the club by closing, there'd be hell to pay.

"Good. That gives me five uninterrupted hours with you."

Huh? The vampire was definitely off his rocker. Especially if he considered shaking down a rogue werewolf as uninterrupted time with her. Cerys shook her head as she crossed the foyer and hit the stairs for the second story. "Not sure how you're expecting tonight to go down Saeed, but we'll be occupied over the next few hours spending some quality time with a stubborn werewolf."

Saeed let out a soft chuckle from behind her. "I don't plan to be here for more than about five minutes."

"Well, that's optimistic." Werewolves were notoriously stubborn. Aggressive. Prone to fights. They were her least favorite assignments because someone always ended up getting hurt before Cerys got her point across. "I was here last week and it took me three hours just to track him down after he bailed out the window."

"No one's bailing." Saeed's confidence was both impressive and a little misguided. "Five minutes. Guaranteed."

A guarantee, huh? Cerys couldn't wait to see how this went down.

CHAPTER
9

Saeed wasn't about to waste an opportunity for time alone with Cerys. Under Rin's ever watchful eye, it had been impossible for him to implement his plan to gain her trust. The faster he could get this matter with the werewolf taken care of the better. He and Cerys had much to discuss and Saeed was through with beating around the bush.

He climbed the stairs behind her to the second story. Her hips swayed with every step and Saeed swallowed down a tortured groan. She had no idea of the effect she had on him. He wondered what it would feel like to have her hips moving on top of him. Pressing down, as she took his cock deep inside of her and rode out her pleasure. Ever since that first taste of her blood, Saeed had craved her. Her open defiance, her fire, her strength and courage had all enticed him. But it was the sadness and despair she buried beneath all of that—the deeper emotions she thought she'd lost with her soul—that drew him to her. It was her darkness that made him want to hold her close to him and never let her go.

Five steps from the second story landing, Cerys paused.

She turned to face Saeed who stood two steps lower and they met eye to eye. She leaned in close and the warmth of her mouth brushed the outer shell of Saeed's ear. A finger of raw lust stroked down Saeed's spine. His fangs throbbed in his gums and the rekindled flames of his thirst licked at his throat. *Later.* Business first, he'd sate his hungers later.

"He's fast. Strong. And a wicked good shot. If we knock, he'll turn the wall into Swiss cheese. The locks are reinforced with steel and the door is constructed with iron and silver rods throughout. It took me twenty minutes to fight my way through last time."

Saeed could no longer resist the temptation as he reached out and threaded his fingers through the thick locks of Cerys's hair. The strands slipped through his grasp like silk as he cradled the back of her head in his much larger palm. Her body stiffened, but she didn't pull away as he gently kept her body against his. His own mouth brushed her temple and Saeed allowed an indulgent moment to inhale her delicious scent. "Five minutes," he assured her once again. "Stay behind me."

Though it pained him to do it, Saeed released his hold. Her body went slack as he brushed past her and mounted the last several stairs to the landing. He turned toward Cerys and raised a brow in question. She pointed a finger to the unit marked 2B. Saeed put a finger to his lips and then flashed a confident smile as he moved almost silently to the werewolf's apartment.

Cerys had been cautious, but she had to have known the werewolf would've scented them the moment they walked into the building. No doubt he was already poised and waiting on the other side of the door, gun drawn and ready to put a bullet into the first body that crossed the threshold. Saeed would gladly take a bullet for Cerys, but he'd be of no use to her if the werewolf managed to plug his body full of silver. And so, he did the only thing he could and got the ball rolling with a healthy dose of honesty.

"I know you can smell me, werewolf," Saeed called toward the door. "I'm here for a moment of conversation and nothing more."

From inside the werewolf's apartment Saeed heard the metallic slide of a gun being cocked. "Tell that fucking bitch if she gets within ten feet of me she's going to feel an iron blade slide between her ribs!"

The insult to Cerys made Saeed's lip curl back in a sneer. He'd vowed to find a peaceful solution to tonight's problem and end what could potentially be a very messy and long standoff before it had a chance to begin. "She's none of your concern," Saeed said. "And mind your tongue when you speak of her."

"None of my concern?" The incredulity in the werewolf's tone was laced with fear. "She's here for my fucking soul!"

"She doesn't have to come through that door to take it." Saeed had no idea how Cerys's power worked, which made his assumption neither a lie nor truth. He took a gamble and hoped that his bluff would confuse the werewolf's senses. "I'm here to talk, nothing more."

"Then why is she here?"

Cerys let out an exasperated sigh. Saeed glanced at her over his shoulder and shot her a stern look. Her fingers caressed the pommel of her dagger as though she were anxious for violence. She painted such a sensual picture that Saeed nearly lost focus of his task. *Later*, he reminded himself. Right now he needed to prove his worth not only to Cerys, but to Rin.

"To bear witness," Saeed said. "And report back to Rin."

"Well she can report back to him right fucking now," the werewolf shouted. "Because I ain't doing shit for Rin!"

"Then perhaps you'll do something for me." Saeed had once been a quick-tempered warrior. A stealthy assassin. Feared and respected alike. With the passage of time, he'd also learned diplomacy. Cerys had become so hardened over the centuries, she knew nothing but violence. Saeed wanted her to know that there was another way. Life wasn't simply black and white.

"Like what?"

The werewolf's tone had lost a bit of its fire. Saeed took it as a good sign. "Open the door for starters. I give you my word no harm will come to you."

"Yeah right," the werewolf scoffed. "And I'm supposed to believe the word of a . . ." He paused. "What in hell are you anyway?"

The werewolf couldn't be very old if he didn't recognize the scent of a vampire. Which made dealing with him both harder and easier without a few centuries' worth of wisdom under his belt. "I'm a vampire." Saeed didn't see any point in mincing words.

"Bullshit."

Cerys let out another long suffering sigh. Saeed turned and gave her a rueful shake of his head. For a creature so old, she had very little patience.

"Open the door and see for yourself." Saeed practically dared him.

"How do I know this isn't a trick?"

Gods. The male was nothing more than a pup. Completely ignorant and too damn foolish to trust his own senses. No wonder his pack had taken him to task. Already, Saeed wanted to throttle him. "I'm a patient male, werewolf, but you're getting on my last nerve. Open the door and you won't be hurt. Continue to behave like a stubborn fool and I'll let my friend swallow your miserable soul."

"You promise you won't let her near me?"

Saeed couldn't help but feel a certain perverse sense of pride that his mate so easily intimidated those around her. He knew she didn't feel the same. That she considered what she was a curse and what she could do, a horrible burden. But there was power in her strength. She'd simply been under Rin's thumb for too long to realize it.

"I told you, you're safe from her. Stop with this foolishness, and open the door." The werewolf was wasting precious minutes. Saeed had asserted himself and his ability to get the job done. The werewolf was making him look bad, and if he didn't get his ass in gear and open the door, Saeed might be tempted to violence.

From inside the apartment, Saeed heard shuffling footsteps move toward the door. It was too soon for optimism. After all, the werewolf was just as likely to pull open the door and put a bullet in Saeed's head. Still, he hadn't run and that was a good sign. Saeed cast a sidelong glance at Cerys. She stood on the fourth to last step, her left shoulder bracing her body up against the dingy wall. Her arms were folded across her chest and pressed the swell of her breasts upward in a tantalizing display. Saeed's tongue flicked out at his bottom lip as a wave of lust crashed over him once again. Gods, his want of her only intensified with every second spent in her company.

The snick of locks disengaging preceded the squeak of hinges and Saeed lent his full attention to the door. A golden brown eye peeked out from the crack in the door and zeroed in on Saeed. He gave a wide smile, making sure to reveal the points of his fangs. The werewolf let out a gust of breath.

"Damn. You weren't kidding, were you?"

Saeed rolled his eyes. Someone needed to teach this young fool how to be a proper werewolf. "You would've known I wasn't lying if you'd learn to properly use your senses."

The werewolf's single-eyed gaze raked Saeed from head to toe. "What do you mean?"

Saeed stepped toward the door. Time to wrap this up so he could spend the rest of the night alone with his mate. He drew on his power as he held the werewolf's gaze. "Open the door," Saeed said. "Now."

The werewolf took a stumbling step away from the door. It closed for a brief moment as he released the chain and then swung it open wide. Saeed got a good look at the male who couldn't have been more than nineteen years old when he'd been turned. He was a child in every sense of the word, and it angered Saeed that Rin had taken advantage of his innocence in the first place. Because of the werewolf's dual nature, Saeed had expected it to be more difficult to compel him. The fact that he'd slipped so easily into Saeed's control was nothing more than another indicator that the male's place was with those who could help him understand what he'd become and how to utilize his own power.

Saeed had already expended three minutes of his five. He wasn't about to waste another second.

"Your name is Nick?"

Cerys watched, transfixed, as the werewolf gave a slow nod of his head. Saeed's voice resonated with power that sparked the air with an electric charge. She'd forgotten how handy it could be to have a vampire around. And not just because he scared the bejezus out of everyone. His large frame took up the entire doorway and his wide shoulders nearly blocked her view. Cerys found herself no longer watching Nick and his dreamy responses as she allowed her gaze to roam freely down the length of Saeed's muscular back. *Hot damn.* The male was fucking *magnificent.* She imagined what he might have looked like in another age. Dressed in ancient robes and armed with a finely-honed scimitar. His enemies must have cowered at the sight of him. He'd been diplomatic with Nick but Cerys knew that had it come down to it, Saeed wouldn't have hesitated to show his teeth.

A pleasant shiver raced down Cerys's spine as she thought once again about the rush of heat that accompanied his bite. Rin kept her on a very short leash. Her opportunities for romantic entanglements had been nearly non-existent. She'd found pleasure when she'd wanted it though, as empty as the experiences had been. Sex just didn't have the same appeal when you didn't have a soul. Sure, it felt good. But it was far from satisfying.

Saeed's bite, however, had been *more* than satisfying.

Gods, Cerys. Snap out of it!

She pushed away from the wall and stood up straight. Her wandering thoughts were dangerous and would only manage to get her into more trouble than she could handle. She focused on Saeed's words rather than his body. That's what they were here for after all. Rin would expect her to report back. He'd want every last detail. And if Cerys failed to remember a single thing, he'd be less than thrilled.

"You owe Rin a favor. Is that correct, Nick?"

Cerys had known many vampires. Many powerful vampires. Somehow, Saeed made them all seem mundane by comparison. Perhaps it was because there were so few of them now. Vampires were interconnected, she knew that much. All that power had to go somewhere when Mikhail had ascended.

"Yes, that's correct," Nick said sleepily. "But everyone knows if you do one favor for Rin he'll get you on the hook for more. I just want to be left alone."

"You should've thought of that before you left your pack and struck your bargain," Saeed said. "You owe him one favor, and you'll do it. No more hiding, no more going back on your word. Do this thing for him and then you will leave the city and return to your pack. You will repent, you will accept your punishment, and you will let those who are older and wiser than you teach you what it is to be a proper werewolf. Do you understand me, Nick?"

Cerys's brow furrowed. She never would've expected this. For centuries, all she'd known was heartlessness and violence. Saeed had shown neither. He'd found a peaceable solution and even went out of his way to perhaps help the young werewolf. Nick was right: Rin would have kept him on the hook for as long as possible. That's how he operated. Saeed might be compelling Nick to do one favor for Rin but whatever small evil it was, at least he'd be free from an eternity of servitude.

Freedom. That's what Saeed had given Nick. Cerys could only hope to know what that felt like. She would feel the weight of her own invisible collar for eternity.

"I understand." The words came slow and quiet from Nick's lips. A more powerful werewolf wouldn't have been so easy to compel, but Nick was young in his supernatural existence. He didn't know how to draw on his own inherent power. His pack might mete out some harsh judgment when he returned, but at least he wouldn't be set adrift in the world with no idea of what he was and what he was capable of.

"Good." The smug pleasure in Saeed's tone sent a fresh round of chills over Cerys's skin. "Tomorrow night, you'll go to Rin. Do whatever is asked of you. And when it's done, put it to the back of your mind. Leave the city and return to your pack immediately."

Nick gave a slow, shallow nod of his head. "Yeah."

"And stay away from magic wielders," Saeed added. "They'll give you nothing but trouble."

Nick's nod of agreement was considerably more robust this time. Thanks to Saeed, the werewolf would live to see another day with his soul intact. He'd never know how much he owed Saeed, but Cerys would remember. The vampire was indeed an extraordinary male.

The air seemed too thin and Cerys assumed it was a result of Saeed pulling back on his power. She took a deep, cleansing breath and held it in her lungs for a brief moment. Saeed turned toward her. His mouth formed a grim line and silver shone in his gaze.

"It's time for us to go," he said.

Like Nick, Cerys gave a slow nod of her head. "Yeah. Let's get out of here."

They left the dingy apartment building and hit the sidewalk. Long silent moments passed, the only sound that of their footsteps. Cerys counted them out. One, two, three, four . . . The brisk rhythm matched the beat of her heart and it managed to calm the nervous energy that pooled inside of her.

"What are you thinking about?"

Cerys turned toward Saeed. "Mercy." She didn't see any point in lying.

"Mercy?" Saeed's brow furrowed.

Cerys gave a small shrug of her shoulders. "Yeah. I was thinking that Rin has no mercy. I don't think he would've understood what you did here tonight."

Saeed cocked a curious brow. "You think I was merciful?"

"Of course." Had Nick refused to play ball, Cerys would've been forced to rip his soul from his body, thereby guaranteeing his servitude. "Don't you?"

"I have no idea what Rin will ask of him," Saeed said. "Steal. Murder. Coerce. Batter, abuse, or worse. Torture . . ." His voice trailed off into silence. Cerys kept her pace to match his as she walked beside him. "Did I show him mercy? Or did I condemn him."

Guilt? Since he had no soul, she couldn't imagine him feeling anything as complex as remorse. Untethered vampires were generally apathetic, something Cerys knew all too much about. Was this new breed of vampires Mikhail Aristov had sired somehow different? Had they retained some part of the ethereal connection to themselves that allowed them some sort of emotion? No. Cerys could see souls and she knew Saeed had none. Not even a scrap of one. He was indeed unique.

"You saved him," Cerys assured him. "What Rin would have done would have been a million times worse."

"Do you think so?" Saeed kept his gaze cast forward.

"I know so," Cerys said. "Rin is the most heartless, cruel male I've ever known."

"I'm going to free you." The no-nonsense statement made Cerys's heart flutter. "Rin will not be your jailer for much longer."

Cerys wanted to laugh. Or more to the point, she wanted to throw her head back and scream her frustration at the sky. Saeed's promise was certainly gallant, and it fit his personality to a tee. But he didn't know Rin, didn't know the lengths he'd gone to possess Cerys in the first place. And he didn't know the lengths to which Rin would go to keep her.

"You should be more concerned with watching your own back." Cerys was careful to keep any inflection from her tone. "If Rin finds out you're going easy on anyone we're supposed to be shaking down, he's going to have your ass."

Saeed gazed at her from the corner of his eye and an arrogant smile spread across his sensual mouth. "You think I'm afraid of Rin?"

No. And that was the problem. "You should be," Cerys replied. "You should be very afraid."

"There's only one thing that scares me." Saeed's voice became so quiet that Cerys had to strain to hear him. "And that is failing to return your soul to you."

Cerys's step faltered. He wanted to do what? "Why?" It hadn't been what she'd intended to ask, but the word slipped from her lips nonetheless.

"Because if I don't," Saeed said, "you will never tether me. And how will I ever prove to you that you are my mate?"

Whoa. In dozens of centuries no one had ever managed to throw her off her game. Saeed had done it with a simple sentence. *His mate?* The vampire was definitely crazier than she'd thought.

CHAPTER
10

Saeed was through playing games. He'd never been one to beat around the bush and he wasn't interested in wasting any more time. Cerys paused on the sidewalk, her mouth slack. He continued to walk and after a moment the sound of her hurried footsteps caught up to him.

"Hang on a second."

Saeed wasn't about to stop. He needed to keep her just left of center so she wouldn't think too hard about what he'd said. They could stand on the sidewalk and hash this out all night. She'd poke holes in his reasoning, find excuses to talk herself out of the truth. He wasn't going to let that happen.

"Saeed, stop!"

Not a chance. The voices of the Collective tugged at Saeed's mind and the dry heat of his renewed thirst burned the back of his throat. Reason became nonexistent as his thoughts lingered on piercing the flesh at Cerys's throat. Stop? Not until they were back at his apartment, away from prying eyes. There was no stopping until he got her alone.

"Surely you're capable of talking and walking at the

same time," Saeed remarked. "You've been doing it most of the night."

"Infuriating vampire," Cerys muttered under her breath.

Saeed smiled. He never would've imagined he could enjoy getting a rise out of her. "You have a curfew, no?"

"What? Well, yeah. But I don't see how that—"

"I'm not willing to waste a single second of time alone with you." Saeed cut her off. "Talk all you want once we get back to my apartment. Because I refuse to let the minutes slip by standing on the sidewalk."

Cerys let out a frustrated breath. "You can't just throw something like that at me and not expect me to want to talk about it right now."

A corner of Saeed's mouth hitched in a half smile. "I never said you couldn't talk. I simply said we weren't going to stop."

"Fine." Cerys fell into step beside him. "We'll walk and talk."

Saeed grasped his hands behind his back as he continued down the sidewalk. "Perfect."

Cerys let out another frustrated breath. Saeed couldn't deny he found her agitation both entertaining and alluring. "I know how vampire mate bonds work. You're soulless until your mate tethers you. I can see souls, Saeed. Sort of a perk of what I can do. And you don't have one. If I was your mate, you'd have your soul back."

"Not necessarily." He found it fascinating that she could see souls. He couldn't help but wonder what they looked like to her. He tucked his curiosity to the back of his mind. "I've found my mate, but her lack of a soul makes the tethering . . . problematic."

"You're certifiable. You know that, right?" Cerys gave a shake of her head. "You're insane if you think I'm somehow your mate."

"Oh, I'm quite insane," Saeed agreed. "But have no

doubt that I believe with every fiber of my being that you are mine."

"Yours," Cerys scoffed. "Like I'm just something you can own. Maybe you have more in common with Rin than I thought."

Saeed frowned. He didn't like being compared to that piece of shit. Cerys wasn't a vampire. She didn't understand the intricacies of the tether in the same way Saeed did. Which was why he needed to prove it to her. "It's not a matter of ownership," he explained. "At least, not in the way you think. You are not my property in any sense of the word. My soul is tied to yours. And yours is tied to mine. It is a connection that can only be severed through death."

Cerys kept her gaze focused straight ahead as she continued to walk. "You seem pretty confident despite the fact neither of us currently has a soul. Pretty hard to tether something that isn't there."

And gods, did it ever frustrate him. "I need no soul to prove it to me. I know in my heart of hearts, and that is enough."

"Your heart?" Cerys gave a rueful laugh. "I don't know about you, but I feel *nothing*."

Saeed's heart broke for her. The absence of his soul might have lent him a certain amount of detachment, but he was far from apathetic. He knew what it was to feel deeply. He'd only been without his soul for months, while Cerys had been without hers for over a millennium. Time and Rin's cruelty had washed away her emotions, nothing else.

"You've chosen to feel nothing," Saeed corrected. He refused to let her talk herself out of any possibilities. "You've done what you needed to do to protect yourself."

She laughed in earnest this time. "Protect myself?" Her incredulous tone scraped against him like fingernails.

"Saeed, I am the thing that everyone protects themselves from."

She thought herself a monster. Unworthy of love. It only made Saeed want to punish Rin more for all of the things he'd done to her. "You are none of the things you think you are."

"Saeed." Cerys gave a sad shake of her head. "I am all of those things and *more*."

Her defeated tone was a fist to his gut. It knocked the air from his lungs and Saeed fought for a deep breath. The Collective had given him glimpses of her. Bits and pieces of her life and history. It had not shown him the deeds she'd done under Rin's command and he knew it was those things that had broken her.

"We all have our crosses to bear. The important thing is not to dwell on the past."

"We're immortal," Cerys said simply. "We can't escape our memories. They follow us through the ages, taunting us."

"There is nothing on the face of this earth that is truly immortal. Never forget that. But because of our long lives, it is not our pasts that live on. Our futures are infinite with infinite possibilities."

She turned her head to face him and the sorrow in her light eyes gutted him. "Poetic," she said with a soft snort. "And enigmatic, just like you."

"For you, I'm an open book. All you have to do is ask."

"All right." The challenge in her tone heated Saeed's blood. "Why are you so sure that I'm your mate?"

She got right to the point. He liked that. "I know for the same reasons that have compromised my sanity. What do you know of the Collective?"

Cerys's brow furrowed. "Nothing."

For as much time as Rin and Cerys had kept in the company of vampires over the centuries it was apparent they shared very little of their secrets with them. Obviously those long dead vampires had known better than to trust Rinieri de Rege. Saeed was more than happy to share his secrets with Cerys. She was, after all, his mate. "If the legends are to be believed, all vampires are created from a single source. The blood that created the first one of us is passed from vampire to vampire. Through that magic, we are all interconnected. And that includes our memories."

Cerys walked quietly beside him. She didn't utter a single word but Saeed knew she listened intently.

"The Collective is the amassed memories of every vampire that has ever existed. Upon our turning, those memories are passed on to us. At first, it's hard to resist the pull of those memories. So easy to fall headlong into lives once lived. I fell victim to that pull and was unable to loosen its hold on me."

"What does that have to do with me?"

Again, right to the point. Saeed smiled. "I found you there. In the Collective. Over and again, night after night, I saw you through the eyes of dead vampires." Saeed took a deep breath. "The fae with hair like fire."

He looked at her from the corner of his eye. She met his gaze for the barest moment before looking away, as though embarrassed. "You saw me?"

"You sound surprised," Saeed said with a laugh. "Rin preferred the company of vampires, did he not? It seems inevitable that you would have a constant presence in the accumulated memories of my ancestors."

"I guess you're right. I had no idea." She turned toward him. "I don't think Rin has any idea either. He'd shit a brick if he knew. Wouldn't like the thought of anyone spying on him even in memories."

"Then we'll keep this between us," Saeed said.

Cerys nodded in agreement. "But seeing me in a bunch of memories doesn't mean I'm your mate."

She would use every opportunity to shut him down. But Saeed's determination could not be squashed. "I felt it." Even now, walking beside her, he was possessed of a sensation of rightness. As though he'd always been meant to be here, walking beside her on the sidewalk. "I feel it now. The return of my soul will confirm what I already know. Which is why I won't stop until I've taken your soul back from Rin and give to you what I know you will give to me."

Gods. Talk about pressure. Cerys stared at Saeed, dumbstruck. He was so confident, so utterly convinced she would tether him. That she was his mate. All because of a bunch of memories. When things didn't go down the way he planned it would ruin him.

"How can you trust the Collective? Aren't those memories what drove you to madness?"

A space of silence stretched out between them. From the corner of her eye Cerys watched Saeed walk, his back ramrod straight, his hands grasped neatly behind his back. So calm. So completely collected. He seemed unflappable. She wondered what it would be like to see the composed vampire come undone.

"I hear the voices even now." His eyes drifted shut for the barest moment. "Calling to me. I used to spend hours there. Searching for you. Waiting for just a glimpse."

Cerys's heart fluttered in her chest. His words affected her even though she didn't want to admit it. To be wanted by such a male was a heady thing. She was undeserving of the honor. Cold. Detached. Dead inside. Soulless.

"How do the others keep the memories from taking over?" She thought it best to veer away from the subject of their supposed tethering and instead focus on the Collective and its hold over Saeed. "Surely there's a way to push them to the back of your mind?"

"There are ways," Saeed agreed. "Feeding regularly is one of them."

A rush of warmth spread through Cerys's limbs. The memory of his bite, the sting accompanied by delicious, searing heat, nearly made her knees buckle. "Everybody needs food." Cerys ate ravenously to help fill the gaping hole where her soul once was. "Helps to keep your strength up, you know?"

"True. Vampires are often possessed of the urge to feed only from their mates, however."

Butterflies swirled in a wild tangle in Cerys's stomach. She couldn't allow herself to be sucked into Saeed's fantasy. Not when reality could so easily swoop down to crush them both.

"So what are you saying? That before you came to Seattle, you starved yourself?" No wonder he found it hard to fight the pull of the Collective. He'd intentionally weakened himself.

"I fed when it became necessary."

A fresh wave of unfamiliar jealousy flared in Cerys's chest. The thought of Saeed's mouth against anyone else's flesh spurred her to thoughts of violence. She cleared her throat and asked against her better judgment, "Who fed you?"

Saeed grinned, showcasing the sharp points of his dual fangs. "Jealous?"

Damn him. "No." She couldn't manage more than the one word.

Saeed chuckled. The warm sound sent gentle shivers throughout Cerys's body. "Sasha and Diego, my closest friends and most trusted confidants, offered their veins when I needed them. I made them vampires and left the well-being of my coven in their keeping."

Cerys still found it hard to believe he had left his life

behind in order to find her. And even crazier that he would abandon so much on an unconfirmed hunch. Then again, Saeed himself admitted that he was far from sane. "When was the last time you fed?"

Saeed stopped. He turned to face her and Cerys's breath stalled in her chest. The intensity of his silver rimmed eyes held her transfixed. Gods, he was magnificent. "From your wrist, that night in my foyer."

Wow. He wasn't messing around, was he? "You should feed." She hadn't intended to say the words but it was becoming apparent that when it came to Saeed, Cerys had no filter. She swallowed against the lump of anticipation that rose in her throat. "Before the Collective gets any louder in your head."

Apparently, he needed no other invitation. Saeed seized Cerys in his arms and spun her away from the sidewalk and into a nearby alley. He pressed her against a cold brick wall and buried his face against her throat. Cerys gasped as his fangs pierced her and she melted against him as a wave of delicious heat rushed through her. Her hands acted of their own volition, wandering up his muscular arms, to his strong shoulders, and the back of his neck. Her fingers dove into the thick strands of his dark hair as she pressed him tighter into the crook of her neck.

She didn't want this moment to end.

He cradled her in his arms as though she were precious. A rare and valuable treasure entrusted to his keeping. His body molded to hers and it felt so damned good that she didn't think she could pull away from him if she wanted to. "Don't stop." The words left her lips in a desperate whisper. "Take what you need to make the memories go away."

She didn't want to care about him. Didn't want to experience the ghosts of emotion that plagued her more and more with every day in his company. She couldn't let this continue, and yet, she did nothing to stop him. Nope. Rather than pull away, she held him closer. Tighter, allowing her fingernails to scrape against his scalp.

With each deep pull of suction, Cerys's mind became a little hazy. Her limbs grew heavy, and her breathing slowed. She'd never known such deep relaxation. Such euphoric bliss. She could float away on a cloud at any second and it wouldn't bother her one bit. Gods, she hoped he never stopped.

Saeed's fangs disengaged from her flesh and his tongue passed gently over the punctures. Cerys swallowed a desperate whimper of protest as he pulled away from her throat. Her eyes came slowly open to find him watching her with that same unnerving intensity that always managed to leave her rattled. He reached up and brushed the palm of his hand over her hair, pushing it away from her face. His gaze searched hers and for a moment, Cerys hoped he'd find whatever it was he was looking for.

"I've taken too much from you."

His voice was a soft caress. Cerys shuddered as she tried to shake the dreamy lethargy that stole over her. "I'm fine." Her own voice carried as much strength as Nick's had earlier in the night. Saeed had compelled her as easily with his bite as he had the werewolf with his power infused words.

"You're not fine." Deep lines of concern marred Saeed's features. "I'm sorry. My control isn't what it should be."

No shit. He'd been practically starving himself. If Cerys went that long without eating she'd decimate an all-you-can-eat buffet in a matter of minutes. Control would be nonexistent. "No more starving yourself," she said, a little too breathy. "It's not good for either of us. I need you at one-hundred percent, all the time. I'll feed you, whenever you need it. No more starving yourself. Okay?"

Saeed's gaze burned through her. "Agreed."

He bit off the single word as though afraid he'd say more. Cerys wished she could crawl inside his head and hear his thoughts. Then again, she might not be prepared for what she might hear.

Cerys didn't know how long they stood there. Her fingers slipped through the silky strands of his hair and wandered to the nape of his neck. As though slowly waking from a dream, some small measure of sense stabbed into Cerys's brain. Her hands dropped to his shoulders and down to her side until the only contact that remained were his arms around her, holding her body against his.

"What you feel is the mate bond." His voice, dark and decadent, held her attention like nothing else could. "And don't try to deny it, because it will be a lie."

A lie, yes. But Cerys couldn't admit even to herself there was more between them than a simple physical attraction. Doing so would lend credence to his belief that they would eventually be a tethered pair. He promised to release her from the bonds of slavery only to replace her shackles with his tether. Out of the frying pan and into the fire, it seemed. Or at least, it would be the case if she believed any of it.

Her spine straightened as she pushed away. Her strength returned and she threw her shoulders back as she disentangled herself from the vampire's hold. "Rin has eyes everywhere," she said. "We need to keep moving."

A deep groove cut into his forehead. His disappointment enveloped her like a too-warm blanket that Cerys was more than eager to cast off. "Our conversation isn't over," he said. "And I still have three hours before Rin expects you."

She was his for the night. Cerys knew better than to argue. She'd learned very quickly that Saeed was a male who expected to have his way. "We can go back to your place," she said. "But only if you order takeout."

Some of the distress melted from his expression and

was replaced with amusement. "You fed me. I'm more than happy to return the favor."

The devilish glint in his dark eyes was a warning Cerys would be wise to heed. Too bad she'd never been very good at that sort of thing.

CHAPTER
11

For a moment, he'd had her.

In that intimate moment—his mouth against her throat, his fangs buried in her delicate flesh, her blood flowing over his tongue—she'd been his.

Saeed had never known anything so powerful. He didn't waste any more time heading back to his apartment. They traveled the last ten blocks as quickly as possible without attracting unnecessary attention to their more than human speed. Cerys seemed just as eager as he was to get back, but then again, it might've been the promise of food that spurred her.

Cerys might not have been convinced of their bond, but Saeed had never been more certain. Fate had played a cruel game with them, and he would do everything in his power to make sure they won.

Before they even hit the elevator, Cerys had her cell phone to her ear and had ordered enough food to feed an army. "Chinese take-out for *days*!"

Her bright smile nearly brought Saeed to his knees. Her usual angry stoicism melted away to give him a brief glimpse of a facet of her personality he'd yet to experience. It was a gift to be treasured. Something for him alone. Her guard was down and she was still a little high from the euphoria of his bite. It was the perfect opportunity to continue to plead his case. He had two and a half hours until she needed to return to Rin, and Saeed planned to capitalize on every second.

They stepped into the elevator and Saeed hit the button for the penthouse. Cerys kept her gaze straight ahead and fiddled with the pommel of the dagger sheathed at her hip. "Thank you for taking care of Nick tonight." Her voice was little more than a quiet murmur. "I know you don't think you did him any favors, but believe me when I tell you he's indebted to you."

Saeed sensed that Cerys's gratitude had little to do with any favors he may or may not have done for the werewolf. "Rin indicated that you weren't an inexhaustible resource. Why is that?"

"There is no power, no resource, on this earth that is inexhaustible," Cerys replied.

Evasive. She'd joked that what she did for Rin was killing her, but was there more to it than that? Anxiety gathered in Saeed's gut. Pressing her on the matter would only create distance between them and undo everything he sought to accomplish tonight. Instead, he let the subject drop, hoping in good time she would explain the meaning behind Rin's comment without him having to ask.

The tether bound their souls, but it didn't create an instantaneous emotional connection. It didn't create trust. Or love. It was an anchor and nothing more. A beacon to bring them together. The rest was up to them.

"Do the fae form mate bonds?" Saeed knew very little about them. The fae were more reclusive and secretive than even the vampires. Their history, their magic and power, were a mystery to him. He was greedy for any little bit of information Cerys would give him.

"No." The staunch formality of her response settled in Saeed's gut like a stone. "At least, not in the way that you might think."

Saeed was beginning to believe she enjoyed giving him cryptic responses. All it managed to do was further frustrate him. "I have no preconceived notions about anything. Least of all, my own tethering. Vampires recognize the mate bond the moment our souls are returned."

Cerys continued to avoid eye contact. "Exactly. So how can you know for sure I would be the one to return your soul to you?"

She would continue to fight him on this until he could provide her with definitive proof. Fair enough. She could thwart him, but she would never deter him. "I don't need a soul. My instinct knows. My heart knows. My mind is convinced."

The elevator doors slid open to the penthouse. Cerys stepped out into the foyer and waited for Saeed to unlock the door and let them inside. "No offense, but without a soul, how can your heart know anything? And I think we both know your mind is a little less than reliable right now."

Her words bit into his skin like tiny sharpened barbs. She meant to push him away with her well-nurtured apathy. "Rin taught you heartlessness." Saeed unlocked the door and pushed it open. Cerys walked into the penthouse without acknowledging him. "It has nothing to do with the absence of your soul."

"You're crazier than I thought if you believe that."

Her openly hostile expression was a far cry from her earlier joy. Saeed knew the emptiness of existing without a soul all too well. A cavern had split open his chest upon his turning and the very essence of his being had been sucked away and replaced with a nothingness so intense, words could not describe it. He'd experienced the numbness. The pale shadows of emotions that lingered within him. Not enough to make him feel whole, only enough to make him ache with longing for what he'd lost. He wasn't discounting Cerys's own experiences. On the contrary, he wanted her to feel some measure of hope that her own gnawing emptiness might soon come to an end. He wanted her to acknowledge he'd awakened something inside of her. That the notion of their souls being tethered was not only a possibility, it was a reality.

"I need some air." Cerys strode through the living room toward the terrace and swung the French doors open wide. "Let me know when my food gets here."

A cool, rain-scented breeze washed through the living room and died as she pulled the doors shut. Her brief moment of happiness had been as fleeting as a ray of sunshine hidden by storm clouds. Cynical. Hopeless. Cold and detached. Cerys had forced herself into a state of emotional inertia. She refused to even ponder the possibility of emotion. Saeed knew the detachment she'd forced herself into. He knew the gnawing need to feel complete. It had driven him close to madness in the course of a few short months. Cerys had lived in the void for millennia. And she'd coped in the best way she'd known how.

Would he ever break through her icy exterior? Would he ever convince her of what he was so certain of?

Saeed settled into an armchair in the far corner of the living room that would offer him the best vantage point to observe the thing he had coveted for so long. Cerys never wore her hair tied back. It was always left long and wild like flames licking down her back. The strands floated in the gentle breeze, fanning out behind her slender form. Even in the absence of sunlight, it shimmered in shades of red, copper, and gold. She appeared delicate and ethe-real against the dark backdrop of night, but Saeed knew better. She was fire and granite. And she belonged to *him*.

She kept her back to him and Saeed continued to watch her for what felt like hours, his eyes caressing the parts of her his fingers longed to touch. His body responded to his wandering gaze as his lust was once again stirred by the sight of her. His fangs throbbed in his gums and his cock stirred in his jeans. The denim was too damned restric-tive and he longed to strip down and lay his bare flesh against hers. *Soon*. Saeed took a cleansing breath to clear his mind. Soon she'd understand and he would no longer be alone in his desires.

A sense of contentment settled over him that he hadn't felt in a good long while as he continued to silently observe her quiet beauty. He would take her reticence over her ab-sence any day of the week.

The low chime of the doorbell flooded Saeed's ears. He'd win back her attention while he fed her and perhaps in the process, earn another of her genuine bright smiles. He answered the door and accepted the hefty bag of Chi-nese take-out before slapping a few bills and a generous tip into the delivery girl's hand. She offered up a quick thanks and a wide grin before heading back to the elevator. Cerys had managed to whittle away another thirty minutes on the terrace. She'd need at least thirty more to get back to Rin. That left Saeed ninety precious minutes with her. A contented smile curved his lips. He only hoped she'd pay as much attention to him as she did the food.

Cerys ignored the doorbell. She kept her focus on the vast city that stretched out before her, the lighted windows of the skyscrapers, the glow of headlights on the city streets below, and the press of people that crowded the sidewalks. Anything to keep her mind off of Saeed. Anything to keep her from fixating on the small seed of hope he'd managed to plant in her chest.

The sooner he left Seattle the better. If Rin found out what Saeed planned, what he thought Cerys was to him, he wouldn't live to see another sunset. Rin would never let her go, and walking away wasn't an option. She was a slave, plain and simple. She'd reconciled herself with the fact she'd never be free long ago. It had taken centuries for her to accept her fate. If she wasn't careful, Saeed's stubborn blind faith and hope would only help to crush her.

If only it were so easy to ignore what her heart wanted her to believe.

Well, her heart was a fucking liar.

The French doors swung open. Cerys kept her back to Saeed but his presence brushed against her senses in a pleasant tingle. Strange how she could be so aware of someone she barely knew. Saeed would say it was fate. Cerys had no idea what to call it.

"Time to feed, little fae." His attempt at a sweet endearment coaxed a smile to Cerys's lips. In his dark, serious tone it sounded a little too sinister.

"Somehow I doubt my dinner is going to be as gratifying an experience as yours was for you."

Cerys turned to face him, eager to see his reaction. Saeed's eyes flashed with silver and his nostrils flared as he inhaled a deep purposeful breath. "On the contrary." Cerys nearly broke out into a sweat from his heated tone. "I've watched you enjoy a meal and I must say it is quite the seductive experience."

She pushed herself away from the balcony as reluctant laughter escaped her lips. For a vampire, Saeed was quite charming. Probably a little too charming. "I think I can safely say no one has ever watched me scarf down a burger and said that it was seductive," she replied with a laugh.

She pushed past him into the condo, her body painfully aware of each and every place it made contact with his.

"It's not the act of eating that I find alluring." Saeed followed her into the condo, past the living room, and into the kitchen. "It's the excitement you exhibit. The utter relief that passes over your features with every bite."

Cerys cringed. That didn't sound very sexy to her. More like pathetic. "Yeah, well . . ." She fiddled with an invisible speck of dust on her shirt. "What can I say, I'm a foodie."

Saeed headed for the cupboard and grabbed a plate before crossing the kitchen to pull out a drawer and retrieve a fork. He placed them both on the granite countertop of the kitchen island and Cerys dipped into the brown paper bag to retrieve the white boxes of Chinese take-out. The salty, savory, and sweet aromas hit her nostrils and her gut clenched. Dinner wouldn't do much to make her feel whole in the long run, but at least it was a temporary fix.

"Your recent food choices do nothing to support the case that you're a foodie." The dry remark earned another chuckle from Cerys and she met Saeed's gaze to find his own eyes sparkling with humor. "I think you'd eat an old boot if it had enough salt on it."

The laughter died in Cerys's chest. When he made comments like that, like he actually *knew her*, it caught her off guard. "Old boots work in a clinch." She kept her tone light so he wouldn't see how his words affected her. "But I like them better with a little Sriracha."

It was easier to be flippant with him. To joke and pretend nothing bothered her. She'd gone too long cold, emotionless, and stoic. Anything deeper than that might break her.

"You do love to deflect, don't you?"

Saeed saw through the pretense. It shook Cerys to her foundation. The only person who knew her better was Rin.

Shame heated Cerys's cheeks. She hated that Rin knew her that well, that she was so transparent to him. He was her jailer. Her keeper. With one hand always wrapped firmly around her leash. Rin couldn't have known her more intimately had they been lovers. And she hated him for it.

"Who's deflecting?" Cerys forced her attention to the little white boxes of food. She opened each individual one and inhaled the aroma of the delicious contents before piling a little bit of everything onto her plate. "Aren't you eating?" She asked without making eye contact. "I don't believe for a second that a little bit of blood is enough to keep you full."

"I don't need food." Saeed drove his point home by letting his gaze wander to Cerys's throat.

"Come on." Cerys pinched a few chow mein noodles between her thumb and finger. She tilted her head back as she brought her hand up and dropped the noodles into her mouth. "Vampires eat. I've seen it."

She remained standing at the bar rather than take a seat at the dining room table. This way, she could keep the countertop between her and Saeed. No need to court disaster and close the gap between them. He mimicked her actions, dipping with his fingers into the box of chow mein. He dropped the noodles into his mouth and chewed. "I can eat. But I can't digest food unless I've ingested blood first."

Interesting. Cerys had always suspected as much but it wasn't like she'd ever asked anyone about it. "But you like food, right?" She found her curiosity getting the better of her. "It tastes good and everything."

Saeed grabbed the fork from the countertop and scooped a bite of fried rice from one of the boxes. "It does," he agreed. "But in truth, no food on the face of this earth can compare to the taste of your blood."

Cerys's stomach did a back flip and a pleasant rush of heat circulated through her limbs before settling low in her abdomen. His blatant statement shouldn't have turned her on, but her thighs were practically quivering from the implication in his words. Damn. It didn't take much for him to get under her skin.

"What does it taste like?" She blurted out the question before she could think better of it. "I mean, besides like you're sucking on a dirty penny."

Saeed's brow crinkled. "Not to me." His gaze met hers and held it. "Your blood is the sweetest ambrosia and I am drunk on it from only a sip."

Gods. Cerys's breath left her lungs in a rush. It was a wonder she hadn't burst into flames. Each word from his lips brought with it a silent challenge, daring her to deny the truth. Saeed was all dark, sultry heat. Midnight in the dead center of summer. "You had more than a sip earlier," she replied wryly. "You seem fine to me."

"You think so?" Saeed's gaze roamed slow and hungry up the length of Cerys's body. "I'm quite drunk. And eager for another taste."

Oh boy. She never should've come back here with him. She was in way over her head and so close to the point of not caring that she could easily stay here all night, Rin's curfew be damned.

"Not sure I can keep up with the demand." Cerys gave a nervous laugh. "You might have to find yourself another blood donor."

Saeed's expression grew serious. "No." The finality in that one word was like a fist to Cerys's gut. "Yours is the only blood I thirst for. I will pierce no other's flesh but yours."

Heat pooled in Cerys's stomach and she swallowed against the lump that rose in her throat. She couldn't deny she wanted him. In fact, she hadn't wanted anything or anyone more in centuries. Saeed watched her with the intensity of a predator. His dark eyes drank her in and she suppressed a pleasant shudder. What would it be like to belong to a male like Saeed? Not as a slave. Or a possession. Not because of her power or the influence she could gain for him. She wanted to know what it would be like to belong to someone for no other reason than she wanted it that way and gave herself freely to him. She'd felt so helpless for so long. Was she brave enough to go after something she wanted, if only this once? Gods, all she wanted was to *feel*.

"Well," the words tumbled from her lips as though she had no choice but to say them. "Are you going to kiss me or what?"

CHAPTER
12

Saeed rounded the kitchen island in the space of a heart-beat. The moment his arms went around her she melted against him, as though her entire body had released a sigh of relief. His mouth claimed hers and Saeed swallowed an indulgent moan. His cock hardened to stone, pressing uncomfortably against his jeans. The hot lust that coursed through him was undeniable. Only his mate could evoke such a response. He refused to believe otherwise.

Her hands reached behind him. One gripped the fabric of his shirt at his shoulder blade while the other dove into his hair. Cerys pressed her body tight against his, grinding her hips into the hard length of his erection. The urgency of her actions spurred Saeed on. His tongue thrust past her lips to taste the honeyed sweetness of her mouth and in the process, one fang nicked delicate skin.

Dear gods! The taste of her blood had no equal. Unable to resist himself, he took her full bottom lip between his teeth and bit down harder, opening four tiny punctures. He kissed her deeply, his tongue dancing against hers as her blood drove him into a frenzy.

"Saeed." Her voice was a breathy murmur against his mouth. He'd longed to hear her say his name, infused with passion. With longing. With want. Instead, he heard nothing but quiet desperation. Pain. Loneliness. Unfulfilled need. "Please." The plea speared into his heart like a stake. "Don't stop."

He had no intention of stopping. Of giving up his quest to make her unequivocally his. Saeed reached for the hem of her shirt and broke their kiss only long enough to pull the garment over her head. The faintest luster painted her skin, so much like the glitter of starlight he beheld in her light eyes. For a moment, Saeed could do nothing but stare. The swell of her petite breasts peeking out from the cups of her bra begged for his touch. She arched her back and pressed against him once again as though to offer her permission.

He craved her like a drug. And he feared he would never find satiation.

Saeed reached up and with the pads of his fingers, traced the outline of one swell. Cerys shuddered and chills broke out over her skin as her breath expanded her chest in quick bursts. He continued his unhurried exploration, his eyes trained on hers. From one breast, to the valley between them and then to the other. Along her delicate collarbone and over one shoulder. Down the length of her biceps to her forearm until his fingertips skimmed her palms and along her fingers. From there, he found the thick waistband of her jeans and he ventured upward. The tight muscles in her torso twitched beneath his light touch. Her stomach clenched and the flesh there vibrated ever so slightly. His hands wrapped around her ribcage and slid upward to cup her breasts through the light fabric of her bra, bringing him back to his starting point. There was still more ground to cover, but Saeed was content to pace himself. Patience was vital lest he scare her away.

Convincing Cerys of their tether was a marathon, not a sprint.

Tears welled in Cerys's eyes. Saeed paused, taken aback by her apparent distress. "You're like a gourmet, five course meal," she said with a rueful laugh. She swiped at her cheeks, brushing the tears away before they had a chance to even fall.

Her words were nonsensical, and yet they pierced his flesh like the sharpest of blades. It was too soon, too fast. "We should stop."

"No." She reached out and grabbed his hand, placing it to the left side of her chest. Her heart pounded. The wild rush beat against his fingertips and the sound of it echoed in his ears. "This is the most alive I've felt in centuries. I don't want you to stop."

Saeed had mourned the loss of his soul for mere months while Cerys had been without hers for hundreds of years. He was ashamed of his own selfishness, his own desperate urge to feel complete when she'd gone so long without. His hand wandered from her chest back to her breast. He brushed the pad of his thumb over the hardened point of her nipple and Cerys's lids drooped. Tonight, he would make her feel. He would give her pleasure, and nothing else.

He put his mouth to hers once again. Saeed kissed her slowly. Methodically. Every slight movement, the angle of his mouth against hers, every flick of his tongue and nip of his teeth precisely placed. He wound his left hand in the length of her fiery red hair as he abandoned her mouth to kiss along her jaw line. His lips found the soft skin at her throat and though he yearned to pierce the flesh there to drink deeply from her vein, Saeed held himself in check. He denied himself the pleasure of her blood in order to focus all of his attention on her.

His right hand abandoned her breast. His fingertips

wandered back down her torso to the waistband of her
jeans. His fingers dipped inside and Cerys drew in a sharp
breath as he ventured further across her abdomen and past
the boundary of her underwear. He loosened the button
and pulled down her zipper to allow his wandering hand
access to the soft flesh of her sex. His fingers slid across
the silken folds, hot, wet, and eager for his touch. Cerys let
out a low indulgent moan that further hardened Saeed's
cock and caused it to throb painfully against his fly. He
would find no relief tonight, but he'd be damned if Cerys
went another minute without.

He found the tight knot of nerves at her core and lightly
circled his fingertip over the surface. Cerys's grip on him
tightened as her body went rigid. She pressed her cheek
against his, and her quick, hot breaths tickled the outer
shell of his ear. Such fire. Such unabashed passion. Saeed
wasn't content to stand in the middle of the kitchen with
his hand thrust down her pants. He wanted her bare, laid
naked before him, so he could worship her the way she
deserved.

She let out a frustrated cry as he pulled away. Saeed
scooped her up in his arms and crossed to the living room
in four wide steps. He deposited her into the overstuffed
chair that he'd earlier settled himself into as he'd watched
her. He bent over her and grabbed her boots to pull them
off. The hollow thump of each one hitting the floor min-
gled with her racing breaths as he unhooked the clasp of
her bra, whisking the garment away from her and depos-
iting it somewhere beside the boots. He took a moment to
admire the beauty of her breasts. Just full enough to mold
to his palms, high and pert, with tiny pink beaded nipples
that begged to be sucked. Pale and lustrous like pearls.

The dry fire of his thirst reignited and his fangs throbbed
in his gums. He wanted to bite. To suck. To glut himself
on her until he was so exhausted that he had no choice but

to succumb to daytime sleep. Later. There would be time enough to satisfy his lusts. And he was anxious to taste more than just her blood.

Saeed went to his knees before her as though in worship. The intensity of her gaze as she watched him stole his breath and caused his pulse to race. He gripped the waistband of her pants and hooked his fingers into her underwear as he dragged them both down her thighs. She lifted her legs to help rid herself of the garments and a growl built in Saeed's chest as he got a glimpse of the delicate, glistening flesh of her pussy.

Magnificent.

Her feet came back down to rest on the floor and Saeed reached between her thighs, gently urging them to part. Her mouth went slack as she let out a breath and her fingers gripped the armrests of the chair. He didn't waste another second and buried his face between her legs. His tongue flicked out and Saeed's eyes drifted shut. She was everything he'd hoped for and more.

Cerys had never been blinded by pleasure but she could safely say she definitely wouldn't be passing an eye test anytime soon. Her head rolled back on her shoulders with the first pass of his tongue as her fingers dug into the plush upholstery of the chair. She'd meant every word she'd said to him. This moment should've been dreamlike, but instead it was as though she'd been woken from a dream. That this was her reality, and her life up until now had been the illusion.

Saeed's mouth was cool on her heated flesh, adding a layer of sensation that took Cerys by surprise. She drew in a sharp breath and held it. Her muscles grew taut and she focused on nothing but the sensation of Saeed's soft, wet tongue as it circled her clit.

"Oh gods Saeed, don't stop."

All thoughts of Rin and the consequences of missing her curfew faded to the back of her mind. Saeed offered her a momentary freedom from her captivity, and she greedily held onto every moment. For a space of time, she belonged to no one but herself. Her pleasure was her own and the only thing required of her was to accept what Saeed offered.

The physical bliss filled that hollowness in a way a double cheeseburger never could. In the past, sex had always been a fairly meaningless act. An itch to scratch and a want to satisfy, but always an empty encounter that was easy to dismiss to the back of her mind. Those experiences had been as hollow as the space in her chest where her soul should have rooted. But in Saeed's kisses, his feather-like touches, the brand of his mouth, she felt the spark of a connection and she found it both exhilarating and frightening.

Her head came up and her gaze roamed down the length of her torso to settle on Saeed's face. His eyes met hers for an intense moment, the dark irises rimmed with brilliant silver. His lids drifted shut as he sealed his mouth over her clit and sucked. The light scrape of his fangs sent a molten rush of heat through Cerys's core and her thighs trembled on either side of his face. Oh, how she wanted him to bite her. To sink the razor sharp points of his fangs into the delicate flesh of her thigh. She welcomed the sting followed by the flash of heat that ignited her blood and softened her bones. He gave her so much pleasure, and all she could do was offer her blood in return.

"Saeed." Her fingers dove into the soft waves of his hair and curled into a fist. A low growl gathered in his throat and vibrated against her pussy, causing a renewed rush of wetness to spread between her thighs. "I want you to bite me." The words were little more than a heated murmur, frenzied and quick. "Do it. I want to feel it."

The gentle rhythm of Saeed's tongue paused. His eyes remained closed as he pulled an inch away as though in indecision. His breath raced, warm pants of breath that caressed Cerys's already sensitive flesh. She didn't release her grip on his hair, but instead angled his head to her inner thigh. She spread her legs wider in invitation, arching her back as she pressed against his mouth. "I know you want it," she breathed. "Take it."

His fingertips dug into her outer thighs as he released his hold and let out a shuddering breath. The pad of his thumb found her clit and brushed against the knot of nerves in an upward sweep at the exact moment his fangs pierced her skin. Without warning, the orgasm took her. She gasped in surprise as she threw her head back. Each deep pull of suction from Saeed's mouth matched the deep pulsing contractions of her sex. Cerys cried out, desperate sobs that grew hoarse in her chest, as the most intense pleasure she'd ever experienced radiated through her. Time stood still. The past disappeared. The future was nothing more than an uncertain blur. All that remained was the present. This precious space of time where Cerys was nothing more than an inconsequential speck in a vast universe. Saeed continued to circle her clit as he fed. He brought her down slowly, his touch becoming lighter, slower, as did the draw of suction against her thigh. His fangs disengaged and his tongue flicked out at her skin. A deep, wracking shudder possessed her and chills broke out over Cerys's skin and she let out a slow breath. She'd never felt anything so intense. Saeed was without a doubt one of a kind.

Cerys expected Saeed to pull away. He'd had her blood, had pleasured her. What was left to do but get naked and go to town? It's what any other male would've done. Instead, Saeed remained where he was. He murmured heated words against her skin in a language she didn't understand.

His native tongue perhaps? The words were rhythmic and beautiful like a prayer, or song. His hands caressed up the outsides of her thighs and around to the insides as he dragged the blunt ends of his fingers down her over-sensitized flesh. He kissed all of the places he'd touched, branding her with each contact. He gripped her hips, laid his cheek to the inside of her thigh, and inhaled deeply as she continued to comb her fingers through the silky strands of his hair.

Such a magnificent male. If only they could belong to one another in the way Saeed believed they could. Cerys had abandoned those sorts of optimistic notions a long time ago. They were each condemned to their fates. Cerys would never belong to anyone but Rin.

Saeed's hands continued their unhurried exploration of her body. Her eyes drifted shut as she allowed herself the indulgence of laying still and reveling in the sensation of his touch. He shifted against her, settling his body into the cradle of her thighs as his palms traveled up her torso against her ribs, over the petite mounds of her breasts, her collarbone, over her shoulders and down her arms to her fingertips.

With the still silence, Cerys's stomach growled. She cringed, cursing her own stupid body for making its other needs known. She looked up to find Saeed watching her, a corner of his mouth hitched in a gentle smile. Amusement sparked his dark eyes that crinkled at the corners. She liked him like this. Clearheaded. Relaxed. His expression soft. She reached up and brushed her thumb along the strong line of his jaw.

One-of-a-kind.

"You're hungry."

Yeah, her stupid stomach had made it pretty obvious. Embarrassment heated her cheeks and she couldn't help but return his gentle smile with a grimace. "I'm always hungry," she replied. "My stomach just chose the wrong moment to be an obnoxious jerk."

Saeed reached up to brush her hair away from her face. His gaze searched hers and Cerys's breath stalled in her chest. "I interrupted your dinner. I apologize."

Laughter bubbled in Cerys's chest but she swallowed it down. She wasn't used to such sincerity. Saeed had just managed to rock her mother-effing world, hadn't asked for a damned thing in return, and he was apologizing? They might have to have a talk about what sorts of things warranted an "I'm sorry."

Saeed's eyes took on that faraway look that signaled his grip on lucidity might be slipping. A tiny knot of worry formed in Cerys's chest, the sensation so uncomfortable and foreign, she rubbed at her sternum as though she could massage it away.

"I saw you." His voice went low and deep, caressing every part of her. "You danced with bright silver swords for a Roman vampire and his entourage. So fierce. So beautiful. And so sad."

Holy shit. Cerys drew in a surprised breath. Hundreds of thousands of memories to weed through. Several lifetimes worth of experiences so easily forgotten, and yet, Cerys knew the exact moment Saeed spoke of. It hadn't been long after Rin had captured her soul and she'd retained some sense of what it was to feel. She'd danced like a puppet on a string, providing a show that was guaranteed to impress the arrogant coven master. Rin had instructed her to be beautiful and graceful, formidable and fierce. Through it all, she'd experienced despair so intense, it had threatened to bring her to her knees.

"Your eyes." Saeed focused on nothing as he stared her. "Pale autumn. Starlight. Your skin. . . ." He reached out to her as though she were an apparition, the tips of his fingers ghosting over her bare shoulder. "Lustrous and fair.

Your hair . . ." Silver flashed in his gaze as he captured a lock of her hair between his thumb and forefinger. "Just like fire."

Tears pricked at Cerys's eyes. His tender words would have gutted her had she been able to feel even a little more. His gaze remained unfocused as though he were back in that memory, reliving the moment alongside her. "Saeed." She cupped either side of his face in her palms as she implored him. "Come back to me. There's nothing for you in the past."

"She'll tether me." Her words had no effect on him. "My soul is bound to hers."

He'd had her blood. That should've been enough to keep his mind clear. Why had he slipped so easily away? A familiar sense of helplessness crept up her shoulders, the weight of which was almost too much to bear. She didn't know how to help him. How to keep him from retreating to a place that no longer existed. She couldn't give him hope when she had none.

Saeed lived in dreams. Cerys had stopped dreaming a long time ago.

CHAPTER
13

Sasha paced the confines of what had once been Saeed's study. The sun would rise in a few short hours, and she was anxious for the oblivion of daytime sleep to put an end to another miserable night. Soullessness wasn't as bad as she'd thought it would be. Honestly, she welcomed a vacation from crippling emotion. It was restlessness that ate at her now. The lack of freedom, now that she was partially responsible for the well-being of their entire coven.

"I don't think your expression is quite sour enough."

Sasha looked up to find Diego's large frame taking up the doorway. She pursed her lips. She could give sour a run for its money. Diego would be wise not to bait her. Her co-ruler was always so damned upbeat. Probably why Saeed had chosen him to rule alongside her. She supposed they offset each other perfectly. Saeed had thought of everything, it seemed. Everything except the empty hopelessness she would feel when he left her.

Did she mourn his loss? Or was it the absence of her own soul that plagued her?

"Mikhail's not happy." She chose to ignore Diego's

comment on her attitude and got straight to business. "Saeed promised to turn three of us and now he's gone and we are short a vampire."

Diego flashed a sardonic smile, revealing the points of his fangs. "Did you really think he wouldn't leave us with a few loose ends to tie up?"

Yes, damn it. It was bad enough he'd abandoned them, the least he could've done was make sure all of his business with the vampire king had been concluded. "I think he should've been responsible rather than chase a dream up the West Coast."

Diego stepped deeper into the study and closed the door behind him. He fixed Sasha with a stern stare and folded his arms across his wide chest. "Would you have done anything less had you believed what Saeed does?"

She hated it when Diego threw logic in her face. He'd always been levelheaded, whereas Sasha let her heart lead the way. She envied his pragmatic nature. His detachment. If only her mind could convince her heart of the truth. Saeed would never be hers. "No." There was no point in lying. She would've left them all hanging without a word. "But this isn't about me."

Diego chuckled. "This is absolutely about you. You're just too stubborn to admit it."

He was right on both counts. Totally sour grapes. She knew her attitude was childish, but she wasn't ready or willing to make an attitude adjustment just yet. "Who should the third be?" She didn't want to talk about her sad, pathetic state anymore. "We have to decide. And we have to choose which one of us will be responsible for turning the candidate."

"Wow. So formal. You really are taking your role as coven mistress seriously, aren't you?"

His mocking tone wasn't amusing. "Someone has to." His eyes widened almost imperceptibly at her harsh words.

"You're so drunk on your own power, you've forgotten your position comes with responsibility."

Diego's lips pursed. She knew he fought the urge to throw out an equally snarky retort. He wouldn't, of course. Diego was much too analytical to devolve into an emotion-driven word war. She also envied his maturity. Right now, she felt more like a spoiled fourteen-year-old than a centuries-old dhampir. Correction: *vampire*. She was no longer the creature she'd once been. Finding a new normal had been tumultuous at best.

"And you're so busy nursing your broken heart, you've failed to acknowledge what you've become."

Diego might as well have plucked the thoughts from Sasha's head. It was true she was so preoccupied with Saeed's absence that she'd spent very little time contemplating the change. "Does the Collective plague you?" Saeed had been unable to resist its pull but Sasha had no such trouble. From the moment of her turning it held very little influence over her. The memories of dead vampires didn't concern her. Probably because she was so damned obsessed with her own life.

Diego shrugged. "Occasionally." He settled down onto the couch where Sasha had had one of her last conversations with Saeed. She tried not to give him an accusing stare as though that stupid couch were some sort of monument that should no longer be touched. "I never succumb to the memories for long though. They interest me, but never master me."

Only Diego could stare into the face of the Collective and respond with an "Eh." Sasha couldn't help but smile. "I don't know what Saeed was thinking. He should've named you alone coven master. I bring nothing to the table."

"You always sell yourself short." Diego gave a shake of his head. "Saeed knew exactly what he was doing."

"Really?" She gave a rueful laugh. "Because I don't know if you've noticed or not, but I don't have *any idea* what I'm doing."

"You're diplomatic. Saeed knew that I'm not."

"You are diplomatic when you need to be."

"Liar," Diego said with a laugh. "I've yet to meet with Mikhail because diplomacy bores me. I see no reason for his endless structure. We shouldn't have to petition for the right to turn the members of our coven. It should be left to our discretion."

She supposed he was a little less diplomatic than she was. "You just don't like anyone telling you what to do."

Diego's dark eyes sparked with amusement. "True. Which is why you're the perfect liaison between our coven and Mikhail. Saeed knew I'd be too abrasive. You on the other hand . . ."

"I'm just a big marshmallow, huh?"

Diego gave her another chiding glance. "Not a marshmallow. You have heart. And I envy that."

"Don't." The last thing he should be jealous of was her stupid emotions. Wasn't she supposed to feel a little more apathetic without her soul? Maybe it just took time for all of those residual feelings to drain out of her. "Believe me, emotions aren't good for anything."

"Sun's about to rise." Diego pushed himself up from the couch and crossed the room toward her. Sasha's own limbs became heavier with the encroaching dawn and she let out a grateful sigh. He stepped up to her and wrapped her in a quick embrace. "You'll soon be tethered," Diego assured her. "And whatever you once felt for Saeed will fade to the back of your mind like the memories of the Collective."

The reassurance was hollow but she appreciated it anyway. "Sleep well." It was all she could force herself to say.

"You too." Diego gave a playful knock to her shoulder. "Tomorrow night will be better."

Empty words. Empty promises. Just . . . empty. Tomorrow night wouldn't be better and neither would the next night or the night after that. She could fake it though. For Diego. For their coven. And maybe even for Saeed.

Christian Whalen checked his phone for the hundred thousandth time. Where the hell was everybody? He hadn't heard a peep from Gregor in over a week. The bastard usually had no problem bugging the everloving fuck out of Christian, but for the past several days he'd been left alone.

Probably not a good sign. Christian was far from being considered a member of Gregor's inner circle, but the least the berserker could do was to hook him up with an update. He hated feeling like he was in a state of limbo. It was worse than waiting on a bookie to come collect. Speaking of which. . . . He was pretty sure he had a few debts that had come due. Too bad his cash cow had gone AWOL.

"Christian, the director will see you now."

McAlister's secretary never said more than those seven words to him. Ah well, he supposed he couldn't charm everyone. She didn't even give him a passing glance as he strode past her desk and two armed guards before entering the director's office. Despite the tentative truce with the vampires, McAlister had done nothing to downplay their beefed-up security. Especially after the massive clusterfuck a few months back when Gregor had tried to ambush his meeting with Mikhail Aristov. Now that the cat was out of the bag, Christian assumed McAlister would be looking for something bigger and badder than a berserker to have his back. He snorted. Good luck with that. With the warlords off their leashes, McAlister was as good as fucked.

Christian waltzed into the room and plopped down into one of the chairs that faced McAlister's desk before propping his feet up on the polished surface.

"Christian." McAlister's testy tone was enough to coax a grin to Christian's lips. "I'd invite you to sit, but what's the point?"

Exactly. Christian never was one for formalities. For the past year, he'd been playing both sides against the middle. An unwilling double agent, he whored himself off to the highest bidder. He was tired of being used as a pawn. Left in the dark and forced to guess. He no longer wanted to play the game, since no one had seen fit to tell him the rules. Especially now that he was almost certain Gregor was searching for Siobhan.

"I know you're busy hiding out in your ivory tower," Christian remarked without chagrin. "But have you noticed the city is absent a few very prominent berserkers?"

McAlister leaned back in his chair as he regarded Christian. Probably trying to decide how much—if anything—he should divulge. Christian reminded himself that he'd catch more flies with honey, and it might not do him any good to antagonize the one male who might have a few answers.

"I've noticed." McAlister was careful to keep his tone neutral. *With a blank expression like that, he really oughtta try poker.* "Did you come here today simply to point out the obvious, or did you actually have something to say?"

Christian swallowed the comeback that sat at the tip of his tongue. *Suck it up and play nice.* "Can we just cut the bullshit?" Okay, maybe that wasn't very nice, but Christian never was one for games. "We both know Gregor's planning something big. His little ambush a while back is proof enough of that. And the fact that he's left the city, presumably without your permission, means the Sortiari have officially lost control of their warlord."

McAlister's mouth formed an annoyed pucker. Finally, a tell from the stoic male. Christian had hit a nerve which meant he might get McAlister to play ball. He wasn't opposed to helping the director further his agenda as long as it got Christian what he wanted. For starters, a few answers. And maybe later, some level of protection for a certain dhampir.

"I find it amusing you don't think I know you've been keeping company with Gregor." Christian tucked away his surprise. He thought he'd been pretty damn stealthy. He guessed it was stupid not to assume that McAlister had eyes everywhere.

"I never denied it," Christian replied. Did McAlister think he'd played a part in the ambush on him and Aristov? "I would've told you if you'd asked."

McAlister snorted. "And *only* if I'd asked."

Christian shrugged. No use contradicting him. McAlister had known when they took him on that Christian was a selfish son of a bitch who served his own agenda. "Not even you can deny Gregor's a scary motherfucker. When the king of the berserkers tells you to do something, you do it."

"King." McAlister scoffed. "Perhaps at one time, but Gregor has no power now."

That might've been McAlister's assertion, but Christian saw a glimmer of doubt in his eyes. "You say that," Christian leaned forward in his seat for emphasis. "But you're just as worried as I am about what he's capable of now that he's finally broken his leash."

Once again, McAlister gave the impression he was none too pleased with Christian's intuitiveness. "You're worried? I would imagine you're jockeying for a high ranking position in his regime."

Under other circumstances, maybe. Christian was an opportunist after all. But Gregor had set his sights on

something Christian coveted. There wasn't a whole hell of
a lot he cared about in this world. Truth be told, he wasn't
even sure he cared about Siobhan. But until he knew for
sure, he wasn't willing to let Gregor get his hands on her.
"Gregor would set the world on fire simply to watch it
burn. I'm not interested in being a part of that."

McAlister's posture relaxed. The slightest spark of
magic tingled Christian's nose and he wondered how much
power the male managed to mask. "You'd light the match
if it benefited you somehow."

Again, not gonna deny it. "Well, I'm not interested."
The opinions of others didn't usually bother Christian.
This time however, McAlister's words got under his
skin. "Gregor's got me in his back pocket, you said so
yourself. I can help you. Do you want my help or not?"

McAlister's eyes narrowed. "And if I chose to believe
for even a *second* that you would be forthright with me,
what would you expect in return for your help?"

Finally, they were getting somewhere. "Answers."

"Answers? What sort of answers?"

That was the problem, wasn't it? Christian wasn't sure
what he was looking for. He had no idea where to start.
Gregor would keep him in the dark. Siobhan would rather
see him chasing his tail. As for McAlister . . . Christian
had to hope that he'd play ball for no other reason than to
save his own neck.

"How is it that Gregor and his lot became indentured
to the Sortiari in the first place? And why and on whom
does he seek vengeance?"

McAlister laughed. It was the first time Christian had
ever heard him make that sort of sound and it shocked the
shit out of him. Who knew the director had a sense of
humor, grim as it may be. "Do you have a month or so to
spare?"

Damn. Obviously Gregor had a laundry list of grievances. "Give me the Cliff Notes version," Christian said. "I'm sure I can fill in the blanks on my own."

"Why do you want to know?" McAlister was nothing if not suspicious.

"Because I don't like being used." The reason was at least partially true. "And I never take a side until I know all the facts." Also, partially true.

"All right." McAlister leaned forward and rested his forearms on the glossy surface of his immaculate desk. "I'll tell you and you can make your alliances from there."

"Aren't you worried I might choose Gregor?"

A dark cloud passed over McAlister's expression. His gaze met Christian's dead on. "What's one more adversary?" he asked. "I've already made enough enemies to last several lifetimes."

You and me both, buddy. On that, they'd found equal ground.

CHAPTER
14

"Saeed. Come back to me."

Gods, how he wanted to. He'd fallen into the Collective unexpectedly. As though a dark chasm had opened before him and he'd had no choice but to fall into it. He had no need for memories when Cerys sat mere inches from him. Living, breathing, soft and seductive, her breath brushing his face as she implored him to return. He truly was mad, wasn't he?

Perhaps not even the tether could save him now.

"Saeed." The smooth timbre of Cerys's voice snapped out like a whip, loud and clear in his mind. "I'm not messing around. Get it together, or I'm going to lay you out."

A smile curved his lips. How he admired her moxie. The voices quieted in Saeed's mind and the image of Cerys dancing with the bright silver swords slowly faded. The surroundings of his condo came back into focus as did Cerys's face, lined with concern. "I lost myself once again." The explanation was as feeble as his failing sanity. "I apologize."

Cerys let out a slow sigh. "You have to stop apologizing." Her earlier worried expression was replaced by a relief so intense it made Saeed's chest ache. "Are you all right?"

No. He wasn't. "I'm fine. A momentary lapse." Another exaggeration. He was suddenly painfully aware of the fact that Cerys sat before him completely naked. He might have been soulless, but that didn't stop the shame that flared hot in his chest. Even untethered, just being in Cerys's presence seemed to stir the remembrance of emotions he'd all but lost. He reached for her clothes and placed them gently in her lap. She might have initiated what had happened between them, but Saeed's intention had been to seduce her. He'd pleasured her in the hopes it would form some bond between them. Instead, all he'd managed to prove was that his madness surpassed his own control. He'd practically abandoned her. Left her naked and confused while he retreated into memories that should no longer have mattered. "Again, I've kept you from feeding. Rin will be expecting you soon."

Cerys's expression fell. Disappointment? Or something else? "Feeding." She gave a slight roll of her eyes as though to add levity. "You make it sound so perfunctory."

She weeded through her clothes and slipped on her bra, followed by her shirt. As she continued to dress Saeed couldn't help but wish he hadn't offered them to her. To cover the glorious beauty of her body seemed a sin.

"It is perfunctory." Saeed thought it best to focus on the conversation and not the perfect roundness of her breasts. "Feed or die."

Cerys shook her head and the ends of her wild red curls teased the very breasts Saeed tried not to notice. "You know, you really need to learn to loosen up. Your stoic, scary vampire routine isn't going to make you any friends."

Saeed cocked a brow. She thought him stoic and scary. He wanted to blame that on the loss of his soul but he knew better. He'd never been particularly warm. Neither had he ever been easygoing. Were those qualities Cerys looked for in a companion? If so, she would find Saeed considerably lacking. His mood plummeted as he tried to hide the scowl that curled his lip. "I'm not interested in making friends."

Cerys pulled on her underwear and Saeed got one last glimpse of her gorgeous pussy before the soft cotton fabric blocked his view. "Only enemies, huh?" she teased.

A smile tugged at the corner of his mouth. "Perhaps."

"You'll give Rin a run for his money." She kept her attention focused at the floor as she stuck one leg and then the other into her jeans before fastening them. Her posture stiffened almost imperceptibly as she spoke of the mage. "You've already got werewolves shaking in their boots."

Cerys was such an enigma to him. She had every reason to be both stoic and scary. A hardened killer who bred fear in those unlucky enough to cross her path. Instead, she carried herself with an almost openly defiant air. As though she refused to let the world see the damage that had been done to her. Such strength. He couldn't help but admire her.

"Eat." She would soon have to leave to go back to her master. In the meantime, Saeed wanted to do what he could to care for her.

"Only if you admit that eating is more than perfunctory, and that 'feeding' sounds way too stuffy."

She wanted him to admit the very necessary act of taking her vein was a pleasurable experience? "I can assure you I would sink my fangs into your throat hourly given the chance, whether I needed your blood or not."

Cerys's mouth softened and the rich perfume of her renewed arousal scented the air. Saeed took a deep breath and held it in his lungs as though he might not have the pleasure of smelling it again.

"Okay then." The breathy quality of her voice sent a

rush of pleasure through Saeed's veins. "I don't know about throats, but I'd definitely sink my teeth into a cheeseburger hourly if I had the chance."

Cerys pushed herself out of the chair and headed back to the kitchen island where her takeout waited. "I'm sure your food is cold by now," Saeed remarked. "I can reheat it for you if you'd like."

"Nah. Cold Chinese food is the bomb. Of course, it's better after it's been sitting in the fridge for a day but counter cooled works too." She snatched a pair of chopsticks from the brown paper bag and dug in with gusto. "Want some?" she asked through a mouthful of noodles. "They're delish."

No delicacy on the planet could be half as delicious as a single sip of Cerys's blood. "Later," Saeed replied. He'd rather simply sit here and enjoy her company for the few fleeting minutes they had left. "I've never kept company with fae before. Your metabolism seems to run remarkably fast. Is that why you need to eat so often?"

The chopsticks with a healthy portion of noodles pinched between them hovered near Cerys's mouth. She looked away as though embarrassed. "My metabolism is as fast as any supernatural creature's. I just . . ." She let out a heavy sigh. "I never seem to feel full."

Saeed's brow furrowed. He sensed her unease and it tore at him. "Your biology?"

She let out a soft snort of derision. "My absence of a soul."

Saeed knew all too well that sensation of emptiness. It had consumed him and sent him into the Collective for solace. Cerys had no such escape and so she used the physical sensation of fullness to replace the spiritual void. For so long, Saeed had thought it only to be a malady that plagued vampires. Up until now, he'd had no notion that creatures like Cerys even existed except in myth. Hers was a unique power. One that was meant to be treated with reverence as well as a fair amount of fear. The matter of one's soul was no triviality. Cerys's ability to steal the soul from anyone she chose was a terrible burden. Saeed had stolen both Sasha's and Diego's souls when he'd turned them. He knew the guilt that weighed on her. A vampire was perhaps the only other creature in this world that could relate to what she could do.

"How did it happen?"

The release of the soul from the body happened during a vampire's transition. The entire process was painful and a little traumatic but there was never a moment when Saeed had recognized or felt the moment his soul left him. Mikhail had drunk him dry and in the moment of near death he had replenished himself with the vampire king's blood. His world had gone dark, and when he woke from the haze of pain and metamorphosis, he'd been . . . empty.

Cerys continued to focus her attention on the box of chow mein. She ate with gusto, polishing it off in a matter of minutes. She moved on to the box of General Tso's chicken and dove in as though completely unconcerned with their current conversation. Saeed knew better, though. He gave her time to gather her thoughts. To eat. To replenish her strength and do whatever she needed to do to fill that emptiness within her.

"I was in the wrong place at the wrong time." She didn't look at Saeed, but rather kept her attention focused on the food in front of her. "Rin saw an opportunity and he took it. He's great at exploiting anyone for any reason. He never goes into any situation without knowing how it will benefit him first. I never went to Rin for a damn thing, but that didn't stop him from finding a way to get his hands on me."

It didn't surprise Saeed a bit. He'd seen firsthand that Rin wasn't above playing dirty to get what he wanted. "He used magic to do it?"

Cerys picked at the chicken with her chopsticks. "He used another *enaid dwyn*. My sister stole my soul and gave it to Rin."

Saeed stared at her, stunned. He couldn't conceive of such a betrayal. A more damaged creature than Cerys Saeed had never met, and he planned to do everything in his power to mend her.

It hurt more than she thought it would to say the words. It had been so long since Cerys had spoken of it that it re-opened wounds she'd thought had scarred over long ago. Saeed continued to stare at her. She tried her best to keep her attention focused on the chicken that had lost its appeal since the conversation began. The hurt, the shock, the sense of unbelievable betrayal seemed as fresh now as it had over a thousand years ago.

"Your sister? How? Why?"

The how was pretty obvious. And really, so was the why. "Rin got my soul the same way he gets everything. Through leverage."

Leverage or not, Cerys wondered for the millionth time how one sister could turn against the other. She never would've agreed to Rin's demand. Hell, she never would've gone to someone like Rin in the first place.

"I thought about it a lot over the years," Cerys said. "And I'd like to think Rin orchestrated the whole thing. Maneuvered my sister into a position where she had no choice but to go to him for help. I know that's probably not how it went down, but it's the lie I tell myself. But that's how Rin operates. He collects favors."

Saeed's countenance grew stern and a storm gathered in his dark eyes. "He helped your sister and requested your soul as payment? Whatever her situation, it must've been dire for her to agree to such a thing." He didn't press Cerys for any more details and she was glad for it. She'd tried to block that day from her memory and wasn't interested in reliving it anytime soon.

"Yeah." Saeed wouldn't get any more explanation than the one word. "She gave Rin what he wanted and has kept a safe distance ever since."

A space of welcomed silence followed. Cerys didn't want to dwell on the past. It never did anyone a damned bit of good. Talking about what had happened, how it had happened, or why, wouldn't change the fact she was stuffing her face with chow mein and chicken in an effort to feel a little less empty.

"Yours was the first?" It wasn't a question. Cerys sensed Saeed simply wanted confirmation.

"Yup. Mine was the first of many. The funny thing about Rin is that he's not without power of his own." Cerys popped a piece of chicken into her mouth and chewed. She might have lost her appetite, but that didn't mean she wasn't going to stuff herself as full as she could manage. "There aren't many mages in the world, even fewer with the ability to manipulate magic in the way Rin can. He rarely uses his own power though. And why would he?" Cerys let out a soft snort. "As long as he continues to capitalize on the desperation of others, there's no need to."

Saeed sat back in his chair and regarded her. "I have found mages to be nothing but secretive. The few that I've encountered have never once exercised their power in my presence. Why is that, I wonder?"

Cerys shrugged. "Your guess is as good as mine."

"In all the years you've been with him, you've never once seen him use his power?"

"Not exactly." Cerys and Rin had a complicated relationship. They shared a certain intimacy despite her burning hatred for the male who claimed ownership of her. "I've seen him call fire to the palm of his hand. He can manipulate water and air as well."

"His magic is elemental?"

"I'm not positive but I think it's where his talent lies." Saeed seemed to contemplate that information, though Cerys didn't know how it would benefit him one way or the other. "Probably not super useful for amassing power."

"No," Saeed said with a gentle laugh. "At least, not the sort of power he wants."

Cerys imagined Rin instilling fear into the hearts of his enemies by calling up thunderstorms and laughed. No, if Rin's magic lay primarily with the elements, he would've simply been another supernatural living among the others. Nothing special. And certainly no one to fear.

And yet, he'd managed to instill more than a healthy dose of fear into those around him. Rin's reputation built with each passing century. Those who encountered him were more afraid of what he *didn't* reveal than what he did.

"Rin is smart, though." Cerys finished off the General Tso's chicken and moved on to the box of honey walnut shrimp. She offered the box to Saeed and he shook his head. Cerys shrugged. His loss, she supposed. Honey walnut shrimp was the bomb. She pinched one between the chopsticks and popped it into her mouth as she contemplated the male who sat beside her. "He knows how to bluff, and he's one of the most ruthless males I've ever met. Who needs magic when you have an assassin at your disposal? If you piss Rin off and have nothing to offer him, he gets rid of you. Plain and simple. That's enough to make anyone wary."

Saeed's brow pinched. "Rin doesn't frighten me. He's nothing more than a coward hiding behind *your* strength."

Warmth bloomed in Cerys's chest. She'd never thought of herself as strong. Her power was both fearsome and terrible, and the only thing it had ever made her feel was shame. "Assassins are a dime a dozen," she replied.

"Anyone with the proper training and enough starch in their spine can do it."

Saeed shook his head. "As though it's that easy. There was a time when I was regarded with fear and not simply because I'd lost my mind." His sad smile tugged at Cerys's chest and she reached up to rub the sensation away. "I made a name and a reputation for myself killing Templars during the Crusades. I killed the unkillable. And yes, I trained, honed my skills, and learned to disconnect my emotions. My heritage—an assumed Muslim targeting the righteous Christians helped to instill fear in my enemies. The climate of the world we lived in and the state of the wars we fought made me someone to be wary of. You'd think those differences wouldn't matter as much in the world we live in now, but they do. We fear those who are different from us. Who believe different from us. My gods are older than any of humanity's and their wars were trifling compared to petty squabbles in the supernatural world. But whereas that fear others felt of me made me noteworthy, it was not what made me effective as an assassin. I was good at it because I was angry and lost and wanted every male who met my blade to pay for what I'd been made to suffer."

There was a darkness in Saeed that Cerys knew all too well. She wanted to argue with him. To proclaim she had no choice but to carry out Rin's orders. That killing brought her no joy. But she'd gone too long without a soul to try and gloss over any of it. She didn't want to feel any kinship at all with Saeed but with every passing second the connection between them grew. How had he been made to suffer? And why did the thought of it make her want to punish whoever had hurt him?

"You're right." She found it difficult to make the admission. "Without that hunger, that need for retribution, the job isn't going to get done. At least, not the right way."

Cerys looked away, turning her attention back to her

food. Her chest burned, reminding her of the sensation of guilt. She wondered at the way Saeed had managed to awaken the barest wisps of emotions she'd thought long dead. Was he right that a fair amount of her detachment had been created by herself?

"You're entitled to your anger. Your need for vengeance. You're entitled to all of it and more. Rin took your power and built his reputation from it, leaving you nothing in return."

Hell yeah! Cerys met Saeed's intense gaze and for the first time in her life felt validated. Rin, that opportunistic son of a bitch, had climbed atop her shoulders and usurped her power. She wasn't jealous of his possessions, his position, or the grip he held on the city's supernatural population. What chapped her ass was that he'd spent centuries diminishing her self-worth. Convincing her she had no value when it was he who was worthless.

"I want him dead." Cerys had never dared to say the words out loud. Always fearful of who might hear. But she knew she could trust Saeed with anything, including her own life. It didn't matter what she said or what she did. He would never judge her. Gods, how liberating that revelation was!

Saeed reached out and brushed the pad of his thumb along her jawline. Cerys's stomach clenched as she recalled their earlier moments of passion and a renewed rush of warmth spread between her legs. Without even trying, the vampire made her wanton. She still didn't believe his claim that they were somehow fated to be together, but neither could she discount the effect he had on her.

"Say the word, and I'll deliver his head to you on a silver platter."

Cerys didn't fight the smile that tugged at her lips. Pretty damned chivalrous—if not a little violent—of him. As much as she appreciated the offer, if anyone was going to make Rin pay for her years of slavery it would be her. "If you managed to pull off that feat, Seattle's supernatural community will throw you a hell of a tickertape parade."

The barest hint of amusement sparked in his dark eyes. "The only thing keeping him alive is your soul," Saeed replied. "As soon as I find it, there is nothing on this earth that can protect him."

Another pleasant rush flooded her. It was totally sick that she found his promises of death and retribution charming. Even a little romantic. The supernatural world was a violent one. There was no place for gentleness, compassion, or civility. The fae were especially wild, considering themselves so far from humankind that they weren't even in the same class. They scoffed at humanity's many rules and guidelines. Their gods were unconcerned with kindness. Perhaps the only ideology they had in common was that the fae believed they reaped what they sowed. But that was the law of nature. The fae needed no books or profits to tell them that.

"It's getting late. I need to get back to Rin." Cerys closed the boxes of Chinese food and stacked them neatly back in the bag. Saeed stood, prepared to escort her back to her keeper. Her heart sank in her gut as she said a silent prayer that Rin would be tired when she got to the club and would want to make it an early night.

"We certainly don't want to keep Rin waiting."

Saeed's sour tone mirrored Cerys's mood exactly. She'd come to admire Saeed over the course of their time spent together, and perhaps she'd even become a little enamored of him as well. What she hadn't told him was that she'd been searching for her soul since the day Rin stole it. She'd always suspected he kept it far away from her, perhaps even thousands of miles. One thing was certain, however, when Cerys did find her soul—and she *would*—she'd put a swift end to Rinieri de Rege's existence.

CHAPTER
15

Saeed hated for the night to end, but it had been a success. He'd managed to earn some measure of Cerys's trust and in the process had strengthened the bond between them. He might not have been able to sense their tether, but he had no doubt it was there. He didn't want to return her to Rin but for the time being, it was necessary to keep up appearances. Cerys's wasn't the only trust Saeed needed to earn. If he had any hope of stealing back her soul he needed to win Rin over as well.

With any luck, his success with the werewolf tonight would put him on the right track.

He walked beside Cerys in silence. They'd opened up to one another tonight and still had barely scratched the surface. Saeed was honored Cerys thought him worthy of hearing one small part of her history and likewise, he was eager to share more details of his own past with her. They had decades, centuries, to learn about one another. In the meantime, his focus was getting them through the next few weeks. Gods, he hoped it wouldn't take that long to find her soul.

A body barreled into Cerys, dragging her into a nearby alley a beat before Saeed could stop it. His heart pounded in his chest as he turned after them and found Cerys pinned against the wall of the alleyway by the tall, bulky form of her attacker.

"It's gotta be worth something to Rin!" Desperation tore through the male's tone. "Enough to buy back my soul."

Saeed ripped the male away from Cerys and slammed him into the opposite wall. He bared his fangs as he drew back his fist, prepared to bash the bastard's face into a pulp.

"Saeed stop!" Cerys's warning shout stayed his hand. "This one's delicate. Besides, I need to hear what he has to say."

Delicate? Saeed dropped his fist to his side but left his other palm on the male's chest, holding him against the wall. "Speak up, and fast," he instructed. "Otherwise, Rin is going to be the least of your problems."

The male's Adam's apple bobbed nervously as he swallowed. He was big, a couple of inches taller than Saeed with maybe a good fifty pounds of bulk over him. Didn't seem as delicate as Cerys thought he was. He didn't smell like a shifter or a werewolf. Neither did the spark of magic linger on his skin. His build wasn't lithe like most fae creatures. Saeed's senses failed him as the male possessed no physical qualities to identify his creed. Curious.

"Berserkers," the male said on a panting breath. "In the city. Looking for Rin. Looking for you."

Cerys's brow furrowed with concern as Saeed met her gaze. His fist clenched tight at his side and his jaw locked down, causing the points of his fangs to nick his bottom lip. Saeed flicked out with his tongue to swipe the blood away and forced himself to relax. He'd tried not to put much stock in Mikhail's ward, Vanessa's, words when she'd predicted Saeed would not be the only one searching for Cerys. Obviously he'd been foolish.

The beast and the madman . . . Even now, the memory of her proclamation left him shaken.

Ian Gregor was in Seattle. Saeed had no doubt about it.

"Berserkers?" Cerys's disbelieving tone gave the impression that the Sortiari's former guard dogs didn't often visit Seattle. "How do you know?"

"I saw them with my own damned eyes." Eyes that shone with fear. Saeed knew very few creatures other than berserkers that could evoke that sort of distress without lifting a finger. "Ten of them. But ten berserkers might as well be a hundred."

The male had that right. Berserkers were killing machines, ruthless, emotionless, with laser sharp focus, and nearly inexhaustible strength. Practically indestructible in full battle rage and not opposed to inciting violence for no other reason than to pick a fight. The whole of the supernatural community avoided them whenever possible. The vampires' mortal enemies, and no longer beholden to Trenton McAlister and the Sortiari; Saeed would be wise to avoid them at all costs.

Too bad Saeed had decided to put wisdom on the backburner.

"Shit." The expletive left Cerys's lips in an emphatic rush. "You're sure? You saw them?"

The male nodded his head so hard Saeed wondered how it was still attached to his neck.

"But how do you know they came for Rin? Or me?"

Saeed sensed the worry in her tone, but Cerys had nothing to fear from Ian Gregor. Saeed would lay down his own life to protect her. The berserker wouldn't get so much as a finger on her.

"I didn't know what they were at first." The male reached up and scrubbed a hand over his face. "I was at that Irish pub in Belltown. You know the one, Mulligan's."

Cerys gave a quick nod.

"The whole group walked in and god, did they stink up the place." The male shuddered at the memory. "Sat down at the bar beside me and they weren't concerned about who overheard their conversation, making me think they wanted word to get out."

Subtlety wasn't exactly Gregor's strong suit. Saeed suspected his plan was to flush Rin out with a healthy dose of fear. Too bad Rin's ego didn't allow for fear.

Cerys leaned in close. Her countenance was fierce, made all the more awe-inspiring by her otherworldly beauty. "That still doesn't tell me how you knew they were berserkers."

Without Cerys, Rin was nothing.

"The musky smell was my first clue," the male replied.

Cerys cocked a brow. "And the second . . . ?"

"Yeah, well, some stupid son of a bitch tried to pick a fight with one of them. A . . . uh. . . . shifter of some kind. I wasn't paying much attention to him. But he pissed the male off at the bar, that's for sure. The fucker pushed out his stool and when he turned around . . ." The male shuddered. "His eyes were completely black. Like a couple of onyx marbles in his head! The color bled out, too. Fanned around his eyes and made him look scary as fuck. The shifter backed off in less than a second. Headed for the door and didn't look back."

Cerys looked at Saeed from the corner of her eye as though searching for some sort of confirmation. He supposed she assumed a vampire would be the best authority on how to identify a slayer. He answered her with a nod. "I know of no other creature save a berserker that possesses those traits."

"I want to know everything you overheard," Cerys said, low. "Don't leave out a single detail."

The male's gaze shifted to Saeed and his eyes went wide as though he'd only now noticed he stood beside Cerys. "Holy shit! Is that a fucking vampire?"

Saeed rolled his eyes. He looked to Cerys as though to ask, "Is he for real?"

"Human," Cerys said by way of explanation. "Kyle's an investment banker."

Human. Delicate. It seemed Rin collected all sorts of souls, not only those of the supernatural community. A tragedy for Kyle; a human's life span was nothing but the tick of a second in comparison to a supernatural creature's existence. Saeed knew there were humans in the world who were privy to the preternatural. Mikhail's assistant Alex was one of them. No doubt this Kyle handled some sort of business transactions for Rin. Once his usefulness wore out, Rin would dispose of him. Either that or he'd die of natural causes first. It was no wonder he tried so desperately to bargain with Cerys now. It was probably his only chance at freedom.

"After the big scary-looking fucker with the black eyes ran off that shifter, it got sort of tense. He had his back turned to the bartender. The others stayed pretty neutral. Then, the quiet one at the far end of the bar barked something at him. Not sure of the language. Sounded . . . dunno . . ." Kyle gave a quick shake of his head as though to dislodge the thought that had apparently gotten stuck there. "Dude sat his ass right down. His eyes changed, went back to normal. The one in charge ordered a round for the bar and everything smoothed over after that."

"Not that your story isn't absolutely *riveting*, Kyle"— Cerys grabbed his shirt by the collar and hauled him closer—"but none of this is worth shit to me. Or to Rin."

Kyle cast a nervous glance in Saeed's direction before

he continued. "The one in charge asked the bartender about clubs in the area. Specifically, the sorts of places people tended to avoid. I figured he was trying to pinpoint places where supes hung out. The bartender ticked off a few names. The Caged Canary, The Last Call down in Belltown, Joe's, and Crimson. The berserker told the others to split up and check each place out. Told them to spread the word that he was looking for a soul stealer."

Cerys released her hold on Kyle's shirt and took a wide step back. Her gaze met Saeed's and a glimmer of concern shone behind her light eyes. The beast had come to Seattle. And it was only a matter of time before he found what he was looking for.

If Cerys missed her curfew, Rin would blow a fucking gasket. By the time she'd manage to get him calmed down enough to relay Kyle's story, it might be too late. Besides, she knew where to find Kyle if she needed to. He wasn't going anywhere. Not while Rin still had his soul.

"Come on Saeed, we're out of here."

"Hey! Wait! What about me?"

Kyle grabbed Cerys by the arm and before she could even react, Saeed stepped in, putting the human none too gently into the wall. He wouldn't be any use to anyone as damaged goods. She appreciated that Saeed had her back, but honestly. He really needed to dial down the intensity a bit.

"Don't damage the merchandise Saeed." She laid a staying hand to his shoulder and the vampire instantly calmed. "Human, remember? Very breakable."

Saeed released his grip on Kyle's shoulder and let out a shaky breath. He really was volatile, wasn't he? She never knew what might set him off or how he'd react. One thing was certain, he didn't appreciate anyone putting his hands on her. Cerys could get used to someone looking out for her like that.

Cerys stepped forward and put her body between Kyle and Saeed. "Go home, Kyle sit tight until you hear from me or Rin. Got it?"

He answered with a nod. "W-what about my soul?"

Cerys's heart sank. Taking this fragile human's soul would've weighed more heavily on her conscience had she had much of one left. As it was, all she could muster was pity. "I'll see what I can do," she said. "But I'm not making any guarantees."

Kyle's expression fell and his gaze dropped to the pavement. "Thank you."

Cerys grabbed Saeed by the hand and without another word turned and left.

"You have *got* to do something about that dark, intense vibe you've got going on, Saeed."

He let out a less than amused snort. "You think I was too hard on him?"

"No, not at all." Cerys rolled her eyes. "You only almost broke the poor guy in two."

Saeed chuckled. And Cerys thought she was hard. Saeed's amusement was downright cold. "Had he hurt you, I would have."

Yeah, dark and intense had nothing on Saeed. "Again, human."

Saeed shrugged. Apparently he had no qualms about damaging someone exponentially more fragile than he was. At least, not where she was concerned. How . . . romantic? She didn't have time to contemplate whether or not Saeed's actions had been chivalrous. The fact of the matter was, Cerys could take care of herself just fine. Kyle's information had her on edge. She needed to get to Rin before one of those berserkers showed up at the club, so they could form a plan of attack. Gods. She couldn't believe she was actually going to alert Rin to a potential threat against him. But if the berserker was truly after her like Kyle had said, she couldn't imagine his plans for her were any more aboveboard than Rin's.

"You know something." She'd seen it in Saeed's gaze. "What?"

"I don't know what I know," Saeed replied.

Well. That was helpful. "Sorry, but you're going to have to give me a little more than that." She refused to let him retreat to that place in his mind that stole his lucid thought. She needed him front and center, five by five. If it took more of her blood to get it done, then so be it.

"An Oracle told me where I could find you, though I must admit her information had been cryptic. She proclaimed I wasn't the only one looking for you."

An Oracle? *Great.* Getting accurate information from an Oracle was sort of like asking a toddler for life advice. "I take it she didn't specifically indicate whether or not it was a berserker trying to track me down?"

Saeed's expression darkened. "No."

She sensed he knew more than he let on. Gods, how she hated secrets. Secrets had gotten her into this mess with Rin in the first place. "Any other pertinent bits of information you'd care to share?"

Saeed rubbed at his temples. "No."

He'd gone from talking her ear off to the silent treatment in the space of a couple of hours. "If you think I'm going to rat you out to Rin, I won't."

Saeed turned to look at her, his brow furrowed before he crossed the street. Cerys followed and he didn't speak until they'd reached Capitol Hill. "You don't think I trust you?"

The question sort of came out of left field. Cerys's step

faltered and she rushed to catch up. "You don't even know me," she said. "You have no reason to trust me."

He brought his fingertips to his temple once again and a ripple of anxious energy traveled the length of Cerys's body. The timing couldn't be worse for him to let his crazy show. Damn it.

"I don't know you?" The hurt in his tone sliced through her. "I've lived lifetimes with you."

She knew he believed there was a mystical connection between them. That they were somehow destined for one another. Cerys could think of worse things than being destined for a life with as magnificent a male as Saeed. Unfortunately, she'd learned long ago the only point of living was to survive one disappointment after the next. She wanted to believe. She just knew better.

"Glimpses of my past through memories isn't living, Saeed." She didn't want to hurt him, but wasn't it best to be upfront? "I could betray you to Rin in a heartbeat and he'd run a stake through your heart before you even knew what had happened."

Saeed seemed unaffected by her words. He continued to walk, his hands resting behind him at the small of his back. Cerys couldn't help but wonder how he'd retained his stiff formality over the centuries. Most supernatural creatures learned to adapt with the changing times. Saeed, on the other hand, had managed to stay firmly rooted in his past. Maybe that's why he had a hard time shaking the hold of the vampire Collective memory. He had no idea how to live anywhere but in the past.

"You would never betray me to Rin."

Such confidence. "How do you know?"

"I have faith in our tether," Saeed replied. "The bond is absolute. Unbreakable."

His unshakable faith in a bond that didn't even exist left

Cerys rattled. Why? It shouldn't matter to her one way or the other what Saeed thought. Perhaps it was that faith, that blind belief that gave her qualms. Cerys had faith in nothing. She believed in nothing. Especially the notion that one soul could tie itself to another.

"And nonexistent without our actual souls," she pointed out. "You said so yourself."

"You'll see." Cerys couldn't help but give a sad shake of her head. His unwavering belief really was something to be admired. "When I return your soul to you, you'll know."

The notion of a tether sounded a lot like slavery to her. She'd been a slave for thousands of years. Why release one bond just to form another? "Don't you think I deserve some measure of freedom Saeed?"

His eyes slid to the side as he regarded her. "You consider a mate bond with me another shackle?"

"Rin made me his property and I didn't have a choice in that. And according to you, the moment my soul is returned, the choice will be taken from me once again. If that's not slavery, I don't know what is."

The bright neon sign that read "Crimson," came into sight a hundred or so yards away. How bad was it that Cerys actually looked forward to a conversation with Rin in order to escape further conversation with Saeed. Not that she found her jailer in any way preferable to the broody, sinfully sexy vampire. Rather, Saeed chipped away at her icy exterior and well-practiced ambivalence. Cerys wasn't ready to face the fallout when she no longer believed the lies she told herself to get through the days.

Saeed's countenance grew even darker. He truly painted a terrifying picture in his anger. She was doing him a kindness by being honest, wasn't she? He might not see it now, but in time, he'd know she was right.

"I am going to return your soul to you." Saeed spoke

the words with the solemnity of a vow. "And when I do, you'll be free to make your own choices. Leave if you must. One thing I will *never* take from you is your freedom."

Yup. She'd pissed him off. Maybe it was for the best. She couldn't afford to lose herself to him.

CHAPTER
16

"Berserkers. You're sure?"

Rin sat up straight in his chair and the air around him sparked with magic. Saeed tried his best to keep a grip on reality and stay grounded in the present but the Collective called. And after his disheartening conversation with Cerys, he wanted nothing more than to leave reality behind.

"Well, I'm not sure," Cerys replied. She took a seat next to Rin, and Saeed clamped his jaw down as he was forced to stand and watch her lean intimately toward him. "Kyle was sure though, and Saeed confirmed his description of the males he saw as accurate. We'd have to see them with our own eyes to be sure but it sounds pretty gods-damned ominous."

Rin cursed under his breath and a renewed spark of magic danced along Saeed's skin. "There is no reason for them to be here unless the Sortiari commanded it."

"Not so." Saeed saw no reason to keep Gregor's break from Trenton McAlister's hold a secret. Word would travel throughout the supernatural community soon enough.

"The slayers have broken faith with the Sortiari. They answer to no one save themselves."

Rin's eyes went wide as he focused his attention on Saeed. "You know this how?"

"It doesn't matter how I know it," Saeed replied. "But it's the truth. Ian Gregor is on a mission for vengeance and he won't stop until not only the vampires are wiped from the face of the earth, but the guardians of fate as well."

A corner of Rin's mouth hinted at a smug smile. "And rightly so. I suppose they do deserve their vengeance."

Saeed didn't disagree. Through the Collective he'd seen many things. One of which being the decision of a single dhampir child to effectively sterilize the Berserkers' race. A sadistic vampire lord had declared his daughter would decide the fate of every berserker female. The child, no more than eight or nine years old, couldn't have possibly realized the implications of her actions when she'd pronounced judgment. The consequences had been far-reaching, however and had brought them all to this moment. Saeed thought again of the woman on the plane and her blind judgment of him based on nothing more than his appearance. The way she perceived him as a threat because of who—and what—he was, was no different than the way Gregor or any other berserker perceived him as a threat. Berserkers saw Saeed and every other vampire and dhampir as a threat to their existence because of their unpleasant histories. Creatures that must be eradicated in order to preserve the berserkers' way of life.

"I still don't see what any of this has to do with me." His attention focused on Cerys. "Or you."

"McAlister is a mage. So are you. Perhaps Gregor seeks to fight fire with fire."

Rin snorted. He tried to act as though none of this bothered him, but Saeed saw something behind his eyes that told a different story. He knew something. Had already made the connection to Gregor's appearance in the city. "Hardly. Mages are entirely unique in their power. Pitting me against McAlister would be more like fighting fire with dirt."

It would've been nice if Rin had given more away in his statement. Maybe some indicator as to who might be the stronger opponent in such a match. Not that it mattered. Saeed was unconcerned with Rin's power. The male could shoot flames from his fingertips for all he cared. It wouldn't deter him from his mission to retrieve Cerys's soul.

"Cerys is a valuable commodity," Saeed pointed out. Rin was a fool if he didn't already know this. "She could be useful to Gregor in a coming war."

"War?" Rin cocked a curious brow. "I suppose a berserker would never go about anything in a very subversive way. Hack, slash. Burn, loot. They're bred to fight. Gregor certainly won't be using mere words to take Trenton McAlister down."

No. He wouldn't. For the first time since he'd met the mage, Saeed recognized the faintest glimmer of fear in Rin's brown eyes. Holding Cerys's soul hostage kept her obedient and by his side, but if someone stole her out from under him . . . the leverage he held over her wouldn't mean a gods-damned thing.

Cerys's gaze met Saeed's. She knew it as well. And the same fear he saw in Rin passed over her expression. She was fearful of capture? Or of being taken away from Rin? The thought that she would choose to stay with Rin caused a low growl to gather in Saeed's chest as a haze of jealousy washed over his vision. That she found Rin's company preferable to Gregor's was understandable. That she might find it preferable to Saeed's made his blood boil with unchecked rage.

A vision of Cerys dancing with her swords in the Roman vampire's court flashed in Saeed's mind, and he fought to hold his grip on reality. It didn't matter if Cerys wanted him. Right now, she needed him. Whether she realized it or not.

"And I thought tonight was going to be boring," Rin remarked. "Cerys, have you ever taken the soul of a berserker?"

She flinched as though stung. It seemed Rin went out of his way to make her uncomfortable. "You know I haven't."

"I wonder if they're harder to extract. Feel like giving it a try?"

Cerys's eyes narrowed into hateful slits. If she truly did prefer a life with Rin to one with him, Saeed must have been more mad and frightening than he thought. "Fuck off, Rin."

Rin broke out into obnoxious laughter that made Saeed want to rip out his vocal cords. "Lucky for us we have a vampire, no?" Rin gave Cerys a playful knock to her shoulder. "Who better to protect you from slayers than their mortal enemy?"

Cerys looked away, uncomfortable. She refused to meet Saeed's gaze, and he didn't know how much longer he could stand here and feign indifference. Rin might've appeared cavalier but Saeed knew better. The mage was afraid Gregor was about to swoop in and steal his prized possession. And he wasn't above throwing Saeed in Gregor's path as collateral damage in order to keep what belonged to him.

"Trenton McAlister was jumped by Gregor and a small war party not three weeks ago."

Rin turned his attention to Saeed. "For a vampire, you seem to know a considerable amount of the Sortiari's business."

Saeed shrugged. He knew Mikhail would want him to keep any information he had to himself. But Saeed needed to make sure Rin trusted him completely. Having Gregor so close would cause his guard to be up. Saeed needed the opposite if he had any chance of locating Cerys's soul.

"I'd hardly call that one little bit of information considerable," Saeed said. "L.A. might seem large, but the supernatural community is relatively small. Gregor enlisted the help of a pack of werewolves in an attempt to steal something from him. He was unsuccessful."

Rin looked as though he hadn't been this entertained in centuries. "What did he try to steal?"

"A child Oracle." It couldn't hurt to tell Rin at least that much and Saeed would protect Vanessa's identity.

"Cerys, we've been living in the wrong town," Rin proclaimed with a laugh. "Shit's going down in L.A. and we're definitely missing out."

"Speak for yourself," Cerys countered with a derisive snort. "I have zero fucks to give about what's going down in L.A."

Rin cocked a challenging brow. "Oh no? The berserker king and greatest warlord who ever lived is in the city to find you. I'd say you might want to consider giving at least one fuck."

Saeed could hardly argue with Rin. He didn't know Gregor's motives in searching for Cerys, but they couldn't be good. Cerys was powerful. Perhaps one of the most powerful creatures Saeed had ever encountered. She wasn't infallible, however. She'd said so herself.

"Don't forget, Rin. I'm not the only one the berserker is looking for."

They bickered like siblings. Antagonizing one another and going out of their way to push each other's buttons. Saeed didn't understand their strange relationship dynamic. Even worse, he couldn't understand why he envied it.

"True. And I can't wait to find out why."

It hadn't taken long for Rin to recover his lost bravado.

The male's entire existence was a fraud. Magic masked Rin's scent, but Saeed didn't need to smell his fear to know Rin was terrified.

"What about Cerys?" Saeed couldn't imagine Rin would play fast and loose with her safety but Saeed wasn't about to take any chances. "Gregor might've been thwarted in his attempt to steal from McAlister which will only make him more determined to be successful here."

"Your concern is so . . . touching." Sarcasm, and a fair amount of suspicion leached into Rin's tone. "Do you always make such fast friends, Saeed?"

Up until this point, Saeed's worth to Rin had been mostly entertainment value. The novelty of once again having a vampire around had pleased him. Now though, with Gregor in the city, Saeed's presence seemed all the more questionable. Gods damn it. If Saeed got his hands on Gregor before Rin or anyone else, he'd rip the bastard's head right off his shoulders.

"Not exactly." Saeed took a measured breath. He was about to tread a very dangerous path. One that could call his alliances into question if Mikhail found out what he was doing here. He would do nothing to put any of his own kind in the path of danger, but neither would he let Rin dismiss him when it was vital that he stay by Cerys's side. "I haven't been completely honest with you."

Cerys's eyes widened by a fraction of an inch but they might as well have bulged out of her head. Rin hid his emotions well however. His expression remained relatively impassive as he studied him, waiting for Saeed to elaborate.

"I spoke with the Oracle," Saeed said. "She sent me here."

What are you doing Saeed? Cerys knew he was crazy, but she didn't think he had a death wish. If he told Rin everything he'd told her, Saeed would find a wooden stake through his heart before he even had a chance to finish his story. She had no doubt the berserkers appearance in Seattle was connected to Saeed somehow. But she'd rather ferret out the details somewhere far away from Rin.

"My office. Now."

Well, shit. Rin wasn't messing around. Cerys stood a second before Rin and pulled her dagger from the sheath at her thigh. She hated playing the muscle card with Saeed after what had transpired between them tonight. To threaten bodily harm to the male who'd recently given you the best orgasm of your life just seemed rude.

"You heard him." She jerked her chin toward the far end of the club. "Don't give me any reason to run this silver blade through your heart, got it?"

Saeed gave a solemn nod of his head. "I wouldn't dream of it. Lead, and I will follow."

The husky undertone of his words sent a pleasant shiver from the top of Cerys's head to the soles of her feet. She needed to retain her usual snarky stance of stoicism if she was going to diffuse this situation with Rin. And Cerys had no doubt that it would get dicey. Especially if Saeed was about to spill his guts about their supposed tether.

A couple of Rin's security staff—two nasty-looking werewolves who'd willingly sworn fealty to Rin—were posted outside the door to the office. One of them reached out and opened the door for Cerys without making so much as eye contact. Most everyone in Rin's inner circle treated her that way. As though she were something below—or maybe even above—their regard. Some supernatural creatures regarded the fae as deities. Cerys packed an extra punch since she was an *enaid dwyn*. Her entire life, all she'd wanted was for someone to treat her as though she wasn't . . . *other*.

Someone had. Saeed.

He'd never once treated her as someone deserving of fear. And whereas he'd regarded her with a sort of reverence—the sort due one's lover or mate—he'd also never put her up on a pedestal and treated her as though she were too sacred to touch. Another ghost of emotion tugged at Cerys's chest, and she willed the sensation away. She needed to get rid of Saeed. Get him the hell out of the city before Rin put him in the ground.

Hell, it might already be too late.

"Sit."

Rin's tone was all business as he barked the order at Saeed. The vampire remained calm as ever, his beautiful face as serene as a midnight pond under moonlight. He took a seat on a ratty chair next to Rin's desk, and Cerys swore that only Saeed could make the old, broken down piece of furniture look regal.

Rin's temper boiled dangerously close to the surface. Saeed's calm demeanor definitely wasn't helping. He either wasn't aware or didn't care that his little comment had managed to spark Rin's ire. Either way, shit was about to get real.

"I don't like games."

Cerys swallowed down a snort. Rin loved to play games. He just didn't like being played with.

Saeed sat in silence. Rin stared him down, and his gaze didn't so much as falter. *Stupid, stupid vampire!* Rin liked to be top dog. Everyone bowed to him. *Everyone.* If he wanted to diffuse what was bound to be a clusterfuck of epic proportions, he needed to swallow his arrogant male pride and play ball.

"If I'd come to you, prostrated myself and asserted that an Oracle had sent me to protect you, would you have believed me? Or would you have instructed your assassin to run her silver blade through my heart?"

"It's not your place to assume how I would or wouldn't

have reacted," Rin snapped. "You came to me under false pretenses."

Saeed cocked a challenging brow. Cerys's stomach did a nervous flip. Damn, the vampire was downright intimidating when he wanted to be. An aura of power, of strength, emanated from him. "I did. But it was Rinieri de Rege who nearly tripped over himself in his haste to once again keep the company of vampires."

Oh Jesus. Cerys could barely keep her eyes from rolling. Was he intentionally trying to antagonize Rin? She couldn't intervene. If she did, Rin would know she'd spent far more time with Saeed—and grown far too affectionate with him—than she should have. He was suspicious enough to come to the conclusion that they conspired against him, and he'd kill Saeed for sure.

"I don't appreciate your disrespect." Rin's lip curled into a sneer. "I've killed others for less."

"Perhaps for once, you should appreciate that I'm not willing to simply placate you like your band of fearful worshipers."

"Placate?" Rin said. "You mean *lie.*"

"I never lied. I simply withheld information."

"A lie by omission is still a lie."

Saeed shrugged as though Rin's opinion on the matter meant little to him. His posture was relaxed as he sat back in the rickety old chair, but Cerys knew he could pounce in a heartbeat. Probably even faster than Rin could react to the attack. In which case, it would be Cerys's job to intervene and protect her master. He owned her soul. She would have no choice but to kill Saeed.

He wouldn't possibly put her in that position, would he?

"Ian Gregor has ears everywhere." Cerys cast a sidelong glance in Saeed's direction. Even she had a hard time telling what was truth and what was a lie. He was *good.* "It's risky enough for me to be in the city. Gregor would happily kill me on sight given the opportunity. I came to you in good faith. That is no lie."

Cerys wanted to give a disbelieving shake of her head. Saeed was definitely filling Rin with a load of bullshit, but she couldn't detect the slightest physical reaction to betray the lie. He was so damned convincing it was scary.

Rin appeared equally convinced. The fire in his eyes dimmed and his posture relaxed. "I'll decide whether or not you came in good faith, after you tell me exactly what the Oracle said to you."

Cerys couldn't wait to hear what Saeed had to say.

"Several weeks ago, Trenton McAlister made an unlikely alliance with Mikhail Aristov."

Rin broke out into raucous laughter. "The director of the Sortiari allying himself with a vampire? You must think I'm a fool to believe that."

"The berserkers have broken faith with the Sortiari. The threat they pose has created the unlikeliest of alliances. Both the vampires and the guardians of fate stand to lose everything if Gregor is successful in his campaign. The enemy of my enemy is my friend. They have no choice but to work together."

No doubt Rin found the prospect of that alliance as unlikely as Cerys did. The history between the vampires and the Sortiari was violent and bloody, and it spanned centuries. Then again, the berserker warlords had carried out the Sortiari's death sentence gladly. If the rumors were to be believed—and Cerys had no reason not to believe—Gregor and his lot had every reason to want every vampire and dhampir that walked the earth dead.

"If Gregor has indeed bitten the hand that feeds him, we're all in for a world of hurt."

Wasn't that the truth?

"His army is ready," Saeed replied. "But even the berserkers will need more than brute strength to defeat an organization whose members are legion. He's collecting weapons, leverage to ensure his success. The Oracle saw your *enaid dwyn* in a vision. McAlister wants her. And so does Gregor."

Yup. Shit just got real.

CHAPTER
17

Word spread fast within the supernatural community. Saeed saw no point in keeping details from Rin that he would eventually find out anyway. Someone like Gregor would not have lived as long as he had without possessing a certain shrewdness. He could try to take Cerys by force, but Saeed suspected the berserker warlord would be much more subversive.

She was a rare treasure. Gregor wouldn't simply let her slip away. Which was why Saeed needed to locate her soul as soon as possible.

"This is all very interesting," Rin said. "But you still haven't told me how you came by the information. I somehow doubt the child simply walked up to your door to tell you this."

This is where things got complicated. It was important to protect Vanessa's identity, especially since Rin showed a proclivity for enslaving those whose power could benefit him. It was bad enough that McAlister and Gregor had both tried to get their hands on the child. Throwing Rin into the mix would only make an already bad situation worse. If Saeed brought any more danger to Mikhail's door, the vampire king would run a stake through his heart before he had a chance to explain himself.

"No, she didn't." Saeed cast a momentary glance in Cerys's direction. He needed to stay as close to the truth as possible without revealing too much. "Gregor recently tried to sway a pack of werewolves to join his cause. They planned an attack on McAlister while he met with the oracle. No doubt Gregor hoped to kill two birds with one stone. A vampire in Mikhail's inner circle happened to be tethered to one of the werewolves. We came to McAlister's aid and in doing so I came in contact with the oracle."

Saeed waited as Rin silently contemplated everything he'd told him. From the corner of his eye, he studied Cerys, looking for any outward show of emotion. Gods, she took his breath away. So inherently fierce. So gods-damned beautiful. So disconnected and hollow. And so deadly she made even the most stalwart of supernatural creatures quake in their boots.

"I've never heard of a werewolf mating with a vampire," Rin remarked. "In fact, I've never known a vampire to take anything but a vampire or dhampir as a mate."

Cerys pursed her lips as she glanced in Saeed's direction. He disregarded her "I told you so" expression as he lent his full attention to Rin. "There are a handful of vampires in existence. It only makes sense that nature would compensate."

"I suppose you're right." As if Saeed needed Rin's acceptance of it to make the fact even truer. "So you were in the right place at the right time. Why did the oracle speak to you?"

Saeed shrugged. "Why do oracles do anything? Their power is as mysterious as they are. The child beckoned me to her and declared that I should come here and find the fae with the hair like fire before Ian Gregor ended her master and used her for his own devices."

Saeed took a chance with that last bit. He'd learned enough about the art of deception over the centuries to know how to bluff without giving himself away. He doubted even his scent would betray him.

"You didn't ask this oracle any questions?" Rin asked. "If someone told me to travel the length of the coast in search of something that might not even be there, I might do a little fact checking first."

"I told you, the oracle is a child. She's not yet old enough to know how to properly articulate her visions. I was happy to investigate. We've been confined to California for two centuries. Now that our numbers have grown, we are afforded the opportunity to venture past those old boundaries. Once I got here, you weren't hard to find. Your reputation might just be your downfall, Rin. If it was so easy for me to find you, no doubt it will be just as easy for Gregor."

"He's right." Cerys spoke up for the first time since they'd come into the office. "According to Kyle, it only took Gregor a matter of minutes to get a list of clubs that might be potential supernatural hang outs you'd frequent." She looked pointedly at Rin. "Including your own club."

Rin folded his arms across his chest in a moment of quiet thought. His gaze passed from Cerys, to Saeed, and back again. It took a sheer act of will for Saeed to pay Cerys no mind. To behave as though she meant absolutely nothing to him when he craved her body, her blood, with every fiber of his being.

"Why kill me? If Gregor is in fact amassing allies, wouldn't I be more use to him alive than dead?"

Rin would be arrogant enough to consider himself a valuable commodity. Again, Saeed got the impression Rin knew a hell of a lot more than he let on. "You're a mage, so is McAlister. Maybe Gregor thinks you'd take his side."

"Without even asking me first?" Rin's amused laughter grated on Saeed's last nerve. He couldn't find Cerys's soul quickly enough for his peace of mind. His need to end the cocky mage increased with each passing day. "Seems a little impetuous, even for a berserker."

Saeed didn't necessarily need Rin to believe that Gregor was a threat to him. But he did need him to realize Gregor wouldn't stop until he stole Cerys out from under him. "Maybe he simply wants you dead so nothing stands between him and what he really wants."

Saeed's gaze went to Cerys and Rin's eyes followed. A sneer curved his lips and his eyes narrowed. "I invite him to try," Rin said. "But he won't get so much as a finger on her."

"Which is why I'm here," Saeed said. "To help ensure that it doesn't happen."

"I have no dog in this fight," Rin said with disgust. "I don't appreciate being drawn into it."

Liar. Rin couldn't cover it this time. He reeked of lies. "You might not appreciate it, but it doesn't change the fact that Gregor is in Seattle and that he wants what's yours." Admitting Cerys belonged to Rin burned Saeed's throat like swallowing acid. She wouldn't belong to him for long, though. He'd make sure of it.

"So what?" Cerys's tone soured. "We pull up camp and leave the city?"

Rin snorted. "There's no fucking way I'm going to let some bloodthirsty warlord drive me out of the city I spent years beating into submission."

Leave it to Rin to let his ego trump safety.

"Well if you think I'm going into hiding, you've got another gods-damned think coming." Cerys obviously had no problem letting Rin know exactly how she felt. "I'll go after Gregor and kill him myself if I have to."

Saeed fought the urge to push up from the chair and tell Cerys that under no circumstances would she go after Gregor. His concern would only throw up another red flag, however. And so, he was forced to sit still in the rickety old chair and pretend as though he couldn't care less one way or the other what Cerys did.

Rin laughed. "And send you right to him?"

Cerys cocked a challenging brow. "You don't think I could do it?" Saeed wanted to pinch the bridge of his nose at her competitive audacity. "I can guarantee you he wouldn't see me coming."

"I have no doubt, my deadly little assassin." Saeed's temper rose to the surface at the endearing tone of Rin's gently spoken words. "That doesn't mean I'm willing to risk you under any circumstances."

That he spoke to her with any measure of affection was enough to make Saeed's blood boil in his veins. Rin had enslaved Cerys, stolen her soul, taken all of her choices from her, and had the nerve to address her as though their relationship was so much more.

"Well then, you'd better think of something. Because like I said, I am not hiding in my apartment until the berserkers leave the city."

If things went Saeed's way, Cerys wouldn't be waiting anywhere for long. He didn't want her any more imprisoned than she already was, but neither was he interested in dangling her right in front of Ian Gregor's nose. "Perhaps it wouldn't be a bad idea for you to lay low for a couple of weeks at least."

Cerys looked at Saeed with disbelieving shock. Of course she would never expect him to suggest such a thing. Especially when he'd been so adamant about freeing her from Rin in the first place. "No." She looked directly at Saeed as she said the one word.

For the love of the gods, she was stubborn! She might not want to be cooped up in a building somewhere, but the least she could do was get her ass out of one of the handful of clubs in the city that Gregor was sure to investigate. Saeed ignored Cerys as he spoke to Rin, "It's up to your discretion of course, but I would at least suggest getting her out of here for tonight."

"I think I need to decide on my own who and what I believe," Rin said after a moment. "I'm not making any decision based on information gathered from a desperate human and a vampire I've just met." Saeed's gut twisted as he realized he was about to be dismissed for the night, leaving Cerys unprotected. "I'll be in touch," Rin said. "In the meantime, get out of my fucking face so I can think."

Saeed stood from the chair. As much as it pained him to leave, he knew he had no choice. He cast one last furtive glance Cerys's way as he headed for the door and pulled it open to leave. He swore to the gods, if Rin let anything happen to her, he would make him pay for an eternity.

"Get rid of him." The words left Cerys's mouth the moment Saeed closed the door. She wasn't worried about him overhearing, all of the offices in the club had been soundproofed. "I'm serious, Rin. Cut him loose."

Rin studied her as though trying to read her thoughts. "He probably hasn't been a vampire for more than a year. Why so quick to end his new life?"

"Jesus Christ, Rin!" Cerys exclaimed. "I meant send him back to L.A. Not run a stake through his heart."

Rin chuckled and it only made Cerys want to lay her fist into the side of his face. She didn't know how much of Saeed's story was actually true—he was damned good at bending the truth—but she was certain if he had a run-in with the berserker or any of Gregor's men they'd be quick to put an end to Saeed's existence. Cerys wasn't worried about losing her own life. Unfortunately, she had value. Saeed wasn't so lucky, and the thought of a world without him in it sent an anxious rush through her bloodstream.

"So you do like him."

Gods. Was there ever a time when he wasn't trying to bait her into doing or saying something? "I like him about as much as I like you," she replied dryly.

Rin laughed a little harder this time. He definitely got off on pushing her buttons. "Honestly, I don't give a single shit whether or not you like him. The question is, do you trust him?"

The crazy thing was, Cerys *did* trust him. He might've been moody, brooding, dark, stuffy, and a few crackers short of a stack, but Cerys inherently knew Saeed would always have her back. He'd never betray her, never turn on her. And she knew without a doubt that he would protect her with his dying breath. A tremor shook her and Cerys let out a shaky breath. *Shit.* The realization convinced her even more that the safest place for Saeed was as far from her as possible.

"Yeah. I do."

"Then why cut him loose?" Cerys found it annoying that Rin often turned to her for counsel. She was his slave, not his gods-damned advisor. "With slayers in the city it seems a vampire would be the perfect companion for you."

"Companion?" Cerys asked. "Or bodyguard-slash-shield?"

Rin hiked an unconcerned shoulder. "The vampire is expendable. You, however, are not."

"You let the slayers kill one of the very few vampires on the planet, and you're going to have more than Ian Gregor to worry about. From what I've heard, Mikhail

Aristov tends to hold a grudge as well." From the sound of it, the berserker uprising had made for some strange bedfellows. She wondered if Aristov would ally himself with Gregor to kill Rin if Saeed happened to die in the crossfire.

"Aristov can make more vampires," Rin said with a flick of his wrist. "You, on the other hand, are one of a kind."

Cerys's gut clenched. Like Saeed, she was a rare breed. But hardly one of a kind. She wasn't interested in arguing that point with Rin, though. Honestly, all this talk of berserkers had her on edge. She wanted to get the hell out of there and call it a night.

"I don't want anyone taking a bullet, a stake, or anything else for me."

Rin's eyes narrowed. "Your first mistake is in thinking you have a choice."

Did she really need her soul back? Living in an empty, unfulfilled, emotionless state for the rest of eternity might actually be a fair trade for the pleasure of running her dagger through Rin's sadistic heart. It wasn't all emotionless, though, was it? Saeed had managed, with all of his crazy disjointed certainty, to awaken something within her she thought lost. It wasn't emotional per se. But it was . . . something. She just wished she knew what.

She'd never find out if she forced Rin to send him away.

"I know you won't form an opinion one way or the other until you've done your own research." Rin was nothing if not thorough. It was how he'd managed to climb so close to the top of the supernatural food chain. "But for what it's worth, I believe Kyle. And Saeed. I don't think it's a good idea for either of us to be out tonight." Rin rolled his eyes. It was easy to be cavalier when using other's lives to protect your own. Cerys's lungs compressed with her slow sigh. "I don't ask you for much." Please. She resisted the urge to laugh at the absurdity of her words. She never asked him for *anything*. "Let's just call it a night and avoid trouble for once."

"All right." She could tell by Rin's magnanimous tone that he'd never let her live down this act of kindness. Asshole. "The club is dead anyway, and I want to hear how it went with the werewolf tonight. I'll order pizza and you can tell me all about it."

Like they were besties sharing secrets at a Saturday night slumber party. *Give me a break*. Saeed's absence had managed to reopen that cavernous void within her. If she didn't do something to fill it, she'd go out of her damned mind. "Double pepperoni. With mushrooms and onions."

"Whatever you want," Rin replied. "I've got to keep you happy."

If he really wanted to do that, he'd give her back her fucking soul.

Cerys followed Rin out of Crimson and climbed into the backseat of his Range Rover. The drive into downtown to the building where they lived passed in silence. Cerys had nothing to say to Rin. At least, nothing that wouldn't land her in a world of hurt. She'd won a victory with him tonight, albeit small. It was best not to push her luck. She got to call it an early night and there was pizza involved. If that wasn't a win, she didn't know what was.

The driver pulled the Range Rover into the underground parking of the swanky downtown Aspira building. Nothing but the best for the mage that owned Seattle. Cerys swallowed down a snort. The place was a veritable prison. With top-of-the-line security and all of the extras money could buy, Rin had set them up in one of downtown Seattle's high rise castles. Rin's place occupied the entire top floor and made Saeed's tiny penthouse condo seem like a shack in comparison. Cerys's own place was situated right below Rin's. A tiny closet of a condo close enough for him to keep an eye on her. She was really living the life, wasn't she?

Since Rin wasn't going to let her hit the sack anytime soon, she rode the elevator to his place. He'd ordered her pizza and she knew he expected an update on his werewolf problem, which wasn't a problem anymore thanks to Saeed. Cerys settled down at the bar while Rin poured himself a drink. His calm arrogance drove her up the damn wall. Sure, the place was better protected than a maximum security prison. But somehow she doubted the best security in the world would manage to keep out a berserker in full battle rage.

"You know, it might not be a bad idea to exercise a little bit of humility. I know you think you're untouchable, but you've never gone up against a berserker before."

Rin took a long drink from the heavy crystal tumbler before setting it back down on the bar and refilling it. "Cerys, your concern for me is touching."

His facetious tone made her want to deliver a kick to his nuts. "Don't flatter yourself," she said. "You've got something that's valuable to me. That's all."

"True." Rin downed his second drink and poured a third. "I suppose you'd better hope nothing happens to either of us."

His veiled threats didn't faze her anymore. Not after so many thousands of years. Ian Gregor might just be the male to put Rin in his place. Cerys just wished his undoing wouldn't inevitably lead to hers as well.

"So does that mean you're ready to believe Kyle and Saeed?"

"No." He sipped from the lip of his glass. "Not yet. I am more than willing to entertain the idea that Gregor has broken his leash and is hungry for vengeance. But I'm more inclined to believe the sky is green than to believe for a second that Mikhail Aristov would ally himself with the very male who issued his death sentence."

Rin was skeptical because it suited him to be so. He always went against the current, took the hard way simply because he could. "For what it's worth, I don't think Mikhail would have any problems allying with the Sortiari. They might have ordered the executions, but the berserkers carried them out."

By the time the guardians of fate had declared war on the vampires, Rin had cleared him and Cerys out of Europe. A fair weather friend to be sure, as soon as shit got dicey he took off. No way would he have risked getting caught in the crossfire. Maybe it was karma coming back to bite him in the ass that he'd landed himself smack dab in the middle of the same conflict he'd run from centuries ago.

"The subject of Ian Gregor is off the table. For now," Rin added. "I want to hear about the rogue."

The least of their problems was a young, terrified werewolf who didn't have the good sense to stay where he belonged. Cerys let out a heavy sigh. Her pizza was taking *for-ev-er*. How could she possibly be expected to get through tonight with Rin on an empty stomach? She drummed her fingers on the granite countertop more to waste a little time than anything. If she had to have a conversation with Rin without the comfort of spicy, salty, pepperoni goodness, she might just go out of her mind.

"The rogue—" The doorbell rang, interrupting her. Relief crested over her, and Cerys said a silent prayer of thanks for Domino's thirty-minute delivery guarantee. A couple of minutes later, one of Rin's staff brought in the pizza box and plopped it down on the bar in front of her. She didn't bother saying thanks. None of Rin's hired help ever paid attention to her anyway. She flipped open the box and filled her lungs with the delicious spicy scent of pizza before snagging a wedge from the sixteen inch round. She tore off the pointed end and said none too gracefully through a mouthful of food, "The rogue was no problem. Saeed took care of him. You can expect him tomorrow night, ready and willing to do whatever task you set out for him."

"How did Saeed get him to cooperate so easily?"

Cerys wasn't the only one who'd forgotten how handy it could be to have a vampire around. "Saeed compelled him," she said. "I was ready to persuade him with my fists before Saeed stepped in. All it took was a couple of words and he had the poor kid eating out of the palm of his hand."

"Poor kid?" Rin tsked. "He knew what he was getting into when he asked for my help."

Leave it to Rin to always cast blame on the victim. No wonder Cerys had spent the past couple thousand years feeling like all of this was her fault. Well, no more. Rin would have been wise to do as Cerys asked and send Saeed away. The passionate vampire had managed to give her hope. And in the hands of someone with nothing to lose, hope was a very dangerous thing.

CHAPTER
18

"I understand your need for discretion, but there's going to come a time when they won't blindly follow your orders anymore."

Ian Gregor scowled at his cousin. Doubt of any kind certainly wasn't welcome, especially from him. "They won't . . . ?" He let the question hang. "Or *you* won't?"

"Fuck you." Gavin kept walking and it was a damn good thing. Both of their tempers boiled close to the surface and Ian couldn't afford their discussion to devolve into a fight. "I've never once called your leadership into question. Or your tactics."

That's because Gavin knew what was good for him. Power surged within Ian, burning through his chest like a cinder. He needed to keep his anger under control, lest it get the better of him. There was a time and a place to utilize that rage, but it sure as hell wasn't here and now. True, they'd gone too long without retribution, but what was a few more months compared to the centuries of suffering they'd endured.

His hopes for an alliance with the werewolves had

turned out to be a huge disappointment. Never in a million years would he have thought one of those bastards would have found himself mated to a vampire. And not only that, but the pack had actually accepted the pairing. The resurgence of the vampire race was stirring up all sorts of shit in the supernatural world. Ian planned to bring a swift end to that change. The werewolves weren't the only faction for him to try and sway. Just like the human world, the supernatural one was full of outcasts. Those searching for belonging, a sense of family, a cause to belong to. Ian would take those unwanted souls under his wing. He would give them what no one else would, and in return, they would give him their undying loyalty. He needed only one thing to start the process that would bring all of his enemies to their knees. And she was somewhere in Seattle.

"Wars aren't won through hasty decisions and hotheaded tactics. Breaking from McAlister was only the first step."

"For some, it was the only step." Ian suspected it took a lot for Gavin to make the confession. "Some no longer wish to live in the past."

Ian's eyes burned in their sockets. Tendrils of heat uncoiled within him like tiny seeking vines. He took a deep cleansing breath, and then another. He could have a simple discussion without losing his shit. "Forgive and forget? Is that it? I don't know about you, but I can do neither."

"No one wants to forgive or to forget," Gavin replied. "But damn it, some of us want to at least *live*. We've been fighting for so long there are days when it seems there will never be an end to it."

Ian knew that weariness all too well. It weighed him down to the point that he didn't know how he managed to continue to put one foot in front of the other. But the moment he stopped, the moment he cast off the mantle of grief and sorrow that fueled him, was the moment his enemies won.

"Without retribution, there will never be closure. We owe it to the souls of the dead to avenge them."

Gavin remained silent. Really, what could he say? Ian knew his cousin would never disrespect the dead by downplaying their tragedy.

"What about the rogue?" He was thankful Gavin changed the subject and steered the conversation back to business. "Do you trust him to remain loyal and to find the dhampir?"

Christian Whalen was a vital part of Ian's plan and also the one possible weak spot. Of all the trackers on McAlister's payroll, Whalen was the best. He found things no one could find with an efficiency that was damn near scary. It grated that so many months had passed and the werewolf had been unable to locate the dhampir female within the confines of Los Angeles. Which made Ian think that either she was already dead—gods, he hoped not—or Whalen was keeping secrets.

"I trust him to be the same self-serving son of a bitch he's always been," Ian replied. "Which is why I'm continuing to keep a close eye on him."

"You think he's playing both sides against the middle?"

He couldn't be sure, but he wouldn't put it past the wily werewolf. "I think Whalen hates being at the end of McAlister's leash as much as we did. But he's a rogue for a reason."

"He's an opportunistic fucker, that's for sure."

Ian nodded. "Whalen is on one side. His own. As long as I keep him happy, he'll give me what I want." A fact that left a sour taste in Ian's mouth. He hated anyone whose loyalty could be bought. Their allegiances turned on a dime, literally. And Whalen's gambling problem only served to complicate things. The son of a bitch went through cash at an alarming rate. And Ian's coffers were only so deep.

"What if he's just stringing you along?"

Unfortunately, that was a chance he had to take. "I'm not so stupid as to think Whalen doesn't have his own agenda. But that doesn't change the fact that he is an integral piece of this puzzle."

"Caden Mitchell is staying in L.A." The words left Gavin's lips in a nervous rush, as though he'd been waiting for the perfect moment to break the news.

The bear shifter was one of McAlister's top dogs. An enforcer with the muscle to back up his impressive reputation, he'd been brought in specifically to protect McAlister during his meeting with Mikhail Aristov several weeks ago. Ian had been unpleasantly surprised to find him at McAlister's side when his band of warlords ambushed the meeting. Along with one of Mikhail's vampires, Caden had managed to keep Ian from one of the other things he'd wanted: a young girl McAlister had proclaimed to be an oracle. Just one short year ago, Ian had had his hands on the child. Even then, McAlister had declared her an item of worth, instructing Ian to keep her safe from harm. It still burned that he'd chosen to disregard the child as important. She'd slipped through his fingers not once, but twice.

There'd been a time, when Ian was still loyal to McAlister, that he'd been sent to upstate New York to fetch Caden and bring him to L.A. The shifter had not so politely declined McAlister's mandate, proclaiming he wanted nothing to do with the Sortiari's dealings with the vampires. Apparently, the big bastard's opinion had changed.

"I'm not concerned about Caden Mitchell." It was true the son of a bitch had caught him off guard and given him a pretty sound ass kicking. The first time, and absolutely the last, that Ian would ever allow himself to not have the upper hand. "He's one male."

"He could be a thorn in our side."

True. But Ian wasn't willing to cross that bridge until they came to it. "One obstacle at a time," he said.

"Find the fae," Gavin said as though he'd heard the order spoken hundreds of times. "Why do you want her? I think we at least deserve to know that much."

It wasn't that Ian didn't trust those in his inner circle. It was simply that he didn't want to jinx the success of his strategy by letting even a single detail slip. He supposed if he wanted to retain the loyalty of his men, he had no choice but to make a small concession.

"The fae connects McAlister to one of his greatest fears."

Gavin turned to him, brows raised in question. "And that is . . . ?"

Gregor pulled open the door to Crimson. Everyone they'd spoken to so far tonight indicated this was where he'd find the mage. Anxious energy dumped into Gregor's bloodstream. He was so close to finally getting something he wanted. "His death." He offered up the simplest reply to his cousin. "The fae is the key to introducing Trenton McAlister to his own gods-damned fate."

For centuries, Trenton McAlister had been maneuvering the fates of others as though they were nothing more than pieces on a chessboard. Ian couldn't wait to see the bastard's reaction when the tables were finally turned.

With Gregor out of the city, Christian finally felt as though he could take a deep breath. He strode through the entrance of Onyx with a pocket full of cash and a sense of anticipation that left him feeling a little buzzed. For once, luck had been on his side and he'd made a killing last night on the BSU-Oregon game. Some people complained about BSU's Smurf-turf, but it turned out to be lucky for Christian. Blue turf forever!

The scent of jasmine hit him before the door even had a chance to close behind him. Gregor was nowhere to be found, he'd hit a winning streak, and the female he couldn't get out of his head was almost within touching distance. It didn't get much better than this.

Though his meeting with McAlister a few days ago hadn't gone quite as well as he'd hoped, Christian knew he'd gained a certain amount of ground with the director. He might've been playing both sides against the middle but ultimately Christian was only interested in helping himself. Or more to the point, helping Siobhan, the very female who happen to be striding across the crowded bar toward him.

Holy fuck, she was absolutely gorgeous.

"What brings you out and about, werewolf?" she purred.

Her sultry tone reached out like a caress and Christian's wolf gave an excited yip in the recess of his psyche. He'd never known a more tempting creature. So sultry and seductive she made him sweat. For months he'd been dying for just a taste which she continually denied him because he wouldn't play her game. Well, not anymore. Christian was more than ready to take their antagonistic relationship to the next level.

He took his time in admiring her. The flowy black miniskirt with matching thigh-high socks and emerald green blouse was much softer than her normal attire. It lent her an air of seductive innocence that damn near drove Christian out of his mind with want. The shirt matched her eyes perfectly, accenting the bright green color in a way that was mesmerizing. He'd never wanted anything or anyone as much as he wanted her and he planned to remedy that unfulfilled want ASAP.

Mine. At least for a night.

Ours.

Christian's wolf couldn't help but to make his opinion

known. Christian didn't know much about mate bonds but he had to assume that if Siobhan were truly his he'd know it in a more immediate and visceral way. He was simply a horny bastard who needed to get off. The wolf didn't understand that. The wolf was sort of an idiot.

"Probably the same thing that brings you out," Christian replied.

Siobhan laughed and the sound was like warm rain on rooftops. "I doubt that," she replied dryly.

It usually didn't take him so long to seal the deal. Siobhan wasn't simply a warm body to take to bed, though. She was a conquest. A rare trophy. Misogynistic? Probably. Christian was too gods-damn horny to care.

"I was looking for you, actually." He didn't see any point in being anything other than honest with her. She'd see through his bullshit in an instant and put an end to this before it even got a chance to start.

"Me?" A space of silence passed between them. "If you came looking for me, it must be because you have something you want to tell me."

She took a step closer and electricity arced in the space between them. Christian's cock perked up, and his jeans suddenly felt a couple of sizes too small. "There is *so much* I want to tell you. None of which is PG rated." Or had anything to do with Ian Gregor. His wolf let out a warning growl at the back of his mind. They'd been sniffing after her for months, and now the bastard wanted him to exercise a little caution?

"I'm not interested in your dirty talk." Siobhan's head dipped and she looked up at him from beneath lowered lashes. "At least, not yet."

He'd seen her defiant, arrogant, haughty, and wild. He'd gladly taken the brunt of her verbal insults, listened to her mandates, and exchanged a fair amount of witty banter. He'd watched as she'd baited him, using another male to tantalize him. He'd never seen this side of Siobhan, though. Soft. Flirty. Coy. *Gods.* Christian blew out a forceful breath. She drove him out of his fucking mind with desire.

His wolf let out another warning growl. He was about to set something into motion that he couldn't undo. Something that could have far-reaching consequences. He wanted Siobhan. Craved her like he did his next high-stakes bet. There was no going back after this. Was he ready for this? Could he handle the fallout?

"I'm ready to play." Christian had no problem throwing caution to the wind. The decision had been made the moment he met her. He'd risk anything to have her, consequences be damned.

Her full, sensual lips spread into a self-satisfied smile. She had to have known all along that Christian would eventually give her what she wanted. A female like Siobhan never went into any situation unless she knew for sure she'd come out the winner. "What made you change your mind?"

"What makes you think my mind ever needed changing?" Christian asked. "Maybe I was just looking for the right moment to show my hand."

Siobhan hiked one shapely shoulder as though she didn't care one way or the other. She had the whole aloof thing down pat. So guarded. So emotionally closed off. It frustrated Christian and made his wolf anxious, though he had no idea why. It's not like he wanted some sappy admission of love or infatuation from Siobhan. But by the gods, it would've been nice if she at least tried to treat him with something other than cool indifference.

That's why you're pissed? Because she doesn't act like she wants you as much as you want her?

In a word? Yes.

Christian's competitive nature was one of his greatest flaws. He had to win. Everything. Every time. He was a sore fucking loser, and yeah, he would've appreciated it if she acted like there was more going on between them than a simple exchange of information.

A dark brow arched regally over one of Siobhan's emerald green eyes. "I can't wait to hear all the details. But not here."

More conditions. More games. Christian gritted his teeth until he felt the enamel grind. If it were anyone else, he would've tapped out and called it a night a long time ago. "Where then?"

Siobhan's husky laughter grated on his last nerve. "Relax, werewolf. We're both about to get something we want. I'm not sure I like you so uptight."

Yeah, well, he wasn't sure he liked her with so many conditions attached. "You're crazy if you think I'm just gonna follow you somewhere so your goon can drink me dry the second you don't have any further use for me."

"Uptight *and* paranoid tonight." Siobhan gave a sad shake of her head. "Why would I possibly allow Carrig to do something as barbaric as that? I thought we were friends."

Please. There was nothing about Siobhan or her big, burly bodyguard that was even remotely civilized. "Friends?" Gods, the sound of that word settled in Christian's gut like a stone. How could she be so cold and indifferent while he felt like he was about to crawl out of his gods-damned skin? "Is that what we are?"

"Well . . ." She reached out and traced a line from his chest to the waistband of his jeans with her fingertip. Christian swallowed hard as his muscles went taut. "I'm hoping we can be a little more than friends."

Damn her. She played Christian like a finely tuned instrument. He had not an ounce of fucking pride when it came to her. Pathetic. He knew better than to trust her, damn it. He knew better than to give into his own foolish wants and desires. He'd known from the moment he laid eyes on her that Siobhan would be his ruin. But Christian was nothing if not self-destructive.

"Lead the way." Christian knew he'd live to regret this. Siobhan was like an out-of-control wildfire. And he ran gleefully toward the flames.

CHAPTER
19

Saeed paced the confines of his living room in an effort to burn off the nervous energy that coursed through him. It had been five hours since Rin had effectively dismissed him, leaving Cerys completely unprotected. The gods only knew where Gregor was. Cerys was formidable, but could she best a berserker in full battle rage?

The sun would be up in a couple of short hours and Saeed would effectively become a prisoner. He cursed that weakness he could do nothing about. He hated to feel helpless. Sunrise would create an uncrossable barrier between him and the only thing in this world that mattered to him. He swore, if Rin allowed any harm to come to Cerys, he would make the mage suffer for an eternity.

Saeed continued to pace. Back and forth, back and forth. The color of the sky outside his window began to lift from dark navy to gray as he made the rounds throughout his condo to shut the blinds and effectively seal out the coming sun. Saeed's limbs grew heavy and his eyelids drooped as the lethargy of daytime sleep began to take hold. His brain buzzed with myriad voices, and Saeed pressed the heels of his palms over his ears as though to block out the alluring sound. How many mornings since his transition had he retreated into the Collective before sleep claimed him? Too damned many to count. Those memories, those voices didn't interest him anymore. Saeed was through with the Collective. But apparently, it wasn't through with him.

"Don't make me do it." Cerys's pleading tone speared through Saeed's chest like a stake.

Rin seemed unconcerned with her distress. He sat beside Saeed, or rather, the vampire whose memories Saeed had fallen into. Kneeling before them was a young male. Silent tears streamed down his cheeks but he remained otherwise emotionless.

"Forgive me Rin," the male said. "Give me the opportunity to prove my loyalty."

"There are no other opportunities. You know that."

Saeed took in his surroundings. He couldn't be sure but he guessed this event had taken place shortly before the Sortiari declared war on the vampires. The when and where were immaterial in comparison to Cerys. Dark circles hollowed her eyes. She was nearly gaunt, thinner than he'd ever seen her. Her usually almost iridescent skin had taken on a dull pallor and her expression was drawn. He'd never seen her so exhausted. So full of fear. So close to the many emotions she'd thought long gone.

She took a timid step toward Rin. "You've used me for too many days. Please, Rin. I need to rest. To replenish my strength." Her voice dropped to the barest whisper. "When will it ever be enough?"

A cruel sneer curved to Rin's lip. "It is enough when I say it is enough." He spoke the words from between clenched teeth. "Do it."

Cerys let out a ragged breath. "Once more," she said more to herself than to Rin. "And then please, let me rest."

If Rin heard her, he gave no outward show of it. Instead, he leaned in toward Saeed. "You think a vampire is the only creature that can banish a soul? Prepare to behold true power."

Saeed tried to lunge forward. To reach for Cerys. The body he inhabited refused to obey and his frustration mounted. That sadistic son of a bitch used Cerys as though she were nothing more than a tool, without a single ounce of care for her well-being. What was wrong with her? What had she suffered to make her appear so ragged?

Cerys turned away from Rin and approached the male. Her brow pinched with regret. "I promise, you won't feel a thing."

Saeed swore his heart stopped beating and his breath stalled in his chest. His stomach tied into an unyielding knot as he waited against his will to bear witness to Cerys's power. He'd never felt more like a slave himself than he did in this moment. Saeed fought the Collective's hold but it held on to him with barbed claws that refused to let go. Like Cerys, he had no choice but to see this moment through to its end.

Almost lovingly, Cerys placed her right palm to the male's chest. A soft pearlescent light shone beneath her fingertips and the male's body gave a slight lurch forward as his back bowed, pressing his chest into Cerys's touch. His head fell back on his shoulders and he let out a slow breath at the exact moment Cerys drew one in. She arched toward him as her head drooped forward. The light grew in its intensity, filling the room with an eerie glow that cast sinister shadows all around them. Cerys sucked in a sharp gasp as she gathered her hand into a tight fist, encasing the light in her grip.

"Give it to me."

Cerys's head dropped to her right and her shoulders slumped. She turned slowly and took several staggering steps toward Rin who waited eagerly, a jar clutched in his outstretched hand. Cerys turned her fist upside down and her fingers slowly opened to deposit the light of the male's soul into the jar. She pulled her hand away and Rin quickly sealed it before placing it on the table in front of the vampire.

"At least when an enaid dwyn takes a soul, one knows where it has gone."

Cerys's eyes rolled back in her head as she collapsed to the cold stone floor.

Saeed let out an agonized shout that fell on deaf ears as he fought to free himself from the body that held him immobile. Rin looked on, barely affected by Cerys's distress. She was nothing more than something to be used and tossed aside.

"Rinieri, what is wrong with her?" Saeed's mouth moved without his permission as he spoke the dead vampire's words.

"It takes a toll, that's all." Rin finally deigned it appropriate to stand from his chair and go to Cerys. Saeed wanted to rip him from her side and tear out his throat with his fangs. "Perhaps I have overused her the past fortnight."

His disregard for her well-being was deplorable. She'd obviously suffered for centuries in a constant state of abuse before Rin had finally had the good sense to use her powers sparingly. He snapped his fingers, and from the dark corner of the room one of his servants appeared, head bowed.

"Take her to her chambers and put her to bed," Rin instructed. "Do not leave her side until she wakes."

The male scooped Cerys up in his arms and carried her

*out of the room. Saeed was desperate to follow, to make
sure she was okay. "You seem a little too smug for my
peace of mind, Rinieri. I won't deny the fae's power is
staggering, but at least when I take a soul—" he cast a
glance at the young male, shivering on the stone floor, his
body in shock from what had been done to him "—it
harms none."*

*"None?" Incredulous laughter accompanied Rin's
question. "I might not have ever witnessed a dhampir's
transition to vampire, but I've heard it's far from harmless."*

*"Painful perhaps," the vampire conceded. "But all
transition brings with it a certain level of sacrifice. The
decision is made freely by both the dhampir and his
maker." Saeed's finger pointed out toward the floor. "That
male's soul was forcibly ripped from his body. Against his
will. Your enaid dwyn pled with you for mercy. And you
instructed her against her will to carry out the act."*

*Rin's jaw squared with anger and a fair amount of
shock. He'd obviously expected to impress the vampire
lord, not draw his disdain. Saeed found himself wishing
the vampire had been angry enough to put an end to Rin.
Of course, ridding the world of Rinieri de Rege wouldn't
have protected Cerys. The world was full of opportunistic sadists like Rin, like Gregor, who would abuse and
exploit her for their own gain.*

*A moment of quiet tension passed before Rin's thinned
lips spread into a tight smile. "Sunrise is not far off, my
Lord," he said with a sneer. "I suggest you return to the
safety of your coven."*

*Saeed turned to leave and he urged the body he had
no control over to stay. He couldn't leave Cerys. Couldn't
abandon her to her fate. It didn't matter that this moment
in time had long since passed. For Saeed, it was now. The
sound of the vampire's footfalls echoed in his ears as he
turned his back on Rin, on Cerys, and the poor male who'd*

yet to overcome the trauma done to him. The floor dropped out from under him and Saeed fell, tumbling helplessly into darkness.

Cerys stepped out of the elevator into Saeed's foyer and rang the doorbell. The sun had just barely dipped beyond the horizon. It shouldn't have taken him so long to let her in. She rang the bell again. Waited. Jammed her finger down on the button once more. Panic tightened her chest as adrenaline dumped into her system. Had he even made it back last night? Or had the berserkers found him somewhere on the Seattle streets?

She turned the doorknob to find it unlocked and let herself inside. A gasp of breath lodged itself in her chest as she raced into the living room and dropped to her knees beside Saeed's seemingly lifeless body. "Saeed." Cerys reached over him and gave him a solid shake. "Saeed!" Louder this time. Gods, how many more times would she find him like this? Unconscious. Unresponsive.

Saeed came awake with a start. His eyes went wide and he came up from the floor in a flash of motion, taking Cerys with him. Her back met the nearest wall with a jolt. Saeed's firm grip on her upper arms was almost painful. A deep groove cut into his forehead as he searched her face.

"He's killing you," Saeed said with a snarl. "Isn't he?"

Cerys had no idea if he was lucid or not. Did he even know who she was? She forced her body to relax. Softened her tone as she said, "It's okay. Saeed . . ."

"Tell me!" His fingertips bit into her skin. "What does it do to you when Rin makes you take a soul?"

Welp, she guessed that answered her question as to whether or not he was lucid. "It-it's complicated," she stuttered.

Saeed's grip on her relaxed. After a moment he let go

completely but kept his body pressed close to hers. He reached up and cupped her face in his palm brushing the pad of his thumb along her cheekbone. His touch was so gentle in comparison to his previous grip. "It's not complicated." His voice hushed to a low murmur. "Tell me."

A knot formed in Cerys's throat and she tried to swallow it down. It shouldn't be so hard to make the admission. After all, it wasn't her fault. But it didn't do anything to assuage her guilt at becoming a victim of Rin's sadistic nature.

"Yes." She replied so quietly she couldn't even hear her own voice.

Saeed's arms went around her and he crushed her against him. He held her as though he could protect her from all of the evils in the world. A sob built in her chest but she refused to let it out. She'd never felt as fragile as she did in this moment. So completely and utterly weak.

If Saeed was this distressed over learning the truth, she doubted tonight would be a cakewalk for either of them. Despite the threat of berserkers in the city, Rin was sending her out tonight to make a collection. Business was business, and apparently not even a band of deadly warlords would deter him.

"I'm going to kill him." Saeed spoke the words close to her ear and his warm breath caused chills to break out over her skin. "I promise you."

Cerys had been bound to Rin for so long that she couldn't imagine an existence without him. She wanted him dead. Wanted her freedom like she did her next meal. Longed for the return of her soul like she longed for the male who held her now. And at the same time, she was afraid. Afraid of change. Afraid of the prospect of being in charge of her own fate, her own choices. Afraid to lose the only constant in her life. She'd always vowed that if anyone were going to kill Rin, it would be her. But, given the opportunity, would she allow it to happen? Could she run her dagger through Rin's black heart? Would she allow Saeed to do it if she couldn't? Or would she stay his hand and spare Rin even though he'd never shown her an ounce of mercy.

"Why were you on the floor?" Cerys couldn't talk about her own situation. She needed her game to be tight tonight and Saeed's concern was definitely messing with her head.

"I fell into the Collective." Such a simple explanation for such a complex matter.

"Fell?" Cerys said with a gentle laugh. "From the looks of it, someone gave you a healthy shove."

A sad smile curved Saeed's full lips.

"You need to feed." Saeed's gaze wandered to her throat and Cerys's heart kicked into full gear. She cleared her throat and kept her tone as level as possible. "I need you clearheaded tonight."

Saeed's brow furrowed. He leaned in close until not even inch of space separated them. "Why?"

It wouldn't do any good to lie to him. He'd smell it on her in an instant and besides, he'd see it for himself later. Cerys bucked her chin up a notch and met his gaze. "Rin is sending me out to make a collection. He wants you to keep an eye on me."

His expression darkened and his nostrils flared. It's not like Cerys thought he'd be happy about tonight's errand, but the least he could do was not treat her as though she had a choice in the matter.

"No." The word was spoken with finality. "I forbid it."

"You forbid it?" Cerys spluttered. Saeed wasn't merely high-handed, he was absolutely out of his mind if he thought for a second he could simply lay down a mandate and she would obey it. "I don't have a choice in the matter."

"I've seen what it does to you." Saeed's voice was a controlled burn. "I will *not* let you do anything to further weaken yourself."

"You've seen it? When? Where?"

"In the Collective," Saeed replied. "You took the soul of a young male and afterward you collapsed to the floor."

The gods-damned Collective. Cerys was beginning to hate the cache of vampire memories Saeed had access to. He was an unwelcome voyeur in moments of her life she'd just as soon forget. "That is a serious violation of my privacy," she snapped. "And I don't like it. How about trying to recognize some boundaries for a change instead of continually poking your nose into moments of my life where you don't belong?"

Saeed's lip pulled back to reveal the wicked sharp points of his fangs. "Between tethered mates, there should be no secrets."

Again with the tether. "You don't even know if it's real!" Tears stung at her eyes and for the first time since she'd met him she felt more than simply a ghost of emotion.

"It's as real as you are." While Cerys couldn't get a grip, it seemed Saeed was unflappable. His unflinching faith frustrated her. How could he believe so wholeheartedly in something he couldn't even prove existed?

"Oh really?" Cerys didn't know why she felt the urge to push Saeed's buttons. Maybe it was because, despite his suspicions, Rin had refused to send him away. Or maybe it was because Cerys couldn't trust her own mind or heart when he was near. "Tell me Saeed, do you have your soul back?"

He flinched as though stung. "You can try to push me away. But it won't work."

That he could see through her angry words enraged Cerys even more. She didn't want there to be a connection between them for the simple reason that Rin would never let her go. She couldn't stand by and watch Saeed live in a constant unfulfilled state while Rin continued to use her and deplete her to the point of death.

"Whatever." It wouldn't matter what she said or what she did. Saeed was too stubborn to quit now. He'd put his own life on the line in an attempt to retrieve Cerys's soul. And if by some miracle he did managed to accomplish the feat, he would be destroyed when she failed to give him his soul in return. "None of this matters anyway. I have a job to do and not much time to get it done. Because of this berserker bullshit he's bumped up my curfew to midnight. We need to get moving. Now. Because I'm not about to suffer his wrath if I don't get the job done."

Saeed took a tentative step back and Cerys shoved herself away from the wall. She pushed past him and headed out the door without so much as a glance backward. She knew he'd follow. Damn him. Since his arrival in the city Cerys had only wanted to protect him. From Rin, from her, from this ridiculous world they lived in. Every attempt to push him away only brought him closer. They were both doomed.

CHAPTER
20

Saeed wished he'd taken Cerys up on her offer to feed him when he'd had the chance. Dry thirst burned his throat as he stepped into the elevator behind her. Resurging anger rolled through him at the thought that he would have to stand by and watch as she effectively took one step closer to killing herself. Rin knew the toll using her power took on her body. And yet he sent her out to do this terrible thing. She was his most valuable possession, and he treated her with such cool indifference that it made Saeed's hackles rise. She was precious. *Invaluable.* Something to be cared for and treasured.

"Here. Drink."

Saeed looked up to find Cerys thrust her wrist toward his face. The defiant set of her jaw and her narrowed gaze told him her wrist was all he would get. He wanted more. Wanted to bury his face in her fragrant throat and nuzzle the softness of her skin as he drank. He needed her naked in his arms, pliant and willing. He'd get none of that tonight, however. It was her wrist or nothing. It showed how desperate he was to have even the slightest contact with her that he would take whatever he could get.

Saeed cradled her delicate wrist in his hand and brought it to his lips. He sealed his mouth over the vein and sucked gently before breaking the skin with his fangs. Cerys wanted this to be a disconnected moment. Saeed had made concessions tonight but this would not be one of them. He gripped the back of her neck with his free hand and guided her head up, forcing her to look at him.

Her lids drooped as her beautiful mouth went slack. She let out a slow sigh that hardened Saeed's cock in an instant. He pulled her closer, holding her as tight against him as he could while he drank. Her eyes never left his and the same electric spark he'd felt the first time he'd tasted her blood sparked between them. Tether or not, Cerys was *his*.

The elevator reached the ground floor, ending their moment much too quickly. With slow, sensual passes of his tongue, Saeed closed the punctures in Cerys's wrist. The elevator doors slid silently open but he didn't budge. Didn't move a single muscle as he continued to hold her gaze, daring her to look away first and break the spell between them.

Only when the doors threatened to slide shut did Cerys thrust her arm out to stop them. A corner of Saeed's mouth hitched in a satisfied smile. She could fight it all she wanted. All of the denial in the world wouldn't change the connection that had been forged between them.

"Lead the way." Saeed held out his arm in invitation. Cerys blew out a frustrated breath as she stepped out in front of him and into the lobby. He followed close behind, admiring the graceful sway of her hips as she walked. He vowed tonight would be the last night she would ever use her power. Rin's hold on her was about to come to an end.

Cerys headed toward Rin's sleek black Range Rover

and pulled open the passenger door for Saeed before rounding the front of the car to take the keys from the valet. "Where are we going tonight?"

"Bellevue," she said. "Can't exactly walk, which is why we're going in this. She climbed into the driver's seat and fastened her seatbelt before sliding the key into the ignition. "I'm on a time crunch, so we need to get moving."

Saeed climbed into the passenger seat and buckled his seatbelt—though he saw little use for it—before closing the door. He had so much to worry about. Rin, Gregor, Cerys's well-being, and the state of their own souls. His stomach twisted into an unyielding knot. He tried to convince himself that if he could just get them through tonight everything would be okay.

Too bad he didn't believe his own bullshit.

The drive passed in relative silence. Cerys kept her eyes on the road and both hands on the wheel. The scent of her anger burned Saeed's nostrils, and her cold stoicism stabbed through his chest. "Do you plan to spend the entire night ignoring me?"

"I have to be back by midnight," Cerys replied. "It's already eight. I don't have much time to get this done and I'm in a shitty mood. So yes, I plan to spend the next couple of hours ignoring you."

He supposed he deserved the biting remark. He was no better than Rin, giving her orders he expected to be obeyed. He knew she had no choice in the matter, and it was his own anger with himself at being unable to help her that had goaded Saeed's words. "I'm sorry."

Cerys snorted. "For what?"

"For treating you no better than Rin." Saeed turned toward her but she kept her gaze focused on the dark highway. "For behaving as though I have any right to tell you what to do."

Cerys's starched posture relaxed as did her death grip on the steering well. She glanced at him from the corner of her eye and let out a slow sigh. "I haven't made a decision for myself in thousands of years. Unless you count my food choices." He appreciated her attempt at levity but there was nothing light or humorous about this moment. "Can you imagine what that's like, Saeed? To have lived as long as I have and be at the mercy of someone else's whims? Can you even comprehend that sort of powerlessness?"

In truth, he couldn't. For most of his life Saeed had been a leader. Even as a paid assassin at the height of the Crusades, he'd retained a certain autonomy. He'd been a dhampir coven master, and for nearly two centuries had no vampire lord to answer to. He'd never known slavery. Had never been bound to another. Even after swearing fealty to Mikhail, Saeed had never been ordered by the vampire king so much as gently urged.

"No. I cannot even begin to comprehend what your existence has been like."

"Well." Cerys let her sarcasm shine through in her tone. "It's awfully big of you to admit it."

She was in the mood for a fight but Saeed refused to give her one. After seeing the effects of what using her power had on her, Saeed knew she would need him by her side tonight more than ever. She'd chided him earlier for not having a clear head. She needed him solid in order to protect her. And he needed her emotionally sound and focused. Prepared for the trauma that was no doubt to come.

"Are all souls the same?" He continued to draw her into conversation. He was hungry to learn more about her, including more about what she could do. "Are some souls harder to extract than others?"

Cerys gave a shrug of her slender shoulders. "It depends. No two souls are the same. I wouldn't say any one is harder to take than the other, but some souls hold on tighter than others."

"The ones that hold on, do they expend more of your energy?" Another shrug followed by a space of silence. "Cerys, you should know by now that you don't have to hold anything back with me. There is nothing you could say, nothing you could do, that would diminish you in my eyes. You can speak to me without fear of judgment. I seek only to understand you."

She didn't address his heartfelt words but when she spoke again her voice cracked with emotion. "Each time is harder than the last. I don't know how many more times I can do it. Some days I'm just . . . tired. For no reason. Rin goes easier on me on those days. Maybe it's because my own soul is gone that it exacts the toll it does on me." Her grip tightened once again on the steering wheel. "Who knows? Rin knows as well as I do that I don't have many more of these extractions left in me. But I think he's too afraid to put me out to pasture. He's afraid of losing the power he's worked so hard to gain. Like tonight. Sending me out to steal a soul even when he knows I shouldn't."

Saeed reached over and laid a comforting hand on her thigh. Her hand dropped from the steering wheel to cover his and she gripped his fingers. Her touch was heaven. Even the most innocent contact resonated with him. "Rin has amassed nothing," Saeed declared. "The power is all yours."

Cerys sure as hell didn't feel powerful. She didn't really feel much of anything except a healthy dose of fear. What had bothered her most about what Saeed had seen in the Collective wasn't that he'd violated her privacy. In truth, it was his reaction to what he'd seen that left her shaken. Pretty hard to downplay your impending death when the guy next to you was freaking out in a way you couldn't allow yourself to do.

She'd learned a long time ago that pleading with Rin for anything was a futile act. He showed no mercy because he had none. She could've thrown herself at his feet tonight. Begged him to spare her. Convinced him that tonight's extraction might be the one that finally killed her. But in the end, it wouldn't have mattered. Rin cared only for the power he'd amassed. And he would do *anything* to keep his hold on it.

"Rin has managed to build his reputation in Seattle. He uses me to dissuade anyone who might think about double-crossing him. But that's all. I'm not powerful, Saeed. I possess the skills to evoke fear."

Saeed turned toward her. His hand disengaged from hers and left her thigh. She missed his touch in an instant. The loss of that small comfort nearly gutted her. He reached up and brushed her hair away from her face as he quietly studied her in the dark interior of the car. "You are strong. Fierce. Formidable. Breathtakingly beautiful. Intelligent. You possess a magic that Rin could only hope to master. Those are the things that make you powerful, Cerys."

She wanted to do something. Say something. Thank him for his kind words. But she couldn't. A knot lodged near her sternum and refused to let the words come out. Saeed made her feel. Something that shouldn't have been possible. The true power was his. She'd been dead for centuries and the broody, half mad vampire had resurrected her.

"Tell me about your coven." They were still about twenty minutes from Bellevue and she didn't think she could talk about herself for another second without losing it completely. She needed to keep her mind off what was coming and the possible consequences of her actions tonight. "I've heard the covens are small and some of them at odds with others."

Saeed continued to idly thread his fingers through the locks of her hair. The sensation was so relaxing it made her want to pull over to the side of the road for a little nap. "My coven was one of the largest in Los Angeles. There were fifty dhampirs under my protection."

"Were?" Cerys asked. "As in there aren't fifty of them anymore or they're not under your protection any longer?"

"No," Saeed replied. "As in they are no longer my coven."

"How does that happen? You just walked away?" Cerys knew he'd left his life in L.A. behind, but had it been so easy for him to turn his back on those he'd once considered family?

"It wasn't an easy decision but one that had to be made." Regret darkened Saeed's tone. "I turned the leadership over to two of my own and left willingly."

"You left your coven on a wild goose chase." Cerys tried to keep her tone light.

"I did. To find you. And though I miss my family, I do not regret my decision even a little bit."

Cerys didn't want to feel anything warm or fuzzy about Saeed's decision to walk away from his coven to come to Seattle. But she had to admit it made her feel wanted. No one had ever made a sacrifice for her before, especially one as big as the one Saeed had made.

"Do you worry about them?"

"Yes." Saeed fiddled with her hair and a chill raced from the top of Cerys's head down her spine. "But I also left the coven in capable hands."

"It must've been hard," she said through the sudden thickness in her throat. "To leave your family."

"The sacrifice was worth it." The rich timbre of his voice resonated through every inch of her. "To find you."

Wow. Cerys blew out a breath. If he kept talking to her like that, his fingers combing through her hair, she definitely wouldn't make it through the night without giving in to her desires. A steady thrum settled low in her abdomen and her body flushed with pleasant heat. With the simplest touch Saeed could evoke an intense reaction in her. She couldn't let herself fall victim to his dark charm again, however. There was only one way this could play out. Saeed might've been optimistic, but Cerys knew neither of them was going to get a happy ending.

"You shouldn't say things like that."

"Why not?" Saeed's attention on her didn't waver. "It's true."

"Because." How could she possibly make him understand? "I don't want to be the reason you left your life behind." *Or the reason for any future regret.* "I'm sure your coven needs you. I don't want to be the cause of any disruption in your life or anyone else's. I ruin enough lives as it is."

She hadn't planned to venture into pity-party territory but she couldn't help herself. She didn't feel guilt per se, but the knowledge was there that every time she extracted a soul, she caused someone's ruination. There were days she was thankful to not have a soul of her own. Otherwise, her guilt would probably kill her.

"My coven has not one, but two vampires to look after them now." Saeed's fingers abandoned her hair and the loss of his touch, no matter how slight, caused a hollow ache in Cerys's chest. "As for ruining lives, you've done nothing but enrich mine."

How? By helping to perpetuate a dream that would never be fulfilled? Their destination came into view and Cerys said a silent prayer of thanks. She didn't know if she could handle another second, let alone another minute cooped up in the car with Saeed before she lost it completely. She vacillated between wanting to tear his clothes off and wanting to force him to leave the city. Nervous energy gathered in the pit of Cerys's stomach as she turned onto a narrow dirt lane and killed the headlights. It was stupid to get herself worked up over Saeed. Especially when she might not even make it through the night.

"We're here." Cerys killed the engine but didn't bother to get out of the car. She kept her hands planted firmly on the steering wheel and took several cleansing breaths. "She knows we're coming." She wanted Saeed to be as prepared as possible for what might go down. "Rin gave her until tonight to step into line. This isn't going to be like the rogue werewolf." Saeed wouldn't simply be able to step in and compel tonight's unfortunate victim. She knew he'd try to spare her from what had to be done but he couldn't. Rin had pronounced judgment and Cerys had no choice but to carry out the sentence.

"You expect a fight?"

And then some. "Rin has had his sights set on her for a while. She controls the largest faction of fae in the state. You won't be able to compel her. And I'm pretty confident she can kick my ass in a fight."

"I can think of no creature more powerful than you," Saeed replied. "What is she?"

Warmth bloomed in Cerys's chest that Saeed would think so highly of her despite the terrible nature of her power. "Breanne is a *bean sidhe*."

Saeed's brow furrowed. Apparently, the vampire didn't have much experience with the fae. In the fae hierarchy, the *bean sidhe* sat at the top of the pyramid. "They're masters of illusion, fierce in battle, and resilient to magic—including mine." Which was why Cerys was pretty sure tonight's extraction would kill her.

Saeed cursed under his breath and his eyes went bright silver. "This is a suicide mission, then. Rin sent the two of us when he should've sent an army."

"Why do you think we're here tonight?" Cerys asked. "To take charge of an army."

CHAPTER
21

Saeed stretched his neck from side to side and rolled his shoulders to relieve the anxious tension that pulled every muscle in his body taut. Rin truly was an ambitious son of a bitch, using Cerys to secure the servitude of not only a single fae, but every soul that answered to her by default. No doubt Rin had been holding the fae's marker for the perfect opportunity to collect on her debt. And Saeed was equally sure that Gregor's appearance in the city was the catalyst.

"If she's resilient to your magic, how do you propose to pull this off?"

Cerys's features appeared even more delicate in the dark interior of the car, her body so much more fragile. She twisted her closed fists over the steering wheel and the leather creaked under the pressure. "I said she's resilient, but not immune. I told you that some souls hold on tighter than others. Breanne's won't be a cakewalk to get. I can do it though."

Such unwavering confidence. Saeed swallowed down a derisive snort. She'd kill herself for Rin and the bastard wouldn't even realize what he'd lost until she was gone. Saeed wanted to lay down another mandate. To tell her he wouldn't allow for her to even try. But the only thing he'd accomplish would be to spark Cerys's stubborn pride. She'd double her efforts to steal the fae's soul if only to prove to Saeed she could do it. Gods, how would he ever protect her?

"We need a plan." Saeed hated to go into any situation unprepared. Now that he knew what they were up against, they could form a strategy. Of course, with Saeed's limited knowledge of the fae he had no idea what to expect. Perhaps all of his worrying was a moot point. It was more likely they'd both die tonight.

"A plan for what?" Cerys opened her door but didn't get out of the Range Rover. "Breanne knows we're coming and she knows what we want. This isn't going to be an ambush."

"Why didn't she run?" It was something Saeed wondered about regularly since he'd arrived in Seattle. So many fools making deals with Rin and waiting around eagerly for their punishments.

"No one runs from Rin." Cerys took a deep breath and got out of the Range Rover. Saeed followed suit and climbed out of the car, rounding the front of the vehicle to meet her. "For Breanne, though, I think it's ego. She thinks she's untouchable."

No one was untouchable. And those with the biggest egos usually went down the hardest. "What will we be up against once we get inside?"

Cerys shrugged and her casual disregard did nothing but spark Saeed's temper. Did she take nothing seriously? "No more than ten is my guess."

Ten? Good gods. "I don't suppose you know anything about them?"

"They're fae. I know that much for sure. Breanne would

never lower herself to keep company with what she con-
siders the lesser supernatural creatures."

Her elitist attitude likely wouldn't help or hurt them in
this situation. "Any trained fighters among them?"

"Without a doubt," Cerys said as though it didn't concern her. "Dollars to donuts half of them will be too afraid
to fight. The other half will give it a good go, but I like
our odds."

He found her overconfidence as frustrating as it was at-
tractive. "And quite a bit of confidence in me for having
never seen me fight."

Cerys gave a flick of her wrist as she headed for the
back of the Range Rover. "Oh, I figure you'll help me out
with one or two of them. I can handle the rest on my own."

Gods, her cavalier attitude was insufferable! Saeed's
heart pounded in his chest at the mere thought of her rushing into battle outnumbered. She opened the hatchback
and the dome light illuminated the cargo space. They'd
brought along a mobile arsenal. She'd certainly come
prepared. Cerys wasted no time in outfitting herself. Two
Glocks strapped to either hip, daggers at her thighs, and
throwing knives shoved into sheaths in her boots. She tucked
a short sword behind her back before she turned to Saeed.

"I brought more than enough for both of us. Take whatever you want."

Saeed was certain the weapons strapped to Cerys's lithe
form weighed more than she did.

"Here." She shoved a weighted vest at him and he took
it from her. "Put this on. Don't want you vulnerable to any
potential stakes, wooden or otherwise."

"You thought of everything, apparently." Except an
actual plan of attack. He put on the vest before he selected
a pair of daggers and a sword from Cerys's arsenal.

"Grab one of the Rugers too," she said. "Believe me,
they'll be armed to the teeth."

Saeed had not been a warrior in a very long time. Not since the Sortiari all but wiped out the vampires. Modern-day warfare held no allure. It took no finesse to aim a gun at your enemy and pull the trigger. He grudgingly took the gun and tucked it into his waistband at the small of his back. He'd use it as a last resort.

"Now what?"

"Now?" Cerys said with a grin. "We go ring the doorbell."

"I understand that Breanne is expecting us, but you're not even interested in a surprise attack?" Saeed couldn't understand Cerys's tactics. They should be doing anything, no matter how small, to try and gain the upper hand. They were going into this situation at a serious disadvantage. From a tactical standpoint, they were screwed.

"Yeah, that's really not how I operate. I don't see any point in pretense."

Pretense? Saeed thought his eyes might bug right out of his head. "Tactical planning isn't pretense, Cerys. It's good sense."

"Eh." Gods. Saeed swore Breanne and her small army wouldn't get a chance to try and kill Cerys. Because he was seriously considering throttling her right now. "What you call planning I call prolonging the inevitable."

"The inevitable?" Saeed did nothing to mask his incredulous tone. "A little pretense, as you so disdainfully call it, could buy us precious seconds and gain us the advantage."

Cerys offered an almost consoling pat to Saeed's shoulder. She closed the hatchback and walked past him, giving him no choice but to follow. "Believe me, Saeed, my presence is shock factor enough. We'll have the advantage."

So damned confident. He almost hoped he'd have the opportunity to prove her wrong, but really, if they walked out of this alive it would be a miracle.

Cerys's demeanor changed the moment she passed Saeed and walked up the long pathway toward the house. She appeared as she had the first time he'd seen her in the Collective. Cold. Calculating. Detached. Focused. So fierce and so gods-damned beautiful she took his breath away. She was the vengeful ghost of his visions, her skin as lustrous as moonlight, her hair a cascade of vibrant flames. If anything happened to her here tonight Saeed would set fire to the world in his quest for vengeance.

The fae's house was tucked in a wooded area far from the main highway. It was much smaller than Saeed expected, more a modest cabin than a mansion fit for a queen. Quarters might be tight when the fighting began, which would make matters a little more difficult. While Cerys kept her gaze straight ahead, Saeed took careful stock of their surroundings, making note of areas that would aid in their escape and others that would offer perfect cover in the event of an ambush. One of them needed to be concerned about how they'd get out of here. Cerys certainly didn't seem to care.

Why? Was she that confident of their success? Or rather, did she anticipate complete failure? Nervous energy dumped into Saeed's bloodstream as he continued to walk and observe their surroundings. The anticipation of battle infused his limbs with adrenaline and awakened his thirst. It was more important now than ever to keep a level head. Cerys's safety depended on it, and he would not fail her.

"Breanne is the only one we'll have to worry about," Cerys remarked as they approached the modest house. "Everyone else will be lesser fae, not half as powerful."

"How do you know?"

"Rin." Cerys let out a snort. "Guess he wanted to make sure I wouldn't be in too far over my head. Breanne's consort, Fallon, would be a serious problem if he was here tonight. Rin found out he'd gone to Spokane to take care of some business for Breanne and made sure his return home would be delayed." She gave Saeed a sidelong glance. "Big of him, huh?"

"Very." Rin's idea of having Cerys's back was seriously perverse. He'd take whatever advantage they could get, however. Saeed might have the opportunity to compel at least one or two of the lesser fae before they had the chance to attack. His main objective was to protect Cerys so she had the opportunity to risk her life yet again to give Rin something he wanted.

Hopefully, this would be the last time Cerys would ever be forced to do such a thing.

If there was an Academy Award for best performance in pretending you have your shit together, Cerys would've been holding that little gold statue right now. Overconfident had nothing on her as she marched up the driveway to Breanne's quaint little cottage in the woods. She couldn't let Saeed see her sweat. Couldn't let him think for even a second she doubted tonight's outcome. On the outside, she was unflappable. Solid as a gods-damn rock. On the inside, she was one step away from losing her shit. Beneath the hard shell of her exterior, Cerys had never felt so fragile.

Breanne's place really was pretty cute. For a moment, Cerys tried to forget why she was here. Instead, she admired the manicured grounds, the natural architecture, and the absence of city sounds. She allowed herself to wonder what it would be like to live this life. To have a little place of her own. To come and go as she pleased with whom she pleased. She sort of envied Breanne. At least, she envied her freedom. And at the same time Cerys couldn't help but resent her for her foolish choices that would steal the freedom Cerys so desperately desired.

Breanne would take for granted what Cerys coveted. Maybe she deserved what she was getting tonight.

Before Cerys could breach the front steps, Saeed reached out and grabbed her by the arm. He hauled her against his wide chest and put his mouth to hers in a crushing kiss that sent her blood rushing through her veins and caused her heart to pound against her rib cage. He kissed her with every ounce of the desperation she felt, and her arms went around him as though she had no choice. His fingers dove into her hair as his tongue thrust past her lips to deepen the kiss. The world melted away. Nothing mattered but this moment. His mouth on hers, the heat of his kiss, her own lightheadedness, and the way he awakened her.

If she had it her way, reality would never barge in to interrupt them again.

Their kiss ended far too soon. Saeed pulled away and Cerys tried to steady her careening world, her breath racing in her chest.

"Promise me you'll be careful in there." Saeed's gaze delved into hers, his dark irises rimmed with silver.

When he looked at her like that, so full of heat and longing, she'd promise him anything. "I promise." She reached out for his hand and pulled it against her chest. Saeed's brow furrowed, and for a moment Cerys just stared and took in his beauty. "But you have to promise me the same." If anything happened to him tonight, she would never forgive herself.

Saeed's full lips spread into a blinding smile. "I promise."

Two simple words, but they seemed like so much more. As though they'd spoken sacred vows to one another, not simply agreed to be careful in the midst of the coming fight. She'd tried to deny it since the moment they met, but Cerys was tired of fighting it. She wanted Saeed. Wanted him as much as she wanted her freedom. As much as she wanted her soul. She could never tell him, though. She could never give even the slightest hint that he meant anything to her. If Rin found out, he would put an end to Saeed, and Cerys knew she would never recover from the loss.

"Get your game face on, Saeed." It was time to put her angst on the backburner and get to work. "Ready?"

He gave her hand a squeeze as she let go and took a step back. "I'm ready."

There was nothing left to say, was there?

Cerys climbed the five steps to the front door and laid her knuckles to the solid planks. She waited several seconds before knocking again, and she sensed Saeed grow tense behind her. It was too early for his nerves to get the better of him. Cerys didn't expect Breanne to rush to answer the door, given what was about to happen to her. Cerys would give her a couple more seconds to be civil before she made the decision to kick down the door.

"Well, shit." Cerys brought her right leg up and as she prepared to kick the door down, it swung open wide. Breanne stood on the other side of the threshold, regal and beautiful. Cerys set her foot down and rested her right hand on the pommel of her dagger. "Hello Breanne, time to pay the piper."

It was no wonder Rin wanted Breanne's soul. Not only was she powerful and influential, but she was absolutely beautiful. Tall and willowy with silver white hair and frost blue eyes, she looked like a creature straight out of a fairytale. Cerys imagined she'd be even lovelier in a hollow, apathetic state. A beautiful portrait of sorrow that Rin would no doubt admire like a prized work of art. Sadistic bastard.

"Tell Rin he'll get nothing from me." Breanne's voice was pleasant and melodic, yet firm. She might have looked delicate, but Cerys knew better. The metal edge of her dagger scraped against the scabbard as she pulled it free. So far, Breanne held the door open only wide enough for Cerys to see her, keeping the element of surprise on her side. But Cerys had a little something up her sleeve as well. Namely, the hulking vampire currently hiding in the shadows to her left.

"You know how this works," Cerys replied. "There's no reneging. You made a deal with Rin and you fell through on your end of the bargain. Now you have to pay up. Rin might have set the price, but you agreed to it, so I suggest we take care of this civilly, so no one gets hurt."

Breanne's icy gaze narrowed. "There's nothing civil about what you've come here to do."

Probably not. Breanne would do what she could to make Cerys lose her nerve. What bothered her the most was that everyone thought she was just like Rin. Cruel. Sadistic. Eager to use her power and lord it over others. No one ever considered the possibility that Cerys acted under duress. That she had no choice but to carry out Rin's orders because she was simply another one of his slaves.

"I can't leave without what I've come here to fetch," Cerys said. "You know that."

Breanne's answering laughter tinkled like wind chimes. "And you think I'd make it so easy for you to collect?"

"You made your bargain with Rin easily enough." It bothered Cerys more than it should have that no one ever seemed to want to pay up. As though they were all genuinely shocked Rin would actually ask payment for services rendered. How could anyone possibly expect anything less after entering into a deal with the devil? Cerys found their indignation insulting. Supernatural creatures should've known better than anyone that you reap what you sow.

Breanne opened the door a little wider as though in invitation. The open floor plan of her cottage wouldn't be too tough to negotiate when the fighting began, but it still wasn't ideal. Upon first glance, Cerys counted at least fifteen bodies inside the living room alone. The odds were stacked more against them than she'd anticipated, damn it.

"If you step past this threshold," Breanne crooned, "I will consider it an act of aggression."

Cerys rolled her eyes. *Please.* She'd known tonight's retrieval wasn't going to be easy, but she'd hoped Breanne would've been at least marginally cooperative. "I was really hoping we could do this the easy way," Cerys said with a sigh.

There was no point in talking. Cerys was on a tight schedule and they could sit here and chew the fat all night. In a perfect scenario, she could force her way into the house, corner Breanne, and extract her soul while Saeed ran interference. That wasn't going to happen, though. The fight would be hard, fast, and chaotic. Outside threats needed to be neutralized before Breanne had a chance to run.

Cerys tucked her right hand behind her back, knowing Saeed watched her. She held up three fingers, two fingers, one . . . and attacked.

Cerys slashed with her dagger before spinning it in her grip and sliding it back into the scabbard. She traded the weapon for the gun at her side and fired off six quick rounds before she'd even crossed the threshold. The bullets, infused with iron, wouldn't kill the fae, but rather would act as a sort of tranquilizer, temporarily immobilizing them and getting them out of Cerys's hair. Her aim was true, and all six went down within seconds of being hit. Breanne stared, wide-eyed, as Cerys blew past her and took out three more fae before hitting the foyer. Cerys chanced a glance backward toward Saeed who also paused in a moment of stunned silence. A smug sense of pride welled within her. She'd told him she'd take out the bulk of Breanne's forces before Saeed even had a chance to engage. She didn't have time to bask in her accomplishments, however. She'd had the element of surprise on her side and now that that was gone the fight would only get harder. Thank the gods she had backup. Despite her confidence, Cerys doubted she'd be able to do this on her own.

Three angry fae rushed toward her and Cerys drew a dagger from its sheath at her left hip as she prepared to engage. Hell, even with backup, they might be screwed.

CHAPTER
22

Saeed didn't waste any time entering the fray. Cerys was by far one of the most impressive fighters he'd ever seen, her motions so fast they blurred in his vision, her aim accurate to a pinpoint, and her dagger skills sublime. Saeed had never been so enamored of her as he was in this moment. She was exquisite. A beautiful force of nature that couldn't be stopped. Gods, how she dazzled him.

Saeed kept one eye on Breanne as he rushed into the living room to curtail the progress of three armed fae headed straight for Cerys. He was surprised they didn't attempt to shoot her on sight and had to assume that like everyone who came in contact with Cerys, Breanne thought to capture her and exploit her. The thought burned through Saeed like fire and he clamped his jaw down tight as he engaged his first attacker. The male fought with the well-practiced precision that came from centuries of training. His sword arm was steady as he hacked at Saeed with a shining silver saber. It was the perfect choice of weapon, considering silver had no effect on the fae but could easily disable a host of other supernatural creatures. They'd obviously anticipated Cerys bringing back up and were well-prepared.

Saeed brought the fight as close to Breanne as possible. All of this would be for naught if she got away and he'd be damned if they had to do this all over again.

"Saeed! Heads up!"

Cerys's warning shout drew his attention and Saeed looked up in time to see the glint of a silver knife rocketing through the air toward him. He ducked to his right and the sound of the knife as it traveled through the air sang in his ear at the same moment the blade nicked the outer shell. He hissed in a breath at the sting of silver but the wound was superficial and managed not to affect him. He straightened and parried with his dagger to block the incoming blow of his opponent's blade. The male's arm moved in a flash as the blade spun in his grip to no longer stab down, but to slash. Saeed adjusted in an instant, and jumped back, narrowly avoiding the blow. He'd been disdainful of the possibility of letting the outcome of the fight be determined by who was a better aim. And after seeing Cerys effectively disable several opponents in a matter of seconds, he could certainly understand the merit of letting a bullet even the odds.

That wasn't his style, though. He had his own weapons at his disposal and his pride demanded he demonstrate to his mate his own prowess in battle.

To compel someone took a certain level of concentration that Saeed was reluctant to admit he hadn't quite perfected. With the Collective's presence a constant in his mind over the past few months, he hadn't found the focus necessary to properly control another's thoughts and actions in a situation such as this with so many distractions. He didn't have the luxury of time, however and he forced himself to focus. The male that rushed him, silver sword drawn, clashed with Saeed in a ring of metal as their weapons met. He held the fae's gaze and drew on his power. "You will sit and not move until the sun rises tomorrow."

A spark of energy ignited in his chest as he felt his suggestion take hold. The male's knees buckled as he went cross-legged to the floor, his sword resting serenely in his lap. Before Saeed had the opportunity to feel any joy over his success, the burn of silver ripped through him as he was attacked from behind and the sharp blade of a dagger sank between his ribs at the side of his torso where the armored vest gaped away.

"Saeed!"

Cerys's concerned shout vied for his attention, but Saeed was too busy keeping the blade from stabbing deeper to acknowledge her. He seized the fae's wrist and twisted until she released her hold on the dagger's grip. She managed to open the wound further before losing her hold and Saeed issued a barked command, compelling her into stillness. He plucked the dagger free from his torso and threw it, burying the blade to the hilt in the opposite wall. Saeed only had enough time to give the wound a quick glance before he was attacked again, this time from his right. Breanne's small army of fae fought with a ferocity Saeed couldn't help but admire. It had been centuries since he'd put his own prowess in battle to the test and he welcomed the challenge, more than ready to prove he was as deadly as ever.

In the meantime, Cerys had managed to disable another two. Breanne had to know the momentum was about to shift and she would soon lose advantage. She'd be a fool not to run and Saeed had to do everything in his power to make sure that didn't happen now. As much as he didn't want Cerys to risk her life by extracting the *bean sidhe's* soul, he knew they both had no other choice but to see this through to the end.

Several shots rang out, none of them fired by Cerys. The fae were no longer interested in hand-to-hand combat and were ready to put a swift end to the conflict. Saeed kicked out with his right foot, shoving his own attacker several feet back. He drew the gun he'd tucked into his waistband at the small of his back and aimed, hitting his attacker in the right shoulder. Gods, he was a shitty shot, but where the bullet hit mattered little. The fae slowed as the iron took hold and he crumpled to the floor in a useless heap. Of the fifteen they'd encountered upon entering the house, only two remained. Saeed left them to Cerys as he turned his focus on immobilizing Breanne.

"Saeed, don't do this. Please."

He stopped dead in his tracks, stunned, as Sasha stood before him. Saeed gave a violent shake of his head and blinked as though to clear his vision. It wasn't the Collective that played with his mind, but something else entirely. He reached out toward Sasha and she took a step back as though wary of any contact with him.

"Come home. To me. Where you belong. We need you, Saeed. *I* need you."

Sasha's soft, imploring tone burned through Saeed like the silver blade that had pierced his torso. Her wide eyes glistened with unshed tears and her chin quivered. This couldn't be real but Saeed couldn't help but engage.

"I can't go back, Sasha." He wished she could understand. "You know that."

Sasha's delicate jaw took a stern set. "She doesn't want you." Her tone became hard. Cold. "Doesn't care about you at all. Why would you waste your time on someone who treats you with such indifference when you can return home with me? I care. *I love you.* I am meant for you, not her."

Saeed had sent Sasha's soul to oblivion when he'd turned her. Her emphatic declarations of love weren't real.

She wasn't real. Breanne's magic had somehow found a way to breach Saeed's mind and call forth an image of her. Faerie magic was foreign to him. It weighed down his limbs and cast a gauzy haze over his thoughts. Saeed knew what he saw could not be real, and yet he found himself drawn into the illusion and helpless to fight its pull.

So much like the Collective, Breanne's illusions had power over him. Was his mind so feeble that he could succumb so easily to Breanne's charm? He cursed his own weakness as he tried to walk past Sasha, only to find himself stayed by her outstretched hand. "Saeed," she implored. "Abandon this quest and come home to your coven."

His step faltered. Doubt scratched at the back of his mind with sharp talons that left his mind shredded and raw. He'd been so certain. His faith so gods-damned unwavering that Cerys would tether his soul. What if after so much fight, so much effort, he returned her soul only to find that his remained trapped in oblivion?

"It's not real, Saeed!" Cerys's voice reached out to him, forceful and clear. "Don't let her in your head!"

Easier said than done. For months, Saeed had lived in a state of blurred reality. Of being unable to differentiate memory from reality. This was no different. Sasha stood before him as true and real as anything he'd seen over the past few months. Saeed took a step closer, and Sasha took a step back. He'd never known her to shy away from him. Another step toward her. Another step back.

"It's a trick!" Cerys shouted the words between labored breaths as she continued to fight. "Pull your head out of your ass before I dislodge it with my boot!"

Saeed's step faltered. He looked past Sasha toward the tall, willowy fae whose ice blue eyes remained trained on him. She was powerful. An illusionist. She'd managed to crawl right inside Saeed's head and weed through his thoughts and memories until she found the perfect ammunition to use against him. Of course he couldn't touch Sasha. She wasn't real.

"Come back to us, Saeed." Tears streaked Sasha's cheeks, but the soulless rarely had tears to shed. "I need you."

Sasha was far too proud to ever plead with him for anything. Saeed pushed forward toward her. He reached out, and shoved his fist through the illusion that dissipated like fog under the sun. Breanne drew in a surprised gasp as Saeed overtook her. He wrapped his large palm around her slender throat as he shoved her none too gently against the wall. He was through playing games. It was time to give Rin what he wanted so Saeed could get one step closer to what he needed.

His fingers squeezed ever so slightly, applying the barest pressure to Breanne's throat. If anything happened to Cerys in the process of extracting the *bean sidhe's* soul, neither Rin nor Breanne would live to see the sunrise.

Cerys was through dicking around. She loaded a fresh clip into her Glock and fired off three successive shots, taking down the remaining fae in a matter of seconds. Breanne knew she was screwed and she'd pulled out the big guns, attempting to put Saeed down by calling forth an image of someone dear to him. Cerys's chest grew tight as her limbs flooded with uncomfortable heat. Who was the female who implored so desperately for Saeed to return home? She had to have been a member of his coven, and someone he'd at one time had feelings for.

Cerys didn't even know the female, and yet she couldn't help but be annoyed by her presence. Angered by an illusion. Cerys swallowed down an angry snort. It seemed the more she tried to convince herself that Saeed meant nothing to her, the deeper he managed to worm his way into her heart.

Without her soul, did she even have a heart with which to love?

There wasn't time for Cerys to contemplate the metaphysics of her current state. She had a job to do, and no matter her misgivings, it had to be done. Rin would expect nothing less than for Cerys to return to him with Breanne's soul contained and ready to be added to his collection. Anxiety twisted Cerys's gut. Doubt and fear scratched at the back of her mind. Her own mortality weighed heavily upon her as she tried not to think too much on what she was about to do. Rin had used her powers sparingly over the past two or so centuries. But tonight's extraction made it obvious he was preparing to make yet another power-play.

Saeed stood not a dozen feet away. His strong arm jutted out to pin Breanne to the wall. His fingers constricted her throat and yet the powerful fae remained for the most part unfazed. Her cool blue eyes looked on him with disdain and her soft, petal-pink lips, curled back into a sneer.

Cerys wanted to tell Breanne not to be a sore loser, but speaking to her would expend precious energy that Cerys couldn't afford to waste. She stepped up beside Saeed and ducked under his outstretched arm. He didn't release his hold on Breanne, but instead took a step closer to press his chest against Cerys's back. The heat of his body warmed her, relaxed her, and put her instantly at ease. Cerys drew in a deep breath and held it in her lungs as she drew on her own power and let it build. Gods, she didn't want to do this. But she had no choice.

Saeed held Breanne with his right hand and so, Cerys reached out with her left. She gently placed her palm on Breanne's solar plexus and released the power she'd allowed to gather in the center of her own being. A wild rush of sensation drained from her body, through her extended arm, and into Breanne. The fae drew in a sharp, pained breath as her jaw clenched and her brows furrowed. She'd barely just begun, and already Cerys felt the depleting effects of her own power.

Saeed's left arm came around her waist as though to ground her. He bent over her and his cheek pressed against her temple. He was her anchor and she allowed him to ground her as her life force left her body and entered Breanne's as she began the process of extracting her soul.

"Cerys, I'm sorry."

Her sister's mournful voice called out to her and Cerys squeezed her eyes tightly shut. She refused to fall victim to Breanne's illusions. Fiona never would've apologized. She hadn't so much as flinched when she laid her palm to Cerys's chest and ripped her soul from her body in order to give it to Rin. Breanne exploited Cerys's hope, not her reality. She'd always wished her sister had regretted what she'd done. She'd always hoped her sister would return and right the wrong. Cerys had given up on wishing and hoping a long time ago. Breanne would not deter her.

Cerys's concentration slipped and she lost the tenuous grasp she had on Breanne's soul. Some were more solid than others, which was what made them easier to extract. Breanne's soul was a gossamer thing, delicate as though it had been spun from cobwebs. Cerys reached out once again, the invisible tentacles of her power reaching and twining around Breanne's ethereal self. Once again her hold broke and Cerys slumped as she felt her own strength leave her body like water being sucked down the drain.

Saeed held her tighter. His firm grip was both calming and reassuring. Another wave of paralyzing fear entered Cerys's bloodstream as she realized she might not be able to do this.

"I've got you." The dark timbre of Saeed's voice rolled over her. "I won't let anything happen to you."

The truth of his words hit her with the force of a

sledgehammer. It was true. If it was in his power, Saeed would never let any harm come to her. Too bad she couldn't be as sure as he was right now. He could protect her from werewolves, shifters, vampires and fae. But the one thing Saeed could never protect her from was her own damned self.

Cerys centered her focus. She couldn't let her thoughts, feelings, or anything else get in the way of tonight's task. She had a job to do, and by the gods she was going to do it. Her chest began to ache from the effort she expended. Cerys gritted her teeth and dug in, doubling her efforts as she fought to extract Breanne's soul. She met resistance as she gave a slight tug and Cerys reminded herself that it wasn't about force exerted, but finesse. Breanne's soul was fragile and so Cerys needed to treat it like a fragile thing. She couldn't simply jerk it free like pulling in a fish she'd hooked on her line. Instead, she needed to coax Breanne's soul from her body. She would only be successful if she could manage to simply coax it to leave.

Cerys's ears began to ring and her heart hammered a desperate rhythm in her chest. Sweat beaded her brow and a sour tang settled on the back of her tongue. She didn't dare open her eyes lest she fall victim once again to Breanne's illusions. Saeed's firm grip on her remained the only constant in the darkness as she envisioned her own inner light reaching out with seeking tendrils to weave with the silvery light that was Breanne's soul.

"Don't fight it." She wasn't sure she spoke the mantra for herself or Breanne. Cerys often wondered if she made the process harder on herself because of her own disgust at being made to do such a horrible thing. She let herself go, banished any notion of harm or regret from her mind. She could deal with those things later. If she lived through this moment. Until then, her only option was to be the cold, detached bitch Rin had trained her to be.

Just a little bit more. . . . Focus, Cerys. You can do this.

Her strength continued to flag but Cerys pressed on. The seeking vines of her power intertwined with Breanne's soul until finally, Cerys felt as though she had a secure grip. The easy part was done. Finding the soul took the least amount of effort. It was separating the soul from the body that took a toll. Cerys wanted to laugh. If she made it through tonight, it would be a miracle.

So many words sat at the tip of her tongue but she couldn't spare a moment of concentration, or energy, to speak them. She wanted to thank Saeed for so many things. For giving her hope when she'd lost it all. For making her feel alive when she thought herself dead. For stirring within her emotions she'd forced herself to suppress, and for holding her tight in his embrace when her own legs couldn't help her to stand.

A knot lodged itself in her throat as Cerys fought for a breath. Her legs went numb and her right hand hung limp at her side. Her head dipped between her shoulders and her left palm remained pressed against Breanne's chest. *Just a little bit more.* She was so close. *Just . . . need to focus.*

A scream gathered in Cerys's throat as she felt Breanne's soul release its grip on her body. Like a rubber band that had been pulled tight and then released, the extracted soul ricocheted as it slammed against Cerys's palm. Her legs gave out from under her, but Saeed held her against him and refused to let her fall. Cerys's eyes opened and she watched as Breanne slumped against the wall. With a shuddering breath, Cerys closed her fingers over the disembodied soul and encased it in her shaking fist. Her right hand hung useless at her side and she cleared her throat which suddenly had gone much too dry.

"Saeed," she rasped. "I need the bottle in my jacket pocket."

Saeed released his grip on Breanne's throat. His hand

dove into her pocket and Cerys averted her gaze from Bre-anne's shocked expression and shivering form. Saeed tried to press the bottle into her palm but Cerys's fingers refused to work. She could barely push the words past her lips as she said, "Open the stopper for me."

He managed to pull the cork from the bottle with his one free hand. Cerys was grateful that he kept his grip on her, holding her upright while she opened her fist over the wide mouth of the bottle. Breanne's soul slithered inside and as the bright, glistening light settled into the bottom of the vessel, Saeed forced the stopper back into place.

"Thanks." She wasn't actually sure if she'd said the word with any coherency as the air seemed to press in around her, compressing her lungs and heart, before her world went dark.

CHAPTER
23

Panic welled hot and thick in Saeed's chest. It stole the air from his lungs and stopped his heart mid-beat. Cerys doubled over in his grasp. Her body hung lifeless and limp like a ragdoll. Breanne stared straight ahead, her expression blank. She slid down the wall onto the floor and her jaw hung slack as gentle tremors shook her body. Saeed hung onto Cerys with his left arm and he clutched the bottle that contained Breanne's soul in his right. He was literally the only body left standing in the aftermath of chaos. And his own shock and worry were so intense it damn near crippled him.

"You're all right, Cerys. You're all right. You're all right. You're all right."

Saeed said the words over and again as though to convince himself. Her heart slowed to the point that he could barely discern its beat and a wave of nausea rolled over him. They were in hostile territory and their enemies wouldn't be disabled for long. Saeed needed to get her out of here. Now.

He shoved the bottle into her jacket pocket and scooped
Cerys up into his arms. She seemed so slight in his grasp,
like a feather that could so easily float away. Bodies littered the floor but Saeed paid them little mind. The fae
would heal in time. Cerys might not be so lucky. A sense of
urgency welled in Saeed's chest as he fled from the house
and raced down the driveway to where Cerys had parked
the Range Rover. He pulled open the passenger side back
door and laid her gently into the backseat, careful not to
jostle her even a little bit. Her chest barely moved with
breath and her skin took on the pallor of death. Saeed saw
no point in living if Cerys didn't survive the night. He
would gladly walk into the sun rather than face a lonely,
soulless existence with only the Collective for company.
He refused to let her die, damn it!

The engine roared to life and Saeed wasted no time in
slamming the car into gear. Gravel sprayed out from under
the tires as he hit the gas and tore out of the driveway. He
had no idea what he was doing. No idea where he was
going. He couldn't take her to Rin. Through the Collective, Saeed had already seen what kind of care Cerys would
receive from her master. He had no other point of refer-
ence, no one to go to for help. They were completely on
their own and Cerys had no one to rely on but him. He
wouldn't fail her. He couldn't. Not when there was so much
at stake.

Saeed sped down the highway toward Seattle. Wet
warmth accompanied a twinge of pain in his torso and he
reached across his body with his right hand to find that the
wound made by the fae's silver blade had yet to heal. He'd
been so concerned with Cerys's safety, his own injuries
had faded to the back of his mind. Saeed's brain went
fuzzy and his grip on the steering wheel loosened. The
Range Rover swerved on the highway, and he jerked to at-

tention, righting the vehicle before it went onto the shoulder. The silver prevented the wound from healing like it should. He had no idea how much blood he'd lost, but his lightheadedness wasn't a good sign.

They were alone, injured, weak, and without allies to come to their aid. Saeed was hundreds of miles from L.A., disconnected from his coven, and far from the epicenter of the vampire race's strength. He couldn't pull over to the side of the road, couldn't risk losing consciousness and being exposed once the sun rose. He had no choice but to keep it together long enough to get them back to his condo. Neither one of them was going to die tonight.

The minutes dragged by like days. By the time they reached his building, Saeed's breathing became labored and sweat beaded his brow. The female who'd caught him off guard had known just where to aim when she drove her blade between his ribs. He was certain he'd sustained internal organ damage. And thanks to the silver, until he did something to fortify his strength, he'd continue to bleed out. Saeed pulled into the breezeway and came to an abrupt stop. He popped open the door and nearly tumbled out onto his ass. He steadied himself and retrieved Cerys from the backseat as the valet came around to the front of the car.

"Park it."

Saeed didn't wait for a response. With Cerys in his arms, he rushed through the turnstile and headed straight for the elevator. His finger stabbed down on the button repeatedly, his temper mounting with each second the doors didn't slide open to let them in. By the time the elevator reached the lobby floor, Saeed's legs felt as though they might give out from under him. He stepped inside and the second the doors slid closed and the elevator gave a lurch to take them to the penthouse, he slumped against the back wall to keep himself upright.

Saeed held Cerys close to his body. He didn't dare look at her, couldn't bring himself to face the possibility that she might not make it. She hadn't so much as stirred since they left Bellevue. Hadn't made a single sound. Her limbs hung limp in his grasp and he supported her head on his biceps to keep it from lolling back. Her heartbeat slowed to a beat or two every minute. The almost indiscernible thump made Saeed's own chest ache with fear.

The elevator doors slid open to the foyer and for a moment, Saeed wasn't sure he'd make it out of the elevator on his own steam. It took a sheer act of will for him to put one foot in front of the other. With Cerys in his arms, he made it through the foyer, past the front door, and into the condo. Thank the gods the blinds were all closed.

By the time Saeed made it to the bedroom, he had nothing left to give. He gently deposited Cerys on the bed before he went to his knees beside her. "Don't leave me." He spoke the words under his breath like a prayer. He'd never needed the tether to prove to him they were meant to be together. From the very first moment he'd seen her in the Collective, Saeed had known. He refused to give up. Refused to let her go. He brought his wrist to his mouth and bit down hard, tearing the flesh. With his fingertips, he urged Cerys's mouth to open as he held his bleeding wrist over her mouth. Had they been tethered, the exchange of blood would have solidified their bond. He had no idea if his blood would heal her. If it would do a gods-damned thing to help her. But he was out of time, and out of options. The room swam out of focus in the periphery of his vision as he stared, transfixed, at the crimson smear of color across her pale lips.

Saeed swayed as a white hot flash of crippling pain stabbed once again into his torso. He felt himself fall but did nothing to cushion the landing. His head smacked sharply against the floor as darkness descended over him.

Not even the Collective could offer him solace now. Saeed was truly lost and within minutes, he'd be dead.

The dark was impenetrable. It pressed in on Cerys from all sides, disorienting her until she couldn't tell if she was right side up or upside down. Chills shook her at the same time sweat beaded her brow. The air around her became too thick to breathe and for a moment, she was convinced she lay hundreds of feet below the earth. Her mouth went dry and Cerys ran her tongue over her lips. Her nose wrinkled at the coppery tang that clung to her taste buds and she shuddered. She tried to open her eyes but her lids were so heavy they might as well have been glued shut. If she could only sleep for a thousand or so years, she'd be fine. If only she'd been given the peace and quiet necessary to replenish her depleted energy stores, she'd be okay. Gods, she was exhausted.

She tried first to wiggle a finger. Her brain seemed disconnected from simple motor function and anxious frustration formed as a knot in the center of her chest. Her toes were equally uncooperative, as were her head and limbs. She lay in a state of paralysis, her body dormant as it healed itself. Only her mind appeared ready to get the show on the road. But no matter how hard she tried, her body refused to obey its commands. She couldn't remember a time she'd ever been so utterly spent.

Maybe she was dead. It would figure that the afterlife would be a cold, lonely, black and desolate space. Life had never done her any favors, so why should death be any different? Okay, so maybe that was a little too bitter. At least if she was dead, Cerys wouldn't have to answer to that son of a bitch Rin anymore. Then again, maybe that's why she was in this empty black place. Seemed pretty impossible to cross over into the afterlife without a soul to make the journey. It would just be her luck that Rin could fuck her over in death in the same way he'd fucked her over in life.

Seriously. The least fate could do was offer up a little lube.

If she was dead, Cerys supposed she'd better try to make the most of it. It didn't look like she was going anywhere anytime soon. At least, not without her soul. This dark purgatory might be a nice place to take a breather. To get a little rest for once in a few thousand years. At any rate, she wouldn't have to sit around and listen to Rin yammer on for hours on end. See? Life—and death—was all about finding that silver lining.

Cerys forgot about the dark. Forgot about her inability to move, the strange taste on her lips, and her own stupid disappointment. She forgot about when or where she might've been and how she'd gotten here. A single image invaded her thoughts. One of dark, intense eyes and full, soft lips. The eyes brightened to brilliant silver. And the lips spread into an indulgent smile that revealed the glinting tips of two sets of razor-sharp fangs.

Saeed.

He'd stayed by her side. Protected her. Risked his own life in an attempt to save hers. In the long run, he hadn't been successful but that was hardly his fault. The odds had been stacked against him all along and Cerys had gone to Breanne's knowing what the outcome would be. Honestly, it was sort of a relief. At least now, he could return to L.A., to his coven, and abandon his quest to free her soul.

Saeed deserved so much better than her.

That didn't mean she didn't still want him, though. Gods, she did. Funny, that even in this place between life and death, she could still yearn for something with such intensity. She could let the memories of her brief time with him keep her company in this lonely place. It might've only been a little over a month, but they'd been the best weeks of Cerys's entire existence. Those memories were precious to her, and nothing could ever force her to let them go.

A flutter of movement drew Cerys's attention. Her index finger moved to brush against soft flesh. She started with surprise, not only because she'd been able to move, but because it was apparent she wasn't alone in this place. She seriously doubted purgatory was the sort of place one inhabited with a roommate. Which meant, she wasn't dead. Not even close. Damn. And she'd been looking forward to a nice, long rest . . .

On the plus side, if she wasn't dead, it meant that Breanne's reluctant soul hadn't managed to do her in. Pretty damned amazing considering how tough it'd been to get the sucker out of her body. Just because she wasn't dead didn't mean she wasn't fucking exhausted. Aside from the slight shift of her body, Cerys still found it difficult to move. Her eyes remained closed and she could barely feel the breath enter and release from her lungs. She still sensed that disconnect from her body. Which, given her soulless state, was a little strange. Didn't she always exist in a state of disconnect?

It wouldn't do her any good to try and force her body to do what it wasn't ready to do. That didn't mean Cerys wasn't anxious as hell to open her eyes and take in her surroundings. Where was she? How did she get here? She had no doubt that the skin she'd brushed her finger against belonged to Saeed. She would know him anywhere. Blind, deaf, barely conscious, and clinging to life by a single thread. The realization struck her with an impact that left her aching. In such a short amount of time, Saeed had come to mean something to her.

Patience suddenly became much harder to maintain. Saeed had been injured during the fight. She'd seen one

of Breanne's bodyguards drive a silver dagger between his
ribs where the vest had failed to protect him. She needed
to see him with her own eyes, make sure he was okay.
Silence pressed in on her ears until it grew almost unbearable. He didn't speak, and as far as she could tell he
hadn't moved. She couldn't even hear the sound of his
breathing. She couldn't quell the panic that threatened to
overtake her. Her own physical state, her own crippling
exhaustion didn't matter. The only thing she gave a shit
about was Saeed and whether or not he was okay.

Come on, body! Get with the fucking program!

Cerys centered her focus on snapping the hell out of
whatever weird supernatural coma held her in its grip. She
might've needed a little recuperation, but all of this was a
serious waste of her time. A spark of power lit in the center of Cerys's being, and she held on to it. Careful not to
disrupt it, she allowed it to grow by small degrees until the
spark became a flame, and the flame a fire. It burned bright
in her center, warming her from the inside out. Little by
little the sensation returned to her extremities down the
length of her arms and legs and into her fingertips and toes.
Her nose wrinkled and her eyelids twitched. One lid
cracked and then the other, to reveal the dark interior of a
bedroom.

She'd never been in this room, but she was certain they
were in Saeed's condo. Jesus, neither one of them had been
in stellar shape at Breanne's cottage. How in the hell had
he gotten them both out of there? The vampire certainly
put the "super" in supernatural. Was there anything he
couldn't do? Cerys was beginning to think she'd been a
little too hasty in ever having doubted him.

"Saeed?" Her voice sounded foreign in her ears. Quiet
and raspy as though it had gone weeks without use. Still a
little too weak for a full range of motion, Cerys felt blindly
on the bed for his hand, or any other part of his body for

that matter. She was sure she'd felt his skin brush against hers, but he was nowhere to be found on the bed. Not lying beside her as she'd expected.

"Saeed?"

Again she was answered by silence, and the fear she'd tried to quell made an unwelcome appearance. Her body was stiff and sore, her muscles ached. Her arms, hands, and fingers refused to work right, as though they'd gone to sleep and she was still waiting for the circulation to return. Numb. Her frustration at her lack of motor skills did nothing but fuel her growing impatience. Where was he? Why didn't he answer her? What in the gods-damned hell was going on?

Cerys flailed on the mattress like a fish out of water. Definitely not graceful, but right now she didn't have a single fuck to give. Her arms flopped like cooked noodles at her sides as she wriggled and repositioned herself so she could look over the edge of the bed. A gasp of surprise caught in her sternum as she took in a dark, immobile form lying on the floor beside the bed.

"Oh my gods!" Saeed lay still as death and a dark crimson stain smeared the bamboo floor. She'd known his wound had been bad, but she never would've imagined it severe enough to put him down. In a less than graceful rush, Cerys slid off the mattress onto the floor with a loud thump. She willed her still numb arms to work as she braced her back against the bed frame and gathered Saeed's head up into her lap. Tears stung at her eyes but she refused to let them fall. *He's okay. He's fine. He's strong.* Did she really think lying to herself would somehow change the fact that he'd nearly bled out on the floor while she lay on that fucking bed, completely helpless and unable to do a damn thing to save him?

His heart didn't beat. His lungs didn't move with breath. His skin was cold to the touch.

Cerys released a breath that ended on a desperate sob. "No." He couldn't possibly be so frail. Not the strong, determined, fierce vampire who'd come to Seattle to steal her from Rinieri de Rege. He'd been cut with the silver blade which had weakened him and kept the wound from healing. The blood loss had taken a toll. That was all. Saeed needed blood, and Cerys was going to give it to him.

She reached for the short knife she'd hidden in her right boot. Her fingers still refused to work properly and it took several tries to get enough of the hilt to pull the blade free. It fumbled in her grasp and landed with the clank to the floor. "Fuck." Cerys tried again, willing her damned digits to function as she managed to grip the hilt once again. She brought the blade to her left wrist and sliced down. The sharp bite of pain coaxed a gasp from between her lips as crimson flashed like a length of satin ribbon and welled over the incision to run in rivulets down her arm.

She'd cut a little deeper than she'd planned but that was okay. She didn't want a few measly drops of blood, she wanted it to pour from her vein like water from a broken spigot. She brought her wrist to Saeed's mouth and pressed it against his parted lips. *Drink.* He didn't move. Didn't so much as twitch. "Come on, Saeed. Damn you. Drink!"

Cerys tipped his head back. If he wouldn't swallow, she'd make sure gravity did the work for him. Seconds passed and then minutes. Wet warmth tickled at Cerys's cheek and she reached up with her free hand to angrily swipe it away. Another drop landed on her cheek, followed by another and Cerys looked up for the source of the annoying drip only to realize it was her own gods-damned tears that trailed down her face.

The soulless had no tears to shed, no emotions with which to feel pain or hurt. So why did her chest ache as though her heart had been smashed into a million irreparable pieces?

CHAPTER
24

The fire in Saeed's throat was quenched as the sweet ambrosia of Cerys's blood flowed over his tongue. Her intoxicating scent invaded his nostrils, too visceral to be a cruel trick of the Collective. He tried to reach for her, to feel the satin glide of her skin against his, but he was still too weak to lift his arm. Too completely depleted of strength to even latch onto her wrist with his fangs. Even his throat refused to properly work. Every beat of Cerys's heart sent a renewed rush of her blood over his tongue, nearly choking him. Had she cut herself to open the vein? If so, she'd cut dangerously deep. Through his bite, Saeed could control the flow. If he didn't heal the wound soon, Cerys would bleed out and everything he'd done to get her to safety would be for nothing.

The lethargy that weighed down his limbs began to subside and Saeed reclaimed some measure of strength. He reached up and gently cradled her wrist in his hand, eliciting a soft gasp of surprise from Cerys as he sealed his lips over the wound and laved it gently with his tongue.

"No, Saeed." Cerys's pleading tone speared through his chest. "Don't stop. You need more."

Stubborn, foolish female. She'd needlessly kill herself in her attempt to save him when she needn't do anything quite so rash. Saeed's thirst was sated, and though his strength wasn't completely replenished, it was a far cry from his previous unconscious state. He cleaned every drop of blood from Cerys's wrist with lazy passes of his tongue as the cut healed. She shivered against him as the fingers of her right hand played idly with the strands of his hair. It almost felt wrong to experience such bliss in the wake of such trauma.

A warm rush of relief flooded his body as Saeed allowed his eyes to drift shut for an indulgent moment. His mouth pulled away from her wrist as his head settled back into her lap, but he kept her hand in his and allowed their fingers to intertwine.

"You need more," she said again. "You're still too weak."

Saeed gave a low chuckle. "And you, on the other hand, are a picture of stalwart strength?" He'd been convinced she was dead. It was a miracle she'd had the strength to pull her body off the bed, let alone force-feed him her blood.

"I'm five by five," Cerys said with a weak laugh. "I could take on an army of fifty angry fae. Just show me the way."

"If I have anything to say or do about it, you won't be stepping foot near dangerous situations of any kind for a good long while."

Cerys didn't laugh this time. Instead, she answered Saeed with solemn silence. "I wouldn't have made it out of there without your help." Saeed had to strain to hear the softly spoken words. "Thank you."

Did she think he would've had it any other way? "Now that I've found you, I don't plan to ever leave your side."

Cerys released her grasp on his fingers. She hugged her arm around her middle as though trying to keep herself intact. "If Rin finds out what you mean to me," she said on a hiccup of breath, "he'll drive a stake through your heart and make me watch."

Saeed's chest grew tight as a surge of warmth spread through him. For so long, he'd longed to hear any favorable words from Cerys's lips. Some indicator that she'd sensed a deeper connection between them. He wanted to shout his elation as well as his relief. He'd earned her trust, her admiration, and perhaps even some measure of affection.

"I'm not afraid of Rin." The only thing Saeed truly feared was losing Cerys, and he'd come dangerously close tonight. "The only creature in this world with the power to harm me, is you."

Saeed reached up to cup Cerys's face in his other hand. Her brow furrowed as she studied him and her light eyes shone like starlight in the dark room. "Me?"

"You are the keeper of my soul. *Qalb ta' qalbi*. Heart of my hearts. You could easily crush me without lifting a single finger."

Cerys let out a slow breath that caressed Saeed's face like a gentle breeze. "You should never let anyone have that sort of power over you, Saeed. Especially me."

"Ah, but I give you that power freely. My soul is yours as yours is mine. And soon enough, our spirits will be united."

"No pressure there." Cerys gave a gentle laugh. "Don't you ever worry that things won't turn out like you planned?"

"I have faith." Never once had Saeed doubted the inevitability of their fates.

Cerys looked away and her expression became pensive. Saeed pushed himself up to sit, still surprisingly a little lightheaded, and took her left hand in both of his. His thumb brushed over the now smooth skin of her wrist. "You cut yourself too deep," he remarked. "You could have easily bled out."

She looked up and met his gaze. "I was in a hurry. I didn't have time to think about the depth of my blade. Besides . . . supernatural creature here. I might be weak and a little slower than usual, but I would have healed eventually."

Saeed brought her wrist to his mouth and kissed her where her pulse thrummed in a gentle rhythm. He breathed deeply of her intoxicating scent and let out his breath in a slow sigh. "Eventually." He let out a soft snort. So cavalier. "I thought you'd died." The admission was harder to make than he thought it would be. The memory of his fear twisted Saeed's gut and he forced the residual anxiety away. He reached up and threaded his fingers through her hair. Her beautiful, flame red hair that haunted his memories, his dreams, and his every waking minute. "I had no idea what to do. How to help you. I had no hope of reviving you. I bit into my wrist and gave you my blood."

Cerys reached up and her fingertips brushed her bottom lip. "I was curious what I tasted when I woke up." Her gaze searched Saeed's and not for the first time he was taken aback by the unabashed wonder in her expression. "I'm not sure vampire blood is a cure-all. At least, not for my problem." A gentle smile curved the bow of her lips. "But I appreciate the effort. It definitely gave me a nice little buzz." Her humorous tone faded into silence. "No one's ever done anything like that for me before."

Icy dread bathed Saeed from head to toe. He'd been so hopeful, so damned optimistic that his blood had somehow helped her. That he'd been able to somehow fortify her strength and reverse the effects of this horrible thing Rin insisted on continuing to put her through.

"You can't ever do that again." It wasn't a mandate that Saeed laid down this time. It was a plea. "You won't survive the next time."

"I know." Those two words were spoken with a solemn finality that caused Saeed's heart to race in his chest. "Rin will cut me some slack just like he always does. Until he comes across someone like Breanne again. Someone he can't afford to lose."

"It won't happen again, because I won't allow it." Saeed wanted Cerys to hear the finality in his tone. "You won't be under his thumb for much longer."

"I wish it was that simple," she said with a sad smile.

"It will be," Saeed assured her. "Because I won't accept it any other way."

Cerys shivered. Saeed reached behind them and pulled the down comforter from the bed to wrap it around her shoulders. She appeared so slight, so fragile, encased within the nest of the fluffy down blanket. Her vibrant red hair framed her face in a wild tangle of untamed curls.

"You always wear your hair this way." Saeed reached out to capture a curl between his fingers. "Why?"

Cerys shrugged. A blush painted her cheeks and she looked away for a nervous moment. "It bothers Rin." She cringed as though she didn't want Saeed to know the truth. "He's so damned fastidious. A place for everything, and everything in its place. It drives him absolutely nuts to see my hair like this. So I wear it this way every single day to show him that there are pieces of me he will never own and can never control."

Soon, nothing, no one would ever control Cerys again. Saeed would make sure of it.

"Do you think I'm petty?"

It mattered to her what Saeed thought. Honestly, she couldn't figure out what he saw in her all. She was a bitter, snarky, emotionally disconnected train wreck with a binge eating problem. Not exactly things that had most guys swiping right.

"I think you're a lot of things," Saeed said. "Petty is not one of them."

"Oh yeah?" Cerys looked away, unable to meet the intensity of his gaze. "Like what?"

Her heart pounded in her chest as she waited for Saeed's answer. They'd only known each other for a few weeks and their time together had been tumultuous at best. He claimed to know her through the memories he'd witnessed, but was that enough? And could the soulless truly ever feel anything?

"You are remarkable. Strong, fierce, powerful. Soft. Delicate, fragile, beautiful. Your eyes are striking. Bright like starlight. Sometimes when you look at me, I find myself helpless to look away even when I try. When you're near, I feel as though I can take a deep breath. You ground me."

Tears welled in Cerys's eyes and her chest constricted with emotion. Emotion she shouldn't have been able to feel. Saeed's presence in her life had brought with it a magic she'd never thought possible. Her soul was gone. She was empty. Void. And yet somehow, Saeed managed to make her feel full.

Being someone's anchor didn't equate to love, though. Rin needed her for her power. Saeed needed her for their supposed tether. She tried not to let bitterness leak in to drown out the warm, fuzzy sensation Saeed caused to bloom in her chest with his pretty words. But Cerys knew need. She understood need. What she craved was to be *wanted*. Not for what she could give to someone. She wanted to be a *choice*. Not a necessity. Or a convenience.

Saeed's voice cut through the silence. Silver rimmed his gaze, creating a soft glow that accentuated his features and made him look even fiercer. "I wasn't at first, but I'm grateful you were unable to tether me."

Cerys studied his dark features. He was the most breathtaking male she'd ever laid eyes on. "Why?"

Saeed's expression grew contemplative as though he searched for the perfect words. "I've never experienced it but through the Collective. But from what I've seen, it's an immediate bond. It creates a certain level of attraction though it doesn't create any sort of emotional connection. It's . . ." Saeed rubbed at his forehead. "The tether takes away choice. It is absolute. Unbreakable. When I saw you in the Collective, I knew you were meant for me. When I walked into Crimson and saw you there, I waited for the return of my soul with anticipation unlike anything I've ever felt. When you failed to tether me, it nearly crushed me. But then I learned your history and what had happened to you and it all made sense. The tether didn't force me to choose you, Cerys. It didn't convince me of what I already knew. I chose you without the tether. I would still choose you even if you never returned my soul to me."

Cerys hadn't cried in thousands of years. Not a single fucking tear. And since the night she'd met Saeed, she'd felt their annoying sting at her eyes more times than she could count. She'd cried like a child at the thought of losing him as she'd forced her blood down his throat. And she cried now, for the sake of the warmth that bloomed in her chest as he said such wonderful, heartfelt things to her now.

It was like he'd looked deep inside of her and knew exactly what she needed to hear. She leaned in and kissed him once. Slow. When she pulled away, niggling doubt scratched at the back of her mind. Saeed seemed to not be bothered by the notion of never being tethered now. But what about later, when the absence of his soul began to wear on him? And it would. Cerys knew all too well the toll it would take on him. He reached up and brushed the tears from her cheeks. What if he never managed to steal her soul from Rin? What if he remained here, tied to her of his own free will, for centuries or longer only to realize he'd made a mistake? What if he grew to resent her? To hate her? Cerys had survived a gods-damned lot over the course of her existence, but she knew she would never survive Saeed's hatred.

"You can't know that." She'd never felt so vulnerable. So very breakable as she did in this moment. "Your faith in the tether makes you think that you would choose me anyway."

"No." Saeed gave her a wan smile and a sad shake of his head. "It's the way you make me feel, right now, without my soul intact that makes me believe without a doubt that I would choose you."

"How do you feel?" Cerys whispered. She was fearful of the answer and yet, couldn't stop herself from asking the question.

Saeed gave her a sly smile. "You make me feel like I've eaten the best meal of my entire life."

Cerys's chest constricted as though the air was being pushed from her lungs. Warmth suffused her and left her flushed and a little shaken. Saeed had so easily put his feelings into terms he knew Cerys would understand. She made him feel full. It was the most heartfelt thing anyone had ever said to her. He made her feel full, too. Full to bursting.

"That part of you that's missing is nothing more than your spiritual essence, Cerys." Saeed's gaze searched hers as he cupped her face in his hands. "Rin didn't take away who you are. He didn't take away your ability to experience. To learn. To feel. The absence of your soul might have created a disconnect, but it never banished any of those things. You've gone too long in a state of numbness, and it's time to reclaim what you've lost."

Cerys came up on her knees and her arms went around Saeed's broad shoulders as she put her mouth to his. There were no words to convey the way she felt in this moment. He'd given her a gift more valuable than all the gold in the world tonight. More precious than any gem. More immense than all of the power Rin so greedily tried to possess.

She would choose Saeed as well. No matter the situation, no matter the circumstances, there was no doubt in her mind that she would choose him. Always.

CHAPTER
25

Saeed could think of nothing that could compare to the bliss of holding Cerys in his arms. Her mouth brushed against his, softly at first, before she leaned in and deepened the kiss. Slow. Sensual. Indulgent. Sweet and seductive. She kissed him with careful precision as though she wanted to remember every single detail in case it never happened again.

The sweetness of her mouth. The petal softness of her lips. The light graze of her teeth along his bottom lip and the way her tongue darted out to tease his brought Saeed's own desires to a fevered pitch that heated his blood and strung every tendon in his body taut. He wanted her with an intensity that he could barely control. Nothing outside of the walls of his bedroom mattered. Not his coven, not Rin, not Gregor or Breanne, and the complications that their many entanglements brought to their lives. Their souls might not have been tethered, but for the first time since he'd met her, Saeed felt as though their hearts might be.

Cerys's hands abandoned his shoulders. Her fingers danced along the back of his neck before they traveled upward to dive into his hair. Saeed had never known a more pleasurable experience than kissing Cerys. Decadent and wicked. Sweet and sinful. Their mouths moved with a synchronicity that served to reinforce everything Saeed believed about their relationship. He'd traveled the world. Lived many lives. Known friends, family, and lovers alike. But he'd never truly felt alive until the day he'd met her.

Saeed was no longer obsessed. This was something more. Something deeper. Cerys's lips parted and her tongue darted out at his bottom lip. He pulled her close as he kissed her, and his arms wrapped tight around her to cage her against him. The lush softness of her breasts pressed against his chest and his cock throbbed in time with the beat of his heart. Their first encounter had been far too brief, and his focus had been solely on her pleasure. Saeed craved the joining of their bodies like he craved her blood. Rin's curfew be damned. Cerys wasn't going anywhere for the rest of the night.

The heavy comforter fell away from around Cerys's shoulders. He reached behind her and grabbed the blanket, tossing it to the floor beside them. He shifted, pulling Cerys across his lap before settling her on top of the blanket. He could've lifted her up onto the mattress, but it would've wasted precious time. Saeed would've taken her in the middle of a field, on a dusty dirt road, the side of a snowbank. Hell, he would've taken her in the middle of the Sahara, grains of sand biting into his flesh, if he'd had to. The *where* didn't matter. The only thing he cared about was that Cerys was with him.

Her legs fell open and Saeed settled himself into the muscular cradle of her thighs. He marveled at her strength, such a juxtaposition to her petite frame and willowy build. Cerys was a warrior. A fighter. All fire and feisty determination. There wasn't a thing about her he'd change, from her snarky cynicism, to her voracious appetite, to the wild, unkempt tangles of her hair that were as much a part of her personality as her smile or laugh.

Saeed's hips rocked in time with the rhythm of their kisses. Even fully clothed, the intense rush of pleasure he experienced was almost too much to bear. He enjoyed the slow burn. The tease of everything he brushed against while being denied the luxury of bare skin. Cerys's hips rolled up to meet his and the tempo of her breathing changed from slow, easy sighs to desperate gasps of breath between kisses. Her hands moved down his torso to grip the hem of his shirt. She tugged it up the length of his body and when she met with resistance, let out a frustrated whimper.

Saeed broke their kiss and pushed himself up to his knees as he crossed his arms in front of him and stripped off his shirt. Cerys's appreciative gaze roamed over his bare torso, sending a rush of pleasant warmth from the pit of his gut outward. Cerys followed suit, stripping off her shirt, and then her bra. The perfection of her breasts had no equal. And Saeed planned to spend a good long while admiring the tender flesh, soft swells, and pearled nipples with his hands, fingers, and mouth.

"Since you're up, you might as well kill two birds with one stone," Cerys suggested with a seductive smile that nearly stole the breath from his lungs. "I can't think of anything you're going to need those pants for tonight."

Gods, the way she spoke. Throughout the centuries, Saeed had always remained so formal. He'd always felt silly trying to blend in when he knew he never would. Cerys on the other hand had seemed to dive headfirst into the modern world. One of many things he loved about her.

Saeed was more than ready to feel the warmth of her naked skin on his. He reached for the button of his jeans and paused before cocking a challenging brow. "You first."

Cerys's low, husky laughter sent a lick of heat down Saeed's spine. "*So* not fair. You've already seen me naked once."

"True. And I have to say it was a breathtakingly beautiful sight."

Cerys looked away, embarrassed. She was reluctant to accept even the most innocent compliment. Sayed vowed that he would shower her with compliments until she got tired of hearing them. "I don't know about all of that," she groused. "But it's still not fair if you get me naked two full times before I even get to see you naked once."

Saeed chuckled. From tonight on, he planned to seize every opportunity possible to see Cerys without her clothes. "I can guarantee you, the sight of me without my clothes isn't half as impressive."

Cerys pursed her lips. "M-hm." Her skeptical tone told him exactly what she thought about his modest claim. "The top half is pretty damned impressive. Now, why don't you lose the pants and let me decide on the bottom half?"

The heat in her gaze rivaled that of the California sun that used to shine down on him. Saeed had no need to miss the beauty of a Los Angeles summer day when he had Cerys. The sun had nothing on her brilliance.

Saeed stood. No way would he let the first time Cerys saw him get undressed be an awkward shucking of his pants while still on his knees. His ego demanded he give her a show worthy of her admiration. He held Cerys's gaze as he kicked off his shoes and socks and unbuttoned his jeans. Her mouth parted on a breath as he pulled the zipper down and slid his hands inside the waistband.

"Has anyone ever told you, you're sort of a tease?"

Cerys's breathy tone ignited his lust just as effectively as a caress. "Never." No one had ever accused Saeed of being playful. Not even Sasha, the one soul in the world he'd been closest to. Everyone in his life had always regarded Saeed as stern, serious, all-business. Cerys made him want to let down his guard. To be playful for a change.

"Well, you are." Her grin became even brighter. "And what's worse? I think you like it."

She was teasing him. Gods, her playfulness drove him wild. It made him want to keep the banter between them going, draw it out until they'd enticed each other to the point that they had no choice but to tear their clothes off and sate their lusts.

"Do you like it?" That was the only thing that mattered to him.

She gave him a coy smile. "Maybe."

Saeed wanted more of this. More teasing, more talking, more playfulness, more kissing, more touching, or exploring, just . . . *more*. They weren't afforded the luxury of time. The freedom to simply be together. All they had were stolen moments, and Saeed had no choice but to make the most out of each and every one.

He was *killing* her! Cerys wondered if Saeed had any idea how truly magnificent he was. He'd only taken his shirt off and worked the zipper down on his jeans and already Cerys thought she might spontaneously combust. She propped herself up on her elbows as her gaze roamed freely over each inch of exposed skin, taking in every hill and valley of muscle that sculpted his chest. Her eyes moved downward along his lean torso to the ridges of his abs and lower still to the deep V that cut into either side of his hips, promising an even more impressive sight once he managed to get his damned pants off.

She liked this side of Saeed. Relaxed. His guard down. Even a little playful. His dark eyes sparked with mischief as he bestowed on her a dazzling smile. He was so beautiful she found it almost difficult to look at him. A sly smile curved one corner of her mouth as she let her fingers trail between her breasts, down the length of her stomach, to settle at the waistband of her pants. "The faster you take off your pants, the faster I take off mine."

Bright silver flashed in his dark eyes. A smug sense of satisfaction traveled through her in a pleasant rush that settled between Cerys's thighs in a deep thrum. She loved that she could get to him with something as simple as a look or a suggestive sentence. Saeed's hands moved slowly, dipping further into his jeans as he swept them over the curve of his ass and down his powerful thighs. His underwear came off with the denim and when he straightened, Cerys blew out a sharp, appreciative breath.

Wow.

A master sculptor couldn't have created a better representation of masculine perfection. Cerys's jaw went slack and for a long moment, all she could do was stare. His lean build didn't sport an ounce of fat. Saeed's body was a mosaic of angles and curves that came together to form a work of art. Cerys committed every detail to memory, from his broad shoulders, to the taper of his waist, to the crisp trail of black hair and his erection that jutted out proudly from his hips. She forced her gaze lower, to his strong thighs, his calves, even his bare feet.

"I've upheld my end of the bargain."

"You certainly have and then some." Cerys didn't waste any more time getting undressed. She rested her back on the floor and thrust her hips into the air as she shimmied out of her leggings. They came off in a whisper of fabric and landed, along with her underwear, somewhere near the foot of Saeed's bed. She flashed him what she hoped was her most seductive smile. "Done and done."

Saeed responded with a low chuckle that coaxed goosebumps to the surface of Cerys's skin. He dropped slowly to his knees and Cerys marveled at the play of individual muscles showcased in the execution of the simple act. His hands met the floor next, and he kept his gaze locked with hers as he crawled up the length of her body. He'd never seemed more like a predator in that moment and Cerys had never felt so much like prey. As though her body had no choice in the matter, her legs fell open. Saeed lowered himself on top of her and the skin to skin contact brought with it another rush of delicious heat through Cerys's veins.

"I want to lie like this for hours." Saeed's breath was warm in her ear as he spoke. "Every inch of our bodies touching."

She knew exactly how he felt. Cerys could stay like this until the sun rose, whispering in the dark, caressing, exploring each other's bodies. Tonight had been an awakening. A realization of everything she'd fought to gain for so long. She wanted to exist in this moment for a while longer. Indulge in the luxury of Saeed's presence.

"Me too." Her voice was small as she made the admission. Embarrassed. "We could, you know. Just lie here. Cuddle."

"Mmm." The hum of his rich voice rippled over her and Cerys shivered. "In truth, it would take an act of will far greater than I possess to lie here with you and not make love to you."

Cerys sucked in a sharp breath and held it. *Make love?* That feeling of fullness—like she'd just scarfed down an entire cheesecake by herself—returned and she took a moment to breathe through the intensity of sensation.

"I know what you mean." Cerys's hands wandered over Saeed's shoulders, down the length of his lean, muscular back as her fingers dipped into the groove cut by his spine. She ventured lower and her fingertips brushed the swell of his ass, eliciting a low groan from Saeed. "I'm getting a little antsy myself."

Saeed lowered himself to her and kissed her. No longer soft or tentative, he put his mouth to hers with intent. Cerys's lips parted as she invited him to deepen the kiss. Their tongues met and parted in a sensual rhythm that bordered on lewd. Heat swamped Cerys's body, her lower abdomen tightened, urgency rose up within her like a tide, and her clit throbbed with every wild beat of her heart.

She broke their kiss as she eased Saeed onto his back and straddled his hips. Saeed sucked in a breath as she rolled her hips and slid her pussy along his shaft. His arms shot out and his hands gripped her hips as his body went rigid.

Cerys smiled. "Do you like that?" The last time they'd been together, Saeed had focused solely on Cerys's pleasure. She wanted to return the favor.

It was a serious boost to her ego that Saeed seemed unable to get his mouth to make words for a couple of seconds. His hungry gaze devoured her as his fingertips dug into her hips. He guided her motion and she slid down his length again, eliciting a low growl.

"Gods, Cerys." Saeed shuddered beneath her. "That feels amazing."

Strange, but there was something infinitely more intimate about what they were doing right now than actual sex. There was a vulnerability to the way their gazes locked, the way Saeed held onto her and the way Cerys let the silky wet flesh of her pussy stroke his length. She continued to give slow, sensual rolls of her hips and she let out a low moan as her own pleasure began to build. She bent over him and put her mouth to Saeed's chest, his shoulder, his throat. Her hips found a rhythm that had them both panting and she continued her exploration with her mouth as she took one earlobe between her teeth and sucked.

"I need to be inside you." Saeed's voice was a desperate

rasp in her ear. "You've brought me to the edge of my control."

Oh really? Cerys wondered what it would be like to see someone as stiff and disciplined as Saeed let loose a little. She propped herself up on his chest as she changed up her routine. Instead of rocking her hips, she moved them in little circles. Saeed's grip on her hips tightened and she lowered herself once again until her mouth hovered above his.

"Do you want to fuck me, Saeed?"

Saeed groaned as he thrust his hips. He hesitated a beat before he responded. "Yes."

"Then tell me."

Saeed let out another frustrated groan as he slid his cock against her. She wanted his inhibitions gone. Wanted him wild and focused only on the moment and their pleasure.

"Tell me, Saeed." She'd beg if she had to. He wasn't the only one who couldn't wait much longer. But she wasn't going to let him get away with holding back, either.

"I want to fuck you."

Gods, yes. Hearing those heated words in his dark, smoky tone gave Cerys a rush. "Say it again." She couldn't get enough.

Saeed thrust up hard and another moan accompanied the intense sensation as the glide of his cock against her clit worked her into a state of wild abandon. She bent over him to change the angle and pressure, and his head came up from the floor as Saeed took her nipple into his mouth. A new layer of sensation exploded through her as his teeth grazed the sensitive flesh. He was tentative, much too gentle with her. Cerys gripped the back of his neck and held him against her. Her quick breaths became desperate gasps. Chills broke out on her skin and at the same time she was flushed with intense heat.

"Bite me, Saeed."

His fangs broke the skin. Cerys's head rolled back on her shoulders. Her hips bucked as she continued to slide her clit over his shaft. The sensation intensified, gathering and building until Cerys could no longer contain it. She cried out as the orgasm swept her up, rolling through her in powerful waves that caused her limbs to quake and her heart to race in her chest. Saeed continued to draw her breast into his mouth, sucking as she rode out her pleasure. His tongue flicked out to seal the punctures as her cries died to ragged breaths. Dear gods. She'd never felt anything like that in her entire existence. She didn't know how Saeed would ever top that . . .

Without preamble, he caught her in his arms and rolled her over onto her back. A low growl worked its way up his throat and she looked up to find his gaze alight with brilliant silver. He entered her in a single, forceful thrust that stole Cerys's breath and made her feel deliciously full. His mouth brushed the outer shell of her ear as he whispered raggedly, "I need to fuck you."

He'd officially just outdone himself.

CHAPTER
26

Saeed's control had been obliterated the moment his fangs pierced Cerys's skin. The sensation of her pussy gliding over his shaft, the softness of her bare skin, her scent, and then, her taste as her blood flowed over his tongue, drove him past reason. He'd become a single-minded beast whose focus centered on finding a way to banish the desperate ache that ate away at him and fill the hollow space that consumed him.

He thrust home and a sense of such intense relief washed over him that it took him a moment to gain his bearings. The sensory overload was almost more than he could handle and the way Cerys's pussy encased his shaft caused a shiver to race from the top of Saeed's spine to the backs of his heels.

"You feel so good, I can barely breathe."

Not that he needed to, but it was the truth. The impact of this moment left him stunned. He'd known with so much certainty that Cerys was meant for him and yet he'd never felt the all-consuming impact of that truth until now. He wanted her with a ferocity that was unlike anything he'd ever felt. Saeed respected order. Self-control. He'd always been calm, unflappable, and self-possessed. But since the moment of his turning, he'd become a creature ruled by instinct and need. The Collective had ruled him for so long, but now it was Cerys who held sway over him. She was the center of his universe.

Cerys hooked her ankles over his thighs and thrust her hips. Saeed sucked in a sharp breath and moved against her, pressing into her as deeply as he could go. She answered with an indulgent moan that sent a tingle over his skin and tightened his sac. She was exquisite. Without equal.

Mine.

Tethered or not, Cerys belonged to him.

"Fuck me, Saeed." Her brazen words reignited his lust. "I want you hard and deep."

He moved against her, slowly at first. It was a sweet torture to force himself to enjoy her body and not simply sate his lust. He pulled out to the tip and dove back in, a slow glide that elicited another delicious moan from Cerys. He loved her passion. Her fire. Her unabashed nature.

He adopted an easy pace, determined to fuck her so thoroughly that she'd never think of another male save him. Cerys's back arched with every deep thrust and her low moans quickly transformed into tight whimpers and desperate cries. She gripped his shoulders, her nails digging into his skin, and Saeed welcomed the gentle bite of pain.

Saeed propped himself up on an arm. He stared into Cerys's eyes, held her gaze and took in her blissful expression with every measured thrust he delivered. Her tongue flicked out at her lips and Saeed couldn't resist but to put his mouth to hers and capture a bit of that sweetness on his tongue. His fangs nicked her and the taste of her blood encouraged him to bite down again, harder. She moaned into his mouth as he sucked at her bottom lip, closing the punctures as quickly as he'd opened them.

Cerys's back arched as she ground her hips into Saeed. He sensed her urgency in every roll of her hips, every tight breath, and her grip on his shoulders as she pulled her body as close to his as she could get it. "More, Saeed." Her desperate plea shot through him like lightning. "I'm so close."

Pride surged in Saeed's chest that he could please her. He fucked her hard and deep, his pace measured but not too slow. Cerys's breath hitched and her body went taut. Saeed took in the sight of her, cheeks flushed, eyes wide, full lips parted with her breath. The natural luster of her skin sparkled in the darkness and only lent to her ethereal aura. She was a goddess. Perfect. Exquisite in her passion. And she was his.

"Oh gods, Saeed!"

Cerys threw her head back as she let out a desperate cry. Each powerful contraction of her sex squeezed Saeed's cock until he didn't think he could take another second of the intense sensation. A rush of wet warmth bathed his shaft and Saeed drove faster, deeper, until his sac grew tight and his thighs shook from the effort. He toppled over the edge a moment after her. He let out a horse shout as he pumped unmercifully into her, riding out his own pleasure as wave after powerful wave crashed over him.

"Mine." The word left his mouth without any thought as to how it might sound. He collapsed on top of Cerys, his own breath racing in his chest as he rested his lips against the outer shell of her ear. "You are mine."

"Yes." Her voice was thick with emotion. "I'm yours, Saeed." She drew in a shuddering breath that made Saeed's own chest ache. "I'm yours."

They were both lost. Both hollow. Both coping as best they could with being incomplete. But in the quiet dark of

Saeed's bedroom, his body resting on hers, the only sound their mingling breaths, he felt whole. It was the closest thing to love Saeed had ever known.

Would he need his soul returned to know for sure?

He pushed those troubling thoughts to the back of his mind. He refused to let doubt or worry ruin the moment. Instead, he focused on Cerys. The softness of her skin against his, the rise and fall of her chest, the sensation of her fingertips as they glided down his spine. Saeed braced his palm on the floor to push himself up and Cerys grabbed onto his arm to stop him.

"Don't." Her voice was little more than a whisper. "Just stay like you are for a while."

Saeed settled back down on top of her and cradled the back of her neck in his palm. "I'm not hurting you?"

"No." Her head came up from the floor as she placed a gentle kiss on his shoulder. "I want to feel your weight against me."

She was so slight compared to his bulk. Despite the comfort he felt, Saeed worried that he would hurt her. He indulged her for several moments before shifting to his side. He wrapped his arms around her, keeping her body close to his as he rolled. He might not have wanted to hurt her, but Saeed still craved the skin on skin contact.

"You have no idea how bad I needed that."

Saeed gave a low chuckle. "I know better than you think." He'd needed it just as badly. "And I'm not even close to sated."

Cerys's fingers teased the strands of his hair that brushed his neck. Saeed let out a slow sigh as he put his lips to her forehead. "Not even close?" He loved her teasing tone. "You must not want me to be able to walk out of here on my own steam."

The thought of shutting themselves away in the bedroom and fucking until neither of them could move only served to reignite Saeed's desire. He reached up and brushed her untamed hair from her face. "The sun will soon be up." A fact he wished he could change. "And I'll have no choice but to sleep."

"What's it like?"

He'd never had to explain the phenomenon of daylight sleep to anyone. "It's not as traumatic as you might think." Saeed knew from glimpses into the Collective that the pull of sleep was different for each vampire. "As the sun rises, I feel an immense sense of exhaustion. Weariness steals over me, my limbs become heavy, and I am relaxed."

"I guess that doesn't sound too bad." Cerys's fingers wandered from his hairline down the back of his neck and across his shoulder. Pleasant chills broke out on Saeed's skin and he drew in a slow breath. "I sort of wish I could feel like that at the end of my day."

"You don't?"

Cerys let out a soft snort. "Hardly." Saeed pulled away to look at her and found her expression so full of sadness that it twisted his gut. "I'm always too wound up to sleep. My brain won't slow down enough for me to relax."

"What do you think about?" Saeed wanted to know every thought she'd ever had. Craved that intimacy with her.

"I think a better question is what don't I think about?" Cerys averted her gaze and let out a slow breath. "Thousands of years of soulless servitude gives a girl a lot to contemplate."

Saeed didn't press her for more. Instead, he gave her a moment with her thoughts.

"Being with you sort of grounds me though," Cerys said as though the admission were tough to make. "I'm not as tense, not as worried, and I don't feel like I have to eat every five seconds."

Two simple sentences spoke volumes. Once again,

Saeed felt a sense of pride that he could offer her some kind of comfort no matter how small. "You should sleep." As much as he wanted to spend the few precious hours they had together in deep conversation, touching, kissing, sucking, Saeed knew the greatest gift he could give her was rest. There would be many more nights spent together. He believed that with his entire being. Once he freed her soul and took her away from Rin once and for all, they could talk, touch, and kiss without worry for as long as they wanted. "I know you're tired." She'd almost died tonight depleting her energy for Rin's foolish greed. Saeed had been no better in his own greed for her body. "Sleep."

"It's past my curfew." Her rueful laughter filled his ears. "How pathetic does that sound? Like I'm a teenager out past her bedtime."

"Rin enslaved you." Anger rose from the pit of his stomach to choke the air from Saeed's lungs. "That's not pathetic, it is an injustice."

"Either way, it sucks."

It certainly did. And Saeed wasn't going to let it continue for a moment longer. "I don't want you to worry about Rin, or anything else tonight. Sleep in my arms, and let me watch over you."

Saeed's offer was tempting. Too tempting. Already Cerys's lids tugged downward, heavy with fatigue. It felt so good to simply lay here in his arms. Feel the comfort of his presence. The protection of his strength.

"If I don't go back, he'll kill us both." Her words lacked conviction and they ran together in a lazy string.

"I think we both know you're much too valuable to him for him to ever consider harming you.

Cerys gave a sleepy laugh. "Maybe. Maybe not. That doesn't mean he won't go after you, though."

Saeed offered up an unconcerned shrug. "He can try to hurt me. He won't be successful, but he can try."

So arrogant. Cerys's lips curved into a smile. "I should go."

"Stay." Saeed's lips found her temple. He kissed her there, down along her jaw line, to the corner of her mouth. "Please."

His arms held her tighter and Cerys had never felt so at ease, so cared for, so sheltered. She didn't want to leave. She was right where she belonged. "Maybe for a few minutes." What could an hour hurt? Rin usually gave her a little leeway when she had a difficult job to do. She couldn't bring herself to move even an inch. Not when it felt so amazing to have Saeed's arms around her.

His contented sigh settled over her like a warm blanket. She was still pretty wiped out from everything that had happened tonight. A few more minutes of rest was exactly what she needed.

"Tell me more about your coven." She loved the soothing quality of Saeed's deep voice. She looked for any excuse for him to speak to her. "How did you become the coven master?"

A space of silence passed. Cerys settled into Saeed's embrace and rested her head against his strong shoulder. She could lie like this forever. The thought of leaving after even a few minutes caused her stomach to tie into an anxious knot.

"I became coven master out of necessity. Not because I had any grandiose plans to amass power." His fingers stroked idly through her hair and Cerys let out a slow sigh. "So many of us were thrown to the wind after the slayers attempted their genocide. We were scattered, directionless, hopeless, and desperate. It was obvious that there was at least one vampire still alive. Otherwise we would've all starved. Mikhail was hidden from us for nearly a century and there were few dhampirs with the fortitude necessary to regroup and protect those of us who were left."

Cerys could only imagine the trauma they must have experienced. Rin had made it a point to keep the company of vampires throughout the years. She had no idea why other than the fact he found them fascinating. But when the berserkers unleashed their fury on the vampires, Rin had made sure to sever all contact. He'd turned his back on those he'd befriended, more concerned with saving his own neck than saving an entire race from extinction.

"At one point vampires populated the world." The lulling quality of Saeed's voice relaxed Cerys much like slipping into a tub of warm water. Her eyelids grew heavier as her breathing became more even. "As our numbers dwindled, so did our territories. The slayers effectively corralled us through our need to draw from each other's strength."

Cerys could see how others would look to Saeed for leadership. He exuded strength and confidence. "I'm sure there are many dhampirs who thought you were a natural choice to lead."

Saeed's gentle laughter rumbled in his chest. "I don't know about that. I merely did what I thought was right and helped to steer us when we had no direction."

One of the things Cerys admired about Saeed was his sense of honor. She'd lived so long in Rin's company, a male who had none. Saeed reminded her there were those in this world who were better than their selfish machinations. Her fingertips stroked from his bare torso up and over the swell of one pec, and across his collarbone. "I'm sure those under your care love you all the more for accepting leadership."

"Perhaps at one time." The sadness in his voice speared through her chest. "I abandoned them when they needed me most."

"Because of me." Guilt welled hot and thick in Cerys's throat. It was selfish of her to want to be here with him in this moment when his coven needed him.

"No." He squeezed her tight against him. "Because I could not remain there while I was incomplete. Because I could no longer lead them when my mind refused to leave the Collective. Because the absence of my soul weighed heavily on me and I knew that its return relied on action."

He'd left his coven with such faith in his success and Cerys feared that once he realized he would never free her soul from Rin's captivity, it would break him. "Saeed." Cerys's heart ached as she forced the words past her lips. "Rin will *never* let me go." The faster he acknowledged that truth, the sooner he could return to those who needed him.

Saeed stroked an idle finger over the swell of her shoulder and Cerys shivered. "Rin has no choice in the matter."

Gods, his confidence. It almost made Cerys believe. "I've belonged to him for so long I can't remember what freedom feels like." Saeed had given her a small taste of what her life could be like without Rin. She couldn't let herself become hopeful. Because Cerys knew their dreams would shatter and, like Saeed, it would ruin her.

"Cerys, I promise—"

"Don't." Cerys put her fingertips to his lips. She couldn't bear to hear him promise her anything. Not when he believed so adamantly in his success while she doubted it so wholeheartedly. It wasn't that she didn't have faith in him. On the contrary, Cerys believed Saeed could move mountains if he put his mind to it. But she also knew Rin would rather kill her himself than allow her to belong to anyone else. "Just let me lie here next to you. Let me feel your arms around me while I rest." She really was exhausted. If she didn't get a little bit of sleep, she wouldn't make it back to Rin's on her own steam.

Her fingers fell away from Saeed's lips. She let out a slow, measured breath and with its release, her body relaxed against him. The thought of forever with Saeed made her feel full to bursting. But the reality was that the only forever they would ever have would be encompassed in minutes rather than centuries.

"Why were you angry at the world? When you were an assassin during the Crusades. What happened to you that made you want to take vengeance on those you hunted?" She'd wanted to know why since the night he'd mentioned it and Cery knew she'd never get another chance to hear the story. Tonight was their forever, and as soon as she could walk out of here on her own two feet, it would come to an end. Tears pricked once again at Cerys's eyes but she refused to let them fall. She refused to taint the beautiful gift of freedom, no matter how fleeting, Saeed had given her with even an ounce of sadness.

"I was angry at humanity." Cerys wondered at his reluctant tone as though he was embarrassed to admit it. "For their religious wars, their prejudices, their secrets and lies. As though the gods care about such petty squabbles." Saeed's words faded to silence. "I was tired of the constant invasions, those who encroached on our peace. Our coven master cared not for the affairs of humans and said we should allow them to annihilate each other, but I couldn't stand by and watch as so many were slaughtered under the guise of a religious crusade. Wars are always about two things: power and greed. I can tolerate neither. And so, I became an assassin and did what I could to send those who didn't belong from the land that I loved because I longed to restore some sort of peace.

"In the end, nothing I did mattered. The course of fate will not be stopped. The Sortiari proved that point several centuries later when they waged war on us. And yet again, I was forced to stand by and watch the slaughter of innocents. Which is why I became a coven master my-self. I wanted to protect those who were left."

Cerys's heart pounded in her chest. He was the most admirable male she'd ever known. She made a vow to her-self in the quiet aftermath of Saeed's story: No matter what happened, she'd do whatever she could to make sure he got back to his coven. Where he belonged.

"I wish I had my soul, Saeed." Cerys fell closer to sleep and she wasn't afraid to say the words out loud. "Because if I did, I think I would love you."

CHAPTER
27

"So, how's everything going?"

Sasha smiled pleasantly at Bria Fairchild. Jenner's mate seemed so delicate, yet outgoing, in contrast to his bulk and quiet intimidation. It made Sasha wonder at the compatibility of each individual tethering. Would she and her mate possess similar qualities or would they be polar opposites like Jenner and Bria?

"We're all fine." Sasha was pretty sure Bria wasn't interested in such a generic answer but that's all she was going to get. "So far there haven't been any hiccups."

Bria gave her a pleasant smile. She acted as a liaison between Mikhail and the thirteen covens. Sort of a social worker, or more to the point, vampire community outreach representative. It was a good idea, in theory. Bria was pleasant and seemed genuinely concerned with everyone's well-being. Sasha liked her. She just wished she was better at showing it. Really, it was Diego who should have been meeting with Bria today. He was the more personable of the two of them and he smiled a hell of a lot more than she did.

"That's good." Bria's reassuring smile was genuine and not rehearsed, which made Sasha feel even worse about her own stoic attitude. "But I'm more concerned with how *you're* doing."

Ugh. Sasha wasn't sure she could adequately convey how much she did *not* want to talk about herself. The most annoying thing about having a conversation with another supernatural being was the fact that you had no choice but to be honest. Or at the very least, find a way to circumvent honesty. If she told Bria she was fine, she'd smell the lie in an instant. Likewise, Sasha wasn't interested in pouring her heart out to someone who was little more than an acquaintance. No matter how nice she might be.

Sasha shrugged. "I'm newly turned, soulless, left to co-rule a coven and turn one of our members while managing my thirst, the Collective, and my own gods-damned emptiness. I'm peachy-freaking-keen."

Bria laughed. "Sounds like it."

Sasha cringed. Her delivery might've been harsh, but it was the truth. What more was there for her to do but to suck it up and do what had to be done? "Is Mikhail unhappy with the way things are being run here?" If that's what this visit today was about, she'd rather they got right down to business.

"Of course not." Bria reached for the glass of water on the end table and took a sip. "I'm not here to spy on you, or check on your coven, or even to report back to Mikhail. None of us knows how to navigate this, Sasha. I'm here to make sure you know that you're not alone. You have help if you need it, and I'm here to listen whenever you want."

If there was one thing Sasha could use, it was a friend. Saeed had been her friend and confidant for centuries and he'd left her as though that relationship had meant nothing to him. "Thank you." Sasha truly was appreciative of

Bria's offer. "I'm fine, though." Just because Sasha appreciated the offer, didn't mean she was ready to take Bria up on it.

"I was thinking . . ." Sasha did *not* like the sound of this. "That I might ask my friend Lucas to stop by."

Nope. She definitely didn't like the sound of this. "Oh, well . . . that's totally not necessary, Bria. Like I said, we're fine. I'm fine. Everything's fine." *Gods, Sasha! Could you have found a way to fit one more "fine" into that sentence?* She wanted to bang her head against the coffee table. Nothing screamed "I'm not fine!" like insisting you were fine.

"Oh, I know." Bria smiled brightly. "It's just that the covens have been separated for so long. With so few of us, it seems like a good idea for us to mingle more, don't you think?"

Again, a task better suited for Diego. Sasha was certain she didn't come across as personable, which made her wonder why in the world Bria would encourage the socialization? "Planning a vampire mixer?"

Bria laughed. "Lucas belongs to Chelle Daly's coven. They recently moved in with Chelle's mate in Pasadena. As the covens begin to spread out, I think it's important to remain connected in some way. Chelle's mate is a werewolf and they live with the pack. Lucas is untethered and I imagine a little lonely at times. I just thought he could use the company."

Interesting. Sasha had heard rumors about Chelle. That the circumstances of her transition had been unique, and somehow she'd managed to break from Mikhail's bloodline. The whole situation was steeped in mystery. Sasha's curiosity almost had her wanting to meet Lucas, if only to get a little dirt. Almost.

"I'm sure he wouldn't want to drive all the way out here from Pasadena."

Bria's mouth formed a pucker. "Has anyone ever told you that you're very stubborn?"

Diego called her stubborn almost on a daily basis. "I'm just not sure I'm ready to start sharing my feelings."

One delicate brow arched over Bria's eye. "Who said anything about sharing feelings? I just suggested Lucas should come over to chat."

Of course that's how it would start. An innocent visit. Hang out. Chew the fat. Share stories, experiences. Forge a relationship that would encourage Sasha to let down her guard and open up. Bria might be all wide-eyed innocence and good intentions, but she was obviously a calculating female. Definitely someone Sasha could like.

"All right. Feel free to send him over." Sasha was fairly certain that even if she told Bria to go to hell, Lucas would show up at her front door anyway. "I'll host a vampire party if you want me to."

Bria hid her amusement behind her water glass and she took another sip. "Let's not get too ahead of ourselves. I'll just throw out the invitation to Lucas and we'll go from there."

Why did it feel like she was being set up on a blind date? "Just so you know, matchmaking services don't work so well for our kind."

Bria responded with a solemn nod. "Don't I know it. I'm not trying to find you a mate, Sasha. I just want you to remember that it's okay to have a little fun."

Bria's words impacted her. For months, she'd moped around the house, mourning the loss of something she'd never really had. She'd allowed Diego to keep her fed and only left the confines of the coven when Mikhail summoned her. This was no existence. It was self-inflicted torture. Sasha brought her gaze up to Bria's and smiled. "Thank you, Bria. I'm glad you came by today."

"Me too. I'm always around if you need me."

"I'll remember that."

Bria rose from her chair and Sasha followed suit. They walked together to the front door and paused in the foyer.

"Call me anytime."

Sasha opened the door. "I will. And tell your friend Lucas he's more than welcome to stop by."

Bria gave a wave in parting and Sasha closed the door behind her. She refused to continue on this morose path. Saeed hadn't thought twice about leaving her. Hadn't even so much as considered the pain his absence would cause, because he didn't love her. At least, not in the way she wanted him to. Life was meant to be lived, and Sasha had spent far too much of hers pining over a male who saw her only as a friend. Well, no longer. She sure as hell wasn't dead, and it was about damned time she started acting like it.

Sasha straightened the silky tunic blouse over her skinny jeans. That she felt out of place and nervous only helped to reinforce she'd lived like a pathetic homebody for far too long. She wondered if she looked like she felt. As though she didn't belong.

Didn't a night out on the town require some sort of wingman? She supposed she should've asked Diego to come out with her tonight, but that sort of defeated the purpose of her new independent outlook. She'd never find the courage to finally go out and live her life if she constantly hid behind the protection of the familiar and comfortable. She was a vampire now. Strong. Fierce. Fearsome. She was not without power. She had no reason to hide. Or sit at home and pout.

"You going inside, or what?"

Sasha looked up, up, *up* until she met the gaze of the male who spoke to her in a deep, gravelly voice. She wasn't adept at identifying the different supernatural factions on sight. His scent was rather musky, which made her think he must've been some sort of shifter. He was certainly far too bulky and muscular to be fae. Sasha squared her shoulders and bucked her chin up a notch. It shouldn't have been such a big deal to walk inside the club. But once she crossed the threshold, there was no turning back. She was tired of being the cautious one, the responsible one, the capable negotiator and diplomat. She wanted to be fun. Wild. Reckless and irresponsible. But most of all, she wanted to be free of her attachment to Saeed. Free of the heartache that plagued her even in soullessness.

"I'm going inside." Now that the words were spoken, she couldn't take them back. Right?

The male smirked as he swept his arm in invitation. "Go on, then. You're holding up the line . . ." He paused as he studied her and his eyes went wide. "Vampire."

Sasha cast an anxious glance over her shoulder to find that there was indeed a line forming behind her. Crap. She didn't waste another second and kicked her butt into gear as she hightailed it into the club. With only a handful of vampires in existence, their presence had a tendency to cause a stir. She'd meant tonight to be a low key trial run. So far, all she'd managed to do was draw attention to herself. Great.

She figured her best option was to start at the bar. It seemed to be the place where everyone gathered, and she didn't think anyone would pay any mind to the fact that she was by herself. Her fingers wandered down the front of her shirt as she once again straightened it. She didn't know why she was so gods-damned nervous. It's not like she was about to walk into the sun, she was in a nightclub for crying out loud. She settled into one of the high stools and rested her arms on the bar.

"What can I get you?"

She had no idea. She was such an inexperienced club-

goer that she couldn't even order a simple drink. Sasha
gave the bartender, a delicately beautiful sylph—at least
that's what she thought she was—what she hoped was
a confident smile. "Oh." She flicked her wrist. "Surprise me."

The sylph studied her for a beat too long. Sasha
squirmed under the intense scrutiny as she realized her
smile had no doubt showcased the points of the dual sets
of her fangs. She waited for the inevitable moment when
the female would realize what she was and make a scene
like the male at the door. The breath stalled in her chest
and she broke out into a sweat. She shouldn't have come
out tonight. She should've just stayed home.

"You look like a lemon drop sort of girl to me," the
sylph said after a moment. Sasha let out a slow breath of
relief as the tension melted from her body. "I'll get that for
you in two shakes."

Thank the gods. At least someone knew the meaning
of discretion. Sasha forced herself to calm the hell down
as she turned on the barstool to take a look around. Vibrant
dance music filled the air, and the heavy bass reverber-
ated in her chest. All around her was activity. Dancing.
Laughing. Talking. Engaging. The energy was conta-
gious and made her feel lighter and less troubled. If she'd
known clubbing would be good stress relief, she would've
done it a long damned time ago.

"Here you go, hon. Enjoy."

Sasha turned and took the delicate martini glass from
the bartender. "How much do I owe you?"

The sylph dismissed her with a wave of her hand. "This
one's on the house. If you feel like running a tab, let me
know."

"Thanks."

Sasha sipped from the glass. The sugar on the rim
helped to temper the tartness of the cocktail as it hit the

back of her tongue, but she still experienced a slight involuntary shudder.

"Sort of a frou-frou drink for such a fierce-looking female."

Sasha smiled over the rim of the glass, remembering how charming it had looked when Bria did it. Then again, Bria had that whole soft, beautiful innocence thing going for her. Sasha never looked anything but severe. She forced herself to make eye contact with the male who spoke to her when what she really wanted to do was turn and put her back to him.

Nope. That wasn't going to work. Not anymore. She couldn't simply turn her back on life.

"Is it?" She smiled wider as she infused her voice with bravado. "What would you suggest I drink?"

She studied the male who took a confident step toward her. Not a shifter. Not a werewolf. Her skin tingled with residual magic. Not fae. At least, she didn't think so. Gods, she wished her senses were keener. He might have been a warlock or a mage. That would explain the static that sparked along her arms.

He grinned. "Fireball."

He wasn't bad looking and Sasha figured that was all that mattered. "Sounds dangerous."

"It can be. But I think you can handle it." He held out his hand. "I'm Simon."

She reached out and shook it. "Sasha."

"Sasha." He let her name roll off his tongue like a slow sigh. "You looking for a little company tonight?"

Was she? Her plan had been to get out of the house and mingle a little. She hadn't really planned on hooking up. Then again, what was that old adage? The best way to get over someone was to get under someone else? Of course, she'd never been over, under, or anything else with Saeed.

Maybe that was the problem. She'd spent too many centuries hopelessly in love and admiring him from afar.

"Sure." Sasha held out an inviting hand toward the empty stool beside her.

Simon settled onto the stool. He motioned for the bartender. "Can I get two shots of Fireball when you get a sec?"

The sylph grabbed two tiny glasses from under the bar and Sasha watched as she poured two shots of the cinnamon flavored whiskey. She wondered if it would be sweeter than the lemon drop. She'd never been much of a drinker.

Simon slid one of the glasses in front of her. "Cheers."

Sasha brought the shot glass up and clinked it against Simon's. She tossed back the drink in a single swallow, spluttering and coughing as the fiery liquor chased a path down her throat. Simon chuckled. His own drink seemed to go down without a hitch. Ugh. She really needed to learn how to not come across as a total loser.

"Well, whaddya think?"

Sasha wiped at the corner of her mouth. Simon's gaze followed the movement and his light eyes shone with heat. His interest bolstered Sasha's confidence and she smiled. "I like it."

The cinnamon-sweet whiskey really was good. Sasha found her mood picking up as Simon signaled their bartender and ordered two more shots. She was actually sort of excited to knock a few more things off her bucket list tonight. One: go clubbing. Two: mix and mingle. Three: drink a little. Four . . . She glanced at Simon from beneath lowered lashes. Who knew what the night might bring?

CHAPTER
28

The sound of wood splintering and breaking dragged Saeed from sleep. The sun had risen. He felt it through every inch of his body. His limbs were heavy, his eyelids were reluctant to open. Not even the urgent plea of Cerys's voice could rouse him.

"Saeed!"

She gave him a desperate shake and adrenaline dumped into his bloodstream. It helped him to become more aware of the chaos that erupted around them even though his body was still slow to respond.

"Rin! Wait!"

A booted foot connected squarely with Saeed's gut and he let out a pained grunt.

"You asshole!"Cerys's outraged shriek hurt Saeed more than a kick to his stomach ever could. They'd fallen asleep, limbs intertwined, nestled on the comforter on the floor. Saeed had meant to stay awake. He'd meant to only let her rest her eyes for a few minutes. Instead, their carelessness had invited Rin's wrath. And Saeed was too gods-damned weak from the risen sun to do anything about it.

"I should run a stake through your faithless heart," Rin seethed. "You think you can take her from me?" His voice escalated to a disbelieving shout. "Try it, and I will end you."

Saeed might as well have been mired in quicksand. He rolled onto all fours and pushed himself to his knees. He'd tear out Rin's throat with his fangs if he had to. He refused to let him take Cerys out of here. Gods, he was weak. Saeed cursed his own fallibility as his gaze met Cerys's. Rin seized her roughly by the upper arm and hauled her against him.

"This." He gave her a rough shake that rattled her. "Is *mine*."

Saeed rocked back onto his heels. He prepared to launch himself at Rin, but as he readied to spring forward, one of the bastard's henchmen ripped the heavy blackout drapes away from the windows. Sunlight streamed into the bedroom and Saeed's back arched as searing pain raced along his bare arms and across his back. Blisters formed on his skin and he gritted his teeth to the point that his fangs punctured his lower lip. Rin thought to deter him with sunlight. Either that, or burn him alive. A cowardly move for someone who supposedly possessed so much inborn power.

Cerys broke from Rin's hold and rushed toward Saeed. She bent low and grabbed the blanket they'd been sleeping on only moments before. She gave him a none too gentle shove and in his weakened state, easily toppled him to the floor. She tossed the blanket over him, effectively blocking out the sunlight that sought to burn him to a crisp. He felt her drop beside him. Her voice was muted through the thick folds of the blanket.

"Don't come after me, Saeed. We both knew this was the only way this could end."

The weight of her body fell away from him and Saeed's

heart clenched in his chest. A vengeful roar gathered in his throat and it ripped free with such force that it shook the walls and tore his vocal cords in the process. The chaos of Rin's invasion died to eerie silence and Saeed was left with nothing but the sound of his own hoarse and tortured shouts.

Curse the gods-damned sun! Curse his own fucking weakness!

Saeed longed to throw the heavy weight of the blanket from his blistered and bleeding body. The pain that wracked his body was nothing compared to the pain of losing Cerys. He was a prisoner. Trapped. Confined beneath the blanket in this fucking room until the sun dipped below the horizon to set him free.

The floor fell out from under Saeed as he toppled toward unconsciousness. The Collective called, and Saeed unwillingly answered as he was sucked away from the pain and anguish of the present and thrown unmercifully into the past.

"Rinieri de Rege, meet Fiona Bain."

Saeed raised an arm that wasn't his as he made the introductions. He studied the delicate fae whose light eyes and fair complexion were so similar to Cerys's. Her hair was a darker shade of auburn, every strand in its place and coiffed to perfection. She held herself with the same proud demeanor, chin held high, her shoulders thrown back, and her spine straight.

"A rare pleasure." Rin took Fiona's hand and placed a delicate kiss against her knuckles. "I've never met a true enaid dwyn *before. I must say, you absolutely radiate power."*

Fiona seemed unimpressed with Rin's gushing praise. Instead, she fixed him with a stern eye and smoothed a hand over the expensive silk fabric of the gown that clung to her hip. "Power, like beauty, is in the eye of the be-

holder." *Fiona took a tentative step back toward Saeed and his arm came around her shoulder as though to offer reassurance.*

Rin smirked. "I disagree. But of course, I'm not here to discuss the matter of power—or beauty—with you. I'm here because you're in need of a favor, no?"

Fiona stiffened beside Saeed and the air soured with her unease. "Yes." *Her reluctant response piqued Saeed's curiosity as much as it invoked his rage. This was the moment that would seal Cerys's fate. The bargain, that once struck, would cost Fiona's sister her soul. Saeed was helpless to stop it and yet, he was forced to witness it. Hell, the vampire whose memory he inhabited had facilitated it! One of his own kind had betrayed Cerys and his anger burned bright and hot.*

Rin's lips curved into a self-satisfied smile and his eyes shone with a greedy intensity that made Saeed fight to move, even an inch, toward the mage. He wanted to pummel him. Tear into his flesh with his fangs. Exact justice for every creature he'd ever exploited. His inability to do anything but watch galled him. He nearly drowned in his own helplessness.

"And what can I possibly do for a creature as powerful as you, Fiona?"

Her eyes darted to the side and her head dropped with shame. "There is a mage . . . whose power I need bound."

Rin's eyes went wide and his smile grew. This wasn't some simple favor Fiona asked, even Saeed realized that. Up until now, Saeed had doubted Rin had any power at all. He used others for their power. If he could bind another mage, or provide the means by which to do it, he was definitely more powerful than Saeed had given him credit for.

Rin stroked his thumb along his jawline as he contemplated Fiona. "Who is this mage?"

Fiona's scent sharpened to the point that it stifled the air and Saeed fought for a breath.

He wondered, as he reached out and gave her hand a reassuring squeeze, what this vampire's relationship to Fiona was . . .

"He's a mage from the clan McAlister."

Gods.

"I can help you." Rin's hungry gaze roamed over her. "For a price."

No! The word resounded in Saeed's mind though it refused to push past his lips. This one moment would no doubt set so many terrible things in motion, he couldn't even contemplate the scope of it.

Saeed turned to Fiona. He took her other hand and bent his head to hers. "Are you certain this is what you want?" Finally, the voice of reason. "Rinieri de Rege isn't the sort to be trifled with. Using one mage to fight another is dangerous."

"I know that." The resignation in Fiona's tone caused Saeed's stomach to twist into an unyielding knot. "I have no other choice."

He let out a slow sigh before putting his lips to Fiona's cheek. She released his hands and turned to face Rin, her demeanor once again confident and fierce. "Let's discuss terms, then. I don't have time to waste."

The floor fell out from under Saeed once again and no matter how he fought to regain the memory, it slipped from his grasp. The weight of the comforter pressed down on him and he breathed in lungfuls of warm air before his mind went dark and the hold of daytime sleep overtook him. One simple bargain. Lives ruined. And Saeed had witnessed it all.

A million curses against Rin sat at the tip of Cerys's tongue. The sight of Saeed, blistered, his skin raw and bleeding, was permanently etched into her mind and nothing she could do would scrub the image clean. Worry vibrated through her, sickened her, and constricted her chest. She could still smell the stench of burning flesh and her stomach heaved. If Rin had killed him . . . *Gods.* Cerys blew out a shaky breath. She didn't think she'd survive the loss.

If she had her dagger right now, she'd drive it through Rin's black heart whether he still possessed her soul or not.

He'd wrapped a sheet around her naked body before he dragged her out of Saeed's condo. Big of him. Like that—coupled with her kicking and boisterous protests—hadn't drawn any unnecessary attention. He'd effectively kidnapped her and didn't give a single shit who watched as he threw her into the back seat of the Range Rover and slammed the door.

Rin jerked open the passenger side door and settled into the front seat, slamming that door as well. "You're lucky I don't wring your neck."

Her indignant fire calmed under the chill of his words. Over the centuries, she'd grown complacent, but that didn't mean Cerys didn't remember Rin's punishments early on in her servitude when she'd done something to anger him. She had no idea how he'd retaliate if she managed to piss him off. He might choose to hurt her . . . or he'd go back upstairs to Saeed and make sure he finished what he'd started.

"I almost died last night." Cerys made sure to keep her voice as calm and level as possible. "I wouldn't have gotten out of Breanne's alive if it hadn't been for Saeed."

Rin snorted. He gave a nod to the driver and the Range Rover pulled out into traffic. "And you showed him your appreciation by fucking him?"

Crass. And meant to rattle her chain. A hot retort begged to be thrown his way but she held her tongue. "Breanne had a small army ready to defend her. If Saeed hadn't been with me, you wouldn't have her soul, and you sure as hell wouldn't have me anymore."

"So I owe him my thanks, is that it? Perhaps even an apology for introducing him to the sun this morning? And Breanne's soul isn't in my hand, so I don't have anything. Yet."

Asshole. Gods, Cerys wanted to slice the blade of her dagger across his throat and watch as he bled out. "The vessel is in my jacket pocket."

In truth, she didn't want to give it to him at all. Breanne was a very dangerous enemy to have, and she and Saeed had both made her shit list last night. She might not have been able to personally retaliate now that she was basically indentured to Rin, but she had equally powerful allies who would likely stop at nothing to reclaim her soul and deliver vengeance upon her enemies.

Rin seriously didn't have an ounce of sense.

Cerys shot an angry glare Rin's way as he dug through her jacket. He pulled the glass bottle from her pocket and examined the glowing essence inside that pulsed as though with its own heartbeat.

"I'm sure you can expect a visit from Breanne soon," Cerys spat. And soulless or not, he should expect the *bean sidhe* to come with her claws bared.

"You secured Breanne's loyalty, but she's the least of my problems." He did nothing to hide the sneer in his tone. "While I was waiting on you last night, I had a visit from Ian Gregor."

Fuck.

"Here." Rin cast a disgusted look over his shoulder as he tossed her clothes into the backseat. "Get dressed."

She never should have let herself fall asleep last night. Saeed had softened a part of her that Cerys had hardened over centuries. He'd made her feel. Encouraged her to hope. She'd let him make promises she knew he'd never be able to keep and by letting her guard down had led them both to ruin.

"Maybe you should be glad I didn't show up last night." Cerys was grasping at straws at this point. Anything to deter Rin's vengeful anger. "Especially since Gregor's looking for me."

"Is he?" Rin's snide tone sent a tremor of anxiety through Cerys's body. "That's what Saeed wanted us to believe."

Cerys didn't even know why she bothered to open her mouth. Every time she tried to put a positive spin on the past twenty-four hours, Rin managed to squash it. All thoughts of modesty went to the wayside as Cerys disentangled herself from the sheet, put on her bra, and pulled her T-shirt over her head. "What in the hell are you talking about?" She'd missed out on a lot over the past eighteen hours or so. It was time to do a little catching up.

"I was too eager to trust the vampire," Rin said. "Certainly a mistake I won't make again."

If he was being vague in an effort to annoy her, it was working. "Oh, but you trust Gregor? Is that it?" Seriously, if Rin was so eager to believe the calculating berserker warlord, she had no choice but to believe he'd come unhinged. "I mean, why not, right? Everyone knows berserkers are incredibly trustworthy."

Flippant? Probably. But Cerys was past the point of caring. Rin had obviously become even more suspicious and paranoid over the years. His insatiable hunger for power might have given him the clout he craved, but it hadn't done shit to secure him any true and honest allies. Rin owned a horde of souls and not a single one of those they belonged to were loyal to him. Cerys included. They'd all just as soon see him dead than protect him.

Rin turned to face her. His eyes narrowed, and his lip

curled into a sneer. "I didn't find Ian Gregor naked and
entwined with *my property* this morning. Already, I trust
him more than Saeed."

Hot, acidic anger bubbled up in Cerys's chest. She was
so gods-damned sick and tired of being referred to as a
possession. As though she were nothing more than some
liquid asset Rin could access on a whim.

"Use me again like you did last night, Rin, and I won't
belong to you or anyone else ever again."

Magic sparked the air and Cerys shuddered. Rin had
gone centuries without expending even an ounce of his
own power. Did it build and swell like water behind the
dam? And what would happen once that power breached
the walls of his restraint?

"Is that a threat?"

Gods, he was dense. He knew her power had a shelf life.
But he was so damned blinded by his greed and inability
to share his toys that he couldn't comprehend exactly what
Cerys was trying to tell him.

"Are you not listening to me, Rin?" Cerys was tired of
playing nice. Tired of kissing Rin's ass. So tired of adher-
ing to behavior he'd spent centuries teaching her. What did
it matter if she defied him? If he forced her to take one
more soul, she'd likely die. If he didn't kill her now, he'd
kill her later. She might as well go out on her own terms.
"I almost fucking died last night!"

Rin turned away. He seemed unconcerned, and a tremor
of fear vibrated through her. Had he found another *enaid
dwyn* to enslave? They were rare among the fae. In fact,
Cerys didn't think there were more than a handful of them
in existence. Fiona might not have had any qualms about
helping Rin to enslave one of her own, but Cerys wasn't
quite so unscrupulous. She was going to die one way or
the other. No way would she ruin someone else's life on
her way out.

"Did Saeed bury his fangs in your flesh, Cerys?"

Rin's tone made the act seem lurid. Something Cerys should be ashamed of. She refused to let him devalue that intimacy she'd shared with Saeed. "That's none of your fucking business."

Rin let out a chuff of laughter. "If he survives the sun, he'll come after you tonight. And when he does, I'll introduce him to the most feared slayer in his history."

Things were quickly going from bad to worse to catastrophic. Cerys prayed Saeed had the strength to survive the sun. And at the same time, she hoped he had the good sense to get the hell out of Seattle and stay as far away from her as possible. His absence would break her. But knowing he lived would make her inevitable death a little easier. And Cerys planned to take anyone who might be a threat to Saeed along with her.

CHAPTER
29

Saeed threw the blanket from his body and sprang from the floor with an enraged snarl. His anger had lain dormant in the oblivion of daytime sleep and now that the sun had set, it burned hot and bright in the center of his chest.

Cerys.

A shout of unadulterated rage escaped from Saeed's lips as he recalled the moment Rin's lackeys had ripped her from his arms. His own inability to protect her only exacerbated his unchecked rage. He needed to get to Cerys. To see her with his own eyes and know she was okay. He had no idea how Rin would retaliate for Cerys not coming home last night. But one thing was certain, if he so much as laid a finger on her, Saeed would make the bastard bleed.

No matter what happened, Saeed vowed tonight would be Cerys's last spent in servitude.

He couldn't take Rin down alone, however. He'd underestimated the mage's greed, ambition, and ruthlessness. Saeed had known many ruthless males over the course of his existence and every single one of them had met their end because their arrogance had weakened them. Rin's arrogance lay in the illusion of his control. Saeed planned to beat Rin at his own game and capitalize on that.

His exposure to the sun had kept Saeed considerably weakened. He needed blood, but since he refused to feed from anyone but Cerys, he would have to wait to replenish his strength. In the meantime, he had no choice but to hedge his bets, and rely on reluctant allies. Hell, when everything was said and done, he might end up as alone as he was now. But he wouldn't know until he tried.

Without a car, the trek to Bellevue wasted precious time. Saeed pushed himself as fast as he could go, a smear of shadow against the backdrop of night. The little cabin tucked in the woods wasn't hard to find, and Saeed didn't bother with pleasantries as he was greeted with open hostility at the door.

"Run a stake through my heart if it pleases you," Saeed said to the angry male who blocked the doorway. "But I'm here because I want to help you reclaim your mistress's soul."

The male looked as though he might do just what Saeed suggested and run him through. Blue-black hair cascaded from the top of his head and brushed his shoulders. Dark brows cut severe slashes over his dark violet eyes. His full lips formed a hard line and his jaw squared with clenched teeth. He stood with the well-practiced stance of a seasoned warrior, one hand resting on the pommel of the dagger sheathed at his side and the other wrapped tight around an intricately engraved silver stake.

"Breanne is not my mistress," the male snapped. "But I don't doubt it would give her a great deal of pleasure to watch you bleed, vampire."

Of that, Saeed had no doubt. "I've come unarmed."

The fae answered with a derisive snort. "Then you're a fool."

"Perhaps." Saeed wasn't here to fight. Or ruffle feathers. "But Rin has something I want. He has something Breanne wants. Not working together to achieve our common goal would be foolish."

The fae sneered. "Having an attack of conscience, vampire?"

"The soulless have no conscience."

Saeed looked past the male to see Breanne slowly making her way down a staircase at the far end of the foyer. Her complexion was sallow and her expression drawn. Her shoulders hunched slightly, making her seem entirely too frail. The aura of power and vitality that had surrounded her was gone and in its place was a dark shroud.

"Did Rin's soul thief die?"

Breanne's question knocked the air from Saeed's chest. Not because she'd asked it, but because of the hope that had accented her words. Saeed knew how the supernatural viewed Cerys's kind and it sickened him. He hated that she was feared and reviled. He hated that she'd lived with so much prejudice because of a power that was as much a part of her as her beautiful starlit eyes and luminous skin. Her power was a parasite that fed from her, stole life from her with every occurrence of its use. And bastards like Rin exploited that power and perpetuated the fear and hate that had followed her for centuries.

"No." Saeed took a step forward and the fae at the door brought the silver stake up in a defensive stance. "And be careful how you speak of my mate, *bean sidhe*."

Breanne's eyes went wide. She said something to the male in a language Saeed didn't understand, and the fae lowered the stake in his hand before stepping aside to allow Saeed into the house.

"Your eyes are empty, vampire, so don't think for a second that I believe Rin's heartless assassin has tethered your soul."

The state of Saeed's soul was no one's business, least of all Breanne's. She could say what she wanted about him. What he wouldn't tolerate, was any slight against Cerys. "I warned you to mind your tongue. Speak ill of her again and I'll make sure your soul is never returned to you."

"Has Rin made you the keeper of his stolen souls, then?"

Saeed didn't have time for this. What he needed to do was swallow his damned pride and do whatever it took to get the help he needed to set Cerys free. "You think she's the enemy, but she's not. She's Rin's victim just as much as you are. Help me, and I give you my vow your soul will be returned to you."

Breanne laughed. The sound was hollow and emotionless, the perfect echo of what she must have felt. He understood her disdain and suspicion, her anger. But all of the anger in the world wouldn't do her any good if she wasn't willing first to help herself.

"You saw what happened to Cerys." Saeed stepped closer to Breanne and her guard dog mirrored his motions. "Extracting your soul nearly killed her. Do you honestly think she would voluntarily do something like that to herself?"

Breanne's gaze narrowed. "You didn't deny that she failed to tether you."

Saeed decided that in this case, honesty was the best policy. "Because she has no soul with which to tether me."

Breanne snorted. "Then we are all Rin's victims. But do you really think I appreciate being used by you any more than I appreciate being used by him?"

Saeed shrugged. Again, he saw no point in trying to deceive her. "I want to use you for a night. A single fight. Rin would use you for eternity."

"And so you think I'd prefer the lesser of two evils?"

"No," Saeed replied. "I think you'd prefer the return of your soul."

The male who watched over Saeed exchanged a furtive glance with Breanne. He sheathed the silver stake and spoke to her in their strange unintelligible tongue. Saeed considered himself worldly and educated. He spoke several languages. But the fae were a mystery to him. The less contact he had with Breanne and her lot, the better. He waited patiently for their conversation to conclude, but every second they wasted was one second too many.

"What do you want from me?" Breanne asked.

"A distraction." Breanne might have been without her soul, but Cerys hadn't taken her power. If Saeed had any chance of freeing Cerys or her soul, he'd need Rin's attention focused elsewhere.

Breanne cocked a brow. "That's all?"

Saeed knew better than to be greedy. "That's all."

Breanne studied him for a quiet moment. She exchanged a glance with the male and Saeed was certain they could communicate without speaking. Again, it meant little to him as long as he was able to secure Breanne's aid.

"Fallon will go with you."

Fallon. Breanne's consort and the male who'd wanted to drive a stake through his heart. "I don't know him." It wasn't that Saeed wasn't grateful, but he'd seen Breanne's power. That's what he needed to distract Rin.

"You don't know me, either." Breanne's haughty response reinforced Saeed's belief that the *bean sidhe* was regarded more as a queen. "And yet, you're so eager to put your trust in me."

Saeed could think of several words to describe what he was feeling right now and none of them was "eager." His reluctant alliance with the fae was born of necessity and nothing else. Saeed had no one to turn to. She was his last resort. He wasn't about to play games with her, though. "I've seen what you can do. How do I even know he'll be of use to me?"

Breanne smirked. "I suppose that's a risk you'll have to take, vampire."

Gods-damn it. In so many words she'd told him to take it or leave it. The sooner Saeed could free Cerys and get her the hell out of the city, the better. He'd had his fill of Seattle's supernaturals.

"All right, then. Let's go." He looked Fallon up and down and said a silent prayer that the male would be of use to him. "You've already wasted too much of my time."

"Don't forget." Breanne leveled her intense stare on Saeed. "If you're successful tonight, you owe me a soul."

Saeed gave a slight inclination of his head. So much relied on his success tonight. First, he'd keep his promise to Cerys. After that, he'd fulfill the rest of his obligations.

"Have you lost your fucking mind, Rin?"

Cerys leaned in close, the words nothing more than a seething whisper after she walked into the club to find a group of berserker warlords seated in the VIP section. She'd only been away for one night and already Rin had gotten pretty gods-damned chummy with the very beasts they should have been avoiding. No doubt he blamed Saeed for bringing all of this to their door when the fact of the matter was Gregor had been searching for them for quite some time. Rin, stupid bastard that he was, had played right into it too. Cerys gave a sad shake of her head. Tonight was the beginning of the end.

"On the contrary, I'm finally seeing clearly."

His overconfident grin made Cerys want to slap the expression right off his face. He had no freaking clue what he was doing. Gregor would bite him in two before Rin even had an inkling he was being devoured as a snack.

"They are the betrayers of the vampire race. You've said so yourself."

"That was then. This is now."

Apparently, Rin wasn't concerned with anything he'd ever said in the past. Funny, since up until now, he had a tendency to love throwing the past in her face. "Gregor can't be trusted."

"Says the one I caught naked with the vampire."

Cerys's gaze narrowed as she regarded him with open hostility. "What's the matter, Rin? Jealous?"

He stopped dead in his tracks and spun on a heel to face her. His hand shot out to grip her throat and his fingers squeezed tight to constrict her airway. Power sparked the air and a cold light glinted in the depths of Rin's brown eyes. He lifted her until her heels left the floor and then her toes. She fought for enough breath to fill her lungs as she clawed futilely at the hand wrapped around her throat. Black spots swam in her vision. Her arms went limp. She was going to pass and out and then what? Would Rin throw her to Gregor and let the berserkers have her?

Rin gave a violent jerk of his arm and brought Cerys's face to his until their noses nearly touched. Thanks to last night's soul extraction, her strength wasn't a quarter of what it should have been. Forget about self-preservation. If Rin closed his fist another inch, he'd snuff her out like a candle.

"Jealous?" If she wasn't already about to pass out from lack of oxygen, his breath would've gotten the job done. "I don't have a gods-damned thing to be jealous about. You. Belong. To. *Me*."

He let go of his hold on the last word and Cerys crumpled to the floor like a puppet whose strings had been cut. She gasped for breath, filling her lungs with much-needed oxygen as she tried to ignore the gaping stares of everyone within a twenty-foot radius. No doubt his little temper tantrum would only help to solidify Rin's reputation as a badass who shouldn't be fucked with.

Cerys didn't give a shit about the gawkers or their whispers that traveled through the crowd at light speed. What she did care about was the five males seated at Rin's table in the VIP section, particularly the one on the left who, unlike his comrades, watched her with an intensity that made her skin crawl.

Ian Gregor.

Had to be. She'd never met him but she knew that look. Want. Rin had looked at her that way the first time they'd met. It wasn't her body he'd wanted. Or her affection. It was power that Rin had craved. She didn't know what Gregor wanted, but it certainly wasn't any of those things. No, Gregor was after something far more basic. Like breathing, or eating. His wasn't a want exactly. It was more of a *need*. And it reflected in the depths of his onyx black soul.

Shit.

Cerys was afraid to wonder if things could get any worse. Especially with the way Rin stood over her, his eyes blazing with unchecked anger. "Get up."

Yeah, she'd get right on that. As soon as the feeling returned to her legs and she could draw a breath deep enough to clear the spots from her vision. "You seem pretty eager to march me over to my new keeper."

Rin kneeled down until his mouth hovered near her ear. "It's Saeed who wants to keep you. Who came here to steal you away." If he seriously didn't think Gregor was here for the exact same reason, then Rin was denser than Cerys gave him credit for. "Now get your ass up off the floor before I grab you by that mop of hair on your head and drag you up!"

She'd just as soon walk across the nightclub naked than let that happen.

Cerys drew on her strength which, to be honest, wasn't much. What Rin couldn't get through his head—what he'd always failed to realize—was that by separating Cerys from her soul, he'd inherently weakened her. Without that light, that essence, she was operating at half capacity all the damned time. She'd been running on fumes for centuries. Unfortunately, she doubted Gregor would be a much better master. He'd likely expend what she had left in a single blaze of misguided glory. Out of the frying pan and into the fire.

Great.

Cerys braced her palms on the floor and pushed herself up on wobbly arms. Damn, she was a real shit show right now. Super impressive. Her legs weren't much more stable and she exhibited all of the grace of a newborn foal as she got to her feet and took several steps away from Rin. If she was about to walk to her doom, she was going to do it on her own steam, damn it.

"You've been building an empire for over a thousand years," Cerys remarked. "And you're about to lose it all in the space of a heartbeat."

Rin's lip curled. Cerys wanted to laugh at his outraged expression. As though he couldn't believe she'd be so ballsy as to continue to talk back. She had nothing to lose at this point. She had no idea whether Saeed was alive or not, and if she extracted one more soul, she was as good as dead. So what did it matter if she threw a little sass Rin's way? Her life was screwed either way.

"Don't worry about my empire," Rin said through gritted teeth. "It's more than secure."

Cerys let out a derisive snort. "If you say so."

Rin raised his hand as though to give her a solid backhand to the face. Cerys simply laughed as she forced herself to brush past him and walk into the VIP section toward Gregor and his men. There was something incredibly gratifying about no longer giving a fuck.

Cerys knew better than to show any weakness as she

made her way to Rin's booth and the berserkers who waited
for her there. She let her attention shift from one male to
the other, as she noted the many similarities in their physical traits. Their expressions remained blank and Cerys
wondered if there was a single one among them who had
ever cracked a smile. Probably not. They didn't exactly
strike her as the happy-go-lucky sorts.

"Not done stirring up trouble all over town, I see."
Cerys saw no reason for pleasantries. "What sort of
bullshit have you been feeding to Rin for the past day?"

She made a point of making eye contact with each one
of them. When her gaze landed on Ian Gregor, she stopped
and stared for a beat too long. She wanted him to know
she had his number. He wasn't in Seattle for any other reason than to stir up shit and it was unfortunate that Rin
was too stupid to see it.

Gregor's chain wasn't so easy to rattle. He certainly
painted an intimidating picture as he refused to acknowledge her and simply stared her down. Lucky for Cerys, her
chain wasn't easy to rattle either.

"Not sure what Rin told you," Cerys made herself at
home and settled into one of the chairs at the table, "but
I'm not for sale." She leaned in toward Gregor conspiratorially and whispered, "I think he's got a thing for me."

Again, she was answered with silence. She leaned back
in her chair and folded her arms across her chest as she
studied the males seated around the table. Rin caught up
and took a seat beside her. She leaned over and knocked
her shoulder against his. "Tough crowd."

Luckily, Rin's buttons were much easier to push. "Do
yourself a favor, and keep your mouth shut."

"Why would I do that?" Cerys blinked her wide eyes
and infused her tone with innocence. "I'm having so much
fun."

Perhaps it showed her masochistic side that she wanted

him to lash out. Maybe even hit her. At this point, anything would be better than the worry that ate her alive. With her own future as uncertain as Saeed's fate, she knew her best bet was simply to ride out the storm. The only problem was, she didn't know if she was capable of doing it. Not when she faced the prospect of losing everything she'd come to hold dear.

"Where's the vampire?" Gregor turned his attention fully to Rin, his own expression less than amused.

"Licking his wounds and readying for battle I imagine," Rin remarked. "I burned the fuck out of him with the sun this morning. He'll show though, we just need to give him a little time."

Gregor leaned forward in his chair. "How do you know?"

Rin cast his narrowed gaze to Cerys. "Because I have something he wants."

CHAPTER
30

Ever since the day Saeed met Cerys he'd felt as though he were racing against the sun and his own gods-damned mind. The number of hours that spanned from sunset to sunrise was out of his control but thankfully, his mind was finally clear. He'd worked so hard to gain Rin's trust, only to have it shattered by his own selfishness. If he'd simply taken Cerys back to the club, and given her over to Rin's care, he might not currently be flying by the seat of his pants and hoping for a favorable outcome despite his lack of planning.

He should've done more to protect her. From Rin. From Gregor. Hell, even from his own damned self.

Saeed was forced to put his trust in a male he didn't know and that bothered him almost as much as his lack of planning. He had no doubt Fallon was every bit as formidable as Breanne suggested. But that didn't change the fact that he was an unknown variable and Saeed's controlling nature refused to allow him to put his trust in the unknown.

"Where does Rin keep his stolen souls?"

Saeed turned his attention to Fallon. If he knew the

answer to that, neither of them would be here right now. "I don't know and neither does Cerys, so don't get any ideas about interrogating her. I suspect only Rin knows the location of the souls he holds hostage."

"This is pointless then." Perfect. All Saeed needed right now was a pessimist. "You lied to Breanne. She'll have your heart for this, vampire."

Pessimistic and dramatic. Saeed let out a sigh. "I lied to no one. I made a promise to return her soul, and I intend to keep it."

"An empty promise when you have no idea where her soul is being kept."

Saeed was beginning to think he'd like to have a strictly nonverbal relationship with Fallon. "I'll find it."

"It might not even be in the city."

"I'll find it," Saeed stressed once again.

"You're annoyingly confident, vampire."

"And you're an insufferable buzzkill." Saeed couldn't help but smile. Cerys had begun to rub off on him and she might as well have put those words in his mouth. "I would've preferred to do this without help, but circumstances have proven that to be impossible. I have one concern and only one, and that is to recover Cerys's soul and get her as far away from Rinieri de Rege as possible."

"So you exploit Breanne to get what you want?" Fallon let out a chuff of disgusted laughter. "You are no better than Rin."

If he wanted to get technical, he was exploiting Fallon. "We have a common goal. An alliance only increases our odds at success."

"What are we up against?" Finally the conversation was moving in the right direction. "Besides Rin and whoever's got his back?"

The ones at his back were the problem. "I could've handled Rin on my own," Saeed said. "There is a small force of berserkers in the city. They currently have Rin's back."

Fallon uttered a curse in his native tongue. Saeed didn't know the word, but he certainly understood the sentiment. "Five berserkers might as well be fifty."

True. But Saeed wasn't going to let that deter him.

"I'm less concerned about the berserkers than I am Rin." Saeed wasn't about to discount the mage's power. "I have no idea what he's capable of. He's guarded himself well, getting by on the powers of others."

Fallon nodded in agreement. He kept his eyes focused on the highway but Saeed knew he was processing everything he said. The drive into the city was tedious at best, but it beat traveling on foot and bought Saeed precious minutes and the time he needed to form a plan of attack. It went against his grain to go into any situation half-cocked. He wouldn't be of any use to Cerys if he didn't have complete control.

"You're right that Rin has kept the scope of his power carefully guarded," Fallon replied. "But I don't see how that makes him different from any other mage. They're all the same. Guarded. Suspicious. Equally mysterious. Power is relative. We're all powerful in one way or another. Our uniqueness is what balances the scales."

A very Zen philosophy considering Fallon's trepidation over the berserkers. Then again, wasn't Saeed counting on Fallon's unique abilities to tip the scales in his favor? His concerns centered less around Rin's capabilities, and more on his hold over Cerys. It gave him a definitive edge in a fight while putting Saeed at a disadvantage. She was his only weakness and if he had any hope at success, he needed to find a way to put his concern for her to the back of his mind.

"Breanne's power is impressive." Saeed figured it was

time he spelled out exactly what he expected of Fallon. "Are your illusions equally as convincing?"

Fallon smirked. "She wouldn't have sent me otherwise. Make no mistake, vampire, I'm here for one reason and one reason only: to ensure the return of Breanne's soul. Don't think for a moment I won't go to any means necessary to accomplish that goal."

Saeed had no problem reading between the lines. Both Saeed and Cerys were expendable. Fallon would sacrifice them both in a heartbeat if it met with his agenda. Saeed wasn't so foolish to think he had any true allies in this fight aside from Cerys. She was a formidable fighter. Skilled and well-practiced. But she was also weakened from extracting Breanne's soul and that put them both at a disadvantage.

"You can expect me to go to the same lengths for Cerys." Saeed was just as determined to get what he wanted and he wouldn't let anything stand in his way.

"Then we understand each other," Fallon replied. "Good."

As they made their way deeper into the city and the Capitol Hill district, Saeed's nerves began to ratchet tight. He was entirely too unprepared. There was so much at stake. The last time he'd seen Cerys, Rin had her by the arm, and dragged her, naked, out of the bedroom. With no tether to connect them, Saeed had no idea whether she was safe or not. If Rin had so much as disrupted a single hair on her head, Saeed would make him pay.

Fallon parked a block from the club. Saeed wasn't sure that the element of surprise would buy them much of an advantage. More likely, it would be the bodies crowding the club that would provide them with a much needed distraction.

"Can you convince Rin to tell you where the souls are being kept?" Saeed had planned to use subversion to coax that secret from him but now that that wasn't a possibility, his only option was brute force. If Fallon could use his illusions to extract the information voluntarily it would be even better.

Fallon gave Saeed a sidelong glance. "One way or another."

He supposed that was all of the assurance—or disclosure—he was going to get. Saeed got out of the car and took a moment to center his focus. He still didn't know if he'd be able to keep a level head once he saw Cerys. The possibility loomed that he'd go into the club and not find her at all. His anxiety crested and Saeed forced it away. He couldn't allow his mind to go there. Cerys was too precious to Rin for him to risk. He wouldn't let her out of his sight.

A vision of Cerys presented itself in Saeed's mind. Her fierce beauty captivated him. Her light eyes held him enthralled. The luminous aura of her skin stole his breath. There wasn't anything he wouldn't do for her. And he was ready to lay down his life for her if need be.

Saeed opened his eyes to find Fallon standing before him. The fae presented him with a pair of daggers. Funny, he would've preferred a gun in this situation. For never having used them in the past, he'd come to appreciate the distance a gun allowed him between him and his enemies.

"Believe me, these are the only weapons you'll need," Fallon said as though he'd read Saeed's mind. "The daggers are enchanted with faerie magic and not only will they guide your hands in battle, they will confuse and deter your opponents."

Saeed could think of no better advantage. "Thank you." He took the daggers from Fallon's hands. With any luck, he'd live through the night so he could return them to Fallon when all of this was said and done.

Then again, if anything had happened to Cerys, Saeed wasn't sure he'd want to live.

Something wasn't right. For the past hour, Gregor's conversation tactics alluded more to stalling than deal making. Could Saeed have been as wrong about the berserker's intentions as Rin was? It seemed to her that Ian Gregor had his own agenda, and no one could guess his true motives.

Her own curiosity had gotten the better of her, distracting her even from antagonizing Rin. There was a civility to the conversation that was almost laughable. As though the two males seated at the table worked secret angles to benefit their own machinations. It threw her off, and as her mind began to wander, Cerys found it hard to focus on anything except her worry for Saeed. Gregor had made it clear that he not only anticipated, but expected Saeed to show up. Why did the berserker want him? It couldn't simply be to kill him. He could've easily taken care of that months ago in L.A.

"Tell me, Rin, what do you know about Trenton McAlister?"

Gregor's question drew Cerys's undivided attention. She cast a furtive glance toward Rin and noticed that he'd perked up as well. A brief look of concern flashed across his features and rightly so. *Shit.* She couldn't help but wonder how Rin would play this. Gregor was old. Perhaps the oldest among them. He'd worked alongside McAllister for centuries. Hell, they might as well have been co-conspirators in the near eradication of the vampire race. There was no way Ian Gregor didn't know intimate details about McAllister's history. He was setting Rin up. Inviting him to lie. Would he take the bait or, for once in his life, would Rin exercise a little gods-damn caution?

Rin gave Gregor an indulgent smile. "I imagine I know as much about him as you do."

Cerys couldn't deny she was a little surprised that Rin had chosen caution. She kept her own mouth shut and simply waited for Gregor to drop the hammer. By no stretch of the imagination was his question an innocent one. Finally, they were getting down to the real reason for him being in the city and it hit so close to home that it caused Cerys's heart to race in her chest.

"Really?" Gregor raised a dubious brow. "Because I imagine you know much more about him than I do."

Heh. Well played, berserker.

"Why?" The word pushed through Rin's lips with open hostility. "Because I am a mage and he is a mage?"

Gregor let out a chuff of laughter. He looked askance at one of his men and smirked. "Because you are the mage who bound his power."

Oh, snap. Cerys's eyes went wide. Gregor wasn't pulling any punches. Rin's expression became noticeably agitated. Cerys wouldn't deny it gave her a smug sense of satisfaction to see him squirm. In a way, she felt a certain kinship with Trenton McAlister even though they'd never met. Their fates were intertwined. Sort of ironic considering the position he held . . .

Cerys watched as Rin forced his expression into a mask of passivity. "Such an act is forbidden within the order of mages."

Good gods. Cerys wasn't sure that was the best response even though Rin hadn't admitted to or denied anything. Gregor was baiting Rin, and though Cerys wasn't sure what he was after, she did know if Rin tried his patience Gregor wouldn't hesitate to separate his head from his shoulders.

"So I've heard."

Gregor was absolutely unflappable. It was no wonder he generated fear wherever he went. Cerys wanted in on the conversation so badly her tongue practically burned with the urge to speak up. Why was he so interested in what Rin had done to McAlister?

"I've always been curious why McAlister kept his mouth shut about it," Gregor wondered aloud. "You'd think he would've called you out on it immediately. Surely the order of mages would have commanded you to release his bonds. Unless . . ." Gregor allowed for a dramatic pause. "It was a sanctioned act."

Sanctioned? Cerys's gut bottomed out. It wasn't possible. Not when Fiona had gone to the lengths she'd gone to to see the act done. She waited for Rin's response, her breath stalled in her chest. A shout built up within her and Cerys bit down hard on her bottom lip to keep from screaming, "answer him!"

"Perhaps you shouldn't speak of matters you know nothing about."

That was it? That was Rin's response? Cerys wanted to throw herself at him and choke the life from him. That wasn't an answer. It was a gods-damned diversion.

"What do you think, soul thief?" Gregor turned his cold gaze on Cerys. "Is this a subject I know nothing about?"

"I think Rin should quit dodging your fucking questions and give you a straight answer." Cerys could no longer hold her tongue. The rage that burned within her threatened to consume her completely.

Gregor turned his focus to Rin and cocked a challenging brow. "Are you dodging my fucking questions, Rin?"

Rin's shocked expression told Cerys tonight wasn't going down the way he thought it would. For once, Cerys could safely say they were on the same page. She'd expected to sit in tortured silence while Gregor negotiated for possession of her. Instead, he'd managed to unearth the most painful memory of Cerys's past and cast a shadow of doubt over every assumption she'd ever made.

"I thought you came here for the vampire," Rin snapped.

"As far as I'm concerned, Saeed has nothing to do with what may or may not have happened to Trenton McAlister over a thousand years ago."

The more Rin deflected, the more certain Cerys became he was hiding something. He was a fucking coward who hid behind the power of others and didn't even have the balls to take care of Saeed himself, instead waiting for the berserkers to kill him. She hoped Saeed was too weak to leave his condo. That he wouldn't show up here and walk straight into an ambush.

"Why I came here is no one's business but my own," Gregor said with a snarl.

"Don't forget, berserker, you came to *me*." Rin's tone escalated as well and the air sparked with magic. "I owe you my thanks for warning me of the vampire's plans to take Cerys, but nothing else."

"You do owe me," Gregor agreed. "And I plan to exact payment."

A cold finger of dread stroked down Cerys's spine. Finally they were getting down to brass tacks.

"I gave you my thanks." Rin pushed out his chair and stood. "And that's all you're going to get."

Gregor's icy smile dropped the temperature in the air by at least twenty degrees. Rin had been pressing his luck all night and Cerys didn't think the berserker warlord would tolerate much more.

"Tell me, Rinieri, if you were to die, would McAlister be set free from his bonds? Would he be free to use his power once again after centuries of being bound?"

Of course. Gregor wasn't interested in returning McAlister's power to him. He wanted to ensure he'd remain in a weakened state. That couldn't be the only reason he'd come here, though. Gods, Cerys wished she knew what he had planned.

"You think you can come in here and threaten me in

my own house?" Rin slammed his fist onto the table for emphasis, rattling the glasses that sat on the surface. "Get the fuck out of here and don't ever show your face in the city again!"

Once again, Rin let his ego get the best of him. Gregor stood from his seat and braced his arms on the table. He leaned forward, a snarl curling his lip. Cerys waited for him to address Rin, but instead, he turned to her. "I'm a staunch believer that punishments should fit their crimes. Haven't you ever wanted to make him pay, Cerys? Show him exactly what it feels like to exist without a soul?"

Oh, shit. Finally, Gregor's intentions were clear. Cerys was as good as fucked.

CHAPTER
31

Saeed had only one chance to do this right. It was now or never, and he hated that he was going in less than prepared. But he had enchanted weapons in his hands, and a powerful—albeit reluctant—ally at his side. The odds might not have been stacked in his favor, but it was as good as it was going to get.

Saeed exchanged a silent glance with Fallon before he pulled open the door to Crimson. A momentary twinge of guilt tugged at his chest as Saeed considered the possibility of innocent lives being caught in the crossfire. He needed the mass of bodies to create a distraction and add to the confusion, however. And he tempered his worry by reminding himself that every patron present was supernatural. This was a tough crowd. A group that could take a considerable amount of damage.

"We can't let anything happen to Rin." Saeed hated that he'd have to protect the bastard for even a second. "At least, not until we know where he keeps his stolen souls."

Fallon gave him a look as though that went without

saying. That might've been the case, but Saeed was going to cover all of his bases.

"Cerys is off-limits as well." He knew the fae wanted retribution for what she'd done to Breanne. Fallon wouldn't waste an opportunity to exact vengeance, given the chance. "Lay so much as a finger on her, and I'll end you."

Fallon inclined his head slightly, and Saeed knew it was all the assurance he would get. He pushed forward in front of the fae, and took point. This was his fight after all and he would not shy away.

Saeed's gaze scanned the club and stopped at the VIP section. His heart beat a mad rhythm in his chest as he caught sight of not only Cerys, but Rin, and Ian Gregor as well. The three of them stood around the square table, their expressions severe, as though in some sort of standoff. The situation appeared volatile and put Saeed even more on edge.

Gregor's nostrils flared and his attention wandered from Rin. Saeed tensed as the berserker's gaze met his and a sly, dangerous smile curved his lips. So much for the element of surprise. Saeed didn't have another moment to waste.

Not a second after Gregor caught sight of him, Cerys whipped around. Equal parts relief and terror flooded Saeed as Rin caught on to what was happening and reached out to snatch Cerys before she could take flight. Thanks to Gregor, Saeed had lost his only advantage.

"Fifty thousand dollars to whoever pierces the vampire's heart!"

Rin was a cowardly son of a bitch. It seemed he couldn't help but enlist others to do his dirty work for him. Saeed froze in his tracks and Fallon came to a stop not far behind him. "Don't worry about me," he said to the fae. "Get to Rin, get what we need, and protect Cerys."

The momentum shifted as chaos broke out. Fallon ran against the current as a horde of bodies rushed at Saeed.

So many eager, greedy bastards willing to do Rin's bidding for a few bucks. His hope of keeping casualties and damage to a minimum evaporated under the violent onslaught headed his way. He had no choice but to defend himself as best he could and put as many of his attackers down as possible.

Saeed brought the daggers up, prepared to fight. A burst of power shot up through his arms and left his limbs tingling with foreign magic. He braced for attack and watched as at least twenty creatures of various creeds rushed at him. The daggers vibrated in his grip and one by one, the bodies rushing toward him slowed. Faerie magic. Certainly useful in a pinch.

Most, but not all, of Saeed's attackers were deterred by the daggers' magic. Five stalwart souls pressed on as the others stopped. A few were armed with daggers and short knives and the remaining two came at him unarmed but with claws bared and ready to shred.

Saeed lost sight of Cerys under the onslaught. He put his worry to the back of his mind as he focused on the fight and self-preservation. His arms moved of their own accord as though in synchronicity with the weapons he held in his hands. Each stab, each parry, each wide swipe of his arm was quick and precise. A blur of motion that caught his attackers off guard and gave him the upper hand.

He didn't have time to waste on Rin's attempt to distract him. Saeed spun as he stabbed, slashed, and hacked. The daggers were perfectly balanced, as though extensions of his hands and served him well as he put down five assailants with ease. His breath sawed in and out of his chest as he pushed toward the back of the nightclub, where Rin held Cerys against her will. Fallon fought to make ground as well, as he encountered a similar roadblock on his way to the mage.

Gregor and his men remained strangely neutral in the

fight. They watched with interest, as though this spectacle had somehow been put on for their entertainment. What in the hell was going on? A large mountain of a body came at Saeed from the left, brandishing what looked to be a broken leg from a chair. Saeed swept his arm upward and caught the male in the face with his elbow. Rin had offered a hefty sum for Saeed's death. He would've thought the berserkers would do the job for free. It didn't add up, and their inactivity only served to keep his focus divided.

"Shit! Get the hell out of here!"

A shout from behind him drew Saeed's attention. The club had quickly begun to empty as one body after another fled from what appeared to be an invisible foe. Saeed had no idea how the *bean sidhes'* power worked, but it was obvious Fallon had somehow managed to project his illusions on many minds at once. For the first time since they'd walked through the door, Saeed felt a glimmer of hope that they might come out on top.

"You wanted him!" Rin's angered shout rose above the din of chaos. "Are you going to kill the vampire, or stand there and watch him?"

Saeed found himself wanting to know the answer to that question as well. Another round of attackers came at him, eager for Rin's bounty, and he once again had to shift his focus to the fight in front of him and not the one beyond his reach.

"Saeed! Behind you!"

Fallon's warning came a second too late. Saeed took a hard hit to his right shoulder that sent him sprawling to the floor on his stomach. He rolled to his left, flipping onto his back just in time to miss the stabbing blow of a splintered piece of wood that shattered when it hit the dyed and lacquered concrete floor. His assailant, a willowy sylph, came at him, her delicate hands formed into claws. Saeed kicked out with his legs and sent her into the air and backward where she landed on a nearby table, temporarily immobilized, but hardly out of commission.

Supernatural creatures weren't exactly easy to stop.

At least he was gaining momentum. Fallon's illusions helped to clear the club and those either unaffected or out of his reach chose to enter the fray or simply watch. Saeed wished the spectators would at least show the common courtesy to lend a helping hand. No one would dare to defy Rin, though. Saeed and Fallon were on their own.

Saeed lost sight of Fallon once again as he faced a fresh and ambitious attacker. Muscle memory took over as he lurched forward with a jab and followed up with a sharp uppercut of the blade that slashed across his assailant's chest. The male backed off as he clutched the wound and turned to run, leaving Saeed a clear path to Rin and Cerys.

He swore to the gods, he was going to cut out the bastard's heart and feed it to him.

Gregor took a tentative step back and his comrades followed suit as though not to impede Saeed's progress toward Rin. Saeed still didn't trust the berserkers, but right now they were the lesser of two evils. His priority was Cerys. Nothing else mattered.

"Take another step and I'll slit her throat." Saeed stopped dead in his tracks as Rin brought the point of a short knife to just below Cerys's jawline. "She's weak, I doubt she'll heal in time if I cut deep enough."

"If you can't have her, no one can. Is that it?" Saeed's patience had reached its limit. He refused to tolerate Rin for another second.

"She won't be any use to me for much longer anyway," Rin offered with a shrug.

Son of a bitch. Saeed weighed his options. Fallon was still at the far end of the club fighting his own battles against those loyal to Rin. The berserkers appeared comfortable in their neutrality. Cerys might have been weak, but Saeed was strong enough for both of them. He took a lunging step forward and stopped as Cerys let out a fearful shout.

"Saeed! Don't move!"

Fingers wrapped around Saeed's shoulder and something sharp pressed into his back. He'd been so preoccupied with getting to Cerys he hadn't even noticed the presence behind him. *Stupid.*

"Rin please." Cerys's pleading tone tore at Saeed's heart. "Let him go. Let him leave Seattle and I promise I'll never leave your side."

She thought to save him, but what Cerys didn't understand was that if Saeed couldn't have her, he might as well be dead.

Rin had maneuvered Saeed perfectly. He'd presented him with a challenge, a gauntlet to run to get to her. He'd known nothing would deter him and that Saeed's focus would be singular, making it easy to put one of his goons at Saeed's back. Rin would take the coward's way to rid himself of Saeed. Cerys didn't know why she was surprised.

She expected Saeed's expression to mirror the betrayal he no doubt felt. Instead, he looked at her with so much tender emotion that it squeezed her heart like a fist. He would never give up. Would never turn his back on her. He would die trying to save her—to protect her—rather than abandon her. If that wasn't love, Cerys didn't know what was. And gods damn it, she loved him too.

Cerys didn't need her soul to tell her how she felt about Saeed. He had brought her back to life from a shallow existence of apathy and had shown her the power of selflessness. Rin would never let her go. Even if Saeed managed to steal her away and flee the city, Rin would come after her. They would never know a moment of peace. She refused to condemn Saeed to such a fate where he would always be on the run, unable to return to his coven, his family. There was only one thing she could do, and that was to repay his selflessness with a selfless act of her own.

"Saeed," she murmured. "I love you."

Cerys turned toward Rin. A smug expression accented his features, but he sure as hell wouldn't be smug for long. His soul glowed like a dying cinder in the center of his chest, a pulsing red pinpoint surrounded by a shroud of dark shadow. What she was about to do would likely kill her, but it would all be worth it if in the process she saved Saeed.

If she had to go out in a blaze of glory, there wasn't any better way to do it than protecting someone she loved.

Cerys slammed the heel of her palm against Rin's chest at the solar plexus. His eyes went wide, and he doubled over as though she'd delivered a punch to his gut. "Cerys! What are you doing?"

His disbelief was almost laughable. So many centuries, bound to him in servitude. In hatred. In dysfunctional codependence. Bound to him because she'd convinced herself that his possession of her soul had also stolen her free will. Well, not anymore.

Cerys was free.

She leaned in close until her mouth hovered near Rin's ear. "I'm giving you a taste of your own medicine," she said. "And it's about damned time."

"Cerys!"

She ignored Saeed's impassioned cry. *Don't worry about me, you idiot. Save yourself!* He needed to focus on the stake currently poised to pierce his heart, not her!

Power flooded Cerys as she felt Rin's soul loosen its hold on his body. The draw on her energy was intense, and Cerys's legs threatened to give out as Rin's soul resisted the extraction.

"Stop! Cerys, stop!"

The sound of a scuffle made its way to Cerys's ears but she forced herself not to look. It took all of her concentration to pull Rin's soul away, and she should've known it would've been stubborn to let go. The knife dropped from Rin's grasp and landed on the concrete floor with a ring of metal. He dropped to his knees and Cerys went down beside him, her palm still pressed firmly against his chest.

"You did this to yourself, Rin." Cerys couldn't bring herself to feel an ounce of sympathy. Perhaps it was a good thing this extraction would more than likely kill her. Cerys didn't know if she'd survive the return of her soul anyway. Not when she would be forced to face the guilt of what she'd done. "You did this to *me*." The shouts of several voices rang out around her but for some reason the words no longer made sense. Cerys pulled from the seat of her power and in one final rush of strength, ripped Rin's soul from his chest. He drew in a sharp gasp that ended on a pained grunt. From his knees, he toppled over like a felled tree and sprawled to the floor.

Holy shit.

Cerys swayed on her knees but she refused to lose consciousness yet. Rin lay on the floor, shaking, in shock, his breath coming in heavy pants. She opened her clenched fist and hovering in her palm was Rin's soul. It was sickly and black, almost sludgy. Like a writhing mass of serpents, it undulated, angry and restless. It made Cerys feel tainted just being in contact with it. Rinieri de Rege was as black and heartless as any creature could be. Not even the berserkers with their inky black eyes and violent tendencies had such dark souls. Not even Ian Gregor, whose vendetta might have been the only thing keeping him alive, was as cold and unfeeling as Rin.

She'd done the right thing by removing his soul. She doubted he'd miss it much. Rin was already as hollow and apathetic as any being could be. What she'd done was effectively weaken him. She might not have been able to bind his power in the way he'd bound Trenton McAlister, but he'd certainly pack less of a punch. Maybe now Rin would finally realize how foolish his use of her had been over the centuries.

"Give it back." Rin's mewling voice echoed the fear of each and every one of his victims. *Her victims.* "Please."

"You made me an accomplice." Each word issued from Cerys's lips dripped with hateful venom. "Gods." She let out a disdainful chuff of laughter. "My soul is probably as tarnished as yours by now."

Rin's soul lurched in her palm in an attempt to fly back to the body that had housed it. She would never allow Rin to reclaim it. *Never.* She clutched Rin's soul tight in her fist and used every ounce of strength and power left in her stores to compress it to the size of a marble.

"What are you doing?" Rin's voice rose to a frantic warble. "Cerys! What are you doing?"

Her strength flagged and her stomach gave a violent lurch. Spots swam in her vision and the sounds around her came to her ears as though she were under water. This was it. Time to blow this Popsicle stand. "I'm doing what I should have done the moment Fiona betrayed me."

The thing that bothered Cerys the most was that she'd never had an opportunity to live her life. And on top of that, what really burned was that she wouldn't get a chance to live it with Saeed.

"It's like Gregor said." Gods, she couldn't believe she was about to quote the heartless berserker warlord. "The punishment should fit the crime. You are guilty Rinieri de Rege, and I pronounce sentence."

Cerys smashed the marble-sized rock of Rin's compressed soul onto the hard concrete floor. Rin let out a tortured shout as particles of black dust rose from the floor and dissipated into the air.

"You can't destroy anyone's life." Cery's breath rattled in her chest as she collapsed to the floor. "Ever again."

CHAPTER
32

Saeed stared in horror as his worst nightmare played out in front of him. The entire scene seemed to unfold in double time, while Saeed moved in slow motion, unable to stop Cerys from extracting Rin's soul and thereby sacrificing her life in the process.

The light went out of her eyes as their gazes met for the barest moment. Her full, petal-pink lips curled at the corners and then parted on a breath as she collapsed to the floor.

Pain unlike anything he'd ever felt ripped through Saeed. A haze of anguish settled over him and his rage burned with such intensity that the tenuous grip he'd held on his sanity snapped. If Cerys died, not a single soul within these walls would survive the night. Saeed would make them all pay. *Every last one of them.*

He fought like a vengeful spirit.

Nothing and no one stood in his way as he rushed through the dwindling crowd of money-hungry attackers and Rin's own loyal bodyguards as Saeed closed the distance between them. Desperation fueled every swing of his arm, every cut, parry, and jab. Each foe who sought to take him down fell beneath Saeed's blade until nothing stood between him and Cerys. She lay lifeless beside Rin's shuddering body and Saeed let out another tortured roar.

The mage had been considerably weakened. Cerys hadn't just stolen his soul, she'd obliterated it. Rin brought his gaze up and it reflected every ounce of anger and hatred Saeed felt. The static charge of magic thickened the air, compressing his lungs until he found it difficult to take a deep breath. An empty, gaping wound had opened in Saeed's chest, and the pain of it was more than he could bear. The desire to kill Rin, to run his daggers through his black heart, almost stole his focus from Cerys. He was consumed with the need for vengeance to the point that nothing else mattered . . .

"Don't let that need consume you, vampire." Saeed started at the sound of Gregor's deep, rumbling voice. He bucked his chin to the right. "Let your friend deal with him. We have more important matters to address."

Saeed turned to find that Fallon had made his way through the fray. He headed straight for Rin and some small measure of good sense cleared the haze of unchecked rage from his mind. His attention went to Gregor once again. The male stood, calmly observing, his arms folded across his wide chest. Was this some trick? The berserker was actually trying to help him? Did his motive really matter? Cerys was dying and Saeed was running out of time.

"I can bring your soul back, Rin." Chills danced over Saeed's skin as Fallon conjured an illusion of Cerys to speak to the still shocked mage. "All you have to do is tell me where you keep your stolen souls. I can use them to bring yours back. You know how these bargains work. It's a simple trade . . ."

Saeed gave his head a violent shake as he forced his attention away from the illusion. He couldn't let that false representation of her distract him. Instead, he needed to heed Gregor's words and let Fallon deal with Rin while he dealt with Cerys. He didn't care why Gregor wanted her saved. They shared in a common goal and that made him—however temporarily—Saeed's ally.

The daggers fell from his grasp as Saeed went to his knees beside Cerys. He gathered her limp, lifeless body in his arms and swallowed down a tortured sob as he pulled her against him. The helplessness that overtook him was more than he could bear. Everything about her was a mystery, from her unimaginable power to the toll it took on her seemingly fragile body.

"It is a wound that will never heal." Gregor took several steps closer and Saeed's hackles rose. "Watching your mate die while there is *nothing* you can do to save her."

Perhaps it was Gregor's intention to kill Saeed with grief? To watch with perverted satisfaction as he lost his mate, much like Gregor had lost his so many centuries ago. The illusion of Cerys still spoke to Rin to his right, entreating him to reveal his secrets in order to save his soul. Rin had watched her destroy it. Would Fallon be able to capitalize on Rin's hopelessness to convince him to take the bait? Did any of it matter if, after all they'd been through, Cerys died anyway?

Saeed bit into his wrist. Cerys was convinced his blood had done little to help her in regaining strength but he had to do something. She was his mate. *His.* The connection between them went beyond their souls. It transcended time, space, and the natural order. If his blood couldn't help her, what was the point of any of it? He tilted her head back and let the crimson drops fall onto her tongue as he said a silent prayer to any god that might listen that she be spared.

For the second time in twenty four hours, Saeed faced the possibility that he might not be able to save her. And again, he knew that he wouldn't survive the loss. "Drink, Cerys." He spoke low to her ear in a pleading tone as though that would somehow change things. "Please."

"Vampires," Gregor said with unmasked disgust. "So arrogant. You think your blood is some magic elixir. A potion that will cure anything. How does that superiority serve you now, Saeed?"

Gregor threw his own inability to save his mate in Saeed's face. It was as cruel a wound as a silver stake through his heart. The pain of it tore through him, eviscerating muscle as it stabbed at his chest. It was a humbling reminder that no being in this world was infallible. Life was precious and delicate whether one lived for sixty or six hundred years. The superiority of his supernatural existence meant nothing in this moment, and it was a cruelty for Gregor to remind him of it.

"Ian! We found it!"

Saeed looked up as two more berserkers entered the club. They crossed to the VIP section and one of them tossed something at Gregor. A flash of glowing light flew through the air over his head. Gregor reached up and swiped it out of the air, to cradle the light in his palm. His eyes met Saeed's, a calculating grin lit his angular face. "Your blood might not save her vampire," Gregor said. "But this will."

A sense of urgency rose up in Saeed to overtake the grief that threatened to swallow him whole. "What is that?" he demanded. "Damn you, berserker! Tell me!"

Gregor held the bottle aloft and examined its contents with an expression of fascination. "This?" he asked innocently. He held the bottle toward Saeed in his outstretched hand. "It's your mate's soul."

How? Had Gregor been searching for Cerys's soul all along? He'd managed to deceive them all, working his own angle while he pitted them against each other. "Give it to me!" Saeed reached out for the bottle.

Gregor pulled his arm back. "It's not going to be that easy, vampire. It's time you and I struck a bargain of our own."

Bastard. Gods, Saeed was so fucking *sick* of the agendas and machinations of users and exploiters. He might as well be making a deal with the devil. If Mikhail ever found out what happened here tonight, Saeed would be considered a traitor and the vampire king would likely run a stake through his heart. Gregor offered Saeed the only glimmer of hope that remained. He had no option but to bow to the berserker's will. Like all of Rin's victims, Saeed was about to eagerly agree to anything in order to get what he needed. He would become beholden to his race's greatest enemy.

"What's your price, slayer?" Like it mattered. Saeed would agree to anything.

A wide smile spread across Gregor's lips. "Take her home to Los Angeles. That's all I want in return."

"Bullshit." The word burst from Saeed's lips. It couldn't be that simple.

Gregor laughed and it made Saeed want to tear the bastard's throat out. "Unlike Rin, I'm a male of my word. This deal struck between us isn't an offer of peace or clemency. If I give you her soul, you must agree to take her to L.A. no later than two sunrises from now. Promise me that, and I'll ask nothing further of you."

"Why? For what purpose?" What was Gregor hiding?

"The why is none of your fucking business." Gregor's native accent intensified with his anger. Black bled into the whites of his eyes and Saeed got a glimpse of the beast who'd nearly eradicated his kind. "Do you want to save her or not?"

"Yes." Saeed would do anything to save her. Including betrayal. "I agree to your terms. Shall I give you a blood oath?"

Gregor scoffed. "I want none of your vampire troths. I know you'll keep your word."

He tossed the bottle carelessly into the air. Saeed's stomach rocketed up into his throat as he scooped it out of the air. He cradled the bottle to his chest before pulling it away to inspect its contents.

Starlight sparkled in the ancient vessel. The same starlight that dusted Cerys's skin and shone in her light eyes. It pulsed in the low light, illuminating her motionless body still cradled against him. Saeed didn't doubt it was Cerys's soul confined inside. He recognized it in an instant.

Saeed broke the wax seal as he pulled the stopper from the bottle. Tendrils of light spilled out of the bottle, twisting and turning in a graceful dance as they covered Cerys's body like a delicate spider's web glistening in early morning sunlight. The light permeated her skin, sinking below the surface and renewing the otherworldly glow that made her appear as though covered in a layer of stardust. Cerys drew in a sharp, gasping breath and her back arched.

As he'd promised, Cerys's soul was returned.

Saeed slumped backward as a force pushed into his chest. He felt full to bursting as the emptiness that had consumed him was flooded and replaced with such a strong sense of self and completeness that it stole his breath. For all of his unwavering faith, the moment of his tethering still sent a momentary sensation of shock through his body. Cerys was his. His tethered mate. The one who'd anchored his soul. Finally, they'd been made whole.

Saeed looked up and his eyes met Gregor's. Whole, but would they ever be truly free? Sooner or later, their use-lessness would run out and when that happened, Gregor's

blind hatred and prejudice would remind him why Saeed—
and possibly even Cerys—needed to die.

"Saeed," Fallon said from behind him, "I know where
the souls are being kept."

Gregor smiled. "Looks like my work here is done.
Gavin!" He called out to one of the berserkers in his group.
"Take Rin." Saeed's jaw went slack. "What?" Gregor offered up an arrogant smirk. "You didn't think I'd leave
Seattle completely emptyhanded, did you?" His sadistic
laughter echoed around him as the berserkers gathered Rin
and headed for the door. "Take her back to L.A., Saeed,"
Gregor said in parting. "Don't make me regret my decision
to let you live. For now."

Cerys drew in a shuddering breath and Saeed's chest
swelled with emotion. She was alive. Her soul was intact,
and their tether was secure. He just hoped all of it was
worth the price he'd just paid.

Cerys took a punch to the chest that registered at about
a+10 on the pain scale. Her lungs expanded with a gasp
of breath that didn't do much to assuage the pain that
radiated from her solar plexus outward. Her back arched
and her arms spread wide as she was flooded with a heat
so intense that for a moment, she thought maybe someone
might have chucked her on her funeral pyre a little pre-
maturely. Brilliant white light encased her body and Cerys squeezed her eyes tightly shut. She turned her head to
one side, but it didn't do anything to shield her. Forget the
funeral pyre. Someone had thrown her into the center of a
nuclear bomb. A storm of hurricane proportions raged
within her, so violent that she couldn't hear anything but
it's untamed rage, and Cerys had no choice but to ride it
out. She just wished she knew what she'd done to deserve
this sort of horrible introduction to the afterlife . . .

Oh yeah. She'd spent the past couple thousand years

helping Rin to destroy and enslave one poor soul after another. She guessed she really was getting what she deserved.

The storm began to wane as did the searing heat that coursed through her veins. The rush of wind in her ears abated to a soft whisper. Her body relaxed and the spasms that racked her muscles subsided. A sense of fullness swept in to replace the pain, as though Cerys had spent the entire day at an all-you-can-eat-buffet and glutted herself to her heart's content. Gods, it felt good. On its heels, Cerys felt a joy so intense that it coaxed tears to stream from her tightly shut eyes to run in rivulets down her cheeks.

"Cerys."

Saeed's voice was like a beacon in a moonless night. The deep vibration and smooth timbre caused her chest to ache with an excess of emotion that filled her close to bursting. *Love*. She was in love with Saeed. And for the first time she didn't simply know it. She actually felt it. In the center of her being. Her very core. Cerys felt her love for Saeed smack dab in the middle of her soul.

Cerys's eyes flew open. She clutched at her chest as she tried to propel herself to sit. She was energized and much too weak all at once. As though her limbs had gone years without use and she was just getting used to her body again. She felt like a squatter in her own skin, the unfamiliar sensation of herself distracting and disconcerting. What in the hell had happened? How had it happened? Her breath caught in her chest as she rubbed once again at her sternum.

"Are we dead?"

It was the only explanation. She and Saeed had died together and the gods had seen fit to send them into the afterlife together. For having passed over . . . he looked a little worse for wear. Cerys reached up and cupped his cheek in her palm. Worry lined his handsome face and shone in his expressive midnight eyes. His black, curly hair was mussed as though he'd raked his fingers through it and blood stained his dark skin where he'd been injured and healed. If he looked this bad, she could only imagine what she looked like. Extracting and destroying Rin's corrupt soul had to have drained her to the point that she looked like a zombie. And she'd seen some scary looking zombies.

"No." Saeed's response was half relieved laughter and half choked out sob. "We're not dead."

"Huh." Saeed's fingers threaded through her hair from the temple to the crown and a riot of pleasant chills broke out over her skin. "Then what in the hell happened?"

Saeed's gaze left hers and darted upward. Cerys pushed herself up on one arm that felt about as stable as JELL-O, and followed his line of sight to where Ian Gregor stood, watching them. How in the hell were either of them still alive? The berserker's eyes went inky black with tendrils that spread outward onto his skin. Just as quickly, the color faded and he gave Saeed a slight incline of his head. A silent moment passed before Gregor jerked his chin toward the door and six males fell into step behind him as they headed for the door. Cerys had been through the wringer, but she was sure there'd been a few less of them here earlier. What the hell . . . ?

She didn't have to be privy to what had happened to know Saeed and the berserker warlord had struck some sort of bargain.

"Saeed," she said, fearful of his response. "What did you do?"

He turned his attention back to her and brushed the hair away from her face. "I returned your soul, like I promised I would."

Of course he had. Because Cerys knew that Saeed would never make a promise to her and not keep it. The strange sensation at the center of her chest gave a slight twinge, not uncomfortable, but as though to alert her to its presence. She rubbed at her sternum and Saeed's brow furrowed as he leaned in and put his forehead to hers.

"You feel it, don't you?"

The physical contact, no matter how simple, felt *so good*. "Feel what?"

He let out a breath. "The tether."

A sob lodged itself in Cerys's throat. Through all of this, Saeed's faith had been unflinching, while she'd doubted. The guilt of that doubt welled hot and thick in her throat. How could she possibly be worthy of him? It seemed impossible, and yet fate had seen its way clear to bind them together.

"Yes."

Cerys pulled away. From the moment she'd laid eyes on Saeed she'd wanted a glimpse at his soul. Now that he'd been tethered, she didn't have to imagine its colors. Her jaw hung slack. A hundred times more beautiful than she'd imagined it.

Brilliant. Vibrant. Dazzling like the Aurora Borealis with as many mesmerizing colors. The aura of Saeed's soul was almost too lovely for Cerys to behold and still, she couldn't force herself to look away.

"You were right." Cerys uttered the words in a hoarse whisper. "I'm so sorry I didn't believe."

There wasn't an ounce of hurt, anger, or disdain in Saeed's expression. "Before you took Rin's soul, you said you loved me."

She had. And she'd meant it.

"We're not done here."

A voice intruded on their private moment and Saeed's expression hardened. A trickle of anxiety entered Cerys's bloodstream. She knew that voice. Had watched as Breanne's consort fought at Saeed's side. He'd been a busy vampire tonight, hadn't he? Making deals with the *bean sidhe* and berserkers alike. *Gods.* Did Saeed have any idea what he'd gotten himself into? Who he was now obligated to?

"I gave you my word." Saeed didn't bother to shift his gaze from Cerys as he addressed Fallon. "I don't plan to go back on it."

Cerys tilted her head up toward Saeed's. "You promised the return of Breanne's soul in exchange for Fallon's help. Is that it?"

Saeed gave a shallow nod of his head. He'd made a rash decision, one that would likely bite him in the ass. The *bean sidhe* were the coldest and most ruthless of the fae. The second Breanne's soul was returned, Fallon would likely kill them both. If anything to prove to their enemies that they weren't to be fucked with.

"Where's Rin?" Cerys had yet to see him since she'd crushed his soul to dust. Having destroyed it, Rin would be nothing more than a shade. Neither living nor dead, a creature that lived between the realms for eternity. She'd condemned him to purgatory, weakened his magic, and stolen the essence of what made Rin, well, Rin. Saeed might have managed to get her soul back, but she doubted Rin would loosen his hold on the countless others he possessed. "He'll never give you Breanne's soul, Saeed."

Saeed put his lips to her forehead. "He doesn't have a choice. He is now the master of nothing and no one. Gregor took him and I doubt Rin will be seeing the light of day any time soon."

There was so much wrong with what Saeed just said that Cerys couldn't wrap her mind around it all. Gregor had taken Rin? And Saeed had let the vampires' mortal enemy just walk right out of here with him? The alliance was so unlikely she wanted to laugh. "Rin will never tell Gregor where the souls are kept."

"We already know where they are," Saeed replied. "Fallon coaxed the location out of him."

Day-um. Shit had gone *down* while she'd been checked out. Cerys had more than enough cause for worry. "Well then," she replied. "I guess we have some work to do."

CHAPTER
33

What Saeed wanted was to get Cerys back to his condo but neither was he willing to let her out of his sight. He'd given Gregor his word that he'd take her back to L.A. immediately, but he couldn't help but feel reluctant. The deal he'd made with Gregor had been rash. He'd been desperate. Cerys was dying and needed her soul to thrive. To survive. He would have agreed to *anything*. The potential consequences for his actions hadn't even registered.

If Mikhail found out what he'd done here tonight, Ian Gregor would be the least of Saeed's problems.

There was so much he and Cerys needed to discuss. She'd said she loved him. The admission was more than Saeed could've hoped for. Since the first time he'd seen her in the Collective, he'd been obsessed. She'd occupied his every waking thought. That obsession hadn't been love, however. Saeed wasn't so foolish as to think otherwise. He'd wanted Cerys. Desired her. Had counted on her to return his soul to him. But sometime during the quiet, stolen moments with her over the past several weeks, Saeed had fallen in love. With her strength, her quiet dignity, her snarky humor, her beauty, her grace, and her perseverance despite everything life had thrown at her.

"Are you sure you're strong enough for this?"

She needed to rest. To recuperate and regain her strength. To adjust to the sensation of being whole after thousands of years of being incomplete.

Cerys reached out to take Saeed's hand in hers and gave it a gentle squeeze. "I'm okay." He gave her a dubious look and she smiled. "Really."

The tether that bound them gave a gentle tug. Saeed admitted he could've used a few quiet moments of adjustment for himself. The reassurance of their connection comforted Saeed, even though he knew it wasn't necessary. He'd known long before his soul had been returned that Cerys was meant for him. His own unflagging faith was more of a reassurance than that sensation in his chest.

Fallon remained stoically silent in the driver's seat, his gaze unflinchingly focused on the road. This night had been one of the longest of Saeed's existence, and it was far from over. "What if we run into trouble?"

Cerys gave a gentle laugh. "I think we've been through the worst of it, don't you?"

Saeed wanted to think so but something told him their troubles were only about to begin. Whether those troubles would be in Seattle or L.A. was yet to be seen. "What I think is that I'm not willing to risk your safety ever again."

"Good luck with that." Cerys laughed again and Saeed wondered how she could continue to be so nonchalant despite everything that had happened. The space of silence passed before she spoke up again. "So, when are you going to tell me what in the hell happened between you and Ian Gregor?"

Never, if Saeed could get away with it. Of course, he knew that would never happen, not when his mate was so headstrong. *Mate*. He realized he'd never allowed himself to truly think of Cerys in such a way before. A smile curved his lips. Cerys Bain was his tethered mate and Saeed couldn't be happier. Finally, everything in his life had fallen into place.

"Later," Saeed replied. He didn't want to have this conversation with an audience. Fallon might've claimed his singular focus was the return of Breanne's soul, but Saeed knew all wouldn't simply be forgiven. He didn't want to give the fae any more ammunition against them than they already had. "When we're alone."

Cerys gave him a look. "You do realize that response isn't exactly putting me at ease, right?"

No, he supposed it wouldn't. Not with her need to find some measure of control in an out-of-control situation. "Patience, love. Just give me a little time to tie up these loose ends and I won't leave out a single detail."

Cerys's gaze warmed. "Love?"

Saeed brought her knuckles to his lips. "As if there was any doubt?" He didn't outright tell her he loved her, because once again he wasn't thrilled about having an audience. Cerys deserved more than a casual admission, and once they were alone he would tell her exactly how he felt.

"We're here."

Fallon broke his silence as he pulled into a gated driveway just outside of the city and brought the car to a stop. Rin might have not have regularly displayed his power, but that didn't mean he never used it. The souls he'd instructed Cerys to take were his most prized possessions. Saeed couldn't imagine getting to them would be a simple task.

"The air is thick with magic." Fallon's tone echoed Saeed's concern. "We should have brought a magic wielder with us."

As if he could've simply picked one up at the corner market. Saeed knew of only one magic wielder, Ronan's mate, Naya, and she was no mage. He doubted she'd be of any use from L.A., however. They were on their own.

"Rin's magic is elemental," Saeed said. "At least we know what to expect."

Fallon snorted. Apparently he didn't share in Saeed's optimism. "That hardly puts me at ease."

He pulled the car to a stop at a large iron gate which Saeed assumed was more to keep up the appearance of security than anything. He didn't know of any supernatural creature that wouldn't be able to leap the gate as though they were simply crossing a puddle. They'd encounter Rin's true security once they crossed it.

"Fallon's right. We need backup. This isn't going to be a picnic."

Saeed gave Cerys a sidelong glance. He knew this wouldn't be easy. In an ideal situation, they would have time to plan and execute. Time wasn't on their side, though. Gregor expected Saeed and Cerys back in L.A. by the sunrise after tomorrow. They didn't have a moment to spare.

"One of Gregor's foot soldiers made it through," Saeed replied. "So we know it can be done."

"Would've been nice if the bastard had seen fit to share those details," Cerys remarked.

On that, they could agree. Gregor had struck a deal with Saeed, but that hardly made them friends. Gregor didn't give a single shit about the other souls Rin held hostage. Helping Saeed to free them was not a part of his agenda. But gods, Saeed wished he knew what Gregor's agenda was.

The paved driveway that led from the gate to the building couldn't have been more than fifty yards. The building itself wasn't elaborate or impressive in any way. Nothing more than a modest outbuilding, which made Saeed even more nervous. The structure had to be well protected. They had no choice but to move forward and pray they could circumvent Rin's security.

"Cerys, how many souls does Rin have in that building?"

Saeed turned his attention to Fallon and waited for Cerys to respond to the fae's question.

"Including Breanne's," Cerys said, "three hundred and two."

Gods. Even if they did managed to circumvent Rin's security, Saeed had no idea how they would return every single soul to their rightful owners before sunrise. "How do we return them?"

Cerys gave him a sad smile. "How did you return my soul to me?"

Saeed's brow furrowed. "I simply freed it from its prison. And it flew to you."

"Exactly. It's a lot easier to return a soul than it is to steal one."

Their gazes met and held. "As easy as tethering a soul?"

She smirked. "Easier."

"Good. Are you ready to right a few wrongs?"

Cerys's smile widened and shone with genuine joy. "Absolutely."

She'd assured Saeed she was five by five, but in truth, Cerys was still a little wiped. Over the past week, she'd gone through the wringer and it would be a couple of months at least before she felt comfortable in her own skin again. The return of her soul had brought with it an intensity to her emotions that had been absent for far too long. Her own residual guilt at having harmed so many at Rin's behest nearly gutted her. Nothing in her world would be right until she did something to undo the hurt she'd caused.

"I should go alone." There was no point in putting both

Saeed and Fallon in danger. This was her deed to do. Her risk to take.

"No." Saeed's response brooked no argument. Cerys should've known he'd never let her go it alone, but she had to at least give it a shot. "We'll do this together, or not at all."

"You'll do this, or face Breanne's judgment." Fallon's icy tone could have frozen flames. "There is no other option."

"Whatever." Gods, *bean sidhe* were so intense. Fallon needed to calm the hell down and let Cerys handle this. "Either way, we're not getting anything accomplished standing here talking about it." Cerys was exhausted. Her emotions were on edge, she felt like an alien in her own body, and all she wanted was to crawl into bed with Saeed and call it a damned night. "We go together, but let's agree on the end game. Get into the building. Free the souls. No matter what, one of us has to do that."

Saeed's narrowed gaze told her he had no problem reading between the lines. "That someone doesn't have to be you." His emphatic tone caused Cerys's chest to swell with emotion. So much that it overwhelmed her. She reached up as her chest tightened and she felt the familiar tug of their bond. That was definitely going to take some getting used to. "Hang back, and let me run point."

Cerys wasn't about to enter into a relationship with Saeed where she expected him to clean up her messes. "I'll run point," she said. "You two just be sure to watch my back." Saeed opened his mouth to protest but she cut him off. "No arguments. I'm doing this. Period. I told you I was okay and I meant it." All right, so that last part was a bit of an exaggeration. "You have to let me fix this, Saeed. Otherwise, it will always be a point of contention between us."

Saeed's expression softened, as though he could see the

logic in her argument. He was a reasonable male, surely he wasn't interested in wasting any more time. "Very well. You run point."

Huh. He'd caved much easier than she thought he would. "Okay, then. Let's do this."

Without thinking, Cerys leapt over the gate. She landed firmly on her feet, a little surprised at her own strength and agility. She'd been running at half capacity for so long, she'd forgotten what she was capable of. She could only imagine how she'd feel after a couple months of rest.

Cerys held her breath as she waited for the first blow of Rin's magical security to hit her. The air was charged with a static tingle and smelled of sulfur, like the heavy air of a summer storm. The sound of two sets of feet hitting the ground preceded a crack of thunder as the sky went bright with a streak of lightning. It struck the pavement not five feet away and the impact knocked all three of them onto their asses.

"Okay . . ." Cerys pushed herself up to stand and dusted herself off. "That could've been worse."

Of course, she'd spoken too soon. Strike after strike of bright white lightning pounded the ground like bombs going off in a mine field. *Awesome*. "Run!"

Cerys took off at a sprint. She zigged and zagged as she avoided one bolt of lightning after the next. The ground shook and her footing wasn't sure but she kept her gaze focused straight ahead and powered through. Saeed and Fallon were both quicker than she was. Their reaction times much faster. They could easily anticipate and avoid the strikes. Cerys could only hope that she could stay even half a step ahead. Every step brought her closer to the outbuilding, and she pushed herself as fast as she could go. Just another fifteen seconds. Ten, and she'd be home free.

At least, she hoped.

The air grew thick with the scent of sulfur once again and the hairs on Cerys's arms stood on end. The crack came alongside the flash of lightning this time and she zigged when she should have zagged. Damn it. *Way to make yourself an easy target you idiot!*

Her breath left her lungs in a violent whoosh of air as she was tackled from the right and taken to the ground. Saeed cradled her in his arms as he rolled to shield her body from the brunt of the impact at the exact moment lightning struck the ground where she'd stood only a moment ago. "Holy shit!" Thunder continued to crash around them as more lightning struck the ground. "That was close."

"Too close," Saeed said against her ear. "Stay near me, please. I don't think a vampire can suffer a heart attack, but neither do I want to press my luck and find out."

Cerys stifled her amusement at his humor. Her stoic vampire was finally starting to loosen up. His timing could've been better, but still . . . Their destination wasn't more than fifteen or so yards away. "Deal. Let's get moving. No use standing around waiting to be struck by lightning."

Saeed's warm chuckle sent chills over Cerys's skin. "Agreed."

Gods, it was so not the right time to be lusting after her mate but Cerys couldn't help herself. It also wasn't the right time for her to realize that Saeed was in fact, her mate. Wow. It was a night of revelations, wasn't it?

"Cerys! Come on!"

Oh yeah, right. She hopped up and took off at a sprint. Saeed kept pace at her side and they ran together toward the outbuilding where Fallon already waited for them. She stayed close to Saeed's body as they navigated the mine field of lightning strikes. Twenty feet . . . ten . . . five. They skidded to a stop under the eave of the roof and Cerys pressed her back flat against the building as she caught her breath. One last angry bolt struck the ground and the world around them rattled before a final boom of thunder trailed off into deafening silence.

"The door is unlocked." Fallon didn't bother to check on anyone's wellbeing. To be honest, Cerys was just thankful he hadn't tried to kill either one of them yet. "I checked the knob but didn't open it."

"Well, I suppose that's one obstacle down." Though it would've been nice if Fallon had actually opened the door to check for a potential threat. She supposed he wasn't going to put his safety on the line, though. Nope, he'd leave the risk to her. Cerys pushed herself away from the building and headed for the door. She reached for the knob and turned it. As she pushed, Saeed jerked her out of the way and turned with her held tight against his body. Gale force winds raged from inside, strong enough to have thrown Cerys's body thirty or so yards away. The howling in her ears drowned out any other sound and the three of them waited, bodies pressed against the building, until the winds died down to nothing more than a gentle breeze.

"Rin's power is diminished now that his soul is gone," Cerys replied. "The magic guarding this place has to be a quarter of what it was when the berserkers came. They must've been battered running this gauntlet."

"I doubt it." Saeed did little to hide his disgust. "Berserkers can take an almost unimaginable amount of damage. I'm sure they made it through with little difficulty."

Probably. Cerys couldn't believe she'd every feel grateful for a berserker's resilience, but she was. At least for now. She hoped the blessing of having her soul returned wouldn't eventually turn into a curse.

"I think we're through the worst of it," she said to Saeed.

Any further attempt to contain elemental magic inside the building would have risked damaging the souls stored inside. No way would Rin have done it. Cerys moved away from the door but Saeed stepped in front of her and shielded her with his arm.

"I'll go in first. When I'm assured it's safe, you can enter."

So gallant. Foolish, but gallant.

"I'm right behind you," Cerys said.

"As am I," Fallon couldn't help but add. *Ugh.*

"Don't worry." Cerys wanted to add something snarky, but she decided to exercise a little caution for a change. "Breanne's soul will be the first one I free."

Fallon leveled his icy gaze on her. "How will you know?"

Cerys suppressed a shudder. "I'll know. Saeed, go ahead. Let's get this over with."

She waited at the threshold as Saeed went inside. Several tense moments passed where Cerys felt like she might crawl right out of her skin. When he appeared in the doorway, she let out an audible sigh of relief.

"It's safe." His voice held a quality of awe that sent a jolt of anxiety through her bloodstream. "Come inside."

Cerys knew what she'd find inside the building but it still caught her off guard. Three hundred and two bottles lined the far wall, all of them glowing with the light of the souls contained within their confines. Cerys recognized every single one and knew on sight which one belonged to whom.

The guilt welled up within her, so hot and thick that she thought it would choke her to death.

"Where is Breanne's soul?" Fallon demanded from behind her.

"There." Cerys pointed to the modern-looking bottle with a rubber stopper closest to her left. The soul glowed and pulsed, glistened like myriad fireflies. "That one is Breanne's."

"How will you return it to her?"

Cerys glanced at Fallon from over her shoulder. The shadows of the darkened room made the angles of his face sharp and almost sinister. Cold and feral. Just like the creature he was. "It will return to her on its own," she murmured. "All we have to do is free it."

"Then do it," Fallon said. "Now."

With his eye on the prize, the *bean sidhe* wasn't interested in pleasantries anymore. Cerys could hardly blame him. She lifted the bottle from its perch and cradled it in her hand. A deep breath inflated her lungs as she pulled the stopper, and she released it as the soul escaped the narrow mouth of the bottle in shining silver tendrils before rising into the air and slipping quickly through the open door.

"There," Cerys said on a breath. "It's done."

"I don't believe you." Fallon's skepticism was going to put a serious kink in the rest of her night. "It can't be that simple."

"It can and it is," Cerys said. "Taking a soul is the hard part. When released from its prison, it naturally wants to return to its home."

"When Breanne gives word that she's once again whole, I'll believe you."

Cerys shrugged. "Suit yourself."

Saeed reached for one of the bottles and Cerys stayed his hand. "Don't." Somehow, she couldn't bear for Saeed to touch any of them. These precious souls that Cerys had so cruelly stolen. "Please. I . . ." A knot formed in Cerys's throat and she tried to speak past it. "I need to do this myself."

Saeed jerked his chin toward the doorway and Fallon took several steps back. Cerys took one of the bottles in her hand—Nick's soul—and turned it in her palm. Saeed laid a comforting hand on her shoulder and Cerys leaned against him. She loved the way his large frame supported her. The way he lent his strength to her.

Crash!

Without thinking, she let the bottle slip from her fingers. It shattered on the concrete floor to release the soul trapped inside. It floated like glowing tendrils of smoke, winding and twining through the air before it slipped past Fallon and out the doorway. Cerys plucked another bottle from the shelf. "Alicia." A desperate nymph with the power to enchant men with the sound of her voice who'd fallen on hard times and gone to Rin for help. The bottle that contained her soul crashed to the floor as well.

Tears welled in Cerys's eyes as she grabbed one bottle after the next. First, they tumbled from her grip, then, she threw them angrily at the floor. With each bottle, she spoke another name. Another victim. Another pathetic creature forced to lived decades—centuries—incomplete. Cerys cried in earnest until her tears blurred her surroundings. Bottle after bottle crashed to the floor until all that was left was a pile of broken glass, her tears, and the guilt she feared she'd never wash from her own tarnished soul.

"Shh." Saeed turned her in his embrace and cradled her against him. "It's all right, love. I've got you. I've got you."

Her arms went around him and she held on to him as though fearful he'd let her go. "I love you, Saeed," she said through her tears. "I love you."

"And I love you." She felt the truth of his words in every fiber of her being. Through the tether that bound them.

It was a good thing, too. Because Cerys had a feeling their troubles were far from over.

CHAPTER
34

Sasha's rebirth hadn't happened upon her turning. No, she'd been reborn the moment she'd cast off the mantle of responsibility Saeed had thrust on her. She was done with playing it safe. Through with being the diplomat. So *over* her role within the coven's structure. It was a new life. And she was finally ready to live it.

"Woohoo!"

She spun on the dance floor, giddy and drunk on blood. She'd found more than a few eager dhampirs to keep her company night after night and they'd all managed to keep her well-fed too. There wasn't much more she could ask for. Except for maybe a refill. Sasha hated it when her glass was empty.

She left her dance partner—a particularly randy shifter—on the dance floor without explanation. Why offer one? She did what she wanted, when she wanted. Sasha answered to no one. Not anymore. Appreciative eyes followed her as she made her way to the bar. She enjoyed the attention. Welcomed it. Saeed had never bothered to look at her with anything other than brotherly affection. The males in the club observed her with open, unadulterated lust. She might take one of them for the night. If it met her mood. Maybe not. Sasha was in control of her own destiny now. She made the rules.

"Can I get another gimlet?" She'd made friends with the bartender, Ani, the sylph who'd offered up her very first cocktail here. Sasha made it a point to drink a different drink every night. It's not like the alcohol did anything to her. Her supernatural liver was just fine, thank you very much, and the blood she'd taken earlier gave her a far better buzz than Tanqueray ever would.

"You're on a tear tonight!" Ani flashed a wide grin as she mixed the cocktail. "What's hot out there right now?"

Sasha leaned in conspiratorially. "Dancing with a sexy shifter right now," she said. "I think he's got a buddy. Want me to hook you up?"

Ani laughed. "Nah. Not tonight anyway. I'm off tomorrow, though. We can hunt for fresh meat together."

"Deal." Sasha took the drink from Ani's outstretched hand and took a long sip. Delish. "See ya in a few. Time to see if the shifter's got any moves he hasn't shown me yet."

"We can only hope!" Ani called as Sasha stepped away from the bar.

"You and me both, sister!" Sasha gave her a silent toast and disappeared back into the crowd.

She'd lost the shifter in the press of bodies on the dance floor but that didn't bother her. There were plenty of decent prospects out tonight and besides, she wasn't sure she wanted someone to warm her bed for the night yet or not. She did need a new dance partner, though.

A body brushed against hers and Sasha turned. She offered up a wide smile to the male who'd ground his hips into her ass, before puckering her lips over the straw poking out of her glass and taking a nice long sip of her gimlet. "Wanna dance?"

His bright smile was all the answer she needed. Sasha swayed to the beat of the music, her drink in one hand, the other brushing the male from his muscular shoulder to his wrist. Over the past several weeks, she'd become adept at identifying other supernatural creatures by her senses alone. She didn't have to use her sense of smell or anything else with this one. Dhampir. One of her own. Well, sort of. And gods, he smelled *delicious.*

Sasha drained her gimlet in a few swallows and discarded the glass on a table near their spot on the dance floor. Why bother with a cocktail when there was something far more delectable for her to put her mouth on?

She gave him a slow perusal, raking him from head to toe with her gaze. She leaned in close and said next to his ear, "To what coven do you belong?"

"Siobhan's."

Interesting. The members of Siobhan's coven generally stuck together. She ruled with an iron fist and forbade any of her members to interact with vampires. This one would be in big trouble if his mistress found out whom he was currently grinding his nether regions against.

"What's your name?" Usually Sasha didn't bother with names. Why? Her recent hookups had been nothing more than one night stands. She wanted to know the dhampir's name, however. Mikhail didn't trust Siobhan and frankly, neither did Sasha. It might be a good idea to become acquainted with someone on the inside.

"Jason."

He flashed another wide, seductive smile that showcased the dainty points of his fangs. Siobhan rarely let any of the dhampirs who fed her pierce her skin in return. But she was feeling feisty tonight and it would give her a perverse sense of satisfaction to have offered her vein to one of Siobhan's own.

Sasha bent her knees and dipped low in time with the beat of the music. She came up slowly, careful to brush the length of his body with hers as she thrust her hips forward and rolled her body upright. The scent of his desire bloomed around her and the dry fire ignited in Sasha's throat. Her secondary fangs slid down from her gums, throbbing with the need to pierce the dhampir's flesh. She wasn't sure if it was her desire to make a little mischief that spurred her on. Either way, Sasha knew she wouldn't be going home alone tonight.

"I'm Sasha." She let her hand wander from Jason's wide chest to the waistband of his jeans. She hooked her fingers over his belt and allowed her knuckles to graze bare flesh. She pulled away and gave him a half smile as she cocked a suggestive brow. Even though she assumed he was a sure thing, she had no problem flirting her ass off to guarantee he'd seal the deal.

"I know who you are." They weren't even really dancing anymore. They stood chest to chest and cheek to cheek as they spoke in each other's ears. "I've been watching you for a couple of weeks now."

"You have?" Okay, so that was a little stalkery, but with the way Siobhan had been rumored to spy on those Mikhail had turned, Sasha wasn't surprised. "And . . . ?"

"And you're by far the sexiest female I've ever laid eyes on."

A total line, but Sasha didn't mind. She had no problem playing hard to get. Especially when she knew her reward would be so sweet. "Won't your mistress be upset if she finds out you're playing nice with a vampire?"

Jason's hand wandered from her hip to the small of her back. His fingertips brushed her ass as he pulled her even closer. Showing his dominance? Sasha appreciated a male who went after what he wanted. "Siobhan doesn't own me," he said with a low snarl.

Oh really? Because Siobhan sure as hell gave a different impression. "Good." Her hand wandered up his arm, over his shoulder to his throat. She brushed the delicate skin with the pad of her thumb before letting her nail scrape against him. Jason shuddered and the scent of his desire intensified once again. "Want to get out of here?"

"Absolutely."

Sasha took him by the hand and led him through the club toward the door. Her night was looking up. Responsibility was definitely overrated.

Siobhan's lip curled as she watched Jason leave the club with the vampire. He followed after her like a dog sniffing after a bitch in heat. The male had absolutely no self-respect, and when he returned to the coven after his night of play, she would be sure to punish him for it.

She tossed back what was left of her bourbon in a single swallow and set the glass on the bar with a little too much force. Her rules weren't made to be broken. She didn't tolerate defiance of any kind. Fraternizing with vampires was akin to fraternizing with berserkers as far as she was concerned. Neither one was better than the other. They were all bloodthirsty, violent, and without conscience.

"Who peed in your Froot Loops?"

Siobhan's lips formed a reluctant smile at the sound of Christian's voice. She supposed she was one to talk, setting down rules that she herself chose not to obey. The game she played with Christian was a dangerous one. She was bound to get burned, and yet she couldn't seem to keep her distance from the flames.

"A foolish dhampir who lacks the good sense not to follow his dick."

Christian chuckled as he bellied up to the bar beside her. His arm brushed hers and a jolt of excitement rushed through Siobhan's bloodstream. He kept his gaze straight ahead as though they were nothing more than two strangers occupying the same space. That's what they were, though, wasn't it? Strangers? The thought soured her stomach. She hated that she wanted more than a stoic acquaintance with the cavalier werewolf. She never allowed anyone control over her emotions. And yet, Christian had easily wormed his way in to seize that power. Not that she'd ever let him know it. He didn't need the ammunition.

"What do you care who he fucks?" His tone sharpened a bit and Siobhan couldn't help but feel a little smug. "Is he your boyfriend?"

Siobhan snorted. "Hardly." She wondered, would he be jealous if Jason had in fact been her lover? "He broke my rules."

Christian snagged the attention of the bartender. "I'll have what she's having," he replied. "And she'll have another." He turned toward her, resting one elbow on the bar. Gods, he was insufferably good-looking. Especially when he adopted that nonchalant stance. "So, what? If you're not getting any, no one can?"

He smiled brightly and it was all Siobhan could do not to kiss him before smacking the expression from his face. She'd never known a male who could push her buttons like Christian Whalen could. Further proof that she'd be wise to stay as far away from him as possible.

"I don't care who he fucks." The bartender set two fresh glasses of bourbon in front of them and Siobhan brought hers to her lips for a slow sip. "As long as it's not a vampire."

Christian grinned. He downed the bourbon in a single swallow and motioned to the bartender for another. "Anyone ever tell you you're a little prejudiced?"

She cut him a look. "Against vampires? Yes."

His confident smirk made her knees wobble. He was a weakness she couldn't afford. Why in the hell couldn't she just walk away? *Because you love the game, that's why.*

"Where's your bodyguard tonight?" Was that concern in his arrogant tone? Christian's gaze scanned the crowd before circling back around to Siobhan. "I told you not to go anywhere without him."

She laughed. It was cute that he thought he could tell her what to do. Their last encounter had ended with Christian confessing that Ian Gregor was looking for a dhampir that matched her description. Siobhan had thanked him by laughing it off and walking away from him. Honestly, she was surprised he was being so civil with her tonight. Especially after she'd promised him a more hands-on relationship in exchange for his information and failed to deliver. "Carrig has other business to attend to tonight. Worried for my safety, werewolf?"

His expression grew serious. "Yes. And you know why."

A tight knot formed in Siobhan's stomach. "Because you think Ian Gregor is combing the city to find me?"

Storm clouds gathered in his gray-blue eyes and he scowled. Apparently, Christian was the only one of the two of them allowed to exhibit a cavalier attitude. Sort of a double standard if you asked her.

"I don't think, Siobhan. I *know*."

He already knew too much about her, and she assumed he'd come to his conclusions through educated guesses. Shrewd bastard. Siobhan couldn't allow herself to share in his concern, no matter how real the threat might be. Ian Gregor was a calculating son of a bitch, but he wasn't smart. At least, not in comparison to Christian. Her werewolf was incomparable.

Hers? She let out a chuff of breath. Not by a long shot.

"So tell me, since you seem to have this all figured out,

why would Ian Gregor possibly want me? He has bigger fish to fry. Trenton McAlister, for starters. Not to mention the number of vampires filling Mikhail's ranks. If you ask me, Gregor should be readying himself for war. Not looking for a female who may or may not exist."

"I don't know why he wants you . . . yet. But don't bullshit me either, Siobhan. I think I deserve more than your duplicity."

"Do you?" Siobhan took another slow sip from the lip of her glass and savored the warm glow of the bourbon as it trickled down her throat. She hadn't fed in days and she found her gaze wandering to the column of Christian's throat more times than not.

The bartender set down a fresh drink for Christian and he tossed that one back as well before slamming the glass down onto the bar. "Whatever." The word left his lips in an angry bark. "Play your games. Deny all you want. Let him track you down. If he gets his hands on you, not even Carrig will be able to save you."

Siobhan had no intention of confirming or denying Christian's suspicions. Information wasn't a two-way street with them. At least, not yet. "He'd better have a good tracker if he has any hope of finding what he's looking for."

"He does," Christian replied. "The best."

"The best, huh?" Siobhan wasn't interested in stroking Christian's ego but truly, she knew of no better tracker. From what she'd been able to find out, the Sortiari valued Christian's services above any of their other trackers. He *was* the best. And she wouldn't deny that it worried her and solidified her plan to gain his loyalty. She couldn't afford for Christian to turn against her. Not ever. "I'm impressed." She allowed the pad of her finger to lightly circle the rim of her glass. "What else are you the best at?"

"Baby," Christian leaned in close and Siobhan filled her lungs with his delicious, spicy scent, "my talents are *many*."

Siobhan experienced another pleasant rush as her stomach clenched tight. They'd been circling one another for months and she was anxious for him to put his money where his mouth was. Would tonight be that night? Disappointment settled in her gut. Probably not. For some reason, she couldn't seem to seal the deal with him. She usually had no problem backing up her brazen promises, but when it came to Christian, something held her back. Siobhan knew that once she crossed the line with him, there would be no going back. Once with him would never be enough. Her want and need would consume her and pull her focus. She couldn't allow that to happen. Not when one wrong move would bring ruin down upon her.

But gods . . . how she craved him.

"I owe you payment for the information you've given me."

"You do," Christian agreed. "But don't worry, I started you a tab. I'll collect. Eventually."

Christian had been forthright with her, coming clean about Gregor and the fact that he was scouring the city for a dhampir that he suspected might be her. She'd promised their look-but-don't-touch relationship would change when he fessed up about who he was working for. Siobhan was a female of her word. One kiss wouldn't hurt . . .

She let her gaze go molten as she stepped up to him. He was a good foot taller than her and she tilted her chin up to hold his gaze while she reached up and let her hand slide from his shoulder, down his arm, to his wrist where the pads of her fingers brushed against his palm. Christian's pupils dilated and his nostrils flared. His enticing scent bloomed around her, awakening Siobhan's own desire to a fevered pitch. Anticipation shivered through her as she leaned in closer . . . closer . . .

Her mouth met his and it was all she could do not to take him to the damned floor. His arms came around her as he thrust his tongue past her lips, demanding that she deepen the kiss. *Dear gods.* His mouth slanted across hers. There was nothing shy or tentative about the way he kissed her. It wasn't a tease. It wasn't playful. No, the way Christian kissed her was a promise and Siobhan hoped to the gods he kept it.

She pulled away with a gasp as she brushed her fingertips across her lips, swollen from his kiss. Her limbs shook and her breath raced in her chest. It took every ounce of willpower she had to walk away from him, but it had to be done. She couldn't lose herself to him. Not now, maybe not ever.

"See you around, werewolf."

Christian's sly grin nearly brought her to her knees. "You can bet on it."

She hoped so.

CHAPTER
35

Cerys could have slept for a month. She had no idea she could feel so exhausted and so happy at the same time. Saeed had seemed almost nervous about putting Seattle in their wake, but not Cerys. The city harbored so many painful memories for her that she doubted she'd ever return. She liked that Los Angeles was an unfamiliar city. No one here knew her, feared her, or made conjectures about her. She was nothing more than another supernatural creature among many. Not even worth a passing glance. The anonymity gave her comfort. It was a fresh start and for once, she was excited to embark on a new adventure.

That didn't mean her excitement didn't come with a learning curve, however.

"What is it, love?" Saeed spoke against her ear in the quiet dark. His warm breath coaxed chills to the surface of Cerys's skin. His wide chest pressed against her back as he tucked her body closer to his.

"I'm okay." She let her fingertips glide over each of his knuckles. "Just finding freedom a little tough to get used to."

Since their return to L.A., they'd kept a low profile. Saeed had given control of his coven to his most trusted confidants and he hadn't wanted to disrupt the new order they'd established here. In fact, he'd done nothing to reclaim his position as the coven's master. He'd told her he would leave that decision to Sasha, Diego, and the members of the coven. From what she'd seen so far, they all adored him. She was fairly certain he'd be running the show again in no time.

"You can have whatever you want." The smooth timbre of Saeed's voice flowed over her like satin. He put his lips to her bare shoulder and she shivered. "Go wherever you want. Do whatever you want. You have no boundaries here. No limitations. The only thing that matters to me is that you're safe and happy."

Cerys had never known a more selfless male than Saeed. His only concern was for her well-being. No one had ever cared for her like that before. No one had ever loved her like he did. There were days she didn't feel deserving of his love. Not after all of the horrible things she'd done for Rin. But there were other times, like now, as they lay entwined in the hours just after sunset, when she felt as though his love had washed her soul clean. In such a short amount of time Saeed had become the weight that anchored her, the focus that centered her, and the calm to her raging storm. She loved him more than anyone or anything in this world.

His happiness was important to her too and Cerys knew something had weighed on his mind and heart since their return to L.A. "You should talk to her, Saeed."

He let out a chuff of laughter. "I would if she ever saw fit to return home."

His response might have been a little melodramatic, but it was true that Sasha spent very little time at the house. Cerys had tried to stay out of coven business in the weeks since they'd arrived. It had nothing to do with her. She simply offered her support to Saeed if he needed it.

"Maybe she just needs a little freedom, too. She'll come around, give her some time."

Saeed's arms went tighter around her as he held her close. "I hope you're right. I worry for her."

So selfless. So caring. So opposite of what she'd lived with for centuries. Cerys turned in his embrace to face him. "She's a big girl. I'm sure she can take care of herself."

Saeed's eyes crinkled at the corners with his smile. "You're right. I worry too much."

Cerys tilted her head up to kiss him. Her mouth moved slowly over his for a long, indulgent moment. Her favorite part of her newfound freedom was knowing her time with Saeed no longer amounted to stolen moments. She could lie here with him like this all night if she wanted to. Kissing, touching, whispering to one another in the dark. She had no one to answer to. Nowhere to be but right here.

And honestly, there was nowhere else she'd rather be.

Saeed rolled Cerys onto her back and settled his hips between her thighs. Her knees fell open as the hard, hot length of his erection brushed against her sex. Cerys's back arched and the sensitive points of her nipples grazed his chest, adding a layer of sensation that coaxed a soft moan from her lips. They'd started off every night of the past couple of weeks this way and it seemed that neither of them could ever get enough.

"There are far too many hours of daylight," Saeed murmured close to her ear. "I can't wait for winter."

A slow smile spread across Cerys's lips. Her head came up from the pillow as she nuzzled his throat before grazing her teeth against his skin. Saeed let out a low growl that sent a rush of excitement through her core. Cerys rolled her hips and she drew in a gasp of pleasure as her clit slid along his shaft. "Oh come on, you haven't exactly been sleeping all day."

The return of his soul and the solidification of their tether had fortified Saeed's strength as well. The sunrise didn't put him down as easily as it used too. Instead, it slowly wearied him as anyone would be at the end of a long day.

"If I had it my way, we wouldn't sleep at all." He entered her in a slow thrust that caused Cerys's back to arch off the mattress.

"How would we spend those extra hours?" Cerys drew in a sharp breath as he pulled out to the tip, and thrust again.

"Like this." He repeated the motion, a slow roll of his hips that nearly drove Cerys out of her mind with want. "Fucking."

He'd certainly loosened up from the stiff, stoic vampire she'd met that night in Crimson. Cerys liked him like this, raw and uninhibited. It turned her blood to smoke and set her soul on fire. "Sounds like a pretty damned good way to spend a day."

Saeed cupped the back of her neck with one hand while he braced the bulk of his weight on his opposite arm. He continued to move at a slow, measured pace as though each thrust of his hips had been carefully thought out and orchestrated. He kissed her. Slowly at first, and then more deeply. Their lips met and parted, tongues intertwined in a sensual dance. His fangs nicked her bottom lip and he let out an indulgent moan. The coppery tang of blood hit Cerys's tongue and her stomach tightened pleasantly as Saeed began to pound into her with more urgency.

"Gods yes. Don't stop, Saeed." Pleasure built within her, twisting and twining as though binding her with a length of satin cord. Every inch of her tightened. The world fell out from under her until all that was left was the two of them and the blinding ecstasy that crested to a nearly unbearable peak. She wanted his fangs buried deep in her throat as she came. "I'm close," she said on a breath. "I want your bite."

Saeed pulled back with a low growl before burying his face against her throat. His thrusts became desperate and wild as his fangs broke the surface of her skin. "Saeed!" Cerys cried out as the orgasm exploded through her, deep pulsing waves of sensation that spread from her center, outward, and left her breathless and shaking.

Her fists wound into the sheets as Saeed fucked her with abandon. Chills broke out over Cerys's flesh from the sensation of his mouth suckling at her throat. It seemed there would be no end to the blinding pleasure that consumed her and to be honest, she didn't want it to end.

Saeed pulled away from her throat with a roar. His body went rigid and his movements became disjointed as a tremor rocked him from head to toe. He shuddered over Cerys as he collapsed on top of her and buried himself as deep inside of her as he could go. The pulsing spasms of his orgasm traveled along his shaft and against the sensitive, swollen flesh of her pussy. Cerys was flooded with delicious warmth as she fell back on the pillows, sated. At least, for now.

She smiled against his shoulder as they came down from the high together, their deep, panting breaths as one. She could lie like this forever. Skin to skin without a single word spoken between them. She thought about all of the lonely years of emptiness spent as Rin's possession. The hollow feeling that never went away no matter how many cheeseburgers, pizzas, or pasta she shoved into her mouth. She'd never felt so full, so sated, as she did now. Saeed was all the sustenance she'd ever need to nourish that part of her. That didn't mean she wasn't still mad in love with a well-made bowl of Phở, though.

"Are you hungry?"

Cerys laughed. Saeed pulled back and gave her a curious look as he brushed the hair from her face. "I was just thinking about food."

"What about it?"

"Just that I don't need it in the same way I used to."

He gave her a soft smile. "And why's that?"

"Because both my soul and my heart are full now."

He put his mouth to hers and kissed her. "I love you, Cerys."

"I love you, too." So much. And she knew that her feelings for him would never, ever diminish. "I wouldn't say no to breakfast, though."

Saeed chuckled. Gods, she loved the sound of his happiness. "What were you thinking?"

"Oh . . . pancakes, eggs, bacon. Maybe some French toast. Coffee . . ."

"Done. We can discuss what's for lunch while we're eating."

How could she have ever doubted that they were made for each other? "Why stop there? We'll plan the entire week's menu."

He kissed her again. Slowly this time. "Done."

Saeed had never known such happiness as he did now. The Collective no longer called to him, the memories no longer held any sway over him. He had his soul and his mate by his side. Worry still gnawed at him, however.

His agreement with Gregor had been so simple: bring Cerys to L.A. and her soul would be hers once again. But why? For what purpose? Something scratched at the back of Saeed's mind. The answer to his question. He'd been given a trail of breadcrumbs to follow within the Collective, but he couldn't make any sense of it.

So many fates intertwined. So many lives disrupted.

McAlister's magic had been bound at the request of Cerys's sister. Saeed didn't know the reasoning behind the request, but it stood to reason there was no love lost between Fiona and McAlister. Did that make Ian Gregor her ally by default? And what was Cerys's role in it all? She'd been an innocent victim, caught in the crossfire of Fiona's dealings with Rin. What purpose would it serve to have her in L.A.? McAlister was already bound. Surely, Gregor didn't want Cerys to take his soul as well. Perhaps it wasn't about Cerys at all, but Fiona . . .

"Saeed?" Cerys's voice blew through his mind like a cleansing breeze. "You okay?"

Her sweet smile and concerned expression nearly laid him low. Gods, she was the most breathtakingly beautiful creature he'd ever seen. They sat together, curled up on the couch, in the study that had once been his office. A movie played in the background—something with superheroes, he wasn't really paying attention—as they spent a quiet evening together. His mind was too full of worry for anything else. Too full of concern for his mate's well-being. He would never let Gregor—or anyone—harm her, but until Gregor's intentions became clear, Saeed would remain on edge.

"I'm fine." For now, all he wanted for her was a little peace and the time she needed to adjust to her new life. "Just thinking."

"About Sasha?"

Ah, yes. The other worry he tried not to address. "She's out of control. This isn't like her to behave this way."

Truly, Saeed had no idea what had gotten into Sasha. Her sense of duty and responsibility had always been so unflappable. It had been hard to believe that she had turned her back on her role as co-leader of the coven, when

Diego had told him. But then, Saeed had seen the evidence of her new carefree attitude for himself. She no longer cared about him, her duty, their coven, *anything*.

"I told you, she just needs to blow off a little steam."

Saeed supposed if anyone knew what it felt like to be confined and pigeonholed it was Cerys. He was prepared to give his mate all of the freedom to stretch her wings and then some. Why was he not able to extend that courtesy to Sasha as well? *She's not your responsibility anymore. You are no longer a coven master.* It was a harsh reminder but a necessary one. He'd stepped down, cast off his own responsibilities in order to search for Cerys. Sasha was his friend and nothing else. It wasn't his place to intervene in her life. He had to allow her to follow her own path.

"I think you're right." Saeed gathered Cerys close to him and tucked her under his arm.

"I mean, what's she doing, really? Partying a little too hard? From the sound of it, she deserves a little fun."

"Diego doesn't think so." In the weeks since Sasha renounced her role as co-leader, Diego had taken over full responsibility of ruling the coven. From what Saeed had heard, he'd done a stellar job, too. "He thinks she needs to stop acting like an entitled child and come to her senses."

Cerys laughed. "Typical male response. He's probably just jealous that he isn't out there with her, sowing his oats."

Perhaps, but Saeed doubted it. Diego was easy-going and charming, he came off as carefree, but Saeed knew better. He never would have left him in charge otherwise. "Diego has suggested again that I take back my position. Permitting the acceptance of the rest of our coven, of course."

Cerys's gaze searched his. "Is that what you want?"

A part of him missed it. "In time, perhaps. Right now,

I'm happy to simply be back with my family, with my mate at my side."

"I'll support you in whatever you decide." She nestled in closer, resting her head against his chest and let out a slow sigh. "In the meantime, we have enough to worry about."

A rush of anxiety spread through Saeed's body. "What do you mean?"

Cerys gave him a look. "Come on, Saeed. I know you made a deal with Gregor to get my soul back. What did you promise him?"

It would do him no good to lie to her and he didn't want to. "I promised I'd bring you to L.A. and nothing more than that."

Cerys cocked a dubious brow. "Why would he want me here?"

"That's what I've been trying to figure out." He hadn't mentioned what he'd seen in the Collective, but it was time he told her. "I saw the moment you lost your soul." She stilled beside him and he tightened his hold on her. "I know that your sister traded it for Rin's services in binding Trenton McAlister's power."

Cerys shivered in his embrace. "I don't know why she did it." Her voice was barely a whisper. "I think they were lovers. Maybe he betrayed her and that's how she took her revenge. I honestly have no idea. Fiona left after she struck her deal with Rin and I haven't seen her since." She let out a rueful laugh. "I don't even know if she's still alive."

Could it be so simple? "Gregor wants you here . . . in the hopes that your sister will seek you out now that you have your soul back and thereby bring her closer to McAlister?"

"It's a possibility." Cerys sat up a little straighter. "It's quite the gamble, though, don't you think? Why would Fiona want to face anyone she'd screwed over?"

Saeed had no idea, but he planned to find out. "I'm not sure, love. But in the meantime, we'll remain cautious and keep our ears to the ground." It was their only option at this point, besides seeking out Gregor and shaking him down for the information which probably wouldn't work out well for anyone.

"Cautious, yes." She reached up and stroked her fingers along his jaw. "But I refuse to live in fear. We aren't going to shut ourselves up in this house and stop living because we're afraid of the future. I won't be anyone's kept thing ever again. Not even yours, Saeed."

He turned and put his lips to her palm. "Never. I would *never* do that to you." He meant it, too. No matter the cost he would never take her freedom from her.

"Good." She smiled coyly and Saeed's cock stirred. He doubted there would ever be a time that he didn't want her with such immediate intensity. "Because we have nothing to worry about. A couple of ex-assassins can manage their shit, don't you think?"

Gods, how he loved her. His fire-haired fae.

"Oh, without a doubt." He put his mouth to hers once again. "Anyone who dares to disrupt our peace will pay a hefty price."

Cerys brought her hand up for a high five and Saeed gave it a slap. "Damn straight!"

They were meant for one another. The perfect team.

"Now that that's settled," Cerys said as she nestled in beside him once again. "What's for dinner . . . ?"

Read on for an excerpt for Kate Baxter's next
Last True Vampire novel

WICKED VAMPIRE

Coming soon from St. Martin's Paperbacks

Ewan grabbed Sasha and threw her over his shoulder. If she was going to act like a stubborn child, he was going to treat her like one. She let out a squeal of enraged surprise followed by a forceful whoof of air. Ewan stepped to the left, into the nearest available room, and kicked the door closed behind him. This was where the shifter intended to take Sasha. And it was certainly equipped for all sorts of erotic play.

Anger rose fresh and hot in Ewan's chest. She'd come here tonight looking for this. He stood, feet planted on the floor, and took in the sight of the room. A sex swing hung from one corner of the ceiling, one wall was adorned with bondage gear. The king-sized bed in the middle of the space was equipped with a sturdy headboard and footboard complete with leather cuffs, long scraps of silk, blindfolds, leather crops and others with feathered tips. It was a room designed for pleasure and the realization that Sasha had willingly sought this out made Ewan's gut tangle into an unyielding knot. Not because she wanted a little wild and kinky sex, but because she'd wanted it with someone other than him.

"Put me down."

Sasha pressed her palms against his ass and pushed herself upward. Ewan's jaw squared and clenched so tight that he felt the enamel on his molars grind. He deposited her to her feet and she took a stumbling step back as she pushed against his chest. She bumped into the foot of the bed and reached out to steady herself on the footboard, rattling the leather cuffs secured there in the process. Ewan couldn't help but picture her laid out on the coverlet, her ankles and wrists secured in place, helpless to do anything but lie there while he pleasured her. His cock stirred behind his fly and his gut clenched as a wave of white hot lust shot through him. He'd agreed to get close to Sasha to protect his other secrets from Gregor. He tried to convince himself that she had no effect on him. That she was nothing more than a curiosity he'd needed to work out of his system. Sasha wasn't a curiosity. She was a fucking drug and Ewan was on the road to becoming an addict.

"What in the hell are you doing here?"

Ewan was taken aback by Sasha's indignant tone. His lust was quickly replaced again by anger. He turned and locked the door before coming back to face her. The last thing he needed was some randy asshole barging in to try and join in the fun. "What am *I* doing here? What in the hell are *you* doing here?"

"I don't need your permission to go anywhere or do anything." Sasha's eyes flashed silver, an indication that her temper was about to crest.

"Oh really?" Ewan knew better than to take her on, but he couldn't help himself. "Did you, or did you not, proclaim that I was your *mate*? Do you often make such claims before seeking out other males to fuck?"

Sasha's eyes went wide. She gripped onto the footboard and leaned forward for emphasis. Ewan's mouth went dry as he looked at her. Her expression, livid eyes bright with silver, face flushed, her breasts pressing against the tight tank top she wore and threatening to spill over the deep V of the neckline. "You sent me away!"

"You bit me!"

Sasha let out a bark of disbelieving laughter. "*Vampire!*" She jabbed a finger at her chest. "It's sort of what we do."

"What? Sink your fangs into your victim's throats without asking permission?"

Sasha's brow furrowed with hurt and Ewan felt a stab of momentary regret. She was right. What she'd done was simply what it was in her nature to do. He couldn't fault her for it and yet, centuries of hate and conditioning had convinced him to do just that. Quiet settled between them, so thick and heavy that it nearly suffocated him. Ewan fought the urge to rub at his chest and instead crossed the space between them and put his mouth to hers.

Ewan had fucked Sasha, but he'd yet to kiss her. Her lips were as soft as he'd imagined, full and silky as she yielded to him. Ewan deepened the kiss, slanting his mouth over hers, forcing her lips to part with his tongue. She kept her grip on the footboard, creating space between their bodies, and a growl built in Ewan's chest. He didn't want an inch of space between them. He wanted her hands on him. Any reservation on her part wasn't acceptable.

As much as he hated to break their kiss, Ewan pulled away. Just enough to speak against her mouth. "Touch me."

Sasha leaned back in a show of defiance. "No."

Ewan's frustration mounted. Passive aggression wouldn't do anything to calm the temper that simmered just under the surface of his control. Before he'd insulted her that night in the stockroom, Sasha hadn't been able to keep her hands off him. Now, as punishment, she withheld what he wanted. Ewan didn't respond well to aggression of any kind. Nor punishment. Hell, he'd defied his own leader, the most feared warlord in supernatural history. He expected nothing less than total surrender from Sasha. There was a time and a place for playing games. Tonight, however, Ewan wasn't in the mood.

That piece of shit shifter had taken Sasha's hand and placed it on his cock. He'd pushed her when she didn't want to be pushed. The bastard was lucky Sasha had stayed Ewan's hand, otherwise, that particular piece of him would have been the first to go. Maybe it wasn't wise to make demands when she'd been faced with unwanted advances only moments before. Ewan wanted to be understanding and gentle and all of those things he expected more sensitive males were, but it simply wasn't programed into his biology to be any of those things. He was burly, demanding, insensitive. Selfish, gruff, and rough around the edges. Hell, maybe he was every bit as bad as that piece of shit shifter. The only difference being that in the short span of two encounters, he already felt a possessive instinct when it came to the spirited vampire. He didn't want another male's hands, lips, or anything else on her. Didn't want another male to so much as look at her with interest.

Ewan wanted Sasha for himself. And that all-consuming, insufferable want was sure to be his undoing.

He wouldn't force her. Wouldn't take her hands and put them where he wanted them like the shifter did. But neither would he plead for the favor. A warlord never bowed to anyone, not even a lover. If he truly was her mate, it was a fact Sasha would have to come to terms with.

He kissed her again. He wouldn't force her, but he'd

sure as hell do his best to persuade her to do what he wanted. Ewan had a tactical mind and he was more than prepared to win this battle of wills. She wanted him. The rich perfume of her arousal invaded his nostrils. She was simply too proud to admit it after being hurt.

Her grip on the footboard tightened as though she needed it to keep her from reaching out. She might not have wanted to touch him, but Ewan wasn't about to impose those kinds of restrictions on himself. He closed the space between them until his body pressed against hers. Gripped the back of her neck with one hand and let the other slide around her back to cup her ass.

Ewan thrust his hips and Sasha allowed an indulgent moan. He abandoned her mouth. Kissed the corner of her mouth, across her jawline, to the base of her ear. "Touch me," he demanded once again.

Her response was nothing more than a murmur. "No."

She punished him for rejecting her bite. If he didn't want her fangs at his throat, she wouldn't give him the satisfaction of her touch.

"If you won't touch me, then maybe I should tie you to this bed?" Ewan slid his hands down to circle her wrists. "Maybe it'll satisfy that stubborn streak of yours." He took her earlobe between his teeth and bit down gently. "Or maybe it'll frustrate you to the point that you beg me to let you touch me."

She let out a soft snort that didn't carry half the confident weight he expected she wanted it to.

His grip tightened and she let out a slow breath as she melted against him. So she liked the prospect of being bound and at his mercy? It would certainly keep those wicked fangs of hers at a safe distance. Heat gathered in Ewan's gut at the memory of that sharp sting followed by a rush of delicious warmth. For something so reviled among their kind, the act certainly hadn't been a hardship to suffer through. That didn't mean Ewan was about to entertain disaster by letting it happen again.

He was more than willing to push his boundaries with Sasha. She was a female who knew her mind and what she wanted. If she didn't like what he was about to do, he had no doubt she'd make it known.

He moved his hands from her wrists to her waist and tossed her over the footboard and onto the mattress. She let out a gasp of surprise but didn't move a muscle as he rounded the bed to stand beside her. He braced his arms on the mattress and bent over her. "Touch me." She knew what he wanted and he'd warned her of what the alternative would be.

Sasha bucked her chin in a defiant show. Gods, that stubborn streak of hers drove him wild. Her eyes met his and flashed with feral silver. "No."

"All right. Have it your way." Ewan reached over her and hooked his fingers in the waistband of her leggings. "You asked for it."

Gods, Ewan turned her on.

The last thing Sasha wanted to do was admit to him that she was more than prepared to beg for whatever the hell he wanted her to. She wanted to touch him so badly that her hands shook and her limbs quaked. When he'd threatened to tie her up, a thrill raced through her. So intense, she thought she might come from his words alone without him having to lay a single finger on her.

She'd come here tonight in search of excitement and found that nothing compared to the feelings Ewan evoked in her. But being here with him—in this place that overwhelmed her senses with sex and desire—was almost more than she could take.

Sasha let out a slow, shuddering breath as Ewan rounded the bed toward her. His hungry gaze devoured her as it raked from her feet, up the length of her body. As he braced his arms on the bed and leaned over her, Sasha's heart raced. Her breath quickened and her senses became awash with his scent, his body, his sheer size as he leaned over her. "All right. Have it your way." His fingertips slid against her skin as they dipped beneath her waistband of her leggings and Sasha's stomach muscles twitched in response. "You asked for it."

Her breath stalled in her chest as he pulled abruptly away. He reached for her feet and pulled off both of her ankle boots, tossing them to the floor along with her socks. Sparks of electricity ignited along her nerve endings as he once again went for her waistband and pulled her leggings and underwear down the length of her legs, stripping them off in one fluid motion. He grabbed her left foot and secured one leather restraint around her ankle. Sasha's breath left her lungs in a rush. Wet warmth spread between her legs as anticipation sent chills over her bare thighs. He rounded the foot of the bed, seized her other foot, and secured it with the other restraint. She'd thought he was full of shit when he threatened to tie her to the bed, but she should have known that a male like Ewan would never bluff.

"This is why you came here, isn't it?" His gaze burned through her as he strode with slow, measured steps to the head of the bed. "To be restrained. To be pleasured. To be fucked."

She'd come here to find a male who'd make her forget Ewan had ever existed. To banish the memory of him once and for all. Instead, Fate mocked her—as usual—by throwing them together once again.

He gripped the hem of her shirt and stripped the sheer, V-neck tank from her as well. He reached beneath her and a smirk tugged at his lips as her back arched to allow him access to her bra. The clasp came undone with a tick

and he pulled that from her as well, discarding it somewhere beside him as he took her hand in his and guided it
above her head so he could fasten the leather restraint
around her wrist.

She barely knew Ewan. He was a berserker. A sworn
enemy. She couldn't trust him and yet, she allowed him to
tie her to the bed frame. Sasha wasn't helpless. It's not
like a few leather straps could actually restrain her. But
that was the point. All part of the game. She could break
free at any time. It was a test of her control. Her submis-
siveness. Her resolve. Would she allow Ewan dominance?
Or would she fold and take back her power?

Her will was just as strong as his. Stronger. She'd show
him what stubborn was. She wouldn't ever beg for the
privilege of touching him. Instead, he'd plead for the favor
of her touch.

"Answer me."

She looked up to find his stern gaze trained on her
face. The soft waves of his light auburn hair fell over his
forehead and she was possessed with the urge to reach up
and brush the locks away. It wasn't wise to provoke a berserker's anger but that's exactly what she was about to
do. Sasha raised her right arm to the headboard and
wrapped her fingers around the metal in anticipation of
being bound.

"That's exactly why I came here," she said, low and
did him one better as she added to his list of lewd acts.
"To be bound. Used. Pleasured. Licked. Sucked. Fucked."

Dark shadows passed over his gaze like storm clouds
blocking out a golden sunset. He rounded the bed and
bound her other wrist, tightening the leather strap until
she felt the bite of the restraint on her skin. "Who here
touched you, vampire? Who so much as laid eyes on your
bare skin? How many here used you tonight?"

Vampire. As though addressing her in such a generic,

impersonal way would somehow hurt her. Ewan had cut her deeply once already. She steeled herself against his words. He wouldn't cut her a second time. His attention wandered from her face in favor of a slow perusal of her body. Suddenly very aware of her nakedness, a chill stole over her, coaxing goose bumps to the surface of her skin and causing her nipples to pearl. The rich musky scent of Ewan's arousal bloomed around her and she breathed deeply of the intoxicating aroma.

Sasha wanted to call him out on it. To point out that it wasn't fair for her to be completely naked while he was fully clothed. But she knew that any protestations would fall on deaf ears. He wanted her to believe that he was in charge. Sasha could play along. For now.

She bucked her chin up and met his gaze with a defiant stare. "Aren't we supposed to establish some sort of safe word before we get started?"

"Safe word?" Ewan smirked. "Oh love, there isn't a word in existence that will keep you safe from me."

He wanted to scare her, but all his posturing managed to do was excite her even more. Everything about him raised the stakes. Took Sasha out of her comfort zone. She'd play this game as long as he wanted to. Anything to keep feeling this way.